ANNA-MARIA ATHANASIOU

SIGNED AND SEALED

The Blackthorn Duet

CONTENTS

SIGNED & SEALED

BLACKTHORN SERIES

DEDICATION

To Nonna –
who loved to read romance novels
but sadly never got to read any of mine

Corona veniet delectis
Victory shall come to the worthy.

1

GUNS BLAZING

After the 20th lap of his pool, Miles hauled himself out of the side and grabbed a towel. No amount of exercise was going to calm his nerves. Not the 40 minutes running on the treadmill or the 20 minutes punching the pads Pierce held up for him. He rubbed himself dry and ran up the stairs to where he found Pierce pouring himself a coffee.

His security guard and friend eyed him over the rim of his cup. "Better?"

"Nope," Miles answered through gritted teeth and crouched down to pet Duke. Not even his furry friend could take the edge off his brimming anger.

"Have some coffee and something to eat," Pierce suggested, pushing a full cup towards him and gestured to the freshly toasted bagels. He knew Miles had hardly eaten anything after they'd got back from the press conference. He had managed to drink his way through a quarter of a bottle of vodka though.

"How much company do we have?" Miles jerked his head towards the street.

"Just a couple."

Miles nodded, then picked up the cup of coffee Pierce had poured for him and looked at his phone. Still no word from Louisa. He'd done exactly what Melissa had told him to do. He'd backed off. After the media frenzy at the press conference and Louisa's signature shutdown – she would do it whenever the going got tough – Melissa had called him in the afternoon.

"How's my favourite ambassador doing?" she asked tentatively.

"Jesus, what a mess."

"Yes, how are you holding up?"

"I don't care about me, Melissa; this is old news for me. I can take anything they throw at me. I just want to speak to Louisa and she's

13

shut me out." He slumped on his sofa and dragged his fingers through his hair. "She's talking about taking a break and… fuck! Sorry, I shouldn't be stressing you out." He was swearing and raising his voice in frustration, when she was supposed to be relaxing and watching her blood pressure.

"It's okay, Miles. Really, you don't need to hold back on my account."

Miles let out a sharp breath, in an attempt to calm down. "I'm not going to just sit back Melissa," he said forcefully.

"Good to hear. I'm on your side completely, Miles." Miles heard the exasperation in her voice.

"Thanks, I just worried that I was being frozen out, you know: closing ranks and all that. She needs me more than anything right now. She always said you lot were a tight set, but man, this is… I don't know." After the last few months of being around Louisa, Miles had begun to understand how the aristocracy worked.

"Look, Miles, I know this is awful but if you go to Holmwood now, the press will be all over it. They're camped out there already. There are still visitors on the grounds and to be honest, you turning up will just fuel the fire, so to speak," Melissa explained softly.

"I see." He didn't – well, he sort of did but his natural instinct was to charge over, protocol, press and procedure be damned.

"Alistair is there and Lady Alice. Louisa just needs a little time to lick her wounds and come clean to her family. You know how private she is. This is her worst nightmare," continued Melissa, hoping she was able to appease him.

"I just want to be there for her," he sighed.

"I know you do. And at any other time, I would've said go up there but… this is how our system works. We close ranks, keep our heads down and wait for it to pass."

"Your system sucks."

"Perhaps," Melissa chuckled. "She's feeling exposed and vulnerable and Holmwood is the best place for her."

"Have you spoken to her? Did she tell you to tell me this?"

"I have spoken to her but she didn't have to tell me anything, Miles. I know her and I know what's best for her. She's… well, she's probably embarrassed too. The scandal is…"

"I'm used to scandal, Melissa. That's why she needs me. She's got nothing to be embarrassed about!" Miles growled. He knew all about embarrassment, the scandal and letting the people you loved down. This didn't even come near to the colossal disasters he'd been part of.

"I totally agree but that's not how she feels. So, just give her some time."

Miles sighed deeply, then muttered. "I'll wait until tomorrow."

"I'll tell you what, I'll call you tomorrow afternoon and see how things are."

"Sure, but if I don't hear from you, I'll be causing a scene and I don't give a shit who records it! Twenty-four hours, that's all I'll concede to."

"Okay."

"Take it easy."

"You too, Miles."

MILES PICKED UP THE bagel Pierce had prepared for him and took a bite. They'd fallen into a familiar camaraderie over the last few weeks, which felt more like flatmates rather than an employer/ employee relationship. Pierce had been his constant companion yesterday, and today he'd never been more grateful for his unassuming presence.

"Any news from Hugh?" Pierce knew this was code for *how is Louisa?*

"I didn't check in yet."

Miles nodded, knowing it was still early. He'd been up since five and if he knew Louisa at all, she'd have locked herself in her suite and kept out of sight. He pulled his laptop across the counter and tapped onto his search engine and typed in Louisa's name. He wanted to know the damage before he spoke to her.

"Motherfucker!" Miles shot out of his seat.

"What?" Pierce stepped around the breakfast bar to see what he was looking at.

"Fucking Gerard turned up at Holmwood early this morning." Miles turned the screen so Pierce could see. There was footage of Gerard arriving in the early hours of the morning. His smug face clearly photographed as his car drove up to Holmwood. It hadn't

15

escaped Miles's notice that Gerard was sitting in the front seat, rather than in the rear, as was normal. He'd wanted the photographers to record him arriving. Miles clenched his jaw and pinched the bridge of his nose. He turned to Pierce and glared at him.

Pierce didn't need any prompting. "I'll tell Hugh we're on our way."

"Yeah, you do that." Miles turned and started towards the stairs. If they set off in the next 20 minutes, they'd be at Holmwood by the latest at nine, an hour before any visitors arrived. "Tell him to make sure they let me in because I'll fucking break the goddamn door down and he can take a shot at me if he wants," he called from the stairs. "That French fucker has ruined her life for the last time. If Louisa doesn't want me there, she can tell me to my face! Is that clear?"

"Crystal," Pierce replied with a smirk.

MILES FORGOT HOW HEAVY the traffic could be at rush hour, even on a Saturday. The usual 40-minute drive ended up being over an hour but at least they'd made it to Holmwood well before opening. At least the weather was on their side today. It had started to rain overnight, which would mean that paying visitors were less likely to brave the weather. The gates opened as Miles's car pulled up, which meant the photographers were unable to get a clear shot. He'd dropped down low in the rear seat as Pierce drove him along with the two other security guards he always had now. Miles held onto Duke and petted him in attempt to calm himself. He'd been trying to keep a rein on his nerves for the whole journey. The last thing he wanted was to make a scene or upset Louisa. He was there to support and reassure her that things would pass. If he'd learned anything over the few weeks, he knew that if Gerard was by her side, and he'd be thinking of any way to get her back and making sure he came out squeaky clean.

"Miles?"

Miles caught Pierce's dark eyes in the rear-view mirror.

"Remember where you are. I know you're pissed off at the moment but the calmer we all are, the better for everyone."

Miles sucked on his teeth and nodded. He knew Pierce was worried that he'd lose his temper and he was thankful he was there to have his back. Hugh hadn't deterred them from coming, which Miles took as a good sign. If there was one thing Miles was one hundred percent sure of, it was that Hugh only had Louisa's best interests at heart. He was glad Hugh was there for her when he couldn't be.

"We're going around the back. The same way we came in the last time." Pierce spoke calmly and in a low voice. Miles was sure this was some tactic he'd learned when having to deal with volatile employers. Surprisingly, his smooth tone was helping. He turned in through the secured gates and waited for them to close before parking up and cutting the engine.

"I won't need a babysitter once I'm in, Pierce," Miles said, unbuckling his belt.

Pierce turned around in his seat and fixed him with a no-nonsense stare. "I'm not your babysitter. I'm your friend. And I will be with you at all times, Miles, for your protection and to have your back," he said firmly.

Miles gave him a smirk and nodded, then opened up the car and stepped out into the secluded courtyard. There was no one about and it was disturbingly quiet. Pierce quickly gave instructions to the other two security and asked them to look after Duke while he and Miles went into the house.

"They all know I'm coming, right?" he asked, looking up at the security cameras.

"Lady Alice, the earl and Lady Louisa know, yes."

"Good. Okay, let's go in. I know the way."

Pierce tapped in the code and the door opened. Pierce led Miles through the corridor but rather than go straight upstairs, like Miles had done the last time, they went through to the ground level of the house and into the grand hallway. Hugh had instructed Pierce to bring Miles to the main house so as to avoid bumping into Gerard, who was staying in Louisa's section, in the same room he'd occupied at the activities weekend. The house wouldn't be opened until 10:30, which was an hour away, meaning there wouldn't be any visitors around either.

"Why are we here? I want to see Louisa," Miles asked, clearly puzzled as he scanned the grand hallway and followed Pierce.

"Hugh asked me to bring you –"

"What the hell are you doing here!" Pierce's explanation was cut short by the sharp familiar accented voice of Gerard. Miles swung around and was faced with the thunderous dark stare of the Frenchman, striding from the dining room into the hall.

"What the hell am I doing here? That's rich coming from you. You're the last person who should be here," Miles scoffed, keeping the volume of his voice in check.

"I'm here to support my wife and family," Gerard retorted, as though it was obvious.

Miles glared at him, knowing full well he was trying to get a rise out of him and he'd succeeded. He took two long strides and was up to him in an instance. "No, you don't get to be here for her, not anymore. You lost that chance. And it's *ex-wife*, you asshole!" He pointed his forefinger in Gerard's face.

"Miles," Pierce said steadily in warning, as he stepped to where they were both standing. The few Holmwood staff that were working in the area quickly retreated out of the way, leaving the three men alone in the vast entranceway.

Gerard waved Pierce off dismissively. "Don't bother yourself, I can handle him."

Pierce shifted his focus to Gerard and arched his brow. *This he'd like to see.* Pierce stepped back and caught sight of Alistair coming in from the drawing-room. He must have heard them or one of his staff had probably alerted him. Alistair halted, seeing the two men in the heated exchange and gave Pierce a questioning look. Pierce gave a slight shake of his head, indicating that there was no need to intervene and Alistair stayed at the threshold, out of sight.

"You'd like to think you can, more like, Gerard. This is because of you. This is all on you and whatever you do now, it's too late," Miles sneered.

"You have no idea what you're talking about. I've known Louisa for over 20 years!" The usually level-headed and aloof Frenchman's voice rose in anger. Miles had hit a nerve and it looked like he wasn't about to stop now.

"That may be, but you have no idea who she is or what she needs."

"Oh, and you do?" Gerard jeered.

"I know better than you do." Miles shook his head in disgust and turned away from him, wanting to calm down. He'd wasted too much time on him and he was about to leave when he thought better of it.

Miles needed Gerard to know what he'd done. He turned back around and stared straight into Gerard's hardened face. "You blew it with her. You can't make this better, don't you see that? This will never be better for her! Fuck. She's destroyed up there." Miles flung his arm in the direction of the stairs that led to her suite. "Right now, I want to beat the shit out of you for doing this to her but I love her too much and that would only make this worse for her and Celeste."

"Trust the American to resort to violence," Gerard answered sarcastically.

Miles huffed at him then shook his head. After everything he'd just said, Gerard had only chosen to pick up on the one thing he could insult him with. *Was he really that obtuse?* "Trust the pompous Frenchman to think he's above everyone else, even his own family," Miles drawled.

Gerard took a step closer to him, seething. "You need to leave."

"I don't take my orders from anyone, especially not from you."

"No, apparently you don't, but if you really care about Louisa, you'll leave her alone. You being here is feeding the media."

"I came in, undetected, in broad fucking daylight, yet you managed to make a spectacular entrance in the dead of night. I'm not feeding the media, *you are*, by design! The media is here because of what you did, not because of me, Gerard. Don't deflect the blame," Miles ground out.

"You have no idea what you're talking about. Coming here, guns blazing. Your reputation will just make everything worse." Gerard threw his hands in the air and Miles narrowed his eyes at him. He was goading and insulting him but Miles wasn't that easily knocked back. He'd been the brunt of criticism, scrutiny and judged by everyone and all out in the open for all to see. He'd grown a thick skin over the years – he'd had to. This uptight, pompous asshole wasn't in a position to judge him.

"My reputation? It's yours that's in dispute. Why are you really here? Are you worried that *your* reputation will be tarnished if your dirty laundry gets a full airing? That your connections with the aristocracy will be severed?"

"Well, you know all about dirty laundry."

"Yes, I do, and every mistake I made was out in the open, in full view. I didn't hide anything and I wasn't *fucking married* at the time," Miles snarled and Gerard stepped up to him with his fists clenched.

"How dare you. I don't have to explain myself to you."

"No, you don't. But you do need to explain yourself to others," Miles spat out, his disdain for this man seeping out of every pore. "You want to take a swing at me?" he goaded.

"Miles, Mr Dupont," Pierce said as calmly as possible. He had moved closer to them as their argument had escalated. Miles shot Pierce a look that said he wasn't about to back down.

"You want to be here for Celeste? That's understandable, but you being here for Louisa?" Miles huffed in his face. "You had 20 years to be there for her and you weren't. Remember that, and live with it. If Louisa wants me to leave, I'll leave, but until then, nothing or no one is going to make me, you got that?" Miles jabbed his finger towards his face and Gerard was about to say something scathing back, but his eye caught sight of Louisa at the top of the stairs. He immediately straightened and plastered a fake smile on his face. It took Miles a second to realise that they had company and he swung around. She'd stopped halfway down the stairs where Celeste was now sitting. She'd heard the raised voices of her father and Miles and had crept down, undetected. Miles's heart dropped. Celeste had probably heard the whole exchange and he cursed himself for not being able to hold back. She looked so young in her ripped denim shorts and Converse, her blonde hair pulled back into a high ponytail.

Louisa patted her shoulder and continued to come down the stairs, while Celeste got up, took a last look at the two men in the hallway, and went back to her room. Miles crossed the floor to the bottom of the staircase and gave Louisa a soft smile. She looked like she'd hardly slept and though she was dressed smartly in fitted trousers and a soft top, this wasn't the immaculate countess of Holmwood everyone knew and was used to seeing. It was *just* Louisa.

"Baby." His simple term of endearment meant so much more. *I'm here for you, I love you, I've got your back.*

"*Cherie.*" Gerard's accented voice made Miles stiffen.

Louisa stopped on the first step and shifted her gaze between the two men. Gerard stood straight. Even in his casual clothing of polo shirt and slacks, he looked the epitome of a wealthy, distinguished, well-bred gentleman. His appearance was immaculate and the expression on his handsome face was, as ever, perfectly composed. Miles, on the other hand, looked wretched. His signature dirty blond hair was dishevelled from the constant raking of his fingers. He was wearing fitted jeans and a light blue T-shirt that made his worried eyes blaze. Paired with the dark blue bomber jacket he was wearing, it suggested he'd thought little of where and who he was coming to see. He'd obviously dressed in a hurry and as Louisa searched his good-looking face, all she could see was pure concern for her. There was no façade, no airs or graces, there was just Miles.

"Gerard."

"Yes, *cherie.*" Gerard stepped up closer and shot Miles a smug look. Miles furrowed his brow and tried hard not to show his disappointment.

"Can you please excuse me? Miles and I have a lot to discuss."

Gerard's face dropped but he quickly recovered, giving her a tight smile and a nod. He turned swiftly and marched towards the dining room.

Louisa shifted her gaze to the man in front of her. He'd come to her when she needed him the most, even when she'd asked him to leave her alone. He knew what she needed more than she knew herself. "So, you don't take orders from anyone, eh?"

Miles blasted her with his megawatt-no-holds-barred smile that lit up the whole room. "Only from you, my lady," he drawled and she gifted him with a small smile.

"Well, in that case, you better come up." She held out her hand for him to take. Miles gently took hold of it and brought it up to his lips.

"Yes, my lady."

2

REVEALED

Alistair smirked at Pierce as they watched Miles follow Louisa up the grand staircase to her suite. "That was quite a show." Pierce stifled a grin at the earl's comment. "I was worried for a moment. I thought you were going to have to step in."

"To be honest, so did I, but my man came through," Pierce said with a hint of pride.

Alistair chuckled, stepping into the hallway. "I've never seen Gerard so riled up."

"Well, he's realising he's losing and he never loses."

"Not sure how we're going to get through this whole mess, though," Alistair sighed and looked up to the upper floor. His heart broke for his sister. How much of what the reporter had said was true he wasn't entirely sure because Louisa, as usual, had been tight-lipped. *Her loyalty knew no bounds,* he thought. Either that or she just didn't want to upset anyone.

"Miles can handle the press. He's had plenty of practice," Pierce said with a shrug, then straightened the instant he saw Lady Alice come through from the library. "Good morning, my lady," he said with a curt nod.

"Is it? Didn't sound like it," she answered dryly and Pierce shot Alistair a look.

"You heard then?" Alistair said with a smirk.

"I was in the library. I think everyone on the ground floor heard. The acoustics in this hallway are surprisingly good," she said with an arch of her brow. "I take it from the way Gerard stormed out, Louisa is with Miles."

"Yes."

"Good. He'll hopefully change her mood."

Pierce stifled a smirk then made an excuse to leave. After working with the Blackthorns for over seven years, he knew when they needed their privacy.

"I'm glad you approve," said Alistair.

"I approve of anyone that makes my children happy and if there's one thing for sure, Miles certainly has that gift. It's a rare thing to find in a partner." Her eyes swept up the staircase. "The American is driven by different motives. Pure motives – that's rarer still. If there's one person who can navigate Louisa through this shambles, it's him."

"I hope you're right. What are we going to do about Gerard?"

"He's going to have to 'suck it up' as they say in America. As Miles said, he had his chance."

Alistair chuckled at his mother, then went to ensure that everything was ready for opening in half an hour. Though he didn't hold much hope for a busy day, even if the heavy rain had turned to drizzle.

"YOU WEREN'T MEANT TO hear that," Miles said the second the door closed to Louisa's suite. They'd walked up in agonising silence, wary there were enough people around who would hear what they both had to say.

"Is that an apology?" she asked quietly.

"Nope, I'm not apologising for what I said. I didn't particularly want you to hear it though."

"I see." She gave a weak smile and dropped her gaze. She was still a little surprised he'd come out here, especially after she'd been so harsh with him and Melissa had told him to give her time. Though, if his past actions were anything to go by, Miles didn't conform or fall in. In fact, most of the time he did the opposite. She had to admit she was pleased he'd disregarded her wishes. Just seeing him had made her almost forget the press conference debacle.

"Louisa, you should know by now that I'm not easily put off."

Her eyes shot up to his handsome face and she scrunched her nose up. His worried eyes softened seeing her so lost and unsure.

"Don't you ever run and hide from me again." He took a step closer. "I don't care what your title is, what you've done or not done. To me, you are *just* Louisa. Do you hear me?" he said firmly, taking another step closer and reaching for her hand. "You will always be *just* Louisa and I'll be there for you – protect you any way I can from whoever and whatever."

Louisa swallowed back the lump in her throat, moved by the sincerity of his words, backed up by his impulsive actions. This was unchartered territory for her. She wasn't used to anyone acting without premeditation.

Miles tugged her towards him, enveloping her in his arms. She instantly melted against him. "I can take it, Louisa. I've been to hell and back and come out the other side and I *swear*, no one will get to you."

He kissed the crown of her head as she took in a shaky breath and for the first time since the horrific press conference, she felt safe. It suddenly all became too much for her and every emotion she'd been holding in came pouring out. He held her tightly as she quietly sobbed against his chest. She'd been so tense, tried so hard to keep her emotions in check, not wanting her family to see how upset she really was. Miles gave her the time to let everything out. He didn't want to push her into an explanation. She'd tell him whenever she was ready.

Louisa pulled back a little and Miles bobbed down, then wiped her tears away with his thumbs. "You forget, I'm bulletproof. Let them come at me, baby, I can take it. I'll take it all for you," he said with a lopsided smile.

Louisa pulled in her lips and nodded. *How had she gotten so lucky?* After everything that had happened, after how she'd behaved, he was still here fighting for her. "Miles, this is just so awful. All our hard work, the Blackthorn reputation, everything has been jeopardised."

He shook his head. "Louisa, it'll pass. Things like this pass," he said as reassuringly as he could. He knew his words were true but he also knew that they'd have a few more bumps on the road. But at least he'd be with her to navigate that journey. "I don't know what the hell went on between you two and to be honest, I know it's none of my business but it's obviously affecting you. If you and I are going to make a go of this, you're going to have to let me know at least some of what we're dealing with." Louisa blinked at him and he gave her a soft smile. "I'm not saying right now but at some point. I can't fight them for you if I don't know what I'm fighting, baby."

"I know. You're right. It's just I've been used to keeping things to myself."

Miles pulled her towards him and kissed her, tentatively at first. His soft lips coaxing against hers. Louisa let out a sigh and slipped her arms around his waist. It was all the encouragement Miles needed. In a swift manoeuvre, he hiked her up against him, urging her legs to curl around him, then strode towards the bedroom. "I hope you don't have any plans for the next hour," he said between breathless kisses.

"None that are important anyway," Louisa said with a giggle as he dropped their tangled bodies onto her huge bed.

"Good, because I've missed you," he said, quickly straddling her and shedding his jacket.

"I missed you too."

Miles looked down at her beautiful face, her dark hair fanning out against the luxurious bedspread, and leaned down so that their faces were a couple of inches apart. "That's the last time you run from me. That's the last time you shut me out. You can't get rid of me that easily, Louisa," he said with a wicked gleam in his eye. And though he meant every word, he didn't want it to sound like the reprimand it was.

"Okay," she said softly, totally enraptured by his determination. He was being forceful without being aggressive, persuasive though not bullish, always thinking of her.

"Okay," he repeated, then gave her a hard kiss.

"Well, you *were* bought and paid for, so you kind of belong to me now," she said with a coy smile.

Miles's face broke out into a huge smile and he let out a husky laugh. "That's right, you did," he said pinning down her hands and gently running his nose against hers.

"Best £50,000 I ever spent."

"I'd better make sure you get your money's worth then."

MILES'S FINGERS RHYTHMICALLY STROKED up and down Louisa's naked back. He was enjoying just being with her in the peace and quiet of her suite. They hadn't been disturbed since he'd burst into Holmwood House over an hour ago but Miles knew they'd eventually have to leave their sanctuary. He was leaving the "when" up to Louisa. It was a rare occurrence for them to have privacy in her family home.

"I need to apologise to Celeste," Miles said quietly. It had been bothering him that she'd heard how he'd spoken to Gerard. Over the past few weeks, he'd built up a comfortable relationship with Louisa's tenacious daughter. She'd always seemed to be on his side. After hearing him put her father in his place though, she might not be as supportive. Added to that, no child should have to hear, for all intents and purposes, a stranger openly berate their parent, regardless of whether it was all true.

"She's tougher than you think."

"Maybe, but she didn't need to hear me roast her father like that. He is her father, whatever else he is."

"She lived with us, remember. She knows exactly who her father is." Louisa tilted her head up to look up at him and he furrowed his brow at her comment that spoke volumes.

"He was unfaithful," he said after a beat. It wasn't a question. It hadn't taken that much effort to deduce Louisa had been betrayed.

Louisa sighed and gave a subtle nod, then nuzzled back into his bare chest, not wanting to catch the pity in his gaze or worse the disappointment.

"A number of times?" Miles asked carefully, unsure if he was pushing her too far. The last thing he wanted was to upset her, especially after she'd seemed to calm down.

The room was so quiet they could hear the gentle patter of the rain and Miles was about to tell her she didn't need to elaborate when her soft voice broke through the silence. "Everyone bought into the dream that we had a fairy-tale marriage." Miles let out a breath he'd been holding. She was finally opening up. "The distinguished, successful businessman marrying the young countess and whisking her off to glamorous life in America. And to be honest it was kind of like that in the beginning." Louisa paused for a second, then she gave a slight huff. "I was head over heels in love with a man who stood out amongst the immature boys who were all I'd met until then. I couldn't believe he was interested in me. I was a very young and inexperienced teen, and I was flattered."

Miles swallowed hard. He'd known she'd loved Gerard but it didn't help hearing her say it. He knew he had no right to be jealous, Lord knows he'd had a technicoloured past, but he'd never been in love until now and her admission stung harder than he cared to admit.

"He treated me like a princess and he loved me. I know it sounds bizarre but he did love me throughout our marriage but he just couldn't seem to love me enough. Not enough to be faithful to me, anyway. I'd like to blame it on his upbringing, his European mentality that deemed it acceptable for men to have extramarital interests, but I think it was more than that. He managed to be with me for five years and then, when I found out about his first affair, I was devastated."

Her voice was soft and surprisingly steady, considering she was revealing a very private and emotional part of her life and Miles again marvelled at her strength. He gave her a reassuring squeeze but kept quiet, afraid that she would stop if he interrupted her. He remembered her saying something along the lines of "If someone talked freely about themselves, it tended to be more revealing than if you asked questions" at their date all those months ago. It looked like today she was proving her theory right.

"I was only young, with no experience and I was alone. Alistair was away on one of his dangerous tours and my parents thought the world of Gerard. So, I drew the conclusion that it was because of me, that I was the problem. I was probably inexperienced and he'd grown tired of me and needed excitement."

Miles clenched his teeth in anger. How could she believe that? How could Gerard let her believe that? All manner of violent thoughts against the arrogant Frenchman came thundering into his head but he managed to keep them in check as she continued with her story.

"So, I tried everything I could to become more worldly and hoped his dalliance would fade. Pathetic, really. I researched, read up on how to be a seductress, how to..." She shook her head and huffed. Appalled at her own story and the lengths she'd had to go through all those years ago, she couldn't even finish off her explanation. "It soon became apparent over the next few years that it didn't matter how creative or assertive I was, Gerard still needed more, or different, or anything else than just me. That time was the worst years of my marriage and I had to behave and carry on as though everything was perfect. I couldn't react, or behave badly, cause a scene. It just wasn't done. I became a recluse and focused on Celeste. We argued – or should I say, I argued; Gerard calmly tried to reason with me and always in private. Apparently, they meant nothing; it was just a passing phase. It was the norm in his circle. Well, it wasn't in mine and I couldn't and wouldn't accept it." Louisa paused and, for the first time since she'd started talking, her voice began to crack.

Miles closed his eyes and tried hard to rein in his anger. His heart broke for her and the years she'd suffered in silence, alone and without anyone she could confide in. Her impeccable upbringing and breeding had trumped her feelings, where saving face was more important than saving herself. No wonder she was so guarded.

"He broke my heart and then shattered it again and again. I know it sounds unbelievable, but I know he loved me more than any of the other women he'd had. He also adored Celeste and when he was with us, he was one hundred percent with us." Louisa took a deep breath and sat up. She wrapped the sheet around her naked body, feeling far too exposed in every way.

Miles shuffled closer to her, ensuring his features didn't give away how unnerved he was. He leaned forward and pressed a kiss to her forehead then gathered her onto his lap, cradling her against him, not wanting any distance between them. Louisa gave him a reluctant smile as he searched her tear-filled eyes, encouraging her to continue. She took in a shaky breath and continued.

"Celeste doted on him and the idea of leaving him and taking Celeste away from him just seemed cruel. The idea of me finding anyone else was also unthinkable. He was the love of my life, even after everything. So, I made the decision to stay for the classic cliché: my child. I made it clear that we were married but lived separate lives. That he was free to do whatever he wanted as long as he kept it quiet and my face was never rubbed in it. Celeste would have both her parents under one roof and to the outside world we were living the fairy-tale."

Louisa focused on the huge window and stared blindly at the rain running down the pane. She could feel the tension in Miles's body and his bright blue eyes staring at her but she was too afraid to see what they might reveal. She was sure any respect for her he'd had vanished. What the reporter had said about her wasn't entirely true but it was close enough. She'd stayed in an imperfect marriage for, what most would have deemed, the wrong reasons. She quickly brushed the lone tear that had escaped and continued her revelations.

"I threw my attention into charity work and kept myself busy, using his contacts to do as much good as I could. I was hoping that he'd see the error of his ways, see how accomplished I was – how valuable, even – that I was worth being faithful for and then in time he'd come back to me. But somewhere along the way, over the following years, I became stronger, more independent. My focus shifted and we grew further and further apart. I got used to being alone, relying on myself for everything. I didn't need him anymore and over time, I'd stopped wanting him too." She gave an awkward shrug and let her gaze flit to Miles's. He gave her a gentle smile and tightened his hold on her, letting her lean on him.

"When Celeste was 15, I asked my lawyer to draft up an agreement that said once Celeste became 18, I would file for divorce and, stated the terms. We'd already been living separate lives for over seven years by then, so it would ultimately mean, after a few signatures, we would be divorced with the minimum of fuss. No scandal. Perfectly civilised and proper. Gerard wouldn't hear of it. He tried everything over the following couple of years to make me change my mind but he'd broken something in me – in us – that was irreparable. For the first time in 20 years, I was in control of our relationship. I'd sacrificed enough to save face, to save any form of scandal or upset of my family, or him. Celeste had had both of us every day: a stable family life, but now it was time for me." In reality, it had taken much longer for the paperwork to be finalised. Gerard had stalled, used excuses of Celeste's graduation, putting off the inevitable. But by the time Celeste was ready to leave for Peru, over six months after her 18th birthday, everything had been set in place.

"Jesus, Louisa. You're so unbelievably strong. So selfless. He never deserved you, your love or your loyalty."

Louisa looked up at Miles's handsome face and all she could see was love and admiration. The first emotion she was more than happy to accept but the latter felt unworthy of her. "I didn't just do it for him, Miles. I had to think of my family here, of Celeste and to be honest, me too. I wasn't ready to leave him. I can't explain it. There were times I did want to. I wanted to pack up and leave him. Make him suffer – embarrass him, even – but when I sat back and took a breath, I realised that acting on an impulse would have a far worse effect on everyone in the long run, including me. And the bottom line was that I did care and love him. I set myself a goal to work to. Which sounds calculated but he was aware of it. I didn't hide my plans from him."

"How did Celeste feel about all of this?"

"She'd lived the last ten years of her life with us, living separately under one roof. She didn't really remember what we had been like before, or rather it was her new normal. In her early teens, when I suppose she understood more, she didn't really question it because most of her friends had divorced parents. The fact we had separate living quarters, in the house, was better than us having separate locations."

"Oh wow, I suppose so." Miles had never been more grateful for his parents and the happy family life he'd had.

"She'd overheard Gerard talking in French to his flavour of the moment and was absolutely stunned. She asked me about it, thinking I didn't know. In fact, she'd agonised over it for a week and it was only when I pushed her to tell me what was wrong, why she'd been so quiet, she finally told me what she'd overheard. I never wanted her to find out. She had her father on a pedestal and she adored him and this hurt her so very deeply, as though he'd betrayed her rather than me." Louisa blew out a breath, remembering how hard Celeste had taken it. Miles threaded his fingers through hers, seeing her struggle and she gave him a thankful smile. "It took me a while to explain to her that this was how our marriage was. That we'd decided this was the best way for us as a family to be. She, like I had at that age, believed that marriage was forever and that being faithful was the only way a marriage should be. I'm pleased to say she still believes that and I didn't ever tell her she was wrong. I still believe in that fairy-tale, even if I've never lived it."

"It *is* the way it should be, Louisa," Miles said earnestly and Louisa nodded.

"In a warped way, that phone call she overheard made it easier for me when we finally divorced. She already knew why; there was no need for explanations or time for us to adjust."

"Didn't she ask Gerard about it?" Miles couldn't believe Celeste would've allowed her father to get off scot-free.

"Oh yes, I think it was the only time Celeste ever raised her voice to her father. It was a difficult six months for them. He'd slipped off the pedestal and he'd, for the first time, not been able to justify his actions. They came to an understanding that she never wanted to meet any woman he was seeing."

"Even now?" Miles asked clearly surprised but also in awe of the young Lady Blackthorn.

"Yes, even now, because she could never be sure if she'd have been around when we were still married."

"Oh."

"That might change. Well, if Gerard finds anyone new."

"And Alistair and your mother, how much do they know?"

"Less than you, though I don't doubt they suspect. We kept it under the radar for all these years; I didn't see the point in tainting what they felt for Gerard. I'd made the decision and it was mine to live with, not theirs. Though in the light of yesterday's press conference, someone knew something, even if their facts were a little distorted."

"Maybe one of Gerard's exes?" Miles knew too well what it was like to be exposed by an ex-lover.

"I doubt it. The time to expose anything would've been when we were together, so that they could force his hand and be with him officially. This was directed at me. They made me out to be a gold digger – which is absurd – and that I enjoyed the ritzy lifestyle – another load of rubbish, seeing as I kept out of the limelight. Sadly, though, that is all that the public will take away from this." Louisa let out a puff of air. She wasn't overly bothered about what people thought of her but it did bother her if it reflected badly on the rest of the family and CASPO.

"Why the hell did he come here?" Miles muttered.

"To show that there is no animosity between us. That we are perfectly comfortable and we support each other. United in our separate lives. Also, it shows the public and the media that, if I was really a gold-digging fame whore, he wouldn't be here."

"Fame whore?" Miles chuckled. Louisa was anything but a fame whore, and he should know, he'd met plenty.

"That's what they call them, isn't it?"

"Yeah, it is." He dropped a kiss to her temple and she sighed.

31

She'd never been so grateful that Miles hadn't listened to her. "Man, this is so fucked up. You can't even defend yourself." He couldn't hide his exasperation.

"I know. Keeping quiet and ignoring it is the only way. If we make a statement, it'll just fuel it. Not that I'd want to anyway. That short outburst yesterday was completely against the norm."

"Whoever got in touch with the newspaper knew enough about your personal life to have them dig a little. One of your staff maybe, or Gerard's?"

Louisa pulled back from his chest and looked into his stormy eyes. The whole situation was weighing heavy on him too. He was searching for a solution to make things better and for someone to blame. "My initial reaction is: no way, they're loyal, plus they've all signed an NDA, but who knows? Hugh is trying to get to the bottom of it but, in all honesty, the damage is done. What will I do if we find out? Sue them... what for? Telling a more colourful version of the truth? It'll only bring it all up again. I don't want or need to explain myself to anyone."

"Then we deflect. We make the concert up front and centre. Get photos out of you smiling and chatting with Gerard and Celeste. Group photos with Alistair and Lady Alice," Miles said with determination.

Louisa shuffled off his lap and thought about his suggestion. "That's an option." She twisted her mouth then said, "Coming out about you and me?"

"What?" Miles's eyes widened in shock.

"Melissa said that would put out the fire in an instant."

"Jesus." Miles swung his legs over the side of the bed and reached for his underwear. "You know... fuck." He rammed his legs into his boxers and pulled them up as he stood then turned around to face Louisa. He was clearly shaken. "Okay, listen to me. There is nothing I want more than the whole world to know that you and I are together... *nothing*." Louisa gave him a shy smile and he gave out an audible sigh. "But to use it to deflect from this... it just tarnishes it. Every time they'll mention us together, it'll have the tagline 'After the scandal of Lady Louisa's divorce' prefixing anything good about us. They're going to think it's staged too or... or they'll end up dragging every story up about me and my past and spin it in such a way that'll make me out to be a gold-digger and… whenever they ask us about our relationship, they'll also ask about this. Does that make sense? It's going to go hand in hand, forever and…"

"I know." Louisa cut him off mid-sentence as he paced around the room. Miles stopped in his tracks and stared at her sitting in a pool of pure white sheets on the grand bed. "I get it and that's exactly why I told Melissa there was no way. You're one hundred percent right. I just wanted to make sure we were on the same page."

Miles strode over to the bed and cupped her face. "You and I are always on the same page, Louisa. Please believe me. I've lived through all this shit; I know how it works. They can have a pop at me but not you, and when we do finally come out, it'll be done for the right reasons." He sealed his statement with a firm kiss.

"I know; besides, I've used you enough to get me out of scrapes… not this time. I think you're right, though; we need coverage of Gerard and me looking happy and unaffected."

Miles nodded, then flopped back onto the bed and looked out of the window. "Well, today's out of the question. No outside shots in this weather."

"No, but we can at least get a plan together for over the next few days. It'll mean us all sitting down and working it out. Can you sit in a room with Gerard?" she asked with an arched brow.

"No problem for me; not sure *he'll* be up for it though."

"He won't have much choice."

GERARD LET OUT A string of expletives as he paced his room. He'd come all this way to comfort Louisa, try and make things better for her and he'd been shunned, pushed to the side in favour of the brash, classless American. This was going to backfire on Louisa and she didn't even realise it. It was all well and good to have someone of that man's status as a pastime – he'd had plenty himself over the years – but to be officially together? Marry… them? That was social suicide. Who did she think she was? Prince Rainer of Monaco? It had worked for him because Grace Kelly's past hadn't been plastered everywhere. Miles came with enough scandal and baggage to fill a fleet of 747s. As if that wasn't enough, Gerard was now having to spend the next few days under the same roof as him.

His patience was going to be pushed to its limits, especially after today's altercation and the meeting they'd had. Miles was lucky that Celeste and Alistair were there, otherwise he'd have been less courteous. Gerard had to admit, though, Miles hadn't said much in the meeting; he'd let Louisa take the lead, only nodding and agreeing on certain points. Maybe he was just a lapdog after all: spineless. She'd definitely tire of that. She was used to having strong men around her. At least he'd be spending time with Louisa. Even if it was for publicity, it was a small price to pay. What Miles's role in all this was, he wasn't sure. Louisa had outlined a few staged scenarios that would be easily seen by the paparazzi that had camped out at the front of the grounds, of the two of them. A decent telephoto lens would easily capture them, as well as undercover photographers posing as visitors on the grounds. Where Miles slotted into this, though, was still unclear. Miles had been right about one thing, though, searching through all the media sites had confirmed that no one knew he was here.

Gerard looked at his watch. It was almost time for dinner. He knocked back his drink and smoothed back his hair. Whatever happened, he wasn't going to let Miles get to him. He would behave impeccably as always. He would plough through the next two days for the sake of Louisa and Celeste, being loyal to the family as he'd always been. He'd play his role, be seen and be photographed, all in an attempt to quash the rumours and reports that tarnished both him and Louisa. He'd been with the Blackthorns through thick and thin over the last 20 years – they weren't about to forget that for this one-hit-wonder who had drifted into their lives. If Miles thought Louisa was going to stick with him and marry him, he was obviously still high and delusional from the substances he'd extensively used. Louisa was worth more than a has-been popstar. He just needed her to see that over the next few days.

MILES TOOK A DEEP BREATH and knocked on the door. He wasn't entirely sure what kind of reception he was going to get but regardless, he needed to make sure his outburst hadn't affected his relationship with Celeste. At the meeting, she'd come in late and had hardly said anything, keeping her focus on her parents, and it hadn't been the right time to talk to her, especially with an audience. But Miles didn't want to leave it any longer than necessary, especially as they were about to have dinner together and spend the next couple of days locked up in Holmwood House. It was a huge house but they'd inevitably cross paths and Miles didn't want there to be an atmosphere between them. It was going to be bad enough dealing with Gerard's animosity.

Nicolas opened the door and gave Miles a surprised smile. "Hey, good to see you," he said, thrusting out his hand. They hadn't seen each other until now. Nicolas had kept out of the firing line while the Blackthorns had been strategizing. Miles greeted him warmly, glad he was here for Celeste. She'd come through from the bedroom to see who it was and stood in the sitting area she had in her suite.

"I came to talk to Celeste, if that's okay?"

Nicolas looked for guidance from Celeste and when she gave a small nod he stepped back in invitation.

"I'll let you two have some privacy," Nicolas said with a tight smile that meant he knew exactly why Miles was there. He gave Celeste a quick kiss on her forehead and shut himself in the bedroom. Miles realised that Nicolas had given them their privacy but was still close should Celeste need him. He was proving to be a good partner for the young Lady Blackthorn.

"Sit down." Celeste gestured to one of the armchairs as she lowered herself into the plush settee. The room was more modern than the rest of the house, though still elegant with exquisite artwork on the walls and a few small sculptures on the large marble fireplace. Celeste had certainly made her own mark and Miles was a little in awe at how accomplished the young lady of Holmwood was. Even dressed in jeans shorts and a simple T-shirt, she still held herself well.

"Thank you," Miles said, relieved she was willing for him to stay.

"What did you need to talk to me about?" she asked before Miles could begin.

"I came to apologise."

"For?" She tilted her head to the side.

"What you overheard in the hallway. It wasn't... that is, you shouldn't have heard that," Miles said in a rush.

"So, you're apologising for me hearing it?" Celeste furrowed her brow, unsure of what he meant. She'd heard raised voices, that morning, from the hallway and crept out, not knowing who was arguing. As soon as she'd exited her suite, the distinct voice of her father was the first voice she heard. It didn't take her long to recognise the second.

"Yeah, look, I'm sorry you heard me speak to your father like that. Regardless of what I feel about him and... well, our differences, it's not nice to hear someone saying those kinds of things." Miles gave an awkward shrug. "This whole thing with your mom is bad enough to deal with, you really didn't need that as well. So, I'm sorry."

Celeste could see he was being sincere. "Thank you." She saw the relief in his face. He really had been worried she was upset by their argument. "I mean, thank you for thinking about me. The things you said... they were harsh but..." She blew out a breath. "Let's just say I'm glad you're here for my mum. I told you before that my papa had his chance and blew it. I take it you know what I meant by that now?"

Miles gave her a nod. He wasn't about to ask her for any more details. He was just glad she wasn't upset with him.

"Growing up, I didn't realise what my mum had sacrificed for me. I do now and though I love my father, I know exactly who he is. It doesn't mean I particularly like to hear it though," she said with a good-humoured huff.

Miles inwardly cringed at her candid remark. "I know, I'm sorry for that."

Celeste brushed off his apology. He had been big enough to come to her, so she was certainly big enough to accept his thoughtful apology. It hadn't tarnished her opinion of Miles; in fact it would probably surprise him to know it had done the opposite. "It's fine, Miles, really. It's the first time I've ever seen my father so worked up but it's also the first time I've ever seen anyone fight for my mum too. I hope you always fight for her, even when she thinks she doesn't want you to," she said wryly.

"That's why I came, Celeste. I've nothing to lose and everything to gain by fighting for her. She's worth it. So, are we good?"

"Yeah, we're good." She gave him a nod and stood up from her chair.

Miles rose out of his seat. "I love your mom, Celeste. You should know that. Anything I do is for her best interests, not mine."

"I know."

"This will pass," Miles said reassuringly.

"I know that too."

"Okay, I'll see you at dinner."

"Yep, one big happy family," she said with a roll of her eyes and Miles chuckled.

"Yeah, right."

3

DAMAGE CONTROL

Lady Alice had never been more thankful for how large the dining room in her wing was. The table could fit 16 comfortably but she only used it whenever she had company, usually opting to eat in her suite. She'd positioned herself at the head of the table and ensured Gerard had her full attention by sitting him to her left. Alistair was next to him and then Louisa. Opposite her father was Celeste, then Nicolas, and finally Miles. They'd strategically seated Miles and Gerard as far apart as possible, though the animosity seeping from every one of Gerard's pores filled the distance and hung heavy in the air. He wasn't about to make a scene but he most definitely made sure Miles knew he'd rather Miles wasn't there.

The rain had finally stopped, but the atmosphere outside was as heavy as it was in the dining room. It meant that tomorrow's plans for the staged outdoor sightings would be able to go ahead. Darcy, who handled all the PR for CASPO, had informed a few of the publications who were supporters of the Blackthorns that there was a good chance they'd be able to catch and photograph the family during the morning and early evenings. Along with Melissa, they'd done their utmost to quash the rumours that there was, in fact, any trouble in the Blackthorn's paradise. The wheels were in motion to flood the media with positive news about the Blackthorns and anything related to CASPO and the upcoming concert. They'd already set up the various press releases of the participating bands, which would headline the numerous publications, ensuring there were only upbeat stories connected to the Blackthorn name.

Lady Alice kept the conversation around the table flowing in her well-practised fashion. She asked about Celeste and Nicolas's trip, sprinkling a few of her own anecdotes of the times she'd also visited Scotland. Miles made a conscious effort to avoid any undue attention. Everyone tactfully avoided talking about what had happened and why they were all suddenly under the same roof. It was almost as though there was an unsaid rule, as they talked about any other topic, from the clearing up of the weather to other places of interest Nicolas should see while he was in the UK – anything rather than address the huge elephant in the room.

Miles ate in relative quiet, only speaking when any conversation was directed at him, a little unnerved at how the Blackthorns were able to conduct themselves in such a detached way. It was such a contrast to the way he was used to. He'd always talked openly about his life, problems and successes with his family. As the dinner wore on, he realised that that wasn't the way here. Everything was controlled and reserved which meant there was always an underlying strain bubbling below the surface. No wonder Louisa had taken so long to open up to him. He kept thinking back to the many times she'd hinted at how the aristocracy behaved and until now, he hadn't seen what she'd meant. He was thankful for Celeste and Nicolas's presence. They'd acted as a buffer between the rest of the dinner guests. Miles couldn't wait to finish and leave the oppressive atmosphere, what with Gerard sending him daggers, Louisa visibly tense and the rest of the dinner guests making polite small talk, all the while worrying that someone would crack under the pressure.

Miles took a sip of the exquisite and no doubt expensive wine and wished it was something stronger and cheaper so that he could just knock it back. He'd zoned out of the conversation, lost in his own thoughts, when he felt a slight nudge of his leg from Louisa. His gaze shot up to hers. She widened her eyes and tilted her head, indicating a question had been directed at him. He quickly scanned the table and realised it was Gerard.

"I asked if you ride, Miles?" Gerard asked again with a stifled smirk. He'd purposely asked him a question, knowing he wasn't paying attention.

Miles wondered why on Earth he was even trying to include him – probably to make himself look good, show he was trying. The conversation had moved onto polo as the dessert was brought out and seeing as he wasn't familiar with the game, he hadn't been paying attention. "I'm sorry. Um, I wouldn't say that. I've been on a horse but I've not really ridden that much." The truth was Miles was wary of the magnificent beasts. He'd had to ride one for a photoshoot many years ago and it hadn't been a particularly good experience. He wasn't about to admit this while Gerard was looking down at him, though.

"Well, you should take full advantage whenever you're here," Lady Alice intercepted, trying to change the subject and put Miles at ease.

"Thank you, I'll certainly bear that in mind," he said with a smile, knowing full well it was the last thing he'd be doing. It didn't escape Miles's notice that Gerard had a smug look on his face. In the meeting, they'd discussed that Louisa and Gerard should ride around the grounds in the morning, all for the benefit of the paparazzi. It was obvious that Gerard was trying to bring attention to Miles's shortcomings. Throughout the dinner, he'd steered the conversation to topics Miles didn't know much about. He'd dropped a few French phrases which were understood by everyone apart from him and Nicolas. Celeste did an excellent job of quickly translating for her beau, which meant Miles also got the benefit.

Miles was pleased he'd sat next to his fellow American; they'd been able to talk a little when the conversation veered to subjects they were both unfamiliar with. What Gerard hadn't realised was that every time he spoke about things that Miles couldn't participate in, he was also alienating Nicolas, which only made Gerard appear even more of an ass.

After an agonising hour and a half, the dinner came to an end. Lady Alice was the first to leave but insisted they stay on for drinks. Celeste and Nicolas saw this as their out, and quickly made their excuses to leave which meant there was Alistair, Miles, Louisa and Gerard left in the dining room.

Alistair was desperate to leave. The last thing he wanted was to partake of benign conversation in a room where two of the guests were ready to kill each other, but he couldn't abandon them with a clear conscience. Gerard looked as though he was happy to stay there all night; any excuse to spend as much time with Louisa, even if he had to tolerate Miles.

Louisa looked tired and drained. The last thing she needed was her ex and Miles to argue, so he made the decision easy for her. "Well, I'm going to take Duke out for a short walk. He must be ready to stretch his legs, and then I'll head up to bed," he said, rising from his chair and rounding the table to where Louisa was sitting.

"I might keep you company," Alistair said, standing up in a rush, to Miles's surprise. "Luna always likes a stroll before bed."

Miles dropped a swift kiss on Louisa's temple. "See you in a bit," he said softly and she gave him a thankful smile. He gave her a wink, then looked up to where Gerard was blatantly staring at him. "Goodnight, Gerard," he said evenly, then headed for the exit. Alistair bid goodnight to Gerard and his sister, then caught up with him.

"Well, that was painful," Alistair muttered once he was sure they were out of earshot. They walked briskly through to the main section of the house.

"Will she be alright on her own with him? I just thought it was for the best for me to leave because if he said anything to me, I wasn't sure I could keep my mouth shut," Miles ground out.

"She can handle him," Alistair said dryly. "Last night, when he came... well, let's just say she put him in his place. You coming here has shaken him and probably made him more determined to fall in. That'll be new for him," he said with a chuckle. "Gerard has never been good at taking orders."

"I thought you were on good terms." They'd reached the far side of the house, where the common room for the security team was. Alistair stopped in front of the door.

"We are. He's been... he helped my family through bad times and I will be forever grateful for that, but it's obvious that he's not been the best of husbands to Louisa."

"Families, eh? They're complicated," Miles said with a chuckle, not wanting to put Alistair on the spot. He'd known Gerard for over 20 years after all; he wasn't about to slate his ex-brother-in-law.

"You have no idea," the earl answered with a roll of his eyes, then pushed open the door where a few of the security team were sitting. They all immediately stood up, a little surprised to see the earl and Miles in their common room. Alistair gestured for them to sit down again, then patted his thigh and called to Luna, who was dozing in her basket. Duke sprinted to his owner and Miles crouched down to pet him.

"Hey, buddy. Let's go for a walk." He caught Pierce's eye. "Has he been okay?"

"Yes, boss."

"I'll take him up to my room after. Thanks for taking care of him."

"Anytime."

It was still light enough outside to see where they were walking. Miles loved the longer summer days in the UK and they were even better out here in the countryside. Duke ran around and rolled in the damp grass as Luna trotted at a more sedate pace.

"He's quite a character," Alistair chuckled.

"Yep, he keeps me on my toes. I need to train him, though. He loves it here."

"I can see that."

The two men were walking side by side. It was surprising how at ease they were with each other. Miles took a deep breath and decided to take advantage of their time together. He didn't know when he'd be alone with Alistair again. It was time to broach a subject he needed to address. "I need to ask you something, though I'm not entirely sure if now's the right time."

"Well, my father always used to say, better grab the bull by the horns before he charges." They'd made it down to the lake just as the watery sun was disappearing into the horizon.

"Your father sounds like quite a wise man."

"He was," Alistair said with a sigh.

"I wish I'd had the chance to meet him. Though from what Louisa tells me, you're very much like him."

"Louisa is being, as she usually is, far too kind. My father was a rare man in the aristocracy. He came to be the earl at the young age of 20, which meant he wasn't influenced by his parents on how to behave as an earl. So, he kind of, as you Americans say, *winged it*." Miles let out a chuckle. "He also married someone outside the aristocracy, which meant he was more in tune with the real world. Something most of them are not."

"Was he in the military too?"

"No, I think he'd thought about it but then my grandfather became ill, so that kind of quashed those plans. He stayed at Holmwood and learned the ropes."

"You like being here though, right? I mean running Holmwood,"

Miles asked. He knew this was Alistair's second choice of career.

"Yes, I do. We're expanding so there are new challenges and it means I'm still active. That's what I miss the most from the military."

"Hmm, I can see that."

Alistair grinned at him. "So, what did you want to ask me?" Alistair picked up a stick and threw it for Duke. "Is it about Amanda?" He turned and looked at Miles.

"No, it wasn't actually, but now that you've opened up that door, maybe I *should* be asking about that."

Alistair let out a laugh. "Looks like I just shot myself in the foot and I've only got one." It was good to laugh after such a tense dinner. Miles once again marvelled at Alistair's laid-back attitude. "Joking aside, she's quite a special woman," Alistair said sincerely as they walked.

"She is."

"That's why I'm being as respectful as I can. We're taking our friendship a day at a time."

"Good to hear. Amanda can handle herself and you don't seem the type of guy who'd hurt her."

Alistair stopped abruptly. "No, I'd never do that," he said, as though the idea of hurting Amanda was appalling.

"I believe you." Miles gave him a reassuring smile. After everything he'd learned about Alistair, he was more than sure his intentions were honourable.

"So, if that wasn't what you were going to ask me about, what was it?"

"Ah, right." Miles cringed. "So, I've never done this and I've no idea of the rules, protocols and that, being a clueless American. The only person I can ask is Louisa and that would kind of defeat the object."

Alistair drew his eyebrows together. "You've lost me."

Miles let out a breath. "I'm presuming it's you I need to ask before I propose to Louisa."

It took Alistair a second to register what Miles had said. "Oh, I see. You're going to ask her to marry you?"

"Yes. You think she's going to say no?" Miles asked, seeing Alistair's shocked reaction.

"No, it's not that, it's just… you only really need to ask Louisa."

"Oh, I thought I needed to ask you."

Alistair shook his head with a grin. "Nope, *she's* the countess."

"I see, I think." He didn't and Alistair chuckled.

"If Papa was alive, *then* it would be expected for you to ask him but to be honest, she's pretty much her own woman and whatever anyone says wouldn't matter."

"Right," Miles said slowly.

"So, you're going to ask her, then?"

"Yes, not in the next few days, not with all this going on. But soon."

Alistair grinned widely and clapped him on the back. "That's good news."

"Only if she says yes," Miles said with a smirk.

"HEY, BABY."

"Hey," Louisa said. Her tone was a little deflated. Even seeing Miles dressed in only his boxer briefs and drinking coffee wasn't enough to lift her spirits. She'd just finished her first fake-for-the-press scenario with Gerard. They'd gone for an early morning leisurely ride around the grounds, in full view of the photographers. Louisa had kept a smile plastered on her face as Gerard periodically peppered their conversation with slating remarks about Miles, all the while keeping a well-rehearsed pleasant expression. She'd told him through her stiff smile that he was very welcome to leave but Miles wouldn't be, any time soon. They were saved from any further arguments by Celeste joining them. This hadn't been the plan but Lady Alice had suggested it the night before to her granddaughter. Even though she was a little late joining them, her presence had had the desired effect. The photographers got their footage of both Gerard and Louisa genuinely smiling as they saw their daughter gallop towards them and it put a halt to their undetected argument.

"You know what? I may make an effort and learn how to ride if I get to see you dressed in those skin-tight jodhpurs. Your ass looks edible in them. They look as though they were sprayed on," Miles drawled, placing his cup on the antique table. He'd been watching them through the window, curious to see if they'd make a good show. It hadn't been easy for him to see how good they looked together as a family but once Louisa had stepped into her suite, he could see the strain on her tired face. He did what he did best and distracted her in his unique way.

"Oh shush." She shook her head and stifled a smirk.

"Seriously sexy," Miles said, widening his eyes to emphasise the point as he stalked towards her.

Louisa's smirk turned into a shy smile as she removed her riding hat and dropped it onto the settee. "Thank goodness I had to wear a riding hat to hide the fact I have sex hair. I badly need a shower. I didn't have time this morning. I smell of sweat and sex."

Miles grabbed her around the waist and nuzzled her neck and she squirmed against his bristly chin. "Now we're talking."

"You've a one-track mind," she giggled.

"I have where you're concerned." And in a swift, well-practised manoeuvre, he hoisted her over his shoulder.

"Animal." Louisa swatted his tight behind and he reciprocated with a light slap on hers.

"Yep. Shower time and then a nice quiet breakfast... alone." And just like that, Louisa had forgotten all the bitter words Gerard had spewed.

HOLMWOOD HOUSE HAD OPENED its doors, which meant the Blackthorns and their guests were keeping out of sight on the top floors. All except Alistair who continued as usual, briefing his staff and wandering around, keeping a watchful eye. Lady Alice had Margot to keep her company, which was usual for a Sunday, while Celeste and Nicolas holed themselves up in her suite, only coming out to have lunch with Gerard.

Louisa and Miles stayed in Louisa's suite – the less contact Gerard and Miles had the better, and Miles was more than happy to stay out of the firing line. As far as the press were concerned, he wasn't even here. It meant he could catch up with a few emails and call up the many people he'd shunned over the last few days. Louisa also had work to catch up on, as well as keep Darcy and Melissa in the loop. Miles smiled to himself, taking in the almost domestic scene he found himself in. Louisa chatted easily, sitting at her no-doubt-priceless antique desk on a conference call, while he set up his workstation at the modest round dining table. They'd been served lunch in the suite and were now enjoying freshly brewed coffee. Louisa opted to use headphones, so as not to disturb Miles, but he'd enjoyed listening to the one-sided conversation. He was in awe of how Louisa was quick to solve problems and suggest new ideas to her team at CASPO, proving again that she was not just a figurehead but a key member of the organisation. He'd tried to keep focused on his laptop but he found his attention drifting to the efficient countess and her new ideas. There was to be a Diamond lounge for special VIPs at the concert. It was to entice all the high society with the deepest pockets to hand over huge sums of money, so that they could rub shoulders with the musicians. Miles also heard that Konran would be doing a press release, which again would hype up the concert and deflect away from the latest scandal.

Miles's attention was drawn back to Louisa as she wrapped up her call. She eyed him listening intently to what was being said and nodded, mumbling that she'd suggest something, then she said goodbye and pulled out her headphones.

"That sounded very productive," Miles said, turning in his seat to face her.

"Yes, things are moving pretty fast. Tickets go on sale next week."

"I hope Melissa isn't overdoing it."

"Ha, that'll be the day. Her mind is working overtime. In fact, she and Darcy had a suggestion that I want to run by you."

"It had better be a better one than us being 'outed'," he said drolly and Louisa gave him a nervous laugh.

"It is but I'm not sure if you'll like it."

Miles furrowed his brow at her comment but before he could ask what it was, his phone signalled an incoming call. "That's Eric," he said, puzzled. It was too early in LA for a call from him.

"Answer it," Louisa urged.

"This weekend is about you."

"Answer the phone; it might be important," Louisa said with a little more force.

Miles swiped the screen and put it to his ear. "Hey Eric, what's up?" He paused as Eric spoke and his eyes flitted to Louisa who had made her way over to the table. "Ah, you heard about that, eh? She's okay. Yeah, she's a tough cookie. We're both at Holmwood." Miles gave her a wink. It seemed that Eric was just calling to see if they were alright after the press conference. "Eric sends his regards."

"Hi, Eric," Louisa called and then watched as Miles continued to listen.

"Oh right, the contract's finalised? Well, just send it to me... Oh, I see. What's the other project? How long are you in London for?" Miles mouthed to Louisa that Eric was in the UK and needed to discuss film schedules. "Oh, well I'm here for the next few days..."

"Ask him to come here," Louisa whispered. Miles shook his head. *He couldn't just invite someone over.* Louisa curled her fingers, gesturing that she wanted the phone and Miles handed it to her.

"Hey, Eric... thank you. So, I understand you need to speak to Miles about a new project? Why don't you come to Holmwood and stay here? We have the room and there'll be no distractions... You're not imposing, I'm inviting. In fact, if I'm not mistaken, Pierce is going to Miles's house today to pick up some clothes for him; he can bring you back with him... Great, that's settled then. See you later." Louisa handed the phone back to Miles with a satisfied look on her face. Miles shook his head and said his goodbyes, telling Eric that Pierce would be in touch, then hung up.

"Well, at least that's all settled. Eric couldn't have timed it better." Miles huffed at her comment, still surprised that his agent was coming to stay at Holmwood, amidst the recent events. "Aren't you a little excited at what the other project is?"

"I suppose, the film is probably hard to follow but hopefully it'll be a good project." Miles shrugged. Eric had been very cagey about the project and insisted on a face-to-face.

"I'm sure it will be. Plus, it'll be good having someone for you to hang out with," she said with a wide self-satisfied smile. At least Eric would keep Miles distracted and away from Gerard, thought Louisa.

"You mean while you're running your empire, my lady?" Miles drawled as he took her hand and pulled her to him.

"Yes, well I have to keep you occupied; can't have my pretty boy bored, now," Louisa said dryly, looking down at him and pushing back his hair off his forehead. He bracketed her legs between his knees and rested his arms around her waist.

"You okay?" he asked with a tilt of his head.

"I am now. Thank you for coming," she said with a sigh.

"Louisa you don't need to thank me for being here for you. That's my job. Well, that and being your pretty boy arm candy," he said with a grin and Louisa let out a light chuckle.

"And you do that sooo well."

LADY ALICE FILLED MARGOT'S cup and handed it to her. It was early afternoon and they'd moved to the airy sitting room that overlooked the beautiful gardens at the rear of Holmwood. The whole area was swarming with visitors as the mid-summer sun shone down, re-touching every elegant piece of architecture, every sculptured foliage and sparkled across the calm lake. The Holmwood grounds were beautiful whatever the weather but when the sun's strokes brushed over them, they became a vibrant masterpiece.

"I'll be glad when Gerard leaves for his dinner tonight. The atmosphere around here can be cut with a knife," Lady Alice said as she sunk back into her luxurious seat. "Thank goodness Celeste and Nicolas are here. They managed to whisk him away for lunch without anyone realising. It was nice to have lunch alone."

"And Louisa?" asked Margot.

"She's been locked up in her suite with Miles after her morning ride."

Margot stifled a smirk. "It's a good job Gerard is off the grounds, then."

The door to the sitting room opened and in strode a flustered Alistair. "Oh, thank God. I need a good strong cup of tea," he said reaching for the teapot. Lady Alice moved forward and placed a slice of cake on a plate for her son, which he immediately took after thanking her.

"Hard day?" Margot asked.

"Well, we've had a 20 percent rise in visitors today. I've had to be on hand and we've got another couple of hours to go," he said taking a large gulp of tea.

"So, the scandal has upped business?" Lady Alice said dryly.

"Alice!" Margot chastised.

"Mama!" Alistair spluttered.

"Well, we have to find a silver lining in all this mess. They may also know that Mr Keane is here."

"I doubt it. He came in undetected, remember?" Alistair reminded her, forking a piece of cake into his mouth.

"Well, he's definitely lightened Louisa's mood. What time is his agent arriving?"

Alistair quickly swallowed and answered. "Pierce has gone to pick him up. He should be here in time for pre-dinner drinks."

"Miles is good for her," Margot said pointedly.

"That he is and his intentions are clear. He only thinks about her and that's what Louisa needs."

Margot nodded at her friend's observation.

"About that. I had a little chat with him last night. His intentions are as serious as it gets," Alistair said taking a seat by his mother.

"You mean he's proposed?" Margot gasped in surprise.

"Not yet but he will."

"He told you?" Lady Alice narrowed her eyes at Alistair.

"Yes, he thought he had to ask permission from me." Alistair chuckled at the thought.

"Louisa has found her knight that will fight for her." Margot gave Lady Alice a wide smile.

"Don't breathe a word," Alistair warned, giving both of them a stern stare.

"You know an engagement will deflect from all this scandal," Lady Alice said nonchalantly.

"Mama!"

"Alice!"

"I'm just stating the facts."

"You sound like Melissa," Alistair muttered.

"You know Darcy has put pressure on Gerard to look supportive of Louisa's work," Margot said raising her brow.

"How's he going to do that. Throw money at CASPO?" huffed Alistair. Gerard had made a good job of avoiding anything that elevated his sister. He'd signed a fat cheque and was hoping that would be enough.

"No, he's going to have to give up something far more valuable: his pride," Margot said with a knowing look.

"Meaning?"

"Darcy and Melissa have thought up another photo opportunity that'll show Gerard's full support of CASPO and the ambassador."

"And Gerard agreed?" Alistair couldn't hide his surprise.

"Well, he wasn't given much of a choice. You know how persuasive Melissa can be," Margot said dryly. Lady Alice stifled a grin at her friend's choice of words. Melissa had all but backed Gerard into a corner and used every kind of subtle blackmail she could, from her 'delicate' condition to expressing how much it would mean to Lady Alice. Gerard had little choice but to accept.

"It'll be good to have a wedding at Holmwood," Lady Alice said whimsically, as she looked out onto the grounds.

"He hasn't asked yet," Alistair said shoving the last piece of cake in his mouth.

"But he will," Lady Alice said, giving her friend and Alistair a wide smile.

"SO, HOW DO YOU want to do this?" Miles gave Gerard a fake smile as they strolled towards the boule green.

"I don't want to do this at all," Gerard gritted out. How the hell had it come to this? Him having to pretend to like the uncouth American and cocky lover of his ex-wife.

"Well, tough shit. We're having to do this because of the crap you pulled. So, suck it buttercup and look like I'm your BFF," sneered Miles.

"You Americans and your love of making up abbreviations." His tone was as condescending as ever.

"You Frenchmen with your holier-than-thou attitude that fucking stinks," Miles countered and Gerard's step faltered. If it wasn't for the fact there were cameras pointed at them and, no doubt, all the Blackthorns watching from the privacy of the top floor, Gerard would have gladly punched him for his insolence. Miles Keane made him want to tap into the temper he'd spent years keeping in check. A gentleman never showed extreme emotions. But just being in the same square mile as him had Gerard incensed.

"Keep smiling, Gerard," Miles jibed, seeing his expression change. "You think I want to be anywhere near you right now? If I never set my eyes on you again, it'd be too soon." He gave a humorous laugh, all the while his perfect fake smile on his face never wavering. Miles hadn't realised how hard acting as though you liked someone was, until this weekend. He was as good as anyone at being polite in certain undesirable circumstances but the past 36 hours of 'playing nice' had pushed this skill to the limit.

The press had circulated the photo-op of Gerard with Louisa and Celeste, which had dampened down the story that there was any animosity between the divorced couple. However, Darcy had suggested that Gerard also needed to be seen as a supporter of his ex-wife's new life and work. So, the perfect scenario would be Gerard with CASPO's famous ambassador. This was how Gerard and Miles had ended up walking over to the boule's green just after Holmwood House had been closed off for the day. They could clearly be seen from the perimeter wall, where a number of photographers had set up.

"How long do we need to be out here for?" Gerard ground out as they walked around, pretending to be absorbed and interested in their conversation. The plan was to have them strolling around the visible area, chatting amiably. Ten minutes Darcy had said would be enough and she'd highlighted their need to look comfortable and happy. *Easier said than done!*

Gerard walked with his hands linked behind his back with his head held high on tense shoulders and Miles strolled loosely next to him with his hands shoved in his pockets, almost enjoying the fact his presence was causing Gerard such a high level of discomfort. Gerard was a sitting duck; if he messed this up, he'd look bad publicly and privately, and Miles took a perverse pleasure in the fact. This was time for payback, not for him but for Louisa.

They both managed to keep a stiff smile on their faces but thankfully the sunglasses they were both wearing hid their true emotions.

"Just another five minutes or so. You think you could put yourself out for another five minutes? How does it feel to realise that the world doesn't actually just revolve around you?" Miles scoffed.

"Shut up. That's really something coming from you. Your career was media lead and supported by hordes of fans. Scandal followed you around like a bad smell." Gerard's fake smile widened. Miles acted as though his cutting comment was something he was considering, all for the cameras, then tilted his head to his walking partner.

"At least any scandal that was attached to me, was about me and hurt *only me*, you arrogant asshole," he said through his stiff smile. Gerard's lips thinned and Miles was sure his eyes behind his dark glasses had turned to slits. "Keep smiling, remember everyone is watching," Miles sing-songed and Gerard's fake smile jumped back onto his face. "You'll be pleased to know I'll make sure our paths hardly ever cross, though."

"You do that. The quicker you're out of here the better."

Miles tilted his head back and laughed heartily. "Oh no, it'll be you that's out of here, Gerard. When I marry Louisa."

Gerard stopped abruptly. "What!"

"Keep smiling," Miles said as brightly as his smile. Gerard allowed his lips to curve up at the edges, just. "I said, *when* I marry Louisa." Miles spoke as though he was talking to a child, purposely trying to aggravate Gerard. "You'll have even less reason to come here. After all, we both know what your true intentions have been all along." Miles turned as he spoke so that they could head back to the house. He was sure the photographers had enough footage by now. He really didn't want to spend any more one-on-one time with Gerard than needed. At least he'd made his intentions perfectly clear.

"She'll never marry you," Gerard said with a humourless laugh after he'd gathered himself.

"Wanna bet?" Miles accentuated his American accent and put out his hand for Gerard to shake. "Take my hand for the cameras, Gerard. You don't want them thinking you're sad and bitter because a better man has stepped into your role, do we now?" Miles goaded. He was sure Gerard's eyes were shooting pure fire at him. Darcy had known exactly what she was doing when she suggested they wear sunglasses this late in the day. Gerard reluctantly took his hand and gave it a hard shake. "She'll marry me because she loves me and I love her." Miles squeezed his hand a little tighter, then pulled it away.

"You're too crass and brash for her." Gerard gave him a sarcastic smirk and began walking back towards the house. Miles fell in step with him pleased he'd obviously gotten deep under his skin.

"That may be but mark my words, Gerard: Louisa and I *will* get married. And just so we're clear, when you receive your invite…"

"Never going to happen," Gerard snapped back.

"*When* you get your invite," Miles repeated a little louder. "Because we both know that Louisa has impeccable manners and she will invite you, you'll politely decline."

"You are not going to marry her. See that up there?" Gerard made a show of pointing up to the sky and Miles tilted his head up instinctively to see what he was pointing at. "Pigs flying." He sneered and Miles let out a loud laugh.

"Ha-ha… such a comedian," Miles said. To everyone looking on from the wall 200 metres away and the house, it looked like two gentlemen shooting the breeze and laughing at each other's jokes. Louisa squinted, taking in the scene while nervously knotting her hands together. She didn't think Gerard would go ahead with the idea. She was still surprised he'd stayed on after the argument they'd had the night he'd arrived. He'd of course come, thinking she'd run into his arms for comfort. When instead, she'd read him the riot act, telling him that she'd always known that one day, every sordid detail would come out that their life was far from spotless. What was worse, the blame had been laid at her feet. Her name had been tarnished because of his less-than-perfect behaviour and that reflected badly on her family name and the work they did. She was put in an impossible situation, where to explain the truth would only make the story escalate, and to say nothing was as good as admitting it was all true. On top of all of that, there was Celeste to think about too.

Today's little PR stunts were all part of Gerard's attempt to make things better. It was no doubt the last thing he wanted to do but for the sake of Celeste and for the name of her family, Louisa knew he'd do what was necessary. Gerard's sense of duty and loyalty were a couple of his better traits, even if he fell short when it came to fidelity. Louisa took in the two men as they strolled back to the house. *What on Earth could they be talking about?* She thought to herself. She knew Gerard all but despised Miles and Miles hadn't held back on voicing his feelings about her ex. Louisa checked her watch. It was almost time for dinner; well, she hoped it would be less tense than the night before.

"You will *not* come to our wedding. I will *not* have *our* day ruined by you turning up like a bad, bent, French Franc." Miles's voice rose with every syllable, all the while he kept his fixed smile.

"The Franc doesn't exist anymore, you imbecile," spat out Gerard.

"My point exactly," Miles said dryly and again Gerard's plastic smile slipped. "Smile for the cameras," Miles taunted and Gerard muttered an expletive under his breath as he forced his mouth to curve. "I will put up with you for the sake of Celeste and out of respect for Lady Alice and Alistair, and because Louisa still cares for you, but I don't have to like you. Step on my toes or interfere in my life with Louisa and I'll expose every one of your dirty secrets." He threatened through his smile. "Are we clear? I've nothing to hide. Louisa and the world know everything about me. You, on the other hand, have managed to keep your female skeletons firmly locked in your *armoire*." Gerard was about to answer him back but Miles didn't give him the chance. They'd speeded up their walk back, both of them eager to get out of everyone's scrutinizing eye. "How arrogant do you have to be to think Louisa would take you back after everything you've done to her? After how you disrespected and hurt her. She told me everything and I swear if I didn't know how much it would upset them all in there, I'd knock you the fuck out."

"Ha! There's the real Miles Keane. The cowboy that can't even ride a horse but thinks he can swagger in here and threaten whoever he wants," Gerard said scathingly.

"At least I don't pretend to be someone I'm not. And what's more, Louisa seems to prefer the rough cowboy." He gave the Frenchman a knowing smirk.

"We'll see. I think we're done here." Gerard patted his back, trying to make it look as though it was a friendly gesture and to everyone looking on it did, except that the pat was more of a hard slap. How Miles didn't flinch, even he didn't know, but he turned to look directly at Gerard as they stopped by the door leading into the conservatory.

"Touch me again and I'll break your fucking arm," Miles ground out with more than a hint of an edge.

"Just trying to be convincing."

"You think you have them fooled, Gerard? They see right through you. Lies always catch up to you. It's called karma and she's bitch with spurs on her boots," Miles drawled, stepping through the French window and coming face-to-face with a worried-looking Louisa.

"Everything okay?" she asked tentatively. Her eyes bounced between the two men. Miles pulled off his sunglasses and gave her a brilliant smile.

"Absolutely," he said cheerily.

"Of course. If you'll excuse me, I need to get ready to leave," Gerard said evenly with a tight smile and made his way to the staircase. Louisa watched him for a second, then turned back to an amused Miles.

"Are you sure everything was okay? Gerard looked tense."

"Probably not used to this kind of performing," Miles said drolly.

"Whereas you're a pro?"

"I try," he said with a cocky smirk, then stepped up to her and kissed her soundly.

"Eric is being entertained by Mama. Are you ready to go in for dinner?"

"Sure." From the corner of his eye, Miles saw Gerard come down the sweeping staircase and out of the house, practically slamming the door. "I have a feeling it'll be a lot more pleasant this evening."

4

REIGN RAIN AND REIN

The atmosphere around Lady Alice's dining room table couldn't have been more different from the night before. Lady Alice was on good form, charming Eric with stories of the Blackthorns that reigned over Holmwood in the past, feeding him historical titbits, scandals and facts that had the whole dining room of guests amused. Alistair chipped in, explaining future plans, while Louisa added her own memories of her childhood days. It was a relaxed and entertaining evening that the American agent found both fascinating and surreal. It was hard not to be awestruck by the grandiose settings, steeped in a rich history and surrounded by priceless heirlooms, furniture and art. His first glimpse of Holmwood House, when he'd first arrived, was confined to the grounds and the back stairs which lead to his beautiful room. Alistair had promised him the full tour in the morning when the grounds and house were free from visitors. Lady Alice had brought out the Blackthorn's finest, knowing the charismatic Eric Schultz would get a kick out of it, which was confirmed by the way his eyes had widened when he'd taken his seat.

Eric's gaze roamed around the room, taking in the opulent chandeliers, magnificent fireplace, pristine linens, antique crockery and silverware. He noticed a crest, carved into the marble of the fireplace, the same crest was displayed in the grand hallway with an inscription running across the bottom. Alistair caught sight of Eric scrutinising the carving.

"It's the Blackthorn coat of arms."

"Fascinating. What does it symbolise?"

"The lion's head is a symbol of our heritage. It's the national emblem of the Netherlands," explained Alistair.

"So, you're Dutch?" Eric couldn't hide his surprise. Miles's brows shot up as his and the rest of the table's attention shifted to Alistair and

Eric's discussion.

"Well, the Blackthorn family goes back to the 1500s. We're related to the Prince of Orange," Lady Alice said with a hint of pride, turning to Eric who was to her left.

"Wow."

"Yes, in fact Louisa is named after one of his daughters."

The whole table turned to look at Louisa. Louisa hunched her shoulders as Miles mouthed 'really?' to her. He'd never dared to delve into her heritage, afraid he'd be even more daunted than he already was. Listening to Lady Alice and Alistair explain the impressive history only underlined the fact, though he was secretly pleased his inquisitive agent was happy to ask the questions he'd been wary of broaching. "Her portrait is in the blue drawing-room. Though our Louisa is far more beautiful," Lady Alice said proudly and Louisa rolled her eyes.

"Oh God, yes. That portrait is hideous! She wasn't a good-looking countess at all," Celeste exclaimed and everyone chuckled. From the way the Blackthorns reacted, it was obviously a family joke.

"And the rest of the crest?"

"There are three Mauritian blue pigeons. They're extinct now but they were coloured red, white and blue, which are the colours of the Netherlands flag and, coincidently, the British."

"And the Americans," chipped in Nicolas, which caused a ripple of laughter.

"And why three?" asked Eric.

"It's a symbol of so many things: heaven, earth and water. Possibly birth, life and death, or the Holy Trinity," Alistair said with a shrug. "To be honest, over the years, the reasoning changed but three has always been a favourable number."

"Very true. The wording isn't Latin, then?"

"No, Dutch," Lady Alice said, then started to recite the words: "*Corona veniet delectis.*" And to the amusement of the American guests all the Blackthorns join in.

"It's been drilled into us from birth," Louisa said with a smirk. "It means, victory shall come to the worthy."

"That's very profound," Eric said.

"All the earls and the countesses have either a seal ring or pendant with our crest on," Lady Alice explained.

"All?" Miles furrowed his brow, remembering the ring Alistair had worn at the activities weekend dance. Louisa nodded.

"We all have one. Some have been passed down over the years and some have been made. Only Blackthorns or the earl or countesses' spouse can have one. That's why Mama has one." Miles shook his head slightly in awe of the many traditions the Blackthorns had. The only tradition his family had was watching the Superbowl together and eating sticky ribs made by his father.

"I find all of this so interesting." Eric took a sip of his wine, totally enamoured and impressed with the Blackthorns.

"We have a book, if you'd like. I think it's in its third edition now. Well, we update it every few years." Lady Alice said brightly.

"I don't think Eric is *that* interested in our history," Celeste said dryly.

"I'd love one, actually," Eric said eagerly.

Lady Alice shot a self-satisfied look at Celeste and answered. "I'll make sure one gets sent up to your room." She patted Eric's arm and he beamed at her.

LOUISA SETTLED INTO THE seat next to Miles and kicked off her shoes, which caused Miles to stifle a smirk as he took a sip of his Armagnac. She'd come a long way in the few months they'd been together. They were sitting in her private suite enjoying an after-dinner drink with Eric, after the rest of the dinner party had retired to their suites.

Eric went through the list of requests for interviews from various magazines and TV shows that had come in since the concert had been announced. He was hoping to pin Miles down for at least one live broadcast, which they could double up as a promotion for his up-and-coming series.

"I'm happy to do the three magazines you suggested but I think I'll pass on the TV shows," Miles huffed.

"Miles," Eric shuffled forward in his seat. "The public need to see you."

"Well, we saw how that went down," Miles answered sarcastically as he reached for Louisa's hand and gave it a squeeze.

"This won't be reporters; it'll be professional interviewers," he said carefully, not wanting to upset Louisa but at the same time wanting to point out the difference.

"It's press, whichever way you look at it."

"I wouldn't put you in a vulnerable position, Miles. Plus, you have a number of projects that need promoting."

Miles let out a breath and slumped back in his seat. He knew Eric was right but after the disastrous press conference, the idea of doing live TV interviews made his heart hammer.

"Let's just see closer to the concert, shall we? I'll tell them we're looking into your schedule."

"Fine," Miles said mulishly and Eric smirked, knowing he would come around eventually. "So, are you going to tell me about this offer? You've been very quiet up until now."

"I wasn't going to jump right in and tell you. You know me better than that." Eric gave him a wide smile and Miles's mood changed, seeing his good friend and agent's face light up in humour. "And besides, we've been talking about the concert. Which also begs the question of whether you'll be performing."

Before Miles could say anything, Louisa answered. "CASPO aren't expecting Miles to perform. His role is as our ambassador."

"Hmm, I see. Well, I was hoping you'd changed your mind because this next proposal might not be so welcome."

"I'm not performing as Keane Sense," Miles said sharply, sitting forward.

"This isn't you performing as Keane Sense," Eric clarified and Miles gave him a nod.

"Just come out with it."

"You've been offered a role on Broadway and the West End playing Donald Lockwood," Eric said softly.

Miles furrowed his brow but Louisa let out a gasp, causing Miles to turn his full attention to her. "*Singing in the Rain*," she said with an excited laugh and Miles gaped at her.

"That's crazy. I don't believe it," he said shaking his head, chuckling.

"What am I missing?" Eric looked between the two of them.

"It's a private joke," Miles explained.

"Oh, okay. A good private joke, I take it?" Eric couldn't hide his amusement at seeing Louisa blush.

"Yeah, you could say that." Miles grinned and for a moment they were transported back to the first evening Louisa had spent at Miles's home and his reckless kiss, in the rain.

Once the surprise of the offer had died down, Eric asked. "Well, what do you think?" Miles gave Louisa a lopsided smile.

"Broadway?" He squeezed her hand, then turned his attention back to Eric. "I live here now." The very idea of being away from Louisa for an extended length of time was impossible, regardless of the offer.

"It's actually six weeks on Broadway, then they bring it to the West end for another six weeks."

"Eric… it's performing. Live performing. I'm not sure I can do it… you know – "

"It's a major role, Miles. You're basically stepping into Gene Kelly's shoes." Eric's voice escalated, interrupting him mid-sentence to make his point.

"Jeez, way to make me feel even more daunted." Miles rubbed his face in exasperation. "When would this be? I have the film shoot in January."

Eric waved his hands dismissively. "In a year's time." He could see Miles was trying to work out if logistically he could do the role. "It'll coincide with the release of the film, so all the press can be done simultaneously," he added, hoping that the idea of joint PR would seal the deal.

Miles turned to Louisa who had kept quiet, not wanting to pressurize Miles one way or the other. The decision was his. She knew he was thinking about being away from her but she'd be able to fly back and forth, if needs be.

"What do you think?"

"I think it's a big role and an honour to be offered it."

Miles turned back to Eric. "Don't I need to audition or something? You make it sound as though it's a done deal."

"It is a done deal. They know you can sing. They know you can dance well enough and the acting will be rehearsed." Miles's eyes widened. He should've known that Eric had cleared any obstacles before he spoke to him.

"This would be what... six performances a week?"

"Seven... Saturdays have matinees," Eric corrected.

"Christ."

"It's a great role, Miles. You wanted to break away from the popstar mould," Eric reminded him and Miles blew out a breath, then turned back to Louisa.

"*Singing in the Rain*." She smiled widely at him and his face mirrored hers in an instant.

"Singing in the fucking rain." Miles shook his head, still unable to believe that this role had been handed to him. It was a sign. "You think they'll have a role for Hugh?" he chortled and Louisa let out a giggle.

"He could play the policeman."

Miles let out a loud laugh.

"Hugh? Who's Hugh?" Eric asked, confused.

"It doesn't matter," Miles said with a shake of his head.

"I don't suppose you have a script, do you?" Louisa asked.

"Of course I do," Eric said and pulled out a thick file from his briefcase and dropped it on the table.

"Read the script, Miles, then take the meeting before you decide," Louisa said softly.

"Louisa, it's performing live seven times a week," Miles said with a hint of sadness.

"In a year's time. Look back to a year ago and see how far you've come," Louisa pointed out.

Eric was thankful that he'd been invited to Holmwood, and that Louisa was by Miles's side when he told him about the offer. "Listen to the countess; she has nothing to gain."

"And listen to your manager," Louisa said with a grin.

"He gets 10 percent; he's got too much to gain," Miles said dryly.

Eric chuckled at Miles's retort. "I'm always on your side. And yeah, the 10 percent is great but seeing you do your thing, knowing it was me that helped you get there, worth more than the 10 percent, Miles. You've always been worth more than 10 percent." Eric lifted his glass in a toast and Louisa clinked her glass against it, then turned to Miles, who reluctantly lifted his glass to hers. They took a sip, then Eric stood up. "I'll leave you to sleep on it. We can talk again in the morning." Louisa wished him goodnight and allowed Miles to see him out of their suite.

By the time Miles came back, Louisa was already in the bedroom changing into her nightdress.

"That's a hell of a role," Louisa said.

"It'll mean I'm away from you," he said quietly.

Louisa stepped up to him and cupped his face in her hand. "No, it won't. I can be with you in New York and pop back and forth. Melissa won't be pregnant, so she'll be back in full force. Alistair has Holmwood covered. Celeste will be at university. It'll be a few months in total, with rehearsals."

"What will you do in New York while I'm rehearsing and performing?"

"I used to live there, remember? I'll have plenty of things to occupy me."

Miles pursed his lips and nodded. All he could think about was that she'd be in New York with nothing to do, while he'd be rehearsing. Gerard would be around. He needed to seal another kind of deal as soon as possible. One with a ring.

Louisa started whistling *Singing in the Rain* and Miles's pondering frown lit up into a huge smile. "That's so crazy, isn't it?"

"I think it's a sign. I think it's a positive sign that this is what you should do next," Louisa said with a soft smile, and Miles knew she meant a sign from Louis.

"Want to read the script?"

"After."

"After?" Louisa asked.

"Yeah, after I seal the deal like I sealed the movie deal." Miles's eyes glittered as he dropped down and hoisted her over his shoulder. Louisa squealed and he marched up to the bed and dropped her down on the luxurious bedspread. Her hair fanned out and she wriggled up to the top as Miles shed himself of his shirt.

"And how's that?" she asked coyly. Miles prowled towards her like a hungry lion ready to devour her. He dropped to his knees on the bed and blanketed his body over hers.

"Let me show you, baby, you're my good luck charm."

MILES STEPPED INTO LOUISA's suite and frowned, seeing her sitting at her desk, engrossed in whatever she was reading on her laptop. "Everything okay?" he asked striding up to her.

Louisa swivelled the laptop so he could see. "I think our plan might be working," she said with a reluctant smile. Miles scanned the screen where a number of publications had articles posted about Louisa and Gerard. Each one of them had various photos of them on horseback, seemingly chatting at ease. The articles reported that Gerard and Louisa had an amicable divorce and he was always welcome at Holmwood. They went on to say that according to their source, who was close to the Blackthorns, that Gerard was supportive of Louisa's work at CASPO and had recently spent a weekend with the families the charity helped. There were a few older photos of Louisa and Gerard together in New York at a gala event and on a yacht in Monaco. Miles remembered seeing the same photos when he did his own research on Louisa, when he'd found out who she was. He then scrolled down to where there were photos of himself and Gerard. The photo of him laughing and Gerard talking with a smile on his face caught his eye. The caption wrote "Mr Dupont and Miles Keane, the new ambassador of CASPO, enjoying their time at Holmwood over the weekend." It looked convincingly like two men enjoying each other's company and Miles gave a smirk, knowing that he knew the truth behind that particular moment. It always amazed and infuriated Miles how the media could twist and create a story to suit them. Today though, he was grateful for their ability to spin their carefully crafted version of the truth.

"'A source close to the Blackthorns'?" Miles said with an arch of his brow.

"Melissa," Louisa said with a shrug and Miles chuckled.

"It seems to have done the trick." Miles dropped a swift kiss on the top of her head. Louisa looked up at him and gave him a relieved smile. Seeing the photos of Louisa and Gerard together, even though he knew they were false, hadn't sat well with him. They looked far too good together and Miles couldn't help but feel unworthy. If the photos were convincing to him, knowing that they were false, he had high hopes that the public would also believe that the rumours the journalists spouted at the press conference were all lies. Seeing Louisa so relieved, though, made the uncomfortable encounters with Gerard more than worth it.

"It's still early days but these will definitely help. Melissa wants me to go to London and be seen going to work."

"You spoke to her? It's only 8:30," he scoffed.

"You know Melissa. She called me just after you left for your run."

"Robert will confiscate her phone if she doesn't slow down." Miles slid into the chair next to her and poured himself a coffee from the beautifully laid-out tray. "So, is that the plan, head back to London?" he asked, eyeing her over his cup. They hadn't really discussed much of their plans past today. Gerard would be leaving before lunch and Eric had to be back in London too. He was hoping to have a few hours with him this morning after Alistair finished giving him a quick tour. Miles glanced at the hefty script he'd left on the table.

"I do need to head back to London." Louisa paused for a beat, then swallowed before continuing. "Gerard is leaving for the city too today." Miles's gaze shot back to Louisa and she gave him an apologetic smile.

"You're leaving together?" he said, trying to keep his tone even, but Louisa saw the clench in his jaw. It was just another photo opportunity. One where they'd be in the same car leaving Holmwood, hopefully cementing their amicable relationship. The problem was that wasn't where the charade would end.

"We're just... um..."

"Carpooling?" Miles said with more than a hint of sarcasm and Louisa's heart dropped. Had it been the other way around she'd be just as upset, probably more so. She was always asking him to bend for her but for how long would he put up with it, before he snapped?

"It's just for the press. He has a meeting and... well I need to be back," Louisa said in a rush and Miles stood up and began to pace.

"Is this Melissa's idea or Gerard's?" He paused his pacing to look at her. Louisa's face dropped and Miles let out a humourless laugh, knowing the answer.

"Gerard suggested it and Melissa thought it was a good idea," she said softly. Miles pursed his lips and ran his hand over his face in frustration. It seemed that Gerard wasn't pulling any punches. He'd only been gone 40 minutes for a run and Gerard had swooped in with a new strategy, in an attempt to save the day. Miles clenched his jaw. He was going to have to be more alert and pay attention.

"So, the two of you will leave this morning?" Louisa nodded. "And he's returning to New York… ?"

"I'm not entirely sure. I know he has a meeting in the afternoon. But after that…"

"He hasn't confirmed anything?" Louisa furrowed her brow and shook her head.

"I see."

"Miles, this is just for the press," she repeated, standing up. Louisa knew how it looked. She'd be spending time with Gerard, alone, no Celeste, Lady Alice or Alistair to buffer them.

Miles nodded slowly, trying to seem calm when he was anything but. He cursed himself for revealing too much of himself to the arrogant Frenchman. This was his way of sabotaging his and Louisa's future. He'd have her all to himself, taking advantage of her vulnerability. He was giving her his full support and using the excuse of "looking good for the press" as a tool to get closer to Louisa. Miles had underestimated him.

"Sure, it is," Miles muttered and Louisa's shoulders dropped. He looked hurt and lost and Louisa felt wretched knowing it was because of her and the situation she was in. She stepped up to him and wrapped herself around him. Miles took a second before he circled his arms around her and dropped a soft kiss on the top of her head.

"I'm sorry you have to deal with all this. It's just for…"

"The press, I know. I get it. It doesn't mean I like it though," Miles sighed.

"I know."

"He's going to stick around for longer Louisa, you realise that, don't you?" Louisa stayed silent because she knew he was right. Gerard had already said he'd be staying for a few more days. Whatever the reasons for Gerard's tactics, it was still going to hurt Miles. "What else, Louisa? What else did he suggest?"

"Miles…" her voice was a soft plea as she pulled back to look up at him.

"Just tell me," he pleaded quietly.

"We'll have lunch somewhere, so the reporters can see us."

"Okay," Miles said carefully. That didn't sound too bad. They'd be out in the open during the day.

Louisa took a nervous swallow and added. "He'll be seen going into CASPO's offices."

"After lunch?" Miles searched her worried eyes, knowing there was something else, something he wasn't going to like.

"No, tomorrow. He'll be staying."

Miles huffed and shook his head. The man had no shame. Never had he been to CASPO's offices. Louisa had told him as much and now, all of a sudden, he was playing the role of interested husband, apart from the fact they were divorced! "So, he really is sticking around, then?" Miles released her and stepped up to the table and reached for his coffee cup. What a way to start the day, talking about Gerard and his cunning ploy. Miles drained his coffee and placed the cup down and turned back to an edgy Louisa. "Where will he be staying?" Louisa looked away from him and began to close down her laptop. "Louisa?" Miles rested his hand on her arm causing her to stop what she was doing, and her apologetic gaze rose to his. It took Miles a second to realise where Gerard would be staying.

"Fuck." He raked his hand through his hair in frustration.

"Miles... it's a big house," she said in an attempt to pacify him as he angrily strode towards the window.

He spun back and narrowed his eyes at her. "Is it? Well, I wouldn't know, seeing as I've never been." The moment he'd said the words he regretted it. He was angry at the situation, at Gerard but not at Louisa, and it wasn't fair to lash out at her, but his patience was running out. The secrecy was getting to him and to make matters a thousand times worse, Gerard could come and go as he pleased, whenever he pleased.

Louisa blinked back the tears that pricked her eyes. The last thing she wanted to do was hurt Miles. He'd done nothing wrong. He was blameless. In fact, he'd done everything he could to make sure she was always protected, putting himself in the path of the firing line for her. His comment stung but he was right: he'd never been to her London home and until now she hadn't realised how much it bothered him.

"We won't even see each other," she said quietly. Miles pinched the bridge of his nose and closed his eyes in an attempt to calm down and avoid seeing Louisa's regretful face. "Miles, we lived together for 20 years and 10 of those we lived separately."

Miles blew out a breath. "Yeah, sure. Like I said, I don't have to like it." He took a deep breath and gave her a lopsided sad smile. "He gets you all to himself, out in the open, stays at your home, after everything he's done to you, what he's put you and your family through... and I get you when you can fit me in... and even then, I'm in the shadows."

"Miles..."

"I know this is not your fault. I know that. But it's not mine either, yet I seem to be the one getting punished," he said with a hint of bitterness and before Louisa could try and reassure him, Miles's phone rang.

Miles reached for his phone and answered it. "Morning, Eric... No, I've been up a while. Look there's been a change of plan. I'll get Pierce and we can be out of here within the hour. We can discuss everything back at mine. Less distractions." Louisa watched on as Miles finished his call, then immediately rang Pierce, telling him of the change to their schedule.

"You're leaving so soon?" Louisa said trying to keep her voice from cracking. He looked so hurt and she didn't know how to make this situation better.

"I think it's best." Miles picked up the script and headed to the bedroom where his things were. He needed a quick shower and to pack.

Louisa followed him, a little lost as to what she could do to stop him. "Miles, you don't need to go."

He pulled out his small case and started putting his clothes in, without much thought. "I just don't want to be around when Gerard and you leave, Louisa." He paused for a moment, then turned to face her. "I know it sounds petty but there's only so much I can take."

Louisa stared into his pensive face. For the first time since they'd been together, he looked dejected. How could she blame him? "I'm sorry you have to deal with all this. It's just..."

"Your life."

67

"Yes, it is."

"I get it but at some point, your life and mine crossed. And I can accept certain things, fall in when it's necessary, put you first, every time. But I can't watch you and…" Miles blinked his eyes for an extended second. "I can't be around when he can have the parts of you I can't. It's not fair for you to ask me to. I want to be the bigger man here but my skin isn't that thick, Louisa." He gave her a sad smile. "It's best if I go. I'm pretty close to knocking that smug look off his face, as it is. He makes it almost impossible to rein in my temper." He reached and pulled her to him, holding her tightly to his chest. "I'm sorry."

"You have nothing to apologise for," Louisa mumbled into his chest. "It's me that should be apologising." Miles rested his cheek on the top of her head, relishing these last moments alone. He had no idea how long Gerard planned on staying but he had no wish to be anywhere near him. He just hoped this whole scandal would disappear and take the arrogant Frenchman with it.

"ALL GOOD?" Eric asked chirpily as their car pulled away from Holmwood House.

"It could be better," Miles said mulishly and focused on Duke, who had settled on his lap. He stroked him gently, hoping it would calm him. They'd managed to pack up and say their goodbyes and thanks to Lady Alice and Alistair. Lady Alice ensured Eric had the large book on the Blackthorns she'd promised him and invited him to come again and stay for longer next time. Louisa had seen them to the car, which had been parked at the rear secluded entrance. She'd also invited Eric back for a visit and once he'd slipped into the car, she turned to a decidedly subdued Miles. He took her face between his hands and gave her a soft kiss, then lowered his forehead to hers.

"I feel like this is goodbye," she said quietly.

"You know where I am, Louisa. I'm not going anywhere." He gave her one last kiss on her forehead and lowered himself into the back of their car. They hadn't made any plans to meet up and Miles hadn't pressed her either. She knew how to reach him. The next move was on her. He'd have to wait backstage for her, in the shadows.

"Smile for the cameras," Eric said brightly and Miles looked up to see approximately 40 reporters loitering just outside the huge gates of Holmwood. They couldn't see into the back of the car where Miles and Eric were sitting. The only photos they'd get were of Pierce and Karl in the front.

"Fucking vultures," muttered Miles and Pierce smirked at him in the rear-view mirror. Miles scanned the lush grass of the Holmwood estate as the car powered away. Even in the misty morning, his keen eye caught sight of a lone man sitting on a horse in the distance, watching their car leave. Miles narrowed his eyes in an attempt to focus on his face, though he already knew who it was. The stiff and proud stance was enough of a giveaway, *Gerard*. Miles clenched his jaw knowing Louisa's ex was no doubt smirking to himself, pleased he'd run him off. But he hadn't run away. He'd made life easier for Louisa, behaved like a gentleman. He'd come to her when she'd needed him, now that she was strong enough to face the world again, it was up to her to run back to him.

"So why the rush to get out of Holmwood?" Eric asked.

"It's complicated," Miles said dismissively.

"Not really. It's very simple," Eric countered and Miles arched his brow at him. "Gerard's the knight in shining armour... to the press anyway. And you're the real hero side piece, hiding in the wings."

"Jesus." Miles shook his head.

"Too brutal?"

"A bit," Miles said dryly. He should've known his perceptive friend wouldn't pussyfoot around.

"Look, you know how this works, Miles, you're no amateur. It's all a façade, it's just you're not used to being the one behind the scenes."

"My ego isn't that big or that fragile, Eric," he huffed.

"No, it isn't but this isn't about your ego, this is about your feelings for Louisa and any threat. You're not in control and you've restrictions to deal with too." Eric gave him a pointed look.

"This whole fucking mess is because of *him* and what *he's* done in the past and I'm the one getting shunned," Miles bit out.

"You're not being shunned. Anyone can see how much she cares for you, loves you. Don't throw a tantrum over something that isn't real," Eric said in a hushed tone.

"He'll be staying at her house in London. And I'm not throwing a tantrum! I'm pissed, okay? Pissed that he can stay and I can't," Miles ground out, then after a beat, added, "He's determined to get her back... he..."

"Fucked up. Louisa isn't a fool. She's not going to run back to him."

"And she's not going to shack up with playboy-ex-drug-addict-popstar either," Miles said with a sneer.

"Ouch! Is that how you see yourself?"

Miles gave a one-shoulder shrug and looked out of the window. "That's how I'm seen and appearances matter, well they matter to the Blackthorns."

"I didn't get that vibe. Lady Alice seemed to like you a lot and Alistair was totally laid back too." Eric patted Miles's thigh to bring his attention back to him. "Plus, you have three big projects that say you're not seen as any of those things." He gave him an encouraging smile. "Miles, listen to me. Stop thinking you're not worthy. Stop dwelling on what you were and focus on what you are and what you can be."

"It's just... pfft... I don't know."

"A lot to take in? Her world?"

"Yeah." Miles looked down at Duke, who'd fallen asleep, and he buried his fingers into his thick brown fur.

"Too much?" Eric pressed. "Is she worth it, all this angst? Can you let her go and see her back with Gerard or some other aristocrat?" Miles shot Eric a look that said there was no way he could let her go and especially to Gerard. "Well then, you need to suck it up. I'm not saying you need to be a pushover, that's not your style, but carry on with what you've been doing. Be present at CASPO, support her, be there for her, even in the background. It takes a strong man to feel confident in the shadow of a powerful woman. From what I've seen and heard, Gerard isn't that man."

Miles swallowed hard and gave a small nod, then turned to look out of the window. It was true, he didn't need to be in the limelight anymore. He'd had his fill of adoration and attention, even if it had been superficial. If the last few years had taught him anything it was that fame was fickle and though he was thankful for his loyal fans, he didn't need them to feel worthy. Not anymore at least. Losing Louis and stepping up for Amanda had put everything into perspective. He wasn't that cocky popstar anymore. And though his past was dug up every time he did anything, he realised it would continue to haunt him until he achieved something else, something that would overshadow his previous self. Meeting Louisa, being part of CASPO had been the first step. The new career path he was taking was because of her. Being with her made him feel stronger, deserving, as though he could achieve anything. She wasn't dazzled by the fame, she saw him, *just* Miles, like he saw *just* Louisa. He'd be happy to live in her shadow, he'd bask in it, as long as she was his.

The car fell silent for a while, with Miles contemplating Eric's words and processing his own introspective thoughts. The lush green countryside gave way to suburbia and as they drove closer to Miles's home in the city, the atmosphere in the car shifted from sombre to a little charged. Even Duke had perked up, the noise of the city waking him from his nap.

Eric had made small talk with Karl and Pierce during the journey, leaving Miles to ponder on his words. He'd known Miles a long time and it was in moments like these he needed some space to cool off. Louis had always been the one to talk him down from his temper or overreaction. He'd been arrogant at the beginning of their career, believing Keane Sense were untouchable, and to a degree, Miles hadn't been wrong. Their collective talent shot them into the stratosphere of fame, and their good looks and sex appeal guaranteed they stayed there. The adoration and the drugs had warped his perspective, inflating his ego with every number one hit, every award and every sold-out concert they performed. In all fairness, since Miles had been out of the limelight, Eric had rarely seen him lose his cool. But tragic loss had knocked his confidence and his certainty. His devil-may-care attitude that he'd worn like a medal had been ripped from his chest and in its place was left a rough and jagged scar that had been patched up well, but was still visible from time to time, especially when he felt out of control and vulnerable. Today's outburst though had nothing to do with his ego, today was about a threat of losing someone he valued, someone he was in love with, to someone he deep down felt inferior to.

"No visitors today." Pierce's low rumble of a voice pulled Miles's attention to the front of the car. "Looks like you'll be free from prying eyes for a bit."

Miles gave him a relieved nod as Karl held up his phone to show Miles the view from the cameras around his home. No reporters or photographers.

Within a few minutes, they'd pulled up outside Miles's home and were inside before anyone realised. Pierce quickly brought in Eric and Miles's cases and then did a quick sweep of the house with Karl.

"Is this what it's always like?" Eric asked, taking a tentative look around. Duke ran into the kitchen and sniffed the floor, then scampered towards his basket.

"I've had to step up security. Mainly because of Louisa but now I'm 'out there'" – he made air quotes and Eric stifled a smile – "there is bound to be someone ready to hassle me."

Pierce came back down the stairs and told them it was all clear, just as Karl came up from the basement confirming the same. Miles told them he wasn't going anywhere for the next few hours, so they were free to go grab a late breakfast and catch up on whatever they needed to do.

"You hungry?" Miles asked Eric, once they were alone, heading into the kitchen.

"Yeah, I could eat. It's too early for lunch though."

"I've some bagels in the freezer and…" Miles opened the fridge and scanned the contents. "Bacon and eggs. How does that sound?"

"Perfect if you also have coffee."

MILES SAT CLICKING ON to every gossip and news site that had any of the latest photos of Louisa. She'd called him as soon as she'd had her public lunch with Gerard, to Gerard's disgust. Louisa hadn't even waited until she was on her own. Gerard sat stiffly next to her in the back of her Bentley as she asked Miles about his morning with Eric. Once they'd returned from CASPO's offices later that afternoon, she called him again. Louisa couldn't physically be with him but she tried her hardest to include him in every way she could and if that meant calling him numerous times a day, she was happy to do it.

Miles pursed his lips at the photographs that flooded his screen. There were various shots of Louisa and Gerard climbing in and out of the car. Far too many of them were of Gerard with his hand on the small of her back. There were a few more of him leaning in close as he spoke to her. Miles clenched his jaw and almost growled. Louisa had told him that Gerard was staying another night and would then be leaving but Miles had his doubts. He seemed to be very comfortable staying under the same roof as Louisa and enjoying both her hospitality and company.

Pierce eyed Miles as he forcefully clicked through each photo.

"What's the plan for this morning?" he asked, hoping to drag Miles's attention away from his laptop. He knew Melissa had set up an interview with a magazine after lunch, which also included a photoshoot. Pierce was glad he'd have something to occupy him. Miles had been in a mulish mood since Eric had left yesterday. Not even a round of poker with Karl and Kurt could shake off his sullen mood.

"Did you see these?" Miles asked, ignoring Pierce's question. He swung his laptop around so he could show him. "He's taking full advantage of the situation. Why doesn't he just fuck right off?"

"You know it's not real," Pierce said carefully, not wanting to annoy his friend any more than he already was.

"Whatever. He thinks he's still married to her."

"Well, she's not." Pierce turned the laptop back to face Miles.

"No, she's not."

"Exactly. Forget about him. Hugh says they hardly speak to each other in the house."

"Did he?" Miles eyes widened at this piece of information and gave Pierce a self-satisfied smirk. Pierce looked uncomfortably away, knowing he'd been uncharacteristically indiscreet. He had never shared anything about what went on in the Blackthorn homes before but he really felt for Miles. Plus, he really didn't like Gerard after the way he'd behaved at Holmwood.

Miles closed his laptop and drained his coffee. "We're going shopping," Miles said, jumping off his stool.

"Shopping? We can get stuff delivered, you know." He watched Miles stride into the hallway and head for the stairs.

"Not this. I'll be ready to leave in 15 minutes. Tell Karl he's driving because you're going to help me."

"Help you buy what?" Pierce called after him as he followed him into the hallway and watched as Miles ran up the stairs two at a time.

"Google the best jewellers in London!" Miles shouted down the stairs and Pierce grinned up at him.

"That'd be in Hatton Garden."

"Then that's where we're going."

KARL PULLED OUT ON to the street and looked up at Miles in the rear-view mirror. Kurt had been left at the house and Pierce was riding in the front.

"Where to?" asked Karl.

"Hatton Garden," Pierce said and Karl shot him a look.

"We're choosing an engagement ring and my man Pierce says he knows the right place to go. I've never bought an engagement ring in London before – come to think of it, I've never bought any ring in any country before." Miles chuckled.

"Well, Hatton Garden is the place to go," Karl confirmed.

"Glad you've got my back, Pierce. Though this is on the low down, right?" Miles's eyes shifted between Pierce and Karl.

"My lips are sealed," Pierce confirmed.

"I'm a vault," Karl said with a nod and a grin.

Within 15 minutes, Karl was pulling into the famous Hatton Garden area of central London, which hosted the lion's share of all the jewellers in the city. Miles watched each shopfront pass by, wondering which one Pierce was going to ask Karl to stop at. Had it been solely up to him, he'd have gone to Bond Street or Oxford Street but thankfully Pierce *knew a guy*. They were all unassuming frontages, nothing like the huge ostentatious jewellers in LA. Pierce signalled to Karl to turn up a small one-way street, then asked him to park outside a smart-looking jeweller with a black awning that had Diamond Palace emblazoned on it. Miles smiled to himself. *Black... perfect.*

Within a few minutes, Miles and Pierce were ushered into a discreet, small room, away from prying eyes at the back of the main shop. There was only one elderly lady customer in but Pierce wasn't taking any chances. Pierce introduced Miles to the manager, a Mr Webb, explaining what he was looking for.

"This is for an extraordinary woman," explained Miles. He wasn't about to spill the beans to the jeweller who exactly, but he wanted to make sure he was clear that the ring needed to be special. Extra-special.

"Of course," the manager said. He'd heard this a thousand times. Every would-be groom thought their soon to be fiancé was extra-special.

"No, I mean it. This isn't for some popstar or model. This is for a woman with class, elegant, exquisite," Miles said, a little more forcefully. He wasn't entirely sure if Mr Webb knew who he was, so he wanted to clarify that Louisa wasn't of the same class as him.

"So, a diamond?" suggested Mr Webb. Miles nodded, then looked at Pierce for approval. Pierce gave him a reassuring smile. "Any cut in mind?" Miles furrowed his brow at the question. Mr Webb explained that he meant the shape and Miles cast his mind back to when he'd researched Louisa and Gerard. He remembered the ring she had was a round solitaire set in yellow gold. Well, he needed the opposite of that.

"Square and platinum. Or oblong?"

Mr Webb gave a nod. "Emerald or cushion cut, maybe. Shall I show you our collections of classic and halo?"

"Sure, sounds good," Miles said and widened his eyes at Pierce. He really didn't know much about jewellery.

"Very good. Take a seat and I'll bring you out a selection."

Miles lowered himself into one of the chairs and indicated to Pierce to sit too. "So how do you know this guy?" Miles asked in a hushed tone.

"My friend works his security here. It's a family-run business."

A few minutes later, Mr Webb came out holding three black velvet trays with a large selection of diamond rings. He slid them onto the table in front of Miles, then pulled out a magnifying glass and switched on the desk light. He meant business. Miles and Pierce shifted forward to get a better look. Miles scanned over the sparkling jewellery, totally overwhelmed. He could've done with Amanda's advice but she wasn't due back from LA for another week.

"They're all lovely," Miles said softly.

"Do we have a budget?" Mr Webb asked.

Pierce shook his head at the same time as Miles said, "Money isn't the problem."

"What about size?"

Miles blanched. He hadn't even thought about that. How was he going to find out what size ring they needed? "Shit... I mean. I don't know."

Pierce stood up abruptly. "I'm on it," Pierce said taking out his phone and walking to the back of the room.

"I meant carat size," Mr Webb said with a hint of amusement.

"Oh, okay, erm..." Miles scrutinized the many rings in front of him. There were simple stones on a band, a few with diamonds on the band, and varying rectangular and square-shaped stones. One particular ring caught his eye. "I like this one." Miles pointed at a square diamond ring surrounded with small diamonds that had diamonds on the band.

"A very good choice, sir. It's part of our Diamond Palace Exclusive Halo Collection. This one is a 2-carat cushion cut diamond on diamond shoulders, from our Malibu range."

"Malibu range? You're kidding me," Miles said with a chuckle. "Well, that's the one, then." Mr Webb plucked the ring from the velvet holder and passed it to Miles. He took it and turned it left and right, letting the light catch on its many facets. Miles turned to an approaching Pierce. "Any luck on the size?"

"Hugh's on it," Pierce said as he inspected the ring Miles held up for him to see.

"What do you think?"

"Impressive."

"But not vulgar, right?" Miles saw the twitch in Mr Webb expression. "Sorry." He turned back to Pierce. "Not too showy?"

"The cushion cut is a classic, sir, as opposed to the emerald cut which is a more modern cut," interjected Mr Webb.

"Well, that sounds right because she's certainly a classic cut above everyone else," Miles said with a wide grin. "It's from their *Malibu* range." Miles gave Pierce a knowing look.

"Seriously?"

"Yeah, what are the chances?" Miles turned to Mr Webb. "I'll take it. Pierce here will let you know the size and once it's ready, he'll come to pick it up." Miles reached into his inside jacket pocket and handed Mr Webb his credit card.

"So, that was a lot easier than I thought it'd be," Miles said, rubbing his hands together, feeling pleased with himself. He needed to be active – scratch that; he needed to be proactive. This was the first step. "Now I need the perfect place to ask her," he muttered almost to himself as Karl navigated their car around the one-way system. "Any ideas?"

"I don't think you need any input from me... you seem to be managing just fine," Pierce answered and Karl mumbled that he had no idea. Miles twisted his mouth and looked out of the window again. It needed to be somewhere special, somewhere special to them and private. *She might say no.* Their schedules were going to be hectic over the next four weeks leading up to the concert and then there were his meetings and interviews, now that his series was due to be aired. And that was all before the news of the film came out too. He'd have to think. If he had the ring, it could be spontaneous. Though he didn't like the idea of just blurting it out. Maybe he should talk to Amanda first. She'd give him a woman's perspective. Miles sighed to himself, his previous excitement fading. *What if she said no?*

5

RECKLESS

"**N**o?"

"No. That's what I said. I'm fine here. We've done more than enough photo opportunities. Melissa already said so." Louisa shifted her gaze back to her computer screen, hoping Gerard would get the subtle hint that she was busy. He seemed to find any excuse to find her after he returned from dinner. She had a mountain of work to get through, as well as look through the emails Melissa had forwarded regarding the concert.

"You could accompany me to the fundraiser," Gerard said as he crossed the threshold of her home office, obviously not taking the hint.

"I can't because I have far too much to organise." Louisa waved at her computer screen and continued to read.

"It would definitely stop any rumours that things are strained between us, *cherie*."

Louisa gave a heavy sigh and sat back in her chair. He really was that obtuse, she thought. He'd actually thought that she'd consider flying back to New York for one of his fundraisers. "I don't doubt it. It will also start another wave of rumours that we're back together again, and we're not." She said the last two words more forcefully, hoping he'd back off. "I'm sure you have a companion that you can take. It's one of the most lavish fundraisers of the year." She looked at him flatly. He wasn't going to get away with casually suggesting her going with him, without reminding him why she would never want to.

Gerard's eyes narrowed at her comment. "Is this because of him?"

"Him?"

"Don't play dumb, Louisa, it doesn't suit you."

Louisa crossed her arms over her chest and tilted her head, trying to work out if he was jealous or just mad that she'd knocked him back. "Miles doesn't demand I do anything, Gerard. He supports me."

"You mean he's your lap dog, like the pooch he brought with

him?" he sneered.

Louisa closed her eyes for a moment and then looked back at her computer. She wasn't going to get into an argument about Miles. "I'm not discussing this with you, Gerard. I cannot have this same conversation with you again," she said dismissively.

"Because you know it's true." Louisa's eyes shot up to Gerard's as he looked down at her. "He doesn't fit in with your world. He has no idea how to behave or what it means to be married to the aristocracy. He'll embarrass you, your family."

"Really?" Louisa stood up from her chair and leaned a little forward. "Well, from where I'm standing it would seem the man who knew *exactly* what it meant to be married to me is the one that's *embarrassing* me, our daughter and my family." Gerard clenched his jaw at her sharp words but before he could reply, Louisa continued. "I married you, you were the love of my life, perfect for me in every way and we lasted five good years." Gerard huffed, stepping back as Louisa rounded her desk. "The rest were a range of bad to tolerable."

"And you think he will give you more good years? You think being married to him will bring you happiness?" he scoffed.

"I can't answer that. But what I do know is that if he asked me to marry him today, I'd do it in a heartbeat." She snapped her fingers in front of his face to make her point. She was done with having to justify her relationship with Miles. He wanted to hear why she was with Miles and wasn't running back to New York with him, he was going to finally hear it. "He puts me first. He looks at me as though I'm his whole world. He looks at me as though I'm special and worth fighting for."

"Don't be a romantic fool. He's just swept away with your title, who you are. He's a common playboy who's landed on his feet." Gerard gave a humourless mocking laugh.

"He looked at me like that *before* he knew who I was. He looked at *me*, *just Louisa*, without any of the trimmings. He's made me see my worth through his eyes and made me experience new things I'd never dreamed of doing. He makes me feel reckless and confident at the same time."

"Reckless? He'll leave you as soon as he's gotten over his obsession." Gerard's voice rose in disgust.

"Well, I married perfect and that didn't work out." She shook her head and reached for her jacket, which was draped over a chair, and slipped it on. She'd had enough, there was no way she'd get any work done now. "At least with reckless I'll have fun along the way," Louisa said dryly and walked towards the door.

"Where are you going? It's past ten."

"I'm off to be reckless," she said, leaving him standing in her office.

MILES CLICKED THROUGH THE photographs the magazine editor had surprisingly sent over for his approval. The article was being rushed through to print, just in time for the concert. It had been a tiring day. Who knew sitting around for hours, while photographers set up shots, adjusted lighting, dressed and redressed you, would be so exhausting? He'd done his fair share of photoshoots when he'd been in Keane Sense but then he'd had the whole band with him and time passed quickly. He was also a lot younger then. Doing it on your own, without a few shots of vodka and a line or two of cocaine, made it drag. The team were very professional and made sure he had everything he needed but when it got to 7:30 and the last of the evening shots were done, Miles was glad to see the back of all of them. He had to admit, the photographer had got some good shots of him with the London skyline as a backdrop, looking all business-like in a blue three-piece suit. There were a few of him walking down a narrow-cobbled London street in more casual attire and the final shots were of him in a tuxedo with his bow tie undone and his shirt open holding his antique trumpet, looking sultry in a smoky nightclub. The magazine had sent the untouched photos for Miles to have and had earmarked the ones they would use for the article. The title of the piece the upscale magazine had written on him was "Keane to be back", a play on words that had Miles feeling a little uncomfortable. He hadn't wanted to make a big splash. He'd have rather caused a few tentative ripples but it seemed the universe had other plans. With his debut series being released just after the concert plus, Eric had bashed out the deal with the film studio and wanted to get the news out as soon as possible, so they'd be cashing in on the exposure; Miles would literally be everywhere.

Miles quickly sent his approval of the shots and then read through the proposal Eric had put together for *Singing in the Rain*. He had to hand it to Eric, he'd outlined every detail and stipulation they'd discussed at length over the last few days. Eric had said the reasons for needing to spend more time in the UK were because of professional commitments. Miles just hoped the theatre director was happy to bend for him because deep down, the more he thought about doing the role, the more excited he got. It had been a long time to feel this hyped about performing. He had to admit the idea of being in front of a live audience still terrified him but he was beginning to crave new challenges. The series had whetted his appetite for new experiences and woken up his ingrained ambition to test and prove himself. The film offer, to play one of his musical heroes, was another step forward towards his new career path and back into performing. He'd be doing what he did best, within an environment he'd feel at ease in. A huge role in a theatre production was a natural progression, a dream come true to any experienced actor or musician, and Miles understood what a tremendous opportunity and honour it was for him. Of course, there was the small, insignificant detail of his fear of performing to overcome. Just thinking about it had him breaking into a cold sweat but he was trying hard not to dwell on it. After all, it was over a year away and like Louisa had said, he'd come a long way in a year.

Miles glanced at the script on his desk. He'd read it a number of times and he had to admit it was good – better than good, it was incredible. They'd taken a classic and put a modern tilt on it. There were notes from the musical director and choreographer outlining what they envisioned and Miles was already picturing the sets and scenes. He picked up his crystal tumbler and took a sip of his iced drink and swallowed, welcoming the smooth burn that soothed his slight spike in heart rate. Was it fear he was feeling, apprehension even or was it excitement? Probably all three, he thought to himself. What he did know was with every moment that passed, if the theatre company wouldn't bend to his demands, he'd be torn between either giving up the role of a lifetime or spending time away from Louisa.

"Hard day at the office, dear?"

Miles eyes shot up to doorway of his office and he was faced with the beautiful vision of Louisa, sheathed in an emerald green dress that hugged every curve, nonchalantly leaning against the door frame.

"Louisa?" Miles gasped and he immediately got up from his chair in a rush. The desk shook a little and Miles steadied his glass as it almost topped over.

"You seem to do that a lot." She chuckled, remembering their first date all those months ago. She was pleased she'd been able to surprise him again.

"That's because you keep surprising me!" he mock-growled as he rounded his desk giving her that megawatt smile that lit up every room, every stage and every stadium. He stepped up to her just as Louisa made a show of pulling off her heels and dropping them. He chuckled and cupped her face. "What are you doing here?"

"Being reckless."

"Now we're talking, that's my kind of behaviour," he drawled accentuating his American accent. Louisa giggled just before he branded his lips to hers, then he unceremoniously hoisted her over his shoulder and strode to his bedroom.

"FUCK ME!" blew out Miles. His chest heaved as he steadied his ragged breathing.

"I think I just did." Louisa let out a gasp and then chuckled. Miles gave a husky laugh, loving the fact he was the only one who saw this side of her. To the outside world she was the Countess of Holmwood, Lady Blackthorn, elegant, well-bred and dignified. But behind closed doors, she was just Louisa: fun, a little bit brazen and a whole lot of sexy.

"I like reckless Louisa," he mumbled into her hair. He slid to the side, then pulled her to him, wrapping his arms around her.

"Do you, now?"

"Yeah." Miles held her close, enjoying the intimacy. Whenever they were together, his mind always wandered to how long they had and how soon she'd have to leave. Tonight's surprise visit had put a great many of his doubts to rest about where he stood. She'd left Gerard at her home and come to him, late at night and unprepared. Miles knew that spontaneity wasn't in Louisa's repertoire, yet over their time together, she'd made bold steps to change that. She'd come a long way in the last few months from her first visit to his home.

Louisa dropped a kiss onto his chest. Every time they were

apart, she felt as though something was missing and for such a new relationship it felt too strong of an emotion. Miles had somehow broken down her defences with his easy and candid manner. It made her feel both vulnerable yet strong at the same time and when he wasn't by her side, she felt at a loss.

"I missed you," she said quietly. "I hated how we left each other, and…"

"And?"

Louisa sighed. "Gerard was pissing me off."

"What did he do?" Miles's voice took on a hard tone.

"Oh nothing, just… Forget it. I really don't want to talk about it or him. He's taken up too much of my time when he doesn't deserve it," she said with a shake of her head and she gazed up at him.

"You'll hear no complaints from me. So, what's the plan? Are you staying?"

"Can I?"

"Of course you can. If I had my way, you'd be here every night, Louisa." He widened his eyes at her and she felt her cheeks heat.

"That sounds kind of nice."

"Kind of?" he said playfully, narrowing his eyes at her.

"A lot, then," she conceded and his face creased up into a brilliant smile that was so infectious she couldn't help but beam back at him. He planted a hard kiss on her lips, then tucked her safely against his chest. "So, tell me about your day; it's far more interesting than mine."

"I had my interview and photoshoot for the magazine today."

"How glamorous."

"Hardly, it was tedious but it will be good for CASPO. I used my trumpet in one of the photos, actually."

"You did?" She turned her head to look up at him, thrilled that her gift had been with him all day.

"Yeah. I can show you the shots later, now that you're staying." He tightened his arms around her as though he was worried she'd change her mind.

"I'd like that."

"Melissa wants to get some interviews done too. Here and in the US."

"Yes, she told me. I'm having lunch with her, Darcy and Joel tomorrow."

"I thought she was on strict bed rest."

"Well, she's coming to my home with Robert and sitting down the whole time. She's been cooped up in her house for too long, she's going crazy, so I thought a change of scenery would help." Louisa pulled back a little as a thought popped into her head. "You should come too."

"To your home?" Miles asked tentatively.

"Yes, it's the perfect cover. You'd be there on CASPO business." Louisa smiled widely, pleased she'd thought of the idea.

"Thank you," Miles said softly. She'd heard his grievance and she was trying to find a way to rectify it.

"Don't thank me yet. Gerard will probably still be there," she huffed.

"Wonderful. Maybe me being there might piss him off and he'll end up leaving," he said dryly and Louisa chuckled.

"Maybe."

"Is that why you're inviting me? To piss him off?"

"No! I'm inviting you because you're CASPO's ambassador and need to be in our meetings. As you pointed out, you've never been to my London home and this is the perfect situation and, most importantly of all, I want you there," she said the last part sincerely.

"Really?"

"Really. Plus, the added bonus is, it'll piss off Gerard too." She stifled a grin and he gave out a husky laugh, then tackled her to her back, hovering over her.

"Louisa, if he says anything to me or you, I won't be able to keep quiet."

"He won't. He'll probably leave."

Miles searched her face for any trace of uncertainty and saw none, then gave a curt nod. "So, did you bring an overnight bag?"

"Nope. See, this is me being spontaneous and reckless," she said and he laughed at her playfulness.

"Hugh is here though, yeah?"

"Of course."

"I guess he'd better go back and bring you some clothes for tomorrow – that's if you're sure you're staying?"

"I'm sure," she said without a second of hesitation.

"Good."

THE MIDDAY SUNLIGHT REFLECTED off the Thames as Pierce drove along its banks. The drive should have been relaxing, what with views of the various parks they passed by, travelling through some of the most prestigious areas of the capital. For Miles though, the journey caused him to tense up with every minute they drew closer to Louisa's London home. Swarms of people were out walking and enjoying the beautiful summer's day as they neared Westminster, taking in the revered sites of the Houses of Parliament and Big Ben but Miles stared blankly out of his window, caught up in his own thoughts. This was the heart of London, not even a mile away from Buckingham Palace and almost next door to MI5, the House of Lords and the Home Office. It brought home to Miles who Louisa was and what she stood for. Her home was in the heart of the British Establishment.

Pierce drove past the BBC Millbank Studios and turned into a narrower street flanked with four-storey period buildings that had, for the most part, unassuming black doors. These were offices or residences of the elite, politicians, aristocrats and the high society of the UK, yet they were unobtrusive while being immaculate. Miles had been outside Louisa's home the night of the CASPO Summer Ball but even knowing its grandiosity, the sight of the majestic Grade II listed building caught his breath. It stood out alongside the other buildings with its ornate stone doorway with pillars on either side of the double solid wooden door. The redbrick contrasted with the stone detailing on every one of the four floors and windows. It was opulent in an understated way and if there was any doubt that the occupants were esteemed, the spiked, black, wrought iron gating around the 50-foot frontage was evidence enough.

Miles stared up at the palatial building, oblivious to the handful of reporters that were skulking further down the quiet street. Karl jumped out of the car and opened up Miles's door, ready to usher him inside. Miles grabbed the beautiful bouquet of summer blooms he'd brought with him and slipped out of the car. He'd second-guessed his decision to bring the flowers, not wanting to draw attention to himself, but even if he hadn't been dating Louisa, he would have brought flowers to her home on his first visit, regardless. He'd been brought up with manners and he almost smiled to himself, thinking his mother would be proud to see him in the newspapers, holding a bouquet. He strode quickly to the door which opened up so fast, he didn't have to break his stride, and was faced with the ever-faithful Hugh. However, Miles's gaze shot past Louisa's trusted bodyguard, taking in the bookmatched marble flooring to the grand sweeping staircase.

"Welcome to Blackthorn Mansion," Hugh said with a smirk, seeing Miles look a little daunted.

"Err, thanks." Miles's gaze drifted to him.

"You good?" Hugh asked, noting his furrowed brow.

"Yeah, sure. Is everyone here?"

"Yes, they're in the drawing-room on the first floor."

"Right," Miles said, drawing out his reply, and Hugh chuckled.

"Come on. I'll show you the way." Hugh turned and gestured for Miles to follow him. "You might like to know that Mr Dupont left for New York this morning." Hugh turned to look at Miles who had a self-satisfied smirk on his face as they climbed up the grand staircase.

"Did he know I'd be here today?" he asked, wondering whether Louisa had purposely told him, so he would leave.

"He asked me this morning what Lady Blackthorn's plans were for today."

"I thought you weren't supposed to tell anyone what she's up to."

"Yes, you're right. A rare mistake on my part. I apologised to Lady Blackthorn when I drove her home from yours this morning. Lucky for me, she didn't seem displeased."

"Rare mistake, eh?" Hugh nodded and gave him a knowing look but kept tight-lipped. "Lucky for me too, I guess. I really didn't want to deal with that arsehole today."

"Lucky all round, then," Hugh said wryly as they reached the first floor. "It's through here."

Miles could hear the distinct voices of Joel and Melissa as he neared the closed door. Hugh opened it up and Miles stepped in.

Louisa immediately stood up and paced towards him. The huge smile on her face was evidence enough that she was pleased he was here. The tension in Miles's stance almost instantaneously disappeared. It had only been four hours since they'd been together and he realised just how much he'd missed her. The sumptuous surroundings faded into the background and Miles focused on a decidedly casually dressed Louisa. He caught up to her, unable to keep a respectful distance, and dropped a chaste kiss on her lips. Louisa seemed unfazed by his greeting and oblivious to their audience of four. Robert and Melissa knew who Miles was to Louisa but he wasn't sure if Darcy and Joel were privy to that particular top-secret piece of information. Well, they certainly were in no doubt who he was to Louisa now.

"I'm so glad you're here," she said softly.

"These are for you." Miles handed her the impressive bouquet in shades of pink.

"They're beautiful, thank you. Come in, we're just starting." Louisa took his hand and pulled him towards the seating area. While everyone said their hellos, Louisa called for one of her many house staff to come and place the flowers in water.

It didn't take long for Miles to feel more comfortable. Darcy and Joel outlined future press releases and the various publications that had been singled out for exclusive interviews. Melissa updated everyone on new sponsors and as well as various high-profile guests who were bidding for the VIP section, which led to Joel re-evaluating the estimated revenue from the concert.

They moved into the dining room and were served by a couple of staff Miles had never met before. He was mindful not to show any excess attention or affection to Louisa and took her lead. The last thing he wanted to do was put Louisa in a difficult position but it was proving to be exhausting, second-guessing every move and look he gave around Louisa. By the time they all retired to the sitting room for coffee, Miles felt drained and was glad when Louisa asked the staff to leave the tray of coffee for her to serve. Finally, he could relax.

"That was a good meeting and Melissa seemed more like her old self. She's finding the constraints of her pregnancy a challenge," Louisa said, after she'd seen off her guests. She was followed into the beautifully decorated sitting room by the housekeeper.

"Yeah, I really feel for Robert," Miles said, darting his eyes around the room from his position by the large sash windows. He smiled tightly as the housekeeper cleared the last of the coffee tray.

"Are you okay?" Louisa asked as soon as the housekeeper left and shut the door behind her. Miles let out a breath and raked his fingers through his hair.

"That was one of the hardest situations I've been in."

"How so?" Louisa asked, puzzled by his comment.

"I kept pulling back from touching you or looking at you too much."

Louisa stepped up to him and scrunched up her nose. This was still new to him, having staff around. Plus, she'd always insisted that the fewer people knew about them, the better she felt though over the last few weeks it seemed to be less important to her. Miles's reckless behaviour was really beginning to rub off on her. "Ah, yes, well I made sure that it was only a couple of staff on today. Sorry about that."

"It's fine, really, I just need to have my wits about me, that's all." Louisa reached for his hand and he grasped it, then tugged her closer so he could finally wrap her in his arms. The restraint over the last three hours had been too hard to bear. He just needed to be able to freely hold her. "I hear Gerard left."

"He did and without me asking him."

Miles chuckled. "I think you have Hugh and his indiscretion to thank for that."

"Hugh has a knack of knowing when he can be indiscreet," she said dryly, then looked up at him. "Do you want an official tour?"

"I'd love one but first…" He bent down and kissed her deeply, taking full advantage of their privacy. "That's better. There is only so much restraint I can take," he said with his trademark smirk.

If the outside of Blackthorn Mansion was considered to be impressive, it paled in comparison to the interior. Louisa had told Miles she'd redecorated when she'd returned from the US and though all of the period features of the residence had been kept, Louisa had managed to add her own unique flair for style to her London home. Antique pieces and priceless art were paired with more contemporary furniture and furnishings, from revered designers, in muted tones that blended effortlessly with the ornate gilded mouldings, rich wooden panelling and original marble fireplaces. Blackthorn Mansion had been in the family since it was built at the turn of the nineteenth century. The then Earl of Holmwood's son had wanted a more manageable home closer to the city centre. Blacks had been the Blackthorns' London residence at the time and was deemed as being too far, in those days, from the centre where the young earl hoped to spend most of his time.

"I personally think he had this built so he could have privacy from the family. He probably had wild parties," Louisa chuckled as they walked up the grand stairway up from seeing the garden and indoor swimming pool in the basement.

"You mean a, like, fuck-pad?"

"No, *exactly* a fuck-pad. It was just before the roaring twenties. By all accounts, my great, great, great-grandfather was a bit of a rake."

"A rake?"

"Womanizer and a bit wild." Miles grinned at Louisa as she continued to walk him through to a large room with a huge screen and soft seating. "Media room," Louisa said, then stepped to where the kitchen was and gestured to him to look inside. There was the housekeeper and one of the other staff Miles had seen clearing up and they smiled warmly at them. Miles smiled back at them as Louisa explained she was giving him a tour, then they started up to the first floor and he followed her as she continued her story. "He died at the age of 42 from falling off his horse."

"Really?"

"Uh-huh. My father said he was probably drunk when it happened. This is the games room. I keep it for Alistair – he likes to meet his friends here and they use it more than I ever do. And through here is my study," she said stepping into the airy room. It was obviously Louisa's study. There was a candid photo of Celeste, her parents, Alistair and Konran altogether perched on her beautiful antique desk. The contemporary blue padded office chair gave the room style and matched the two armchairs in front of the desk. Miles took in the photos and wondered whether his photo would ever earn a place on her desk. "Papa always used to joke that he'd survived the First World War, yet died from too much drink," she said with a chuckle, continuing her story. "So, my great, great-grandfather became the Earl at 19."

"Is that an elevator?" Miles asked, a little stunned that such a house had one.

"Uh-huh. It goes to all the floors," Louisa said as they started up the stairs.

"Oh wow. So, your great, great, great-grandfather was a party animal? I feel like my past is tame, listening to your family's history."

Louisa gave a soft laugh as she led him up to the next floor. "They were all a little wild, by all accounts. It was kind of part and parcel of being in the aristocracy. Except Papa."

"Why's that?" They'd reached the second floor and Louisa stopped outside a wooden door that contrasted with the white gleaming marble flooring. The afternoon sunlight filtered down the central stairwell from the magnificent cupola that dominated the top floor, ensuring each of the floors had natural lighting.

"He became the Earl young too. My grandpapa did things to excess and died from a heart attack. Papa didn't want to be like the earls before him. Plus, he didn't have an arranged marriage – he married for love. Mama was a commoner and probably grounded him. He wanted to break the cycle."

"Well, he succeeded. Both you and Alistair are hardly wild. That'd be my department," he said with a widening of his eyes. Louisa laughed and opened the door to what looked like another corridor.

"Yeah, but I'm certainly seeing the advantages of being reckless," she called over her shoulder in a teasing tone.

"You do, eh? Am I bringing out the wild side of the Blackthorns that's buried deep inside you?" he joked, enjoying her playfulness.

"Talking of being buried deep inside me. This is my bedroom." Louisa opened up another door and revealed a sumptuous bedroom dominated by a huge bed, decorated in pale blue and light grey.

"Jesus Louisa, you can't say shit like that when I'm trying to be well behaved." Miles rubbed his hand over his face and blew out a breath.

"Behaving is overrated. I've had first-hand experience." Louisa closed the door with the bump of her hip and leaned against it. Miles turned around and let his gaze take in every detail, from her full wavy hair, over beautiful face, down past her simple ivory top and matching trousers, to her polka dot stilettoes.

"You've a house full of staff..."

"This room is pretty soundproofed," she said, kicking off her shoes.

Miles clenched his jaw. "They'll know I'm up here..." He stepped closer, trying to be the gentleman she deserved when in all honesty, he had the most ungentlemanly thoughts running through his head.

"They'll all be down in the basement, unless I call for them." Louisa reached for the hem of her top but Miles shot his hand out and stopped her.

"Haven't you got things to do?" He couldn't believe he was actually trying to stop her from undressing and making excuses not to make love to her. He shook his head at the thought of what he'd become. Rewind to over six years ago and he'd have probably fucked her on the billiard table, in the games room, with the door wide open for all to hear and see. *Boy, how times had changed... the popstar was the sensible one and the countess was being brazen!*

"You know, I've never had to work so hard at convincing a man to sleep with me," Louisa said, stifling a smirk as she threw back his similar words from their very first date at Blacks. Miles let out a husky laugh and pulled her to his chest.

"Louisa... I don't want to make things difficult for you."

"I know, and thank you for thinking of me and my reputation, but after the week I've had... I just want to forget about what people think."

"By having sex with me?" he said and she looked up at him.

"No, by losing myself with the man I love." Miles's face softened and he gave her a gentle kiss, then pulled back. "I can always call an escort agency for them to send round their best gigolo," she teased and Miles's jaw dropped open.

"Lady Louisa Blackthorn, you did not just say that!" Louisa let out a giggle and he hoisted her over his shoulder and headed to the bed. "I hope this room really is soundproofed because you're really going to get it and the whole house will hear you," Miles threatened as he dropped her on the bed. Louisa wriggled up to the top and started to remove her clothes.

"You know you're the only person I've ever talked about gigolos with," she said with a laugh as Miles swiftly shed his shirt and toed off his shoes.

"I bloody hope so!" He laughed at the ridiculousness of their conversation. *A countess and a popstar talking about gigolos! No one would believe him.* Miles unzipped his trousers and dropped them unceremoniously to the floor as Louisa rid the last of her clothes and flopped back onto the bed, totally naked.

"I told you before, I do many things with you I've never done before."

Miles whipped off his boxer briefs and crawled up the bed and laid himself over her. "I take it making love with an ex-popstar, in the afternoon, is one of them." He rubbed his nose against hers and flexed his hips and she closed her eyes, relishing the intimacy she craved with him.

"And with the curtains open," she muttered and Miles paused.

"Shit, should I close them?" He went to get up but she gripped on to him.

"The glass is tinted. No one can see in." Miles relaxed against her and she opened her eyes. "Always thinking about me."

"You have no idea," he mumbled and branded his lips to hers. He was sick of overthinking. All he wanted was a few hours of uninterrupted time with her. Miles longed for when they'd be able to do and be as they pleased. He understood her life had structure but it was times like these, where she bent the rules, messed up the order and behaved freely that Miles cherished the most. This was who Louisa really was and every moment he spent with her, he fell even deeper in love.

His fingers skimmed down her side, causing goosebumps to flare up in their path. Louisa shivered, then shifted her legs so that Miles could nestle himself between them and he deepened the kiss. She loved the way he kissed her, softly at first, then more urgently, like a switch had been flicked, making him lose control. To the outside world, he was a man with a questionable past, an American bad boy with a pretty face and cheeky confident comebacks but to anyone who knew him, Miles was far more complex. He gave his all to whoever or whatever was important to him. His love was potent and though he had to water down his emotions in public, when they were alone, Louisa felt the fully undiluted intensity of his feelings.

Miles cupped her behind and pressed her up to him. She could feel his hot, hard length against the top of her thigh and she bucked up towards him, eager to hasten the pace, but his full weight held her exactly where he wanted her. Outside she took the lead but when it was just the two of them, behind closed doors and in bed, he took charge.

He wasn't selfish or overly dominant, he just knew exactly what she needed and made it his mission to sate her.

"Don't rush me," he breathed into the shell of her ear, causing her to shiver again. He reached for her hands that were roaming over his back in frustration. He loved her like this, a little crazy with lust, her skin flushed, soft and pliable, yet fiery with desire. Miles raised them slowly as he worked his lips in open-mouth kisses down her neck and across her collar bone. He laced their fingers and stretched their joined arms over her head and she moaned.

"Miles, let me touch you."

"You will, when I've gotten you soft and ready," he mumbled against her silky skin.

"I'm ready," she groaned in frustration and she felt his smile against her breast a second before his lips closed over her nipple. He gently sucked and she felt its effects shoot down to the apex of her thighs. "Oh god!" She arched up and Miles took pleasure in seeing her respond so strongly to his touch. He tightened his grip on her hands as she squirmed beneath him, then deliberately rubbed his length against her most sensitive spot. "Miles!" she called out and his eyes found hers as she looked down at him. They flared with male satisfaction, he hadn't even entered her and she was already close to becoming undone. Miles slid up against her again and this time they both let out a tormented moan. "Miles, I can't hold on." Her voice was shaky, betraying how close she was to the edge.

"I've hardly touched you," he said in wonder, then flexed his hips and Louisa let out a whimper. She was so highly strung; he could feel her practically vibrating beneath him. Their constant restraint was an aphrodisiac, it was as though Louisa stored up all her sexual tension and let the valve burst open the moment they were alone and Miles revelled in it.

All she needed was a particularly skilful move from Miles, a deliberate stroke, the smoothest of motion up and down against her and he had her convulsing beneath him. All Miles could do was watch with wide eyes as she fell apart.

"Christ you're so sensitive, so beautiful." He kissed her hard as she rode out the pulses, then released her hands so he could cup her face. He shifted down a little and Louisa moaned as the tip of his erection brushed against her opening. In one smooth, slick manoeuvre, he pushed inside her. Their eyes locked and they both moaned in sexual satisfaction. Miles pulled back a little and rested on his elbows so he could fully see her face as he slowly pushed in and out of her at an unhurried torturous rhythm. When he made love to Louisa, he didn't want to miss a thing. He loved watching her expressions and listening to her breath quicken. He relished the taste of her skin and her unique feminine scent that intensified with every heated moment. Every moan and shudder were locked into his memory and her words of love were branded to his heart.

"I love you," he said, his voice hoarse with emotion. Louisa cupped his jaw and pulled his forehead to hers.

"I love you," she whispered. Miles let his eyes drift down to where their bodies joined and hissed.

"Look how well we fit, baby. We're perfect."

Louisa looked down at the erotic sight of Miles's toned and tanned body entering hers. His body was made for this, every controlled movement, every thrust and withdrawal, perfectly executed to elicit as much pleasure as possible. It was too much sensory overload and Louisa had to close her eyes in an attempt to shut out the intensity.

"Miles…" she gasped, arching up towards him, feeling her second orgasm build.

"I know, baby. I feel you. Look at me, Louisa. Let me see you."

Her eyes slowly opened at his plea and took in his savagely handsome face. His eyes were ablaze with masculine triumph as she splintered into a second mind-blowing orgasm. Miles followed almost immediately, slowly pulsing into her, riding out their last moments of pleasure.

6

WORST KEPT SECRET

Four weeks before the concert.

Miles Keane was seen arriving at the London residence of Lady Louisa Blackthorn, Blackthorn Mansions in the heart of Westminster. The CASPO ambassador arrived at midday dressed in a light casual suit (Armani, see stockists below) carrying flowers, for what seemed like a casual CASPO meeting. The summer concert, to be held at Holmwood House, is weeks away. Head of PR Miss Darcy Aldridge, and Joel Hardman, lead accountant, arrived earlier along with Lady Blackthorn's good friend and member of the CASPO board of directors, Mrs Melissa Hindley and her husband Mr Robert Hindley, CEO of the Hindley Group. Sources close to the Blackthorns confirmed that the meeting was a progress report and set up at the residence for the ease of Mrs Hindley who is eight months pregnant (see photos below).

Miss Darcy Aldridge confirmed that all the arrangements for the highly anticipated concert were on schedule but would not confirm if Mr Miles Keane would also be performing. Miss Darcy said, "Mr Miles Keane has been instrumental in the organisation of the concert. His role is ambassador for the charity and his expertise has been invaluable to all involved."

In related news, TuKon is now in the European leg of his sold-out tour. His final tour dates will be in the UK, finishing at the charity concert he and Mr Keane have instigated and collaborated on. TuKon has been making appearances on talk and radio shows over the last few days, using every opportunity to promote the charity concert. The first tickets go on sale at 8am GMT this coming Monday, see link below.

PIERCE STEPPED INTO MILES'S office and took one look at his furrowed brow and knew he was searching for articles about the meeting.

"We need to set off if you want to beat the traffic. I checked and the flight's on time."

"Yes, sure. I could've gone on my own," Miles said, still scanning his screen.

"Hugh's strict instructions. I'm driving you."

Miles ignored Pierce's statement and waved at his computer screen. "Did you see these?"

Pierce walked over to the desk and peered over Miles's shoulder. "You knew the reporters were there."

"Darcy, Melissa and Louisa have never mentioned that they're fielding questions about whether I'm performing." His tone was a mixture of irritation and disbelief.

"I'm sure they get asked all manner of questions. It's Darcy's job to deal with them. Come on, let's leave. I packed up all Duke's things too," Pierce said, straightening up. The last thing he needed was for Miles to start worrying about what the press had to say.

"Thanks, you didn't need to."

"I'm kind of attached to the little guy. I'm going to miss him." Pierce gave a shrug. They were taking Duke to stay for a few weeks with Amanda and the children, now that they were arriving back from their holiday. Miles had a number of engagements to attend and it would mean Duke would be alone for the best part of the day.

"I'll just grab my overnight bag and we can head off. I can't wait to see them."

The whole journey from Heathrow Airport to Amanda's home took just over two hours. The children were so excited to see their uncle and fill him in with an almost blow by blow account of their holiday. He'd spoken to them practically every day while they were away but they still felt the need to re-enact every detail. Miles sat back and enjoyed the attention. He'd missed them so much. This was the first time they'd been to LA without him. Amanda chipped in from the front seat; she'd purposely let Miles sit in the back so that Grace and Louis would have his full attention. She kept chuckling along with Pierce, who found the whole trip highly amusing.

The flight and car journey had taken its toll and by the time they'd arrived home, the children were tired and hungry. Miles ordered in

Italian, while Amanda dealt with the unpacking, and kept the children amused with the help of Duke. Once Grace and Louis had eaten, Miles quickly bathed them and had them tucked up in bed. They were asleep in seconds, to the relief of Amanda.

"That was a tough flight back. There's only so much you can entertain them with on an 11-hour flight." She slumped into her chair and reached for her glass of wine.

"I'm usually with you." Miles twisted his mouth, feeling a little guilty. For the last five years he'd been with her on every trip.

"We managed." She waved her hand in the air dismissively as Pierce strode into the kitchen.

"I've done a sweep of outside. I'll go up to my room and come back before you both go to bed."

"Thanks," Miles said, and Pierce left them to catch up.

"Beer?" Amanda asked, getting up and heading to the fridge.

"Sure. You don't want to go to bed. You must be exhausted."

"I am, but I want to hear all your news, in detail. Tomorrow the kids will be full-on and we probably won't get a chance." She stifled a yawn. She loved going to their Malibu house but the jet lag really took it out of her. Amanda reached for a beer and popped the cap, then headed back to the table. "So, tell me everything about the musical."

Miles grinned at her genuine enthusiasm. She'd been with him from the beginning and any success he'd had, she had always felt part of it. Miles went through what the deal entailed and his worries about performing and she listened without interrupting. She'd learned over the years to be his sounding board and more often than not, when he'd aired his worries, Miles felt less daunted.

"I can't believe it! Broadway and the West End." Amanda clinked her glass against his beer bottle.

"Don't. I'm kind of just sliding through it all. If I really think about it, I get palpitations."

"Miles, you'll be great. Better than great, you'll smash it," she said excitedly and Miles chuckled.

"The press are hounding Melissa and the CASPO staff about me performing at the concert," he said quietly, picking at the label of the beer. Amanda leaned forward, suddenly concerned.

"You said you wouldn't."

His gaze lifted to hers. "Don't worry, they haven't even mentioned it to me. It just came up in a recent article." Miles blew out a breath and pulled at the label. "You know the thing: making me out to be difficult."

"The article said that?"

"Not in so many words. But there was a not-so-subtle dig." Miles pursed his lips and shrugged, trying to make light of it but Amanda knew it was bothering him. She knew he'd feel as though he was letting everyone down.

"What did Louisa say?"

"I haven't talked to her about it. I'll be calling her later. I know what she'll say. She'll tell me to ignore it. That CASPO don't expect me to perform and it's just the media trying to rattle me."

"She's right."

"Maybe."

"There's no maybe about it. Louisa knows how these things work. She's had first-hand experience of bad press."

"I do feel as though I'm kind of passing the buck, if you get what I mean. Though Louisa has been adamant that I only do what I feel comfortable with." Miles shifted in his seat and took a drink from the bottle he'd been preoccupied with.

"I love that woman, she's a keeper," Amanda said wittily raising her glass and taking a sip of wine, hoping her words would put him at ease. Miles gave a wide smile at his sister-in-law's antics.

"I love her too and you're right, she is a keeper. I even bought a ring."

"What!" Amanda choked on her wine and spluttered. Miles got up quickly and patted her back. "You're only just telling me this now? We've spoken every day!" she cried, once she'd recovered.

"I think this kind of news warranted a face-to-face," he answered dryly.

"We've been together for almost six hours!"

"I didn't think it was the right thing to say in front of everyone," he countered and rolled his eyes.

"I suppose. Pierce might let it slip out to Hugh."

"Oh, Pierce knows; he went with me to choose the ring. And so does Hugh; he got the size," Miles said sheepishly and Amanda's jaw dropped.

"What! Who else knows?"

"I asked Alistair." Miles cringed waiting for her reaction.

"Alistair! He never told me anything," she said incredulously.

"Well, I think he was being discreet."

"Jeez, who else knows before me."

Miles leaned forward and narrowed his eyes at her. "So, you two have been in touch, then?"

"Oh no, you don't get to change the subject." Amanda waggled her finger at him. "I want all the details. I leave for a few weeks' holiday and all this happens? That's it: I'm never leaving you again." She mock-glared at him and Miles chuckled.

"Gerard knows."

"Are you kidding me right now? The ex knows before me? Why would he know, anyway?"

"I sort of lost my temper and spat it out." Miles explained to her how the photo opportunities at Holmwood had gone down and how Gerard had goaded him.

"He is a bit of an arsehole." She made a face and took another sip of wine.

"You'll get no argument from me. I want to punch that smug face of his so fucking bad," Miles muttered and Amanda almost choked again. She quickly swallowed and fixed him with a determined gaze.

"Back to the ring and the proposal. I think I should be asking you who doesn't know."

"Apart from you, you mean? Well, Louisa doesn't."

"Oh, you're hilarious," Amanda said sarcastically and Miles let out a laugh.

"I'm sorry. It was spontaneous. I was angry and felt so out of control. But I knew I wanted her to be with me forever, so I went and bought the ring."

"It better be some special ring."

"It is. Here, I've got a picture of it." Miles picked up his phone and brought up a picture of the ring. He'd purposely taken a photograph to show her.

"Oh Miles, it's beautiful."

"I have good taste," he said smugly with a wink.

"That you have. So, when are you going to pop the question?" Amanda rubbed her hands together in excitement. She'd waited long enough for her wayward brother-in-law to settle down.

"Some time before the concert."

"That's in less than a month." Amanda twisted her mouth as she thought about it. "Any plans where?"

"In LA."

"How the hell are you going to get her to go out there again with everything happening here and the lead-up to the concert?"

"I'm not sure but I've Pierce, Hugh, Alistair and now you to help me figure it out," Miles said, with a self-satisfied smirk.

Amanda laughed at his ridiculousness. "Oh my God! This is so exciting and Holmwood is such an amazing place to have a wedding!"

"She hasn't said yes yet," Miles reminded her and Amanda waved her hand dismissively.

"She will."

MILES SETTLED ONTO HIS bed and sent off a message to Pierce, saying he'd turned in for the night. It was still early but Amanda was exhausted and he wasn't in the mood to watch TV, even if Pierce was happy to keep him company. Miles pulled his laptop closer and began searching the various media sites to see if there were any more scathing articles about him not playing at the concert. Why was the public or the media so fixated on him? How did they expect him to play any of his Keane Sense material when a key member of the band wasn't here? Miles rubbed his face and then checked on his emails before his scheduled call with Louisa. She had a conference call with the charity she was part of in New York and was going to call him once it was over. He checked the time; it was almost 10. Miles quickly replied to his last email and changed out of his clothes. He'd just slipped under the covers when the video call from Louisa came through.

"Hey, you're in bed already?" Louisa said in surprise, seeing him bare-chested and propped up against the bedhead.

"Just now. I'm so rock and roll."

"Aren't you just?" Louisa laughed and leaned back in her office chair admiring the view of his mussed-up hair and toned chest.

"Amanda and the children were so tired. So, I came up to bed. No doubt they'll be up at some ungodly hour tomorrow."

"How are they?"

"They're good. The children have grown. God, I hadn't realised how I'd missed them. They never stopped talking though. I couldn't even get a word in."

"I'm sure."

"How was your conference call?"

"Boring. They want me over for some event this month, an art exhibition, but it a few days before the concert." Louisa rolled her eyes, then sat forward again. "Anyway, forget about that. Tell me Amanda's news."

"I managed to tell her all about *Singing in the Rain* – she freaked out. I think she wants me performing more than anyone."

"She remembers you in front of an audience, how good you were."

"Thank you. Eric is subtly putting pressure on me to do a TV interview. The magazines are good but a TV show has more impact. I think the production company of the series want me to do it too, even though I never signed anything to say I would."

"The film producers might not be so lenient," Louisa said softly and Miles nodded.

"They're not. I still haven't signed the contract. They want the full dog and pony show." He blew out a breath and rested his head back.

"Oh Miles, will you pull out of the deal?" He looked a little lost and she wished she was with him. Had he been at his home she might have been tempted to go around. She was glad he was with Amanda. She always seemed to have a calming effect on him.

"Shit, Louisa, I want this role so bad but the thought of being at film festivals and on talk shows… I don't know how well I can handle them." He straightened up and gave her a weary smile. "I've also pretty much told Eric that *Singing in the Rain* is a yes. He's negotiating down to the last minute of my time but it's just stalling tactics."

"Stalling? What for more money?"

"No, I don't need more money, I need the time to get used to the idea." He pulled in his lips and let out a sigh.

"I know how you feel. When I came back to the UK, my mother

was constantly pressurising me to become the patron. I wanted to, very much so, but I stalled for almost six months until I finally said I was ready."

This was the first time Miles had heard this. He'd presumed that they'd timed the takeover of her role to coincide with the ball. "Why did you stall?"

Louisa sat forward and rested her chin on her knuckles. "I didn't think I could do it. I didn't want to be out in the public eye. I'd enjoyed being in Gerard's shadow. It was safe. I also didn't want to fail. I wasn't lying when I made that speech at the ball. My mother's shoes are hard to fill. It was her and Papa's charity. I didn't want to muck it up."

Miles's brows drew together, hearing her talk so candidly about her insecurities. She'd always come across so self-assured, especially where her duty was concerned. She'd been born into the role of countess and always performed her duties flawlessly. Miles couldn't believe she'd held back from being the patron. "What changed your mind, made you say yes?"

Louisa leaned closer to the screen and gave a soft smile. "A cocky American ex-popstar with a cheeky smile." Miles let out a husky chuckle and she grinned back at him. "Getting to know you and learning about what you'd been through. Then seeing you decide to take the plunge, face your fears, it made me want to do that too."

"Louisa." He mildly shook his head, flawed by her revelation.

"Well, I couldn't be upstaged by our ambassador, could I?" she joked and Miles chuckled.

"It's the other way around. When you're in the room, I gladly fade into the background and follow your lead. What you do, how you are, I'm in awe of you. It's because of you I took the first steps to being in front of an audience again."

"Looks like we're good for each other then, doesn't it?"

"We're more than good. We're perfect."

"Yes, we are." Louisa gave him the sweetest smile and added. "Once this concert is over, no more hiding."

"I don't intend to." If Miles had his way, they'd be officially together before the concert. He just needed some way to get her to his Malibu home.

HOLMWOOD AND ITS GROUNDS were at the height of their glory. Holmwood was beautiful all the year round but in the summer, when the sun spread its generous rays over the lush grass and made the surface of the lake sparkle, it was magnificent. Miles scanned the vast grounds that had recently been full of visitors, taking in its beauty. The sculptured gardens were in full bloom and as he strolled through them, he picked up the fragrant scent of the light pink rose bushes named Miss Alice. Louisa had told him her father had had them planted in honour of her mother. He still couldn't take in the vastness of the estate but with every visit, he was becoming a little more familiar with it.

The staff moved swiftly around the grounds in golf carts, emptying bins and collecting any errant pieces of rubbish. The boats on the lake were being moored and cleaned, ready for the next day and the horses were let out to roam around their gated field. In the distance, Miles could see Alistair and Amanda riding towards the woodlands and he smiled to himself. Alistair had invited her and the children down for a few days which meant it was also a perfect opportunity for Miles to meet Louisa, though she had yet to arrive from London.

Miles made his way to where Celeste, Grace and Louis were patting the horses and feeding them pieces of cut apple. Louis squealed with laughter as the horses nibbled against his palm. It amazed him how comfortable they'd become here. They'd visited a handful of times, yet were at ease in the vast estate. A lot of that was due to Alistair and Lady Alice. They made Amanda very welcome and though she was still in awe of how the Blackthorns lived, she'd certainly felt more at ease.

"Thanks for watching them," Miles said, as he reached where they were standing. Celeste had volunteered to take the children to the horses while Miles finished off a call.

"No worries, it must be a new feeling for you." Celeste subtly gestured with her head to where Alistair and Amanda were. "Being the gooseberry."

Miles let out a soft laugh. "Yes, well I have been a gooseberry before where Amanda is concerned, so I'm used to it."

"You think they'll end up together?" Celeste whispered after a beat, mindful of the children but in all honesty, the horses had totally captured their attention. One of the stablehands had come out and was chatting to them, leading them to where the most docile horse was.

"Would that be so bad, a Keane marrying a Blackthorn?" Miles tilted his head to the side and regarded her.

"No, not at all," Celeste said quickly, worried she might have offended him.

A wide smile stretched over his lips, obviously pleased with her response. "Good to know," he said with his trademark wink and Celeste furrowed her brow, wondering why he felt the need to make sure she was comfortable with the idea. Miles turned to search for Grace and Louis, worried that he might have given too much away. They were happily helping the stable hand brush one of the horses. Celeste stepped into his line of view with her eyes narrowed.

"Wait a minute. Were you talking about Amanda and Alistair just now or about you?"

"Me?" Miles feigned confusion.

"Yes, *you*. You and Mum. Are you…?" She stepped a little closer and scrutinized his expression but his sunglasses were doing an excellent job of hiding his eyes, so she couldn't be completely sure, until Miles twisted his mouth and gave an awkward on shoulder shrug. "Oh. My. Freaking. God!" She cried out, then slapped her hand over her mouth.

"Calm down, I haven't asked her yet," Miles said in a hushed rush, looking around to make sure the outburst of the tenacious Lady Blackthorn hadn't been heard.

"But you will?" she stage-whispered and Miles gave her a nod.

"I will. Soon," he said quietly, feeling a little uneasy talking about proposing to Louisa with her daughter.

"Why are you stalling? Is it the whole countess thing?" Celeste asked, without any regard and Miles took a second to respond, a little intimidated by her directness.

"That doesn't help," he said dryly and Celeste pulled a face, which caused Miles to chuckle. He was still getting used to Celeste's unconventional manner. "I actually wanted to ask her at my home in Malibu."

"Oh, I see. When will you be going next?" she quickly asked.

"I haven't planned anything. Our schedules are hectic and the concert is a month away. I wanted to ask her before, so we could announce it afterwards. If she says yes, that is."

"She'll say yes." Celeste rolled her eyes at his comment. *Did he really think she'd say no?* "Hmm. Maybe she could come with me to New York. I'm spending five days with Papa before the concert, then Nicolas is coming back with me. We're starting university in September."

Miles widened his eyes, a little surprised that she was thinking of ways to help with his proposal plan. He also wasn't too thrilled with the idea of Louisa being anywhere near Gerard. "Not sure I want your mom spending time with your father when I'm about to propose."

"Oh Miles, she won't be. They're well practised in avoiding each other, even under the same roof. She keeps him at a distance. She doesn't stay at Papa's, even if he offers." Miles mulled on her candid comment. He'd forgotten how perceptive Celeste was. She'd grown up with her two parents, living together but having separate lives. "She's different with you," Celeste said with a wistful smile.

"Good different?"

"Yeah, even Granny notices." Miles stifled a smirk, obviously pleased with her remark. "You don't need to look so smug about it," she teased and he chuckled. "I'm sure there's some event she's invited to in New York. She always had a full calendar when she lived there. Maybe I could persuade her to go with me," Celeste said thoughtfully. "Then it's down to you to get her to LA."

Miles stared wide-eyed at her, stunned she was actually scheming ways to get her mother to the US so he could ask her to marry him. "I actually don't have anything I need to go there for," he said carefully, caught off guard by the direction of their conversation.

"Well, think of a reason, or create one," she said in a deliberate tone and rolled her eyes. Miles laughed at her determination but when he thought about it, she was right, this could actually work. "You're thinking about it, aren't you?" she said smugly.

There was no denying it: he was. "Not a word to anyone. It's bad enough that other people know."

"People? You mean Amanda? Well, she might tell Alistair." Celeste gestured to where Amanda and Alistair were now ridi towards them.

"Actually, Alistair knew before her."

"What! How did that happen?"

"I thought I had to ask his permission," Miles said sheepishly and Celeste let out a laugh.

"Ah, I see. Well, if Alistair knows, Granny knows for sure."

"You think?" Miles said in horror.

"Pretty sure."

"Oh shit."

"I wouldn't worry. She likes you."

"She does? How do you know?"

"She and Aunt Margot are always singing your praises. Aunt Margot will definitely know too."

Fuck!

Miles rubbed his hand over his mouth and chin. "This is the worst kept secret ever."

Celeste giggled. "Don't worry, they won't say anything. It also means you can't back out." She gave him a knowing look. He responded with an 'are you joking' look over his sunglasses and she grinned at him.

"I just hope I can propose before someone lets it slip. You have to swear not to tell her."

"Mum's the word… hah, she is, actually." She chuckled at her own joke and Miles shook his head. She really was just a fun-loving 19-year-old, albeit a very privileged 19-year-old, but grounded and probably a little worldlier than most young women her age. "Don't worry, I'm good at keeping secrets. It comes with the territory. Speaking of Mum…" Celeste gestured to the house and Miles turned to see the
date black Bentley driving through the gates in the distance. "I think
's her arriving. Just in time for drinks before dinner." Miles shaded
s and watched the sun bounce off the chrome trim of the classic
k, I'm going to be a bridesmaid!" Celeste sing-songed and
k-glared at her.
!"
ry." She grinned at him, then skipped to Grace and
to get Louisa to the US before one of her family let
ng r.

MILES WASN'T SURE WHOSE idea it had been to have a barbeque but he was grateful. He enjoyed being in the grand dining room at Holmwood. It was a surreal experience, but casual dining outside was more his style and definitely more child friendly. He was sitting on the terrace looking out towards the grounds, watching the children throw balls for Duke. Amanda kept her eye on them from her seat nearer to the edge and closer to where Alistair was mixing drinks from the trolley. Louisa was overseeing the table of salads and sides as the chef set up the grill. Alistair played host, ensuring everyone had drinks and Miles had the distinct feeling every activity and arrangements today, and no doubt the next couple of days, were all his doing. The casual dinner tonight, horse riding lessons tomorrow, boating on the lake and there was talk of a helicopter trip too. All tailored to entertain and cater to the children and no doubt impress Amanda. This was "courting", as Lady Alice had once said, Blackthorn-style, and from the happy look on Amanda's face, it seemed to be working. Not that Amanda needed grand gestures – quite the contrary. When she'd meet Louis, they'd been living in a two-bed apartment over a laundrette and had lived off street food and pizza, studying hard and playing music even harder. She used to come around with homemade British-style food she'd made and they all used to sit on the floor, around the coffee table, digging into shepherd's pie or stew and dumplings, drinking beer out of the bottle. She'd been starry-eyed from the very first time she'd clapped eyes on Louis and today, Miles could see the start of that very same look whenever she stole a gaze at Alistair. Miles wasn't sure how far their relationship had progressed but there was certainly a familiarity between them that was obvious to him and, no doubt, the rest of the Blackthorns. It was definitely early days and obvious that both of them were treading carefully as they stepped into areas they hadn't thought would cross their paths again. There was too much at stake, too much to lose for them to rush into anything, other than a friendship. For now at least, anyway, but Miles hoped that there would be more, for both of them. Amanda undoubtedly deserved a secon chance at happiness and Alistair had earned the right to find somec he could love and who would love him for the honourable, good ı he was.

Lady Alice sipped her gin and tonic and cast her eye over the terrace, smiling wistfully. It had been a while since she'd seen her family so happy. Alistair was being sociable and the perfect host, a role he usually left to Louisa. He'd even donned long trousers, which was a rarity, and replaced his usual worn polo shirts with a casual button-down, with the sleeves artfully rolled up. His beard was trimmed and his hair had been cut, still long but decidedly more stylish. It had been a long time since Lady Alice had seen her son take an interest in himself and a woman. He'd never been short of women admirers and had dated plenty over the years leading up to his accident. None had been particularly special to him. He'd been young and had had years in front of him before he thought about settling down. He'd used the excuse of his military career for not wanting to marry and leave his wife behind as he moved around the world. In all honesty, Lady Alice had always thought that there wasn't a woman who could measure up. After his accident, Alistair became a recluse and depressed, then the sudden death of his father, as he was slowly coming to terms with the hand fate had dealt him, had thrown him into the role of the Earl of Holmwood and he'd had to focus on the business and his family duty.

Alistair's personal life took a back seat while he recovered physically, emotionally and mentally. His military training had put him in good stead for his role, as well as the years working alongside his father. Most believed he'd embraced his role out of his fierce sense of duty, some closer to him realised he'd risen to the challenge, using his work as a crutch to help him move forward with his life. But those who knew him well understood that Holmwood was his life raft. He needed it as much as Holmwood needed him. Working and making Holmwood a success gave him a reason to get up every morning. It purpose to his life. His father had worked the estate and made it s for his children. Alistair committed himself to increasing his ccess, to ensure that the future of Holmwood was financially nto the future, even if he was unable to secure an heir to gacy. He'd far exceeded his own expectations and now e in his life where he needed something other than ction.

to where the large grill and the chef were and

offered to help, just as Celeste came to join them for dinner. She'd stolen away to call Nicolas, who was back home in the US for a few weeks. Before long, the Keanes and the Blackthorns were grilling up their dinner, making jokes and settling into a comfortable casual dinner. There on the beautiful terrace, in front of the grand sixteenth-century Holmwood House, the blue-blooded Blackthorns and the Keanes ate dinner and drank vintage wine, laughed, shared stories and enjoyed each other's company.

Lady Alice took a moment to take in the joyful tableau of her family and their guests, wishing her husband was there to witness how far they'd come and how well they were doing. When he'd died, Alistair had only just been starting to make a recovery and Louisa's marriage had turned to one of convenience. The late Earl was troubled by his children's unhappiness and his inability to be able to help them. He'd be proud of how they'd turned their lives around, how far they'd come. A rebel himself, he would've relished the company of Miles and loved seeing how he brought the slight recklessness out in Louisa. Most of all he'd be thrilled that Louisa had found a man who loved her for who she really was and would equally fight for her and bask in her glory. Seeing the young bloom of romance between Alistair and Amanda would have been the icing on the cake for the late Earl. The thought that Alistair would never find a worthy partner had always been a worry to him. The Earl wanted what he had for his son. That fateful bomb blast hadn't only shattered his leg and spine, it had shattered all his hopes of that happening too. It would take a special kind of woman to accept and truly love Alistair. As Lady Alice watched her son laugh so freely, she felt sure that Amanda might just be that very woman.

"Are you alright, Granny? You're very quiet," asked Celeste quietly, taking a seat next to her on one of the outdoor sofas.

Lady Alice gave her a wistful smile. "Just thinking about Grandpa."

"I miss him too."

"He'd love this, seeing everyone happy. Seeing Alistair happy especially." Lady Alice gestured over to where Alistair was lifting Louis in the air, turning him around and making helicopter noises. Louis shrieked with joy as Grace and Amanda laughed at their antics.

"Yeah, I think there's something there, don't you?" Celeste widened her eyes and Lady Alice nodded, then shifted her gaze to where Miles and Louisa were sitting close together on another of the sofas, laughing too.

"It would seem that the Blackthorns have a soft spot for the Keanes, including me," Lady Alice said conspiratorially and Celeste giggled.

"Yeah, me too."

"We'd better make sure we don't scare them off then, hadn't we?"

"DON'T WORRY ABOUT PERFORMING. You know what the press are like." Konran dragged his palm over his short black hair and gave Miles a reassuring smile. "We'll give them some juicy bits of information to keep their focus on what's really important; the money we'll be raising and the cause it's for." For a young man and one who was so new to the crazy music business, Konran knew exactly what the score was and how to play the game where the press were concerned. Miles hadn't been that keyed in at his age and he was glad he'd decided to talk to him about his worries. Miles had spoken to Eric and Amanda about him feeling the pressure and they'd supported him but hearing it from a fellow musician was what Miles needed. "Besides, there's no room in the line-up for you anyways," he joked and Miles chuckled.

"Looking forward to playing in Barcelona tonight?"

"Man, I love Europe. It's so... I don't know... cultured. Everything's historical or classy. Every city is different," he gushed. They tried to catch up at least twice a week with video calls, firstly for a progress report but mostly because they enjoyed bouncing ideas off each other. They'd grown closer over the last few weeks, plus Konran got a real kick out of knowing *the* Miles Keane video-called him.

"Enjoy it, kid, it's the best time, touring, seeing and experiencing new places." In the background, Miles could see Margie walking around the high-end hotel room in a bathrobe. She waved at him and then went off-screen.

"Yeah, it is but we don't get that long. I'm gonna need a month's vacay to see all these places properly."

"So, you and Margi, eh?" Miles gave him a smirk and Konran gave him a wide toothy grin.

"Yeah, she's special."

"She is, I'm happy for you, man."

"Thanks. How about you and Lady B?"

"Louisa?"

"Yeah, well I wasn't talking about Celeste!" He let out a laugh, then seeing Miles's surprised expression, he quickly added, "Don't worry, Celeste told me you and her mom were together."

"She did, did she?"

"Yeah, my girl and me are tight. She tells me everything."

"Well, in that case I don't need to say anymore," Miles said dryly, really not wanting to get into his personal life.

"That's cool, you're keeping it on the down-low. I can appreciate you don't wanna have the press all over it."

"Exactly."

"So, Malibu eh?" Konran did a bad job of suppressing his huge grin.

"Oh fuck, Celeste told you?"

"Uh-huh. Like I said… tight."

"Not a fucking word." Miles mock-glared and pointed at him.

"I won't tell a soul." He made a cross sign over his heart and Miles rolled his eyes. This was getting out of hand. Everyone who knew they were together knew he was ready to propose. "But for the record… I'm so stoked."

"She hasn't said yes yet."

"Man, that deal is signed and sealed, brother." He let out a hearty laugh and Miles couldn't help but chuckle at his enthusiasm.

7

DISTRACTIONS

Three weeks before the concert.

Tukon recently posted on his Instagram account the final line-up for the CASPO concert and links to the CASPO charity for donations. It hasn't escaped hardcore fans of Keane Sense that Miles Keane is noticeably absent from the line-up. It was speculated this would be the first time he would perform since the tragic loss of his brother, five years ago in the Alice Tully Hall shooting. Since Miles Keane was appointed ambassador, the revered charity has seen a sharp uprise in donations and interest. The charity's social media accounts have hit over three million followers since his ambassadorship. The concert and the inclusion of high-profile celebrities has brought a new wave of donators and supporters as well as a 'Keane' interest... pun intended. Mr Keane is absent from all social media but is often featured in the CASPO account in his ambassador's role.

TuKon recently announced that future profits from his music would be donated to CASPO and ACTS (Association for Children with Talent and Skills) the charity that sponsored his education in New York. It is estimated both charities will receive over $20 million each year based on the number one rapper's earnings this year.

In related news, Lady Louisa Blackthorn, patron of CASPO, officially opened an urban garden funded by CASPO. The rundown area in the inner city of Birmingham has recently been re-landscaped for nearby residents to enjoy and a playground created for children.

The neglected area has been totally transformed and future upkeep will be funded by the charity. Lady Louisa Blackthorn looked elegant in a salmon dress with flowered sequins over the shoulders by Ralph and Russo, one of her favoured designers (see picture below). After officially opening the gardens, she spent time amongst many of the children and parents, many of them single, who will benefit from the *garden. Lady Louisa expressed her thanks to the eight local residents who created the garden, and will be subsequently employed full-time for its upkeep.*

The Blackthorn family have always been working aristocrats. The Earl of Holmwood was in the Royal Airforce and is a decorated war hero. He now runs the Holmwood estate after losing half his leg in an accident during his final tour (see pictures below).

PIERCE PUSHED THE DOOR open and quietly slipped into the music room, trying hard not to distract Miles. Over the last few days, Miles had locked himself in the room whenever he could, playing snippets of music on his piano and scribbling lyrics on a dog-eared pad. Miles was old school when he composed: he wrote lyrics faster than he typed and took comfort in the slight resistance a pencil gave, as opposed to a ballpoint. Miles hummed to himself, then let his fingers gently press the keys before rubbing out and rewriting notes on the music paper. He caught sight of Pierce and stopped.

"Sorry, I didn't mean to disturb. Thought you might want a top-up and something to eat." Pierce indicated to the laden tray before placing it onto the low table.

"Thanks, you didn't need to."

"You've been in here for four hours," he pointed out and Miles furrowed his brow and looked at his watch.

"I lost track of time." Miles put down his pencil and stretched out his stiff shoulders. The smell of freshly brewed coffee beckoned him.

"Your phone has been buzzing. I only answered to Eric and Konran. Nothing urgent, except Eric." Miles lifted his brow and made a gesture with his hand for Pierce to elaborate. Miles reached over to where the tray was and picked up the cup of coffee and took a sip, savouring its smooth taste. *Had he really been at it for four hours?*

Pierce's voice interrupted his thoughts. "He said, and I quote, 'Tell him to sign the film contracts and stop fucking about.'" Pierce stifled a grin and Miles rolled his eyes. He could only imagine what other things he'd said to his trusted bodyguard and friend.

"That's all?"

"No, he also told me to make sure you didn't look at the media sites."

"You're not my babysitter," Miles huffed, a little annoyed that Eric was trying to coddle him.

"I kind of am," Pierce said dryly and perched himself on the edge of one of the armchairs. "But I told him you were working, that's why you weren't answering. I didn't want to hurt the poor guy's ego," Pierce said with a smirk. Eric didn't need to know that Miles was closely monitoring any sites which mentioned or discussed the fact that he wasn't performing.

Miles gave a nod and was thankful he had the perceptive Pierce to make his excuses. "What did Konran want?"

"He said he had an awesome idea and wanted to bounce it off you," Pierce said in an excited voice, imitating the vibrancy of the rapper, then chuckled.

"He's got so much energy. I remember being like that when I was his age."

"Weren't we all?" Pierce said and Miles nodded, then let his gaze focus on the music he'd been writing. "I'm no musician but that sounded good."

"Thanks, it's getting there. Funnily enough, it was after my last conversation with Konran that gave me the inspiration. His energy must be rubbing off on me," Miles said with a shake of his head.

Pierce rose from his seat and headed to the door. "I'll leave you to it. Mind if I leave the door open? I like listening."

"Sure, and thanks for that." Miles gestured to the tray with the sandwich and beer on.

"Make sure you eat it," he said but Miles had already turned his attention back to his scribbling.

MILES SIGNED HIS NAME on the various marked pages of the hefty contracts that had been gathering dust on his desk. He slipped the copies into the box file and shut the lid. He'd have them couriered tomorrow. It was coming close to 10 and he knew Louisa would be finishing off her various calls and meetings and waiting for his call. He'd already let Eric know he'd be sending him the contracts for the film but Miles wanted Louisa to know as soon as possible. The film studio would probably want to send out press releases once they received their copies, letting the world know. It'd be open season again and no doubt he'd have a collection of press camped outside of his home.

Within a few minutes, Miles was in his bedroom and calling Louisa. She was in her bedroom at Blackthorn Mansion, just over a mile from where he was. It annoyed him that they were so close yet still so far from each other.

"Hey, you done for tonight?" Miles asked.

"I've a few more emails to reply to but nothing urgent. They can wait until tomorrow." She yawned, shuffling up on her bed to rest her back on the plush headboard.

"I saw the footage of you in Birmingham today. You looked beautiful."

She smiled softly at him. "Thank you. It was a good day for CASPO today. That area was crying out for attention. Those children have no place to play that's safe."

"What's on for you tomorrow?"

"Lunch at Blacks with a few sponsors. We need bigger donations." She shook her head dismissively. "Forget about me, what have you been up to?"

"I finally signed the film contract."

"Oh Miles, that's wonderful. How do you feel?"

"Scared shitless," he answered dryly and they both chuckled. He loved the fact he could be as candid as he wanted with her.

"I know you don't want platitudes and believe me, I'm not saying this just to make you feel better, but Miles, you're really going to be amazing in this. It's the perfect role." Her gaze held his through the screen and for that moment he felt he really could achieve anything.

"Thanks. I also spoke to Konran before he went on stage tonight."

"He's in Paris?" Louisa's brow furrowed as she tried to remember.

"Marseille, Paris next."

"I can't keep up." She shook her head and Miles grinned.

"The press are talking about his donation, which is exactly what we need."

"He's a smart cookie, timing the announcement in the run-up to the concert."

"He is. He also ran something else by me."

"Oh?"

"He suggested we co-host the concert." Miles narrowed his eyes at her, then added, "You knew."

Louisa scrunched her nose and nodded. "He asked me about it, wanted to know what I thought. I told him the decision was all yours."

"It'll certainly stop the constant speculation about me performing," Miles said with a hint of bitterness. They still hadn't let up on that particular line.

"Don't read the articles, Miles. They're just trying to get hits on their sites. It's bullying. No one at CASPO, me, anyone expects you to do anything more than you're already doing."

"I know," he said with a sigh. Konran had said the exact same thing to him and he appreciated their support. Maybe presenting wasn't such a bad idea. *A minute on stage every half an hour... he could do that, couldn't he?*

MILES WAS NEVER MORE thankful for having Konran a.k.a. TuKon in his corner. The news of his future donations shifted all the focus on him and for a few days, anything Miles Keane-related was old news. They had a new story to write about and Konran made sure he was available to talk about it and CASPO, whenever and wherever. When Miles caught up with him as he prepared for his last date in France, he'd simply said that he'd learned to use the press, instead of them using him. Give them something, so they forget about what you don't want them to talk about. Deflect and save up announcements for exactly that purpose. Miles had to hand it to him, he was shrewd for someone so young. When he'd asked him how he'd become so smart, he simply said he'd learned from the best, the Blackthorns.

"They work the press like no one I've ever met." Konran grinned at Miles from his phone. "Sure, it's different in our industry but it still works. Did you ever hear that it was Lady B who paid for my education?" Miles shook his head. "They made sure no one knew. Had you even heard of or seen Lady B when she was in the US?" Miles thought about it and Konran was right, she'd kept off the radar until she was ready. "She kept herself out of everything. That press conference is the only blip they've ever had and to be fair, it wasn't their doing.

But they still managed to quash the rumours, deflecting them with the photo ops." Konran leaned closer and lowered his voice. "If you decide to do the co-hosting, they'll forget that you're not performing. If you don't want to do that, we'll give them something else to talk about. I've learned to turn a negative into a positive."

"Are you quoting motivational quotes to me?" Miles joked, his voice rising in surprise.

"Yeah, man. There are so many of those sayings I love, like, 'Fake it 'til you make it'."

"Change the game, don't let the game change you," countered Miles. Konran let out a hoot.

"Ooh, Macklemore... good one!"

"I know my rappers too, you know," Miles said dryly.

"Okay, what about one of my personal favourites, 'I have nothing to lose but something to gain.'"

Miles grinned at the young man who he'd become to see as his friend. He had to admit his energy was infectious. "Eminem?"

"You do know your rappers!"

"I've been around a long time." Miles chuckled. "Believe it to achieve it. That's what Louis always said," Miles added more soberly.

"That's a good one."

"Yeah, I think someone wrote a book with that title a few years ago but Louis was saying it long before that," Miles said with a hint of pride.

"Louis sounds like he was an awesome man. I wish I'd met him."

"He was. He's in my thoughts and with me every day."

"I get that. My dad is with me too. I feel like he's sitting on my shoulder cheering me on or guiding me. Kind of like Jiminy Cricket." Konran chuckled.

"What was he like?"

"He was a big, strong guy but he never used his strength to hurt anyone. He always worked hard and never wanted any handouts. He had a plan, always had a plan, and worked on it every day. The day he got shot, he'd secured a loan to start his own security business."

"Jesus, I'm so sorry for your loss," Miles said softly. To lose your father so tragically and when you were so young must've been hard, Miles thought to himself.

117

"It taught me to grab any opportunity that came my way. Accept the handouts but still work hard too – and now I have the chance to pay it forward."

"He'd be proud of you."

"Oh, I know," Konran said with a wide smile and Miles realised he really meant it.

"About the presenting, I think it's a good idea," Miles said tentatively.

Konran nodded his head and beamed. Even on the small screen of his phone, Miles could feel his excitement. "You know it is. We're gonna blow their minds." And he then did an impression of a bomb exploding with his hands and made the noise too.

Miles let out a laugh. "Are you sure you're not on something?" he teased.

"I'm high on life, man. No drugs, a beer after the show and my family all around me, that's all I need," Konran drawled.

"You are one of a fucking kind, Konran."

"So are you, Miles. Let's tell Darcy and then let's get the concert producers into a meeting. We've three weeks to get ready."

"Yeah, we need to give the press a distraction."

"We sure do, my man."

OVER THE NEXT FEW days, Miles locked himself in his music room and composed to clear his mind. If he focused on his music, he could forget about being on stage in front of thousands of people. He had meetings every day either with the scriptwriters via video or his acting coach at home. The concert organisers and producers were also contacting him every day with ideas they thought would work well for the concert. Miles was second-thinking his decision to co-host until he spoke to Eric who assured him this was probably the best way for him to get used to a live audience again. The introduction to each act would be scripted, with the option for him and Konran to ad-lib. They'd have an autocue too and if he faltered, Konran would be there to help him out.

Miles's decision to have a more active part in the concert couldn't have made Eric more pleased. The film producers were biting at the bit to announce the new film. They had their megastar lead, they had their director and the other major roles in the film were being negotiated. Once Miles Keane was announced, any wavering A-star actor would jump at the chance to work alongside him. The series producers would also profit from the announcement but as always, in the entertainment business, it was all about timing. Miles had been off the radar for five years but in the last six months, he'd done a high-end advertising campaign for a luxury watch brand, been seen at prestigious fashion events, taken on the ambassador's role at CASPO, filmed a six-part documentary series and was an integral part of the biggest charity concert of the year. Now that Miles was on board to co-host the concert, the film announcement could wait for just before the concert, for maximum impact. Eric didn't want to flood the media just yet; they'd have plenty of opportunity to keep the media occupied over the next few weeks. With the film producers happy, Eric's next task was to get Miles to the US so he could finally sit down with the musical's director. He hoped his powers of persuasion would work because with any luck he might even get Miles to agree to a talk show appearance.

"How's your schedule looking for the week before the concert?" Eric asked casually but Miles wasn't a fool. If Eric wanted to know what he was up to he had something in mind.

"Why do you ask?" Miles answered cagily.

"I was hoping you could come out and sign for *Singing in the Rain* in person. Meet with the director, get a feel of the whole team. They're eager to meet you."

Miles put his phone onto loudspeaker and looked at his computer diary for the week before the concert. He had his acting lessons, which he could reschedule and some conference calls which could be done from anywhere. "When exactly? Because I need to be back by the Saturday."

"I think they're flexible. Let me lock in a date. Wednesday could work." Miles mulled over the idea. This might be the opportunity he was looking for. If he could persuade Louisa to fly out on Tuesday, meet with the director, then fly to LA, have two days together and be back in the UK on Saturday. Just in time for preconcert preparations and rehearsals.

"I wanted an excuse to come out, to be honest," Miles admitted, surprising Eric.

"Yeah? You homesick?"

"Not exactly but I did want to go to LA," Miles said vaguely.

"Oh. What's in LA?"

"My home," Miles deadpanned.

"Ha-ha. What's going on, Miles?"

"I want to take Louisa there."

"I see, a mini-break. She must be stressed."

"Yeah, there's that too."

"Miles, is something wrong? Is Louisa alright?"

"She's fine, she's perfect in fact. So perfect that..." Miles paused for a beat. He couldn't believe he was telling yet another person. "I'm going to propose and I want to do it at my home."

"Miles! That's, jeez, that's brilliant news."

"It will be if she says yes, otherwise it'll be awkward," Miles said with a hint of sarcasm.

"So, your plan is the keep her there until she agrees? I didn't think there was any woman on this Earth that would turn down Miles Keane," Eric joked.

"Louisa isn't any woman."

"No, she's not. I'm really happy for you Miles. She's exactly what you need."

"Thanks. It'll certainly give the press something to write about."

"Ha, I'll say." Eric beamed, then added a little cautiously. "I wanted to run something else by you."

"JIMMY KIMMEL!"

"Yeah, apparently he's been asking Eric since I recorded the series. And now with the concert..." Miles gave Louisa a lopsided smile. He was surprised at how giddy she was. "Eric thinks it's perfect timing."

"This is huge," Louisa said as she paced around his kitchen, clearly excited at the prospect. She'd managed to arrange an unscheduled visit on her way back from her lunch at Blacks. Miles was making coffee for them, taking a break from working on his music and seizing the opportunity to throw the idea of them spending a few days in LA at her.

"I've done Jimmy Kimmel's show before, you know," he said with an arch of his brow.

Louisa stopped pacing. "Oh God, of course you have. How silly of me. You were always on chat shows. Celeste watched them incessantly, drove me mad."

Miles laughed at her uncensored comment and she giggled, realising how bad it sounded. "It was a while ago, though." Miles gave a one-shoulder shrug and then placed her coffee cup on the kitchen counter and patted the stool for her to sit on. He took a second to take her in as she took a sip of her coffee, then edged up onto the high stool. She looked all business-like in a form-fitting skirt, heels and a silk blouse. Very ladylike but still sexy as hell, especially as the skirt had risen up over her delicate knees.

"So, will you do it?" she asked, placing her cup back down, oblivious to his wayward thoughts.

"I think I should."

"Well, at least you know him."

Miles stepped up to where she was sitting and swivelled the stool so she was facing him. He took hold of her hands and gave them a gentle rub. This was the perfect time to ask her. There were no distractions, he had her to himself and she didn't have anywhere to be. He had the rest of the day, evening and night to persuade her. "Would you come with me?"

"On the show!" Louisa's eyes widened in horror and Miles let out a husky laugh.

"I meant to LA, but sure, why the hell not? I'm sure Jimmy would be thrilled," he said with a smirk, then gently brushed her hair off of her forehead. He dropped a kiss on her mouth and she smiled against his lips.

"No, to being on the show," she said with a slight shake of her head at her misunderstanding.

Miles nodded and waited for a response to whether she'd be able to come. "It's the week before the concert," she said drawing her brow together. He slowly let his hands drift to her thighs and he frowned at how restrictive her fitted skirt was.

"I know," he said while pushing her skirt up a little so he could spread and step between her legs. "I'm thinking of going to New York first. Eric wants me to meet with the musical's director, then fly out to LA and stay a couple of days."

"Oh, I see."

Miles slipped his hands over her hips and leaned to graze his nose over the shell of her ear. "I can do the show and head back a couple of days before the concert."

"Miles…" Louisa breathed as he dropped feather-soft kisses against her neck, causing her to shiver.

"We could have some uninterrupted time together. No distractions, no staff, just us." He punctuated every point with soft kisses across her collarbone.

"Sounds like heaven."

Miles murmured his agreement, then knelt down and prised off her shoes, letting them drop with an unceremonious clatter. She smiled down at his handsome face and cupped his jaw. "What are you doing?"

"Making you comfortable. You're not leaving until you say yes," he said with a hint of a challenge.

"You want me with you?" Her voice quivered as Miles turned his head and kissed her palm.

"Always."

Louisa's heart soared at his unequivocal response. "I'll make it happen."

8

CONCERT COUNTDOWN

Two weeks to the concert.

*C*ASPO recently announced that TuKon and Miles Keane *will be co-hosting the sold-out summer charity concert, Concert for CASPO, due to be held at Holmwood House in two weeks' time, ending any speculation that Miles Keane would be performing. The concert idea was proposed by the two megastars at the beginning of the summer and the two musicians have been at the forefront of the organisation. With an A-list of musicians lined up to be part of the concert of the year, it is guaranteed to bring in huge donations for the revered charity. Miles Keane was appointed as ambassador of CASPO in June by the Countess of Holmwood, and has had a huge impact on the charity's profile.*

Netflix will be airing his recently filmed interviews with bygone popstars in a 'where are they now?' six-part docu-series, Keane's Interest, *this September. The series is a candid look at stars who have fallen on hard times. This will be the first time Miles Keane had taken on this role of interviewer and begs the question: is this a new path in his career?*

No stranger to interviews himself, the Grammy winner singer-songwriter has been notably absent and tight-lipped. Miles Keane has had a love/hate relationship with media in the past, and recently was present at the press conference where a reporter made accusations about the advantageous relationship Lady Blackthorn had with her ex-husband, Mr Gerard Dupont businessman and multimillionaire. His lack of interviews since the incident would seem to be a deliberate move at snubbing the media, making the adage 'Treat them mean, keep them keen' (pun intended) more than apt. We get the message, Miles, but throw us a bone!

MILES RANTED OUT HIS anger while Amanda listened

patiently. It had been a while for her to see him so vexed. In the old days, Miles had always been the more vocal band member, arguing and acting up when things didn't pan out how he expected. Louis, in contrast, had been the calm voice of reason that had kept the band, and his wayward brother, on an even keel. Since his months in rehab though, Miles had learned to keep his emotions in check. When he'd come out, Amanda remembered him saying he'd wanted to be an example to Grace and Louis junior. He wanted to be as good a father figure as he could be, by instilling his late brother's qualities and traits. Today though he almost seemed to be like his old self again. Amanda put it down to the newfound interest in what *the* Miles Keane was doing and that the press were still focusing on his silence rather than on his involvement. There were also the new projects he'd committed to, which she knew were preying on his mind. They were huge and high-profile and would have him permanently in the public eye, somewhere he'd successfully avoided being over the last few years. The whole world would be watching, waiting and wondering whether he could pull off this new diverse career path he was carving out for himself. There was no doubt about his musical talent – he had the accolades and millions of sold records to prove and validate that. But these were new roles in areas he'd never been tried and tested in, and with the media vying for anything to sell magazines and get hits on sites, Miles knew he couldn't just be good, he had to be outstanding. That was a lot of pressure for someone who already had issues with public performing. As if that all wasn't enough, he had to witness Louisa being constantly in the public eye and just the mention of the press conference or her ex sent Miles into a tailspin. He couldn't even defend her or come to her rescue because as far as the public were concerned, Miles Keane was just the ambassador of CASPO and Lady Louisa Blackthorn was the patron – they were colleagues and nothing more. Amanda knew he was feeling out of control. His five years of living a reclusive life with her and the children was abruptly coming to an end. As Miles had said to her before, it was open season, which he was used to handling, but when it touched his family or the woman he loved, he wasn't about to sit back and let them take shots. He'd been there, done that, got the scars to prove it.

"We give them news that I'll be co-hosting and they still bring up the press conference?" he growled at the computer screen. "Throw them a bone? Seriously? They haven't left Louisa for a second, camped out by her home. I've got at least five loitering outside my house." Miles threw his hands in the air in frustration. "I can't believe I'm going to say this but we'd be better off in LA. Thank goodness Louisa's agreed to go. I'm telling you, the minute she says yes, that's it, we're going public and then see them come at her and bring up her 'advantageous relationship'. Fuckers. I'll kill them with my bare hands."

He took a deep drink from his crystal tumbler, hoping it would calm him down. He didn't particularly like sounding off but he was feeling frustrated and being cooped up in his home wasn't helping either. There was only so much he could do to keep himself occupied. The only thing that brought him some peace was his music. With his emotions on red alert, he'd channelled everything into his writing.

"Is she upset?" Amanda asked tentatively. She didn't like seeing him so wound up. He didn't have the children as a distraction, which in the past had worked – or Duke, for that matter.

"Putting on a brave face. I hate that whenever they mention her, they bring up *him!* She's her own woman, for fuck's sake. She can buy and sell him a thousand times over and they just dismiss her worth."

"Alistair said they've always had the policy of not reacting. It's kind of an unsaid rule."

"I know. Louisa told me they've never given statements in their defence. And I get it, the more you engage, the more they come at you but fuck if it doesn't try my patience."

"Once the concert is over, they'll find something else to focus on."

"Probably our engagement," he shot back mulishly and Amanda scrunched up her nose. He was right. Once that news hit, they'd be bringing up his colourful past and wondering what Lady Blackthorn saw in the ex-drug addict, playboy, popstar.

"There's no *probably* about it. That's going to be huge. It'll be like Grace Kelly and Prince Rainer but in reverse."

"Louisa's better looking than Prince Rainer," Miles muttered and Amanda giggled, glad he hadn't totally lost his sense of humour.

"She sure is. You know she called me and asked if I could take a bigger part in the concert's organisation? Did she tell you?" Amanda narrowed her eyes at him as he tried to look impassive.

"She might have," Miles said quietly.

"Miles! Did you put her up to it?"

"Nope." He shook his head, confirming the fact because it was true. Louisa had thought up the whole idea without his input. "I just asked if she thought Alistair could manage while she was with me in the US. She said he had a whole team of staff and he'd manage perfectly with the physical side but he could do with moral support. I kind of dropped your name saying you were the best at keeping up my morale and that was it. She wanted me to ring you but I said you might say no to me." He pulled a face and Amanda glared at him but she couldn't deny that he was right.

"Well, Melissa called and said I was *desperately* needed," Amanda explained. "Seeing as she was only working at 'half throttle' – her words, not mine."

Miles chuckled because he could totally imagine Melissa's upper-class business tone. She always laid it on thick when she wanted a favour and no one ever could say no to her. No doubt Robert was hovering over her as she spoke too. "She's right. Melissa is a pro and runs CASPO like a well-oiled machine but she's supposed to be taking it easy."

"Yes, she pointed that out to me too. Basically, guilting me into it, and then I got a follow-up call from Louisa." Miles's eyes widened. "She said something along the lines of it being a personal favour."

"Sounds like Blackthorn blackmail," Miles said drolly and Amanda hummed in agreement.

"How do you feel about being there for a few days without the kids?"

Amanda let out a breath and gave a half-hearted shrug. "Guilty."

Miles's expression softened. He knew how hard it was for Amanda to move on with her life. She'd sacrificed so much already and the longer she continued just living for her children, the harder it was going to be. "Your parents are going to love having them to spoil," Miles said, hoping to help alleviate any guilt she had towards the children.

"I know, but it's the first time I'll have ever left them."

"Well, take them with you, then."

"I thought about it but if I'm there to help, be part of the team, I can't be worrying about whether they're alright."

"Look, your parents could bring them down to Holmwood by the time I return on Saturday. It's literally four days. It also means you get uninterrupted time with Alistair." He smirked and her cheeks turned pink.

"Another reason to feel guilty," she mumbled looking away from the screen.

"Amanda, you have nothing to feel guilty about. It's been five years. You deserve some time to yourself and the possibility of finding someone. I'm not saying Alistair is it, but he could be," Miles said softly.

Her eyes drifted back to the screen and she sighed. "He really could. I think that's why I feel guilty."

Miles's eyes widened at her admission and then he gave her a wide smile. "Really?" Amanda gave an awkward shrug. "Well, maybe four days alone with him will make your mind up."

"Not quite alone. There'll be the 30 staff, guards, CASPO employees, volunteers, Lady Alice and no doubt Margot."

Miles chuckled because it was true. "Yeah, that's true, but hopefully you'll get some time together?"

"You know, this is all your fault," Amanda said pointing at him through the screen.

"Mine? How?"

"You're whisking Louisa away."

"Nice try. As you said, Alistair has an army of staff. I think it's Melissa matchmaking or maybe he asked her to ask you."

"You think so?"

"Pretty sure."

LOUISA HELD UP AND admired the purple T-shirt which was part of the new uniform for everyone working at the concert. It had the tasteful "C 4 C, Concert for CASPO", embroidered in ivory on the left and on the back was "Crew for CASPO". She laid it out on her desk next to the concert T-shirt, racerback vest, baseball cap, hoodie, keyring, armband and beanie. She couldn't believe how quickly the manufacturer had produced the various merchandise items and uniforms. From Darcy's reports, the items were also flying off the shelves, so to speak, on the CASPO website too.

Her phone vibrated with a call on her desk and the smiling face of Alistair, sitting at the cockpit of his helicopter, lit up her screen. A photo she'd taken of him at the activities weekend.

"Hey, Action-man," she teased.

"Hey, Lou-lou," he countered, using her childhood nickname. "We just got delivery of all the merchandise. Thank goodness we can store it all out in the paddocks until the sale booths are erected next week."

"It's lovely, isn't it? Maybe put some in the gift shop."

"Good idea. We're having an impromptu meeting this afternoon. A concert countdown update, as the organisers called it. Mainly the gang, those who want to help out and I wondered if you could make it too."

"I doubt it. I've got so much to finish up here and I'll be away for five days next week so I'm trying to finish off as much as I can."

"Ah yes, I forgot you're swanning off, leaving me to deal with it all," he said wryly.

"I'm not even worried," she replied nonchalantly. "I hear you'll be having a special guest to help you out while I'm away, so don't try and make me feel guilty. And to be fair, I'm sure you'd prefer Amanda's company to mine."

There was a second of silence and then he asked, "Are you meddling?"

"It was Melissa's idea, I just made it happen," Louisa said quickly, hoping she hadn't ruined any possibility of her brother and Amanda getting together. She couldn't think of a better match for him. All his previous girlfriends had been from similar circles, the aristocracy, and Alistair had had very little in common with any of them. Amanda was a breath of fresh air. She was genuine, caring, intelligent and down-to-Earth, exactly like her brother. The chances of Alistair ever meeting a woman like Amanda were slim, so the fact that fate – or CASPO, actually – had brought them together was in itself an amazing stroke of luck. And from how they'd both behaved, it was obvious there was a small spark between them. It might just be a small flicker right now but Louisa hoped after a few days together, it would be fanned into a brighter glow.

"I'm quite capable of asking out my own dates, Louisa," he said in a mildly exasperated tone.

"I know you are; you just don't actually do it," she said with a little force. "So, Amanda coming to help, asked by CASPO, means there's no pressure, just the two of you working on the concert. Totally innocent." She didn't want him to feel as though this was a blind date, where he was expected to be charming and attentive. She was giving him the opportunity and letting him decide on his involvement.

"Thanks," he muttered and Louisa smiled to herself. She knew he was secretly thrilled Amanda was coming because her mother had rung and told her he'd organised new clothes for himself. Something he rarely ever did.

"She was all too pleased to be asked," Louisa added, hoping it would make him feel less daunted.

"Yeah?"

"Yes, you idiot. She likes you! Make sure none of your gang mess it up for you either," she said with a huff.

"Ha, I'll keep them busy, don't worry. We've all the trailers arriving for all the bands to change in and use next week, so I'll have them organising and kitting those out."

"Yes, Hugh told me." Every morning Hugh gave Louisa a full rundown of the developments and Darcy called every evening with a progress report.

"Hugh is having kittens. This is his worst nightmare," Alistair said with a chuckle.

"I know. Who else did you rope in?"

"The usual suspects: Gils, Tim, Eddie and Gordon."

Louisa smiled to herself. She was glad Alistair had his trusted friends with him on such a huge event. "How is Gordon?"

"You mean other than heartbroken?" Alistair said with a hint of sarcasm and Louisa told him to be quiet. She still couldn't believe Gordon was still hung up on her after 20 years. She also couldn't believe she hadn't noticed and that Alistair had never told her. "Well, Emily seems to be doing better. She needs to keep on her meds and stay in the clinic, though I think they've a long road ahead, that's if they stay together after this. But he's supporting her for now."

"That's good to hear, it can't be easy."

"No. Talking of not being easy, Darcy wants a huge firework display," Alistair said with a shudder. "Just the thought of loud banging and popping is bringing me out in a cold sweat. Even Hugh is a little dubious."

"Oh heck! That won't do." Louisa needed to talk to Darcy about avoiding any kind of display that was loud. Since coming back from Afghanistan, Alistair was uneasy around any form of explosive noises. As well as that they had a great number of horses and animals on the grounds and she didn't want them traumatised either. "Maybe we can think of something else? I don't think Miles will appreciate it either. A laser show, possibly?"

"SO, WHAT DO YOU think?" Miles stared at the wide smiling face of Konran that practically filled his screen.

"Dude it's awesome! I'm honoured, truly. Thanks for letting me know."

"Not a word to anyone," Miles said firmly.

"I swear." Konran made a cross over his heart and Miles gave him a nod. Their video calls were every other day now and had forged a close friendship over the last few weeks. Miles looked forward to hearing about the places Konran had visited. Seeing the familiar cities through fresh eyes made Miles think about the times he'd had and, in some way, relive them.

"We leave on Tuesday but we'll be back on Saturday. So, we can talk more when I get back."

"This is so exciting." Konran beamed.

"To be honest, I'm nervous."

"Nah Miles, you've nothing to be nervous about. Lady B, she's gonna be blown away!"

"I hope so."

"I know so." Konran said with a pointed look.

"I'm no Sting," Miles said dryly and Konran let out a loud laugh at the reference to Louisa's crush.

"No, man, you're *the* Miles Keane!"

Five days before the concert.

MILES RESTED HIS HEAD back and glanced towards the window. There was a respectful hush around the first-class cabin and Miles was sure it was because *the* Countess of Holmwood was on board. Whenever he'd travelled over the years, the cabin crew were always friendly and chatty, almost bordering on familiar. They felt that they knew him somehow – celebrity did that; it made you accessible and for nearly 15 years of his life, that was how it had been. However, on the two occasions he'd travelled with Louisa, the crew's smiles were reserved and it was almost as though they were on their best behaviour, like when a headmaster came into a classroom. They spoke in a hushed cordial tone, as though speaking any louder would be the ultimate faux-pas. He smiled to himself at the thought of the crew being nervous around Louisa. If only they knew what she was really like. It probably didn't help that they also had four security with them too. Hugh, Pierce, Karl and Kurt were seated further down, closer to the steward's station. Pierce would be staying with Miles while he was in New York whereas Hugh, Karl and Kurt would stay with Louisa and Celeste.

Miles shifted his attention to Louisa who was now napping to his right. She'd dropped down the pod screen between them so they could chat during their dinner but she was exhausted after all the preparations. Once they arrived in New York, she'd have a full day and evening too. He was glad she was getting some rest. He wanted her relaxed by the time they reached LA.

It had been a busy run-up to their trip and they'd hardly seen each other. Snatching a few hours here and there, so Miles had hoped they'd have had at least the flight to catch up on. He carefully lifted up the screen, giving her more privacy and opened up the other side of his so he could get up and stretch his legs. He needed another coffee and rather than call one of the crew, he decided to go to the back himself. As he rose from his seat, he caught sight of Celeste swinging her legs out of her pod and she smiled widely at him.

"You want anything? I'm going to get a coffee while I stretch my legs," he asked.

"I'm good but I think I want to walk a bit too. I'm a bit stiff." She stifled a yawn and flexed her shoulders. The two of them walked towards the back... to the horror of the cabin crew, who scrambled to get to them.

"Mr Keane, is everything alright?" one of the air stewards asked.

"Yes, I'm fine. I thought I'd come up and get a coffee. Stretch my legs too."

Almost as an afterthought, the pretty air steward glanced at Celeste. "My lady, is there anything you need?"

"No thank you. I'm just keeping him company," she said with a smirk. *Could she be more obvious?* thought Celeste as she watched two of the stewards prepare Miles's coffee. *Really? Two of them needed to make it?* Miles made polite small talk with them as they gushed and hung on his every word. *Were we going to be on time?* Miles asked, *Oh yes.* One of them shamelessly fluttered her eyelashes at him and Celeste rolled her eyes. *Any idea on the weather?* Miles took his coffee and the other steward answered. *It looks fine.* Miles thanked them and turned to where Celeste was leaning against an empty pod with her eyebrow raised.

Maybe this wasn't such a good idea after all. The crew carried on hovering around them, keeping a close eye on them in case they needed anything. Miles caught sight of Pierce sniggering and Miles mock-glared at him as Pierce batted his eyelashes at him, imitating the air steward. Celeste giggled, then gestured with a jerk of her head to their seats and they headed back to their pods.

"It's a good job Mum's sleeping," Celeste whispered. "She'd have given them a hard stare. Is everyone always so shameless around you?"

"I don't really notice it." Miles shrugged.

"That's because you think it's the norm. Go out looking normal and less..." She waved her hand in front of him, sweeping from his face to his body. "You'll soon realise what it's like not to have everyone fawning over you."

Miles's brows rose up sharply. "Erm, excuse me but aren't you a countess? *You* get everyone fawning over you," he said with a pointed look.

"Ha. Believe it or not, while I was in the US, I was pretty much under the radar." They'd reached Celeste's seat and she leaned against it. "Mum made sure of it. I had as normal an upbringing as possible and I was always out of the media. It's only since I came back to England that people have got to know me a little. This opening is my first official event since I graduated high school. Nicolas didn't even know anything about my family, even after we started dating." She pursed her lips at him and crossed her arms over her chest.

"Really? How's he feel about who you are, now that he knows?" Miles asked, surprised at her response. He'd presumed that Celeste had moved around within the typical upper-class circles.

"Well, he met me in Peru and like I said, had no clue, which was good. I've always worried about whether my wealth and title would be the draw. Even when I told him my father had his own business, he didn't ask what he did."

"Celeste, you're an amazing woman."

"Thanks." Celeste scrunched up her nose at his comment and for a second, she looked like Louisa did whenever she was embarrassed.

"Believe it or not, I do remember you all those years ago."

"Yeah?" Celeste's eyes lit up.

"Uh-huh. I remember... hazily," he said with a widening of his eyes and Celeste giggled. "Eric said you were coming and we all groaned. The last thing we wanted to do was entertain a spoilt brat who was 10 years old."

"Wow, Mum was right, you were a dick back then."

"Ha-ha. Your mom was a hundred percent right. Anyway, you were so sweet and so unguarded. I was a little taken aback. But you still had this graciousness about you and I remember how ladylike you were with impeccable manners. Kind of made *me* feel like the spoiled brat."

"I told you before we Blackthorn women are hard to forget." Celeste punctuated her comment with a nod.

"That you are." Miles lifted his coffee cup in a cheers gesture and took a sip.

"Going back to what you asked about Nicolas. He's getting used to it. Though to be fair, he knows I won't need to take on the role for a long while yet."

"So, you two are serious?"

"It feels right but I won't make the same mistake my mum made. I'm going to do my thing and Nicolas can be with me. If we make it through the next three years, then who knows?"

"That's very level-headed of you."

"Maybe, but I do love him and I know he loves me – the real me, that is, not all the extras," she said with a soft smile.

"Like flying first class?" Miles arched his brow and Celeste chuckled.

"Yeah, he freaked out when we flew out in Papa's plane last time."

"I bet he did. He seems like a good guy though." Celeste nodded with a wistful look on her face and then sighed. Miles grinned at her and took another sip of his coffee. Lady Celeste was well and truly smitten.

"So how do feel about the interview?"

Miles rocked his head side to side. "Honestly, I'm nervous as hell. This whole trip is going to be so stressful."

"Because of the interview?"

"Partly. I have meetings in New York for a new project, which is a big deal."

"Oooh, can you tell me?" Her eyes lighting up in excitement.

Miles cringed slightly. "I'd rather announce it all when we've signed. Don't want to jinx it."

"Sure, I get that."

"And then there's the interview."

"But you've done Jimmy Kimmel loads of times before."

"Yeah, but it's been a while."

"Well, at least Mum will be there."

"Well, she kind of won't be. I don't want anyone knowing she's in Malibu. It could cause all sorts of problems. So, she'll be hiding out at my home while we do the recording."

Celeste furrowed her brow. "I thought it was live."

"No, they record it and then air it at night. We'll watch it together later at my home."

Celeste narrowed her eyes as though she was trying to piece a puzzle together, then widened her eyes. "Wait a minute, is this when you're going to... Oh my God, with everything going on I forgot all about that. That's why you're so nervous!" she said, as if she'd had a eureka moment.

"Jesus, Celeste, be quiet." Miles looked around to make sure Louisa couldn't hear.

"Sorry. This is so exciting," she said, almost jumping on the spot, and Miles laughed softly at her reaction. She really was just a normal teenager, unguarded and genuine.

"It will be, if it all goes without a hitch," he said with a shake of his head.

"Oh. My. God! Miles Keane is going to be my stepdad," she stage-whispered, then clapped her hand over her mouth. Miles stared at her for a beat, then let out a husky laugh, he hadn't even thought about that. He'd be a stepdad!

9

PLANS IN PROGRESS

*A*fter over almost five years of silence, Miles Keane, singer-songwriter, winner of 11 Grammys and 15 number one hits, will be a guest on Jimmy Kimmel Live! this Thursday. The popstar's last interview was on this very show days before his band performed at the Juilliard graduation, where both he and his late brother Louis Keane are alumni. Miles Keane suffered a gunshot to his shoulder and Louis Keane was killed along with another eight people at the Alice Tully Hall shooting.

The host said, "I feel honoured to have Miles Keane back on my show." The show will be recorded in the afternoon and aired the same evening. Miles Keane recently arrived stateside for a few days, in the run-up to the Concert for CASPO, which he will be co-hosting with the number one rapper TuKon.

The question on everybody's lips is whether Miles Keane will perform at the concert. Until now, the spokesperson for CASPO has confirmed the A-list line up, which does not include Miles Keane, though the remaining Keane Sense band members, Josh Ashley and Mick Doherty, have confirmed they will be at the concert as guests in support of the charity. Speculation is growing as to whether they will be playing, even though they have denied any plans to perform.

In related news, TuKon completed his final European tour dates and heads for the UK today. His band will play four dates before their final performance at Holmwood House in the most anticipated concert of the summer.

GERARD SIPPED HIS DRINK and looked out onto one of the most exclusive views of the city of New York. There weren't many people who could boast they had a six-storey house on the Upper East Side. Central Park was a stone's throw away and every luxury store was within walking distance. When they'd bought the house over 20 years ago, Gerard had never envisaged he'd be living in it alone. For the last eight months, he'd busied himself, worked longer hours and taken trips away, so that he didn't need to spend so much time in his beautiful house, because it was a house now, not a home. A home had a heart, life and laughter running through it and since Louisa had moved out and Celeste had left to start a new chapter of her own life, none of that existed anymore. The priceless artworks and luxurious furnishings didn't keep him company, they didn't check up on him to make sure he'd eaten, they didn't ask about his day and they didn't know when he needed a sounding board. His marriage to Louisa had ended up being one of convenience but Gerard had always known Louisa cared and loved him. He still couldn't believe that she'd made a new life for herself and was moving on.

His eyes shifted to his open laptop and he scowled at the recent articles that seemed to be flooding the Internet. There wasn't a news site or gossip column that wasn't reporting on everything Miles Keane was doing. From being hidden away for five years, he now graced the most prestigious news sites right across the board, to the sleaziest. His pretty face was plastered everywhere, from the luxury watch commercial he'd filmed, to paparazzi pictures of him visiting the CASPO offices and Blackthorn Mansion. With the concert days away, his every move was documented and with that, reports on Louisa soon followed. How their relationship hadn't been leaked was a mystery to him. Maybe it was because it seemed so unlikely, a blue-blooded aristocrat with an ex-drug-addict popstar, or maybe it was because the Blackthorns knew how to nip any scandal or slanderous reporting in the bud – he knew how much power they yielded, he'd seen it and experienced it first-hand. The recent scandal of their marriage seemed to have been forgotten. Gerard was certain that it was down to the Blackthorns' involvement.

When Louisa had called him to confirm she would be coming to the gallery opening, he was pleasantly surprised, believing she was coming to support him, until he realised that Miles would also be in the US. News of his first interview since the shooting was everywhere. Louisa was being careless – if they were staying at the same hotel, it wouldn't take too much for some nosey reporter or hotel staff to put two and two together. *Was this her idea or was it his and how had the Blackthorns allowed it?* If there wasn't a slip up in New York, then how were they going to conceal her visit to his home in Malibu? Louisa had told Gerard that she was going to fly out the following day after the gallery opening. He'd presumed she'd be staying with Celeste, then flying back out with her and Nicolas, in time for the concert.

Gerard strode over to the bar and poured himself another generous measure of cognac, then headed to where his laptop was set up. He quickly pulled up his schedule for the weekend and scanned it. A business lunch on Saturday, a date with one of his regular hookups in the evening and golf on Sunday. All things he could reschedule. Gerard had had no intention of going to the concert but with all the hype and constant attention Louisa was receiving, he needed to be around, even in the background. He had to show his support, and if she'd made the effort to come to New York, even if it was for an ulterior motive, then the decent thing to do was to reciprocate.

He picked up his phone and called his assistant. "Cancel and reschedule my plans from Friday to Tuesday and make sure the plane is ready to take me, Lady Blackthorn, my daughter and Nicolas to London. Send an email to Melissa Hindley, informing her I will be at the CASPO concert and if she needs my help, I'm available from Friday when we arrive." He'd let Louisa know his change of plans tonight at the gallery and hopefully he'd be able to persuade her to fly back with him and Celeste and avoid LA altogether. It would further quash any rumours that they had a strained relationship. If Gerard arrived in the UK with Celeste and without her, he'd insist it would look strange after being seen together.

Gerard rested back in his leather armchair and stared at the latest photos of Miles Keane and Konran together. It looked like a screenshot of a video call that Konran had recently posted on social media of them obviously discussing the concert, he'd tag-lined it 'planning in progress'. The particular site was reporting that the two megastars had formed a close relationship and speculated whether they'd collaborate musically in the future. They all seemed to have forgotten Miles's sordid past, the drug-taking, the womanizing, fights and bad behaviour. Gerard took a large drink from his heavy crystal glass. Miles Keane was muscling in on his family and friends. He was becoming part of their lives and with every day he was apart from Louisa and his family, the easier it was for Miles to get his feet under the table. Well, he wasn't about to sit back and make it easy for him. Miles might be the star of the show, up front and centre but Gerard would be waiting, backstage, in the wings.

10

RULE BREAKER

Four days before the concert.

*I*t seems Miles Keane has been splitting his time between the US and UK. He was seen with his friend and manager of 15 years Eric Schultz in New York, dining at the exclusive Gabriel Kreuther off Bryant Park. Sources close to Mr Keane say he is in the process of closing a number of lucrative and high-profile deals. Miles Keane has been the face of the luxury watch brand Tempus (see photos and link), and has been seen at London and New York Fashion Weeks. The megastar of one of the most popular bands of his time has been absent for over five years after he was injured and tragically lost his brother in the Alice Tully Shooting but with his recent appointment as ambassador of CASPO, and involvement in the summer concert, it looks like we'll be seeing a lot more of him.

Miles Keane will be the guest star on Jimmy Kimmel Live!, *the first talk show he has done since his return to the entertainment world earlier this year.*

In other related news, Lady Blackthorn, the patron of CASPO, was seen yesterday with her daughter Celeste and ex-husband Gerard Dupont at the showing of a new collection of art and sculptures from students sponsored by the ARTS charity. The ARTS charity has sponsored hundreds of talented children over its 10 years. The collection is on show for four weeks and has already caused a sensation in New York and interest from collectors. Lady Louisa Blackthorn and her daughter Celeste will be returning to the UK in time for the concert.

"THIS IS A BIT decadent." Louisa ran her hands over the plush cream leather of her chair and let her eyes wander over the luxurious interior of the private jet. She could see the air steward had started to prepare their drinks as the aircraft levelled out.

"A perk of signing the contract. I wasn't going to turn down a private jet to LA. It also means we can get off the plane and into the car without anyone seeing you." Miles smiled up at the air steward approaching with an open bottle of champagne and two crystal flutes. She placed them on the table in front of them along with a plate of hors d'oeuvres. She made quick work of pouring the light blush liquid and they thanked her before she paced to where Hugh, Pierce, Karl and Kurt were sitting.

"They really offered you the plane as a perk?" Louisa said in surprise, once the steward was out of earshot.

"Yeah." Miles picked up a glass and passed it to Louisa, then took his own.

"Well, here's to you, the new Don Lockwood, and smashing it on Broadway and the West End." They clinked glasses and took a sip. "How do you feel?" Louisa asked over the rim of her glass.

"Scared shitless," Miles said without hesitation and then they both chuckled because he'd said the same thing when he'd signed the film deal too. Miles shook his head, indicating he really didn't want to talk about it, then asked her about the gallery opening she'd attended the night before. He didn't want to go over his anxieties again – he'd had enough of talking them through with Eric all day yesterday. Miles had had to put on an air of confidence when he'd met up with the director and producers. They were thrilled he was going to be part of the ensemble. They made him feel as though it was an honour to have him. When Miles had suggested that he was the one who should be honoured, they wouldn't hear of it. It made him think back to the conversation he'd had with Celeste and the fawning he was often subjected to. If he was honest he hadn't really thought about it until she'd quite brutally pointed it out. It was sobering. They were taking a chance on him, a big gamble. He'd never done theatre before but yet they seemed sure he was the perfect fit. His songwriting, singing and number one hits were enough of a resume, apparently. They'd seemed to forget his well-documented meltdowns, bad behaviour and constant appearance in every gossip column. They either had a short memory or didn't care. Maybe it was his celebrity the show needed? He would never be sure which one was the reason they'd asked him, maybe it was a combination of all of them. Miles still felt the role had fallen too easily into his lap.

Now he was on his way to do his first television show interview in five years. Another item on his agenda he wasn't comfortable about doing, but he was trying to focus on after the interview. If all went to plan, tomorrow at this time he'd be engaged to Louisa. He instinctively let his eyes roam to his jacket, draped over the opposite seat where he'd placed the ring in the inside pocket. He'd carried the ring around with him since Pierce had collected it for him, never letting it out of his sight.

Miles listened to Louisa talk animatedly about the artworks and sculptures she'd seen and the interest they'd had from some prestigious collectors. He loved her passion for the projects she was involved with. She wasn't just a figurehead, she genuinely took interest and listening to her was the best distraction against his building anxiety and the voice inside his head.

What if she says no?

"Look, let me show you," Louisa said pulling him out of his worrying thoughts. She picked up her phone and opened up the gallery icon. She began to click through the photographs Celeste had forwarded to her, of the different pieces on display. Miles looked at each one and agreed with her that there were some excellent pieces. He also noted that there was the odd picture with Gerard just off to the side.

"How was Gerard?" He tried to sound casual but even to his own ears, he knew he sounded agitated.

"He was…" Louisa blew out a breath and slightly shook her head.

"What?" Miles narrowed his eyes at her reaction and knew whatever she was going to say, it was going to annoy him.

"He's coming to the concert." Louisa took a gulp of her champagne and shifted her head to look at Miles. She hadn't known when would be the best time to tell him but she was glad to get it out. *Better sooner rather than later,* she thought.

"I thought he couldn't come," Miles said evenly, trying not to show any emotion.

"Well, apparently now he can," Louisa said, obviously irritated at her ex's change of heart. "So, he's flying out on Friday night with Celeste and Nicolas." Louisa drained her glass and set it down. She was annoyed and Miles took pleasure in the fact that Gerard was pissing her off. She furrowed her brow as though she was debating whether she should say more. Miles was about to ask her what she was thinking when she turned to face him. "He's just doing it because... because he's behaving like a petulant adolescent that didn't get his own way and..." She stopped abruptly and blew out another breath. "You know what? Forget it. I don't want to ruin your good news, this monumental moment." Louisa reached for the bottle of champagne but Miles got to it before her and poured her some more and topped up his own flute. The air steward started to rush over, appalled she'd not been paying attention but Miles waved her away politely, telling her they were fine pouring their drinks for themselves.

"Louisa you can tell me anything, you know that, right?" He said sincerely, hoping she'd confide in him a little more about her ex-husband. He didn't need the information to dislike Gerard any more than he already did, but he did want Louisa to feel she could tell him, without being judged or lectured. Miles wanted to know everything, so that he was on an even footing with Gerard. It was as though he was being left out of the loop where he was concerned, which meant he couldn't defend or protect her. He needed to know all the facts when the truth of it was he felt left in the dark; maybe that would change after tonight.

Louisa took a deep breath, annoyed with herself for blurting out her frustrations. Today was supposed to be about Miles. She knew these few days were important and she'd agreed to be with Miles so she could support him in any way she could. She couldn't be at the studio but at least she'd be at his home waiting for him once he'd finished. The flight was supposed to be a time for them to relax and for her to distract him. They were only half an hour into their six-hour flight and she'd already botched it up. Once the interview was done and they had the next day together she'd vent her anger, but not now. Today, Miles needed *just* Louisa, without the French baggage! "I know and at some point, I will tell you everything, but not today," Louisa said with a determined tone and Miles gave her a nod. Maybe today wasn't the right time but at least she'd said she would, and that was as good as a promise. Louisa picked up her flute and shifted around to face him. "Today is all about you, your future role on Broadway and Jimmy Kimmel!" She beamed at him, her worried eyes lighting up with genuine excitement and Miles lifted his flute to hers.

"Oh God, don't remind me."

"Scared shitless?" Louisa said with a smirk and Miles let out a low laugh.

"Absolutely, ma'am," he drawled, accentuating his American accent, then took a drink from his flute. "Maybe I should lay off the booze," he said with a cringe as placed his glass down. "I don't want to turn up drunk for my *first interview in five years*." He made quotation marks when he said the last five words. That was all he'd read in every article about him since it was announced. That and a reminder of how Louis was killed. He just hoped the producers of the show understood that he wasn't going to talk about his past. This was about his future. He twisted his mouth to the side and added. "Though to be fair, that was pretty much how I used to turn up on the last few times I was on Jimmy's show."

"Nooo!" Louisa gasped.

"Yep. And high." Miles had the decency to look embarrassed.

"I let my daughter watch those!"

"You also let your 10-year-old daughter have a photo with me, even after I'd wiped cocaine from under my nose."

"Oh God, you're right. But she would've been heartbroken not to meet you. You were a dick that night." She mock-glared at him and he gave her his patented megawatt smile.

"Yep, a bona fide, card-carrying super-dick. I hope I've changed since then."

"You have." She leaned closer and dropped a chaste kiss on his lips, surprising him. "You're now my bona fide, card-carrying super-dick," she said stifling a giggle and Miles's jaw dropped.

"Lady Blackthorn are you being crude?"

"I blame the champagne."

"Makes a change from the Lafite." Miles grinned at her reference to their private joke.

"It does. I love that we're on a private plane and we can be just us," Louisa sighed.

"Me too, though I kind of wish we didn't have Hugh and the guys with us. They kind of kill the romance." Miles widened his eyes and Louisa let out a giggle.

"Next time, we get a jet with a separate room," Louisa said in hushed excitement and Miles let out a husky laugh. She was just too cute when she'd had a couple of glasses of wine. She let her guard down and became the carefree, happy go lucky Louisa he knew.

"God, I love you." Miles dropped an unhurried kiss on her lips, then pulled back before getting too carried away. She was right, next time they had to have a separate room.

"I love you too, super-dick," Louisa whispered dreamily.

"I can't wait to show you *my* super dick," Miles said dryly and Louisa let out a laugh.

THE LA SUMMERS WERE brutal and Miles was glad they'd literally walked off the jet's stairs and straight into a waiting air-conditioned limo. They were driving straight to the El Capitan Entertainment Centre on Hollywood Boulevard, where the talk show was filmed. The plan was to drop Miles off with Pierce, then Louisa would be taken directly to Miles's Malibu home with Karl and Hugh. Kurt would return later to collect Miles and Pierce, once he'd finished his interview. The whole trip had been precision timed to avoid any paparazzi finding out Louisa was with Miles. The limo had fully blacked-out windows and was big enough for Louisa to stay well out of sight. She'd travelled in faded jeans, sneakers and a white T-shirt. Her hair was hidden in a C for C baseball cap and her large-framed sunglasses hid her face. Her most unladylike outfit to date, which was purely precautionary. No one knew she'd flown out to the West Coast apart from her family but Miles didn't want to take any chances.

Louisa clasped Miles's hand and gave it a squeeze. She really wished she could be with him. He gave her a strained smile, then lifted her hand to his lips. It meant the world to him that she was here, even if she was being whisked away the minute he was out of the car. Miles's eyes darted to Pierce, his trusted bodyguard and friend who was talking quietly into his phone at the far end of the limo. Pierce gave Miles a reassuring nod. Security would be tight at the studio but the nod Pierce had given him was in reference to the arrangements for Miles and Louisa's evening. Miles stifled a smile and looked out of the darkened windows as the car travelled towards the city and ticked off the items on his to-do list for this trip. *Sign the contracts... check. Get Louisa to Malibu... check. Arrange for a romantic dinner... check. Do the interview... in progress. Ask Louisa to marry him... tonight.*

Kurt pulled up outside the studio and Miles's eyes widened in surprise at the crowd that was waiting outside. He darted his eyes to Pierce who gave him a reassuring nod, then turned to Louisa. "I'll see you at home, baby." He leaned down and gave her a tender kiss.

"I love you, super-dick," she whispered and he chuckled. It was just what he needed to ease his nerves.

"I love you too." He gave her that sexy wink that had her squirming in her seat, then gave a nod to Pierce. Pierce spoke into his sleeve and the door opened up, letting the harsh California summer sunlight flood the interior. Miles slipped on his sunglasses and turned to Louisa as Pierce stepped out onto the pavement.

"Showtime." Louisa smiled widely at him and then gasped at the roar of the crowd as he stepped out of the car and into the sunlight. The noise instantly dulled as the door closed with a thud and Louisa swivelled to look out of the window. There were hundreds of fans all shouting for Miles and he graciously waved at them. All the while, Pierce and four studio security kept close to him. For a moment, it looked like Miles was going to head straight to the studio but then he slowed down and said something to Pierce who stiffened, then nodded. Louisa squinted through the glass and her heart rate began to rise. *What was he doing? Had he changed his mind?* She was glad they hadn't driven off immediately. Her questioning gaze shot to Hugh who had now shifted closer to the window. "What's he doing?" she said in a panic.

Hugh spoke into his sleeve, hoping Pierce would inform him but before he could get an answer, Miles had paced to where the fans were waiting and held out his hand. They went crazy, snapping photos of him on their phones and handing him envelopes, flowers, soft toys and books to sign. Louisa let out sigh of relief. He was just taking time to talk to his fans. It hadn't been his plan to do it. He was just focused on getting inside the studio but seeing his fans he was overcome with a sense of duty. They'd stuck with him through all his highs and lows, he could spare them a few minutes of his time to thank them personally.

Louisa's attention shifted to Hugh, hearing him talk.

"Thanks, Pierce, see you later."

"What did he say?" she asked.

"Apparently Miles wanted to speak to the fans," he said with a hint of amusement. "I think Pierce had a mild heart attack."

"Well, you know Miles; he's always been a bit of a rule-breaker." Louisa grinned.

"Yeah, amongst other things," Hugh said with a smirk.

11

SHOWTIME

Miles Keane arrived at the El Capitan Entertainment Centre on Hollywood Boulevard this afternoon, straight from the airport, where he'll be appearing for the first time after a five-year absence, on the Jimmy Kimmel Live! show. Mr Keane stopped and spoke to a few of the fans who had waited patiently outside the famed studio. He was looking relaxed dressed in a camel suede bomber jacket over white jeans and T-shirt, (get the look, see stockists below). Sporting a C for C baseball cap, one of the many pieces of merchandise for the Concert for CASPO (see link below), he signed a few autographs and posed for photographs and seemed in good spirits. The summer concert he and TuKon instigated is four days away and is said to raise over £10 million for the charity CASPO. Tomorrow TuKon will play his final date of his sold-out world tour, then head to Holmwood. The line-up includes Dua Lipa, Maroon 5 and Sting. The concert will be live-streamed around the world and is the biggest charity concert this millennium. A spokesperson from CASPO suggested that the concert may be a regular feature on the Holmwood House calendar. The late Earl of Holmwood started the charity with his wife Lady Alice over 30 years ago. It looks like the present countess is carrying on her parents' good work.

"WE'RE READY FOR YOU, Mr Keane," the stage assistant said, popping her head around the door. Miles gave a questioning look to the makeup artist as she dabbed his brow with powder.

"You're fine. Here let me take the tissue off." She reached into his collar and pulled away the tissue that had protected his crisp white shirt. Miles thanked her and then straightened his light grey and burgundy polka dot tie, then stood up from his chair. The makeup artist held out the jacket of his dark blue pinstriped three-piece suit and after he thanked her, he slipped it on, then buttoned it up. He adjusted the ruched burgundy and white detailed pocket square in the mirror, patted his breast pocket where he'd place the engagement ring, then turned to the waiting stage assistant.

"Looks like I'm ready as I'll ever be," he joked, trying to cover up his nerves. This would be the first live interview he'd done in the US since the shooting, and right now he wished Louisa was backstage with him, instead of sunning herself by his pool.

Miles was led through to the side of the stage, out of the audience's sight. Jimmy Kimmel was taking a satirical dig at a recent scandal surrounding a prominent CEO of a tech company. Miles took a couple of deep breaths while the audience's laughter erupted.

"Hey, you okay?" Miles turned to see the very welcome and familiar face of Eric walking towards him. "Sorry I'm late," he whispered.

"Hey, I didn't know you were coming."

"I wasn't but when Lady Blackthorn calls, even I jump. I know I'm not as good looking as her but I make a good understudy." Miles gave a hushed chuckle. Just having Eric here made him feel a thousand times better and he was thankful for Louisa's foresight. He really needed someone in his corner and as Eric pointed out, he was no Louisa but very welcome all the same.

"Thanks." The single word held so much more meaning than gratitude. Eric had always been next to him, standing in the wings, watching his back and taking on the role of advisor, protector, confidant and friend. He wasn't Louis either but he'd tried to fill as much of Miles's late brother's shoes as possible. Eric was glad Louisa had called him. He patted Miles's arm, then nodded to the stage as Jimmy Kimmel started his introduction and mouthed, 'you're up'.

"My next guest has too many talents to list. The front man to a worldwide successful band. Singer-songwriter of 15 number one hits and winner of 11 Grammys for best song, best video, best band, best album and best performance over his 10 years with Keane Sense." Jimmy paused while the audience clapped and cheered. "After a five-year break, a recent article titled 'Keane to be back' says it all. He's recently been appointed as the only ambassador to the charity CASPO in the UK and has just completed a six-part series for Netflix." More cheers were heard and Miles took in another calming breath. "As if that wasn't enough, he has been instrumental to putting together a charity concert with TuKon and a string of A-listers this weekend on the grounds of a British stately home, Holmwood. I'm honoured to be his first television interview since his comeback. Please welcome Miles Keane!" Jimmy Kimmel stood up and rounded his desk as Miles took his first steps onto the stage and into the blinding lights.

The audience's claps and cheers were almost deafening as Miles turned to smile and wave for the first time to the audience, who were now all on their feet. Jimmy waited, allowing him to have his moment before pulling him into a hug. "It's great to see you," he said quietly in his ear.

Miles thanked him, moved by his genuine words and the audience's reaction. While the audience still cheered, Miles unbuttoned his jacket, giving a final wave and mouthed his thanks before taking his seat.

"That was some welcome. You've been missed," Jimmy said with a soft laugh and the audience cheered again.

"It sure was," Miles replied with a wide grin.

"It's a great honour to have you here today."

"Thank you. It's been a while." The audience chuckled and Miles reached for his glass of water and took a welcome sip, using it as a delaying tactic to calm his nerves.

"Man, you haven't aged at all." The audience laughed at Jimmy's observation. "It's true."

"It's all that cool weather in the UK, away from the harsh sun."

"Sure, it is... nothing to do with good genes."

"They help." Miles gave a throaty laugh.

"How are your folks?"

"They're good. Probably watching right now."

"Probably?" Jimmy said in mock offence, playing to the audience and they lapped it up. "So how are enjoying living in the UK?"

"I'm loving it, though the US is still my home. I'm learning to appreciate both countries. I still have a home here."

"And the rest of the family. How are they?"

"They're so good. Grace and Louis are growing up at a ridiculous speed and I'm lucky to be part of their lives."

Jimmy gave a nod but didn't push any more. "So, you've done a fair bit of diversifying over the last year," he said dryly.

"You could say that," Miles replied with a cheeky smile.

"Firstly, your role as ambassador to CASPO. That's quite a responsibility."

"You saying I'm not up for the challenge?" Miles replied in good-humoured mock-offence.

"God, no!" Jimmy put up his hands and Miles chuckled, thankful for the host's easy manner. "Over the last two months, since you were given the role, the charity has seen a marked increase in donations and its profile has become more visible."

"Well, I'm pleased that that has meant single-parent families are seeing a direct benefit to my involvement." The audience clapped at his response.

"Indeed. How *did* you get involved?"

"It was all Amanda's doing. She's been volunteering and raising money for a while and asked if I'd be interested. I was lucky that the Blackthorn family thought I'd be a good fit."

"Well, you must've made quite an impression because in three days, the Blackthorns are hosting the concert of the year at Holmwood House." The audience clapped as photos of Holmwood House were projected onto the screen behind the host. "That's quite a venue!" Jimmy said, acting up to the audience who respond with an approving murmur.

"Believe me, the pictures don't do it justice. It is a magnificent estate and we're lucky to be able to host such a concert in these grounds."

"And it's one hell of a line-up, selling out as soon as the tickets were released."

"TuKon is also a huge contributor." There were some screams from the audience and Miles chuckled. He'd forgotten how fun this kind of interview could be.

"He's a big name. Have you two met?"

"Yeah, we have, a few times. It was his idea to put a concert on and he asked me to be a part of it."

"Now the biggest question on everyone's lips is…" Jimmy turned to the audience and paused for dramatic effect, causing the audience to jeer him on. "What's it really like rubbing shoulders with the aristocracy?"

Miles chuckled along with the audience, knowing that this wasn't the question on everyone's lips. The endless speculation whether Miles would be performing hadn't stopped the rumour mills from churning. Miles himself had continued to be tight-lipped and as far as everyone in the know and at CASPO was concerned, he hadn't changed his mind. "The Countess and Earl of Holmwood are some of the nicest and down-to-Earth people I have ever met. They take their roles seriously but at the same time are as generous in their time as in the funds and influence they have."

"We can see that. It's an amazing charity, I've seen the work they do. So, apart from being part of this concert phenomenon, you've also recorded a six-part series due to be aired in mid-September. How did that come about?"

Miles explained how he was approached to be the presenter and once he was on board, he also took the role of executive producer. Miles explained in brief, the concept and a small clip was shown of the first episode.

"You've kind of broken out of your mould."

"Yeah, it was interesting being on the other side, interviewing I mean."

"Do I need to worry that you'll be vying for this chair," Jimmy said eyeing the audience with mock nervousness.

"You never know, Jimmy." The audience laughed at Miles's response and he gave them that megawatt smile that had earned him the title of Sexiest Man Alive in People Magazine.

"Now I hear it on the grapevine that you've been in a few meetings here in LA and New York. Are you able to let us in on what those were about?" The audience oohed at this new piece of information.

"It has been a busy few weeks and I have been offered a couple of exciting projects." The audience jeered in response, encouraging Miles to elaborate.

"You're killing us, Miles… you can't tease us like that." Jimmy looked to his audience in support and they of course rose to the challenge.

"Okay." Miles made a show of conceding, earning him applause. He had the audience eating out of his hands now. "I accepted a film role to play Chet Baker which starts filming in the new year." The audience clapped loudly at the news and a few let out a whistle.

"Oh, wow, that really is a different direction again."

"Yeah. It's an honour really. He was my and Louis's idol, so I have big shoes to fill." A number of black and white photos of Chet Baker were shown as Miles gave Jimmy and the audience a few details about the director and cast, explaining that it was a biopic of the artist in his later life.

"Any other projects you'd like to share?" Jimmy asked hopefully, having been given the go-ahead by Eric. Miles twisted his mouth as though deciding whether to reveal any more, playing to his audience.

"I have one but we've only just finalised it this week and I'm not sure I can say anything yet," Miles teased and his gaze found Eric standing off stage who nodded at him.

"Oh, come on, we won't tell anyone, will we?" Jimmy joked and the audience replied with a resounding 'no'.

"Ah, okay, seeing as I know you won't blab and I've always been a rule-breaker," Miles said with a cheeky wink and the audience cheered. It took them a few seconds to calm down but as soon as there was a lull, Miles said, "I just signed up to play on Broadway for six weeks next fall, in the role of Don Lockwood in *Singing in the Rain*."

The audience went wild and Miles shook his head at their response. Once they quietened down, Jimmy said, "I think they like the idea." Miles chuckled. "That's quite a change for you."

"It is. I like to keep everyone guessing on my next move." His comment gained him a ripple of laughter.

"So, will you be relocating to the US permanently?"

"No, that's not on the cards at the moment. My family are in the UK and I want to be as close as I can to them."

"Well, Miles, it's been a huge pleasure to have you back. You've certainly come back with a splash. I wish you every success in your new roles and hopefully you'll be back soon to tell us all about them."

"That would be my pleasure."

"Miles Keane, everyone!"

The audience cheered again, whistling and giving him his second standing ovation.

"Thank you all so much."

The program director ordered the cameras to stop rolling and Jimmy leaned in closer. "That went well."

Miles blew out a breath and shook his head. "It never gets any easier," Miles muttered as he stood to unclip his microphone and powerpack. He handed it to the sound engineer and turned back to Jimmy. "Thanks again for going easy on me."

"It was a pleasure."

Miles could hear a few of the audience calling his name, now the cameras weren't rolling. "I'll just go and say hi."

"Sure, I'll come with you."

Miles gave him a thankful smile and they both jogged down to the tiered seats to the delight of the crowd.

THE HOUR-AND-A-half drive back to his home felt endless, even with the phone call to Louisa letting her know how the interview went. Now that he'd gotten his first interview out of the way, Miles was anxious to be at home with Louisa. The next two days would be hectic and these were their last few hours to be alone. Once they arrived at Holmwood tomorrow, they'd be surrounded by staff, family, colleagues and a multitude of people, trying to get the grounds concert-ready. Not to mention the entertaining of the A-listers playing. The Blackthorns had opened up their house for a few of the bands to stay. Security would already be tight as well as being convenient for the artists, plus it was a thank you from the Blackthorns for their support of CASPO.

The sun had already set by the time Kurt pulled into Miles's driveway. He'd made arrangements for a late dinner to be delivered and set up for their last evening. Karl had been left behind to oversee everything with Hugh. No one knew Louisa was staying in Malibu. As far as anyone knew, Lady Louisa Blackthorn was still in New York. His stomach tightened just thinking of the importance of tonight. It was his last chance before they left for the UK tomorrow.

Miles stepped out of the car and bid Pierce and Karl goodnight, then headed towards his front door. He paused for a moment taking in a deep breath.

"Everything alright?" Pierce asked, seeing him hesitate.

"Yeah, it's a big night," Miles said over his shoulder.

"You did good today. It went well, very well."

"Thanks, but I meant..." Miles's eyes shifted to the front door.

"Oh." Pierce gave him a huge smile, understanding why Miles was nervous. "I wouldn't worry. You totally got this." He gave him a wink, then gestured to the door with his head. "No time like the present."

Miles blew a breath up his face suddenly feeling the weight of the suit and tie he was still wearing from the interview. He felt stifled in the heat and humidity of the late summer evening. He put the key in the lock and turned it, then slowly opened the door.

The first thing he caught sight of was the dining table set up for two. The dark moonless sky was a perfect backdrop to showcase the central candles on the table and the lanterns scattered around the terrace. Karl had done well, if the night went as he'd hoped and planned, Karl would be in for a bonus. Miles loosened his tie and popped open the top button, stepping further into his home. His eyes drifted to the kitchen where he could see the various dishes warming in the oven. Thankfully, dinner had already arrived, though at the moment the last thing his clenched stomach needed was food. There was the faint sound of the shower running from his ensuite as he padded towards the stairs and started to make his way up, quickening his pace as the sound suddenly ceased. Miles stepped into his bedroom just as Louisa came through from the bathroom. She'd piled her hair messily in a haphazard bun and the fluffy white towel contrasted with the golden tan she'd acquired today. She gave a soft gasp, seeing him there, and then immediately smiled.

"Sorry, I didn't mean to startle you." Miles gave a grimace and she shook her head.

"I didn't expect you for another ten minutes. It went well, then?"

"Yeah, it did." He gave her a wide smile and Louisa all but ran to him, meeting him halfway. She wrapped her arms around him as Miles picked her up and spun her around. "I'm glad it's over, though." He gave her a hard kiss and let her slip down his body. "Thanks for calling Eric."

"I wanted to be there for you and I was so frustrated being here and you there. I think I interrupted his dinner plans." Louisa made a face.

"Well, he wasn't going to let *you* down."

"No. I kind of gave him no room to argue."

Miles let out a laugh. "I like having Lady Blackthorn in my corner."

"Well, we are quite formidable when we need to be," she said in her best official posh voice. Miles growled and nuzzled her neck and she squirmed. "Stop it, you're tickling me!" Miles pulled back and grasped her face between his hands and gently kissed her until she was breathless, then rested his forehead on hers.

"I'm also glad I have *just* Louisa in my corner too."

"Me too. I love being *just* Louisa." Her eyes flitted down his body. "Aren't you a little overdressed?"

"Yeah, I could do with wearing less. You, on the other hand, are perfect as you are." He widened his eyes and she chuckled.

"I'll put on a robe. I'm not eating dinner in a towel."

"Spoilsport." Miles pouted and she rolled her eyes at him, stepping back.

"Go and have a quick shower while I set up dinner and then you can tell me all about it while we eat."

"So bossy," Miles said, narrowing his eyes.

"Yep, that's me: bossy Blackthorn at your service." She gave a salute and Miles laughed at her playfulness. She dropped her towel and Miles stopped laughing and openly raked his eyes over her naked body. He took a step towards her and Louisa put up her hand. "No further: shower, dinner and then" – she swept her hand down her body with a flourish – "dessert," she said coquettishly and Miles groaned.

"Louisa, not fair!"

She pivoted around, pulled her robe off the bed and walked slowly towards the door dragging her robe behind her.

"Chop, chop. I'll meet you downstairs," she said over her shoulder and Miles narrowed his eyes at her and shook his head. She was such a tease and he lapped up every second of it.

"Not sure I like bossy Blackthorn," he called after her as she left the room.

"I guarantee you will... once you've had dessert," she called back and he let out a loud laugh. *Who was he kidding?* He loved every kind of Louisa Blackthorn, from the haughty to the naughty and everything in between. She was perfect.

DINNER WAS DELICIOUS, NOT that Miles's concern tonight was the quality of the food. Miles had chosen from one of his favourite restaurants he had often frequented that was a little further up the Pacific Highway. Eating out was not an option for them but his beachfront property more than made up for their restrictions on dining. It also meant Louisa could be dressed in a simple white robe and he in nothing else but a pair of lounge shorts – casual dining at its best. And on a night like tonight, he wouldn't have wanted it any other way. Miles wondered if he'd ever want to dine out again. He'd become accustomed to having Louisa to himself and cherished their private time together. There were few places they could be alone and uninterrupted. He'd gotten used to Hugh and Pierce being around, though they tried to be as invisible as possible, but when he was at Holmwood or at her London residence, they were constantly on show.

They dined on cooked oysters, steamed buttered lobster and sipped on vintage champagne, celebrating his first interview and his role in a Broadway musical. Miles smiled as Louisa talked animatedly about her recent conversation with Melissa. Her heavily pregnant friend had been moved into Holmwood and set up in the room next to Louisa's suite. Louisa had brought in round-the-clock nursing staff to ensure she was well looked after and monitored, to the relief of Robert. It meant Melissa was still involved with the concert but at least there were enough people on hand to help. She felt guilty for leaving her to come with Miles to the US but everything was under control. Alistair and her team at CASPO were more than capable and she was a phone call away.

Louisa had dominated their dinner conversation, which was unusual, but Miles seemed introspective and she felt that the weight of the day was playing on his mind. He'd made huge commitments that he'd announced to the world and she was sure his mood was him second-guessing his decision.

"You're very quiet. Is everything okay?" She asked as she stood up to clear their plates.

"Yeah, I'm fine," Miles said, rising up to help her. "Here let me. Why don't you go and sit on the terrace?"

"It'll be faster if we both do it," she said softly, then rested her hand on his arm. "Are you sure you're okay? You've been... is anything bothering you?" His bright blue eyes lifted to see her concerned expression.

"Kind of." Louisa furrowed her brow at his answer and Miles gave her a soft smile. "Let's leave these for later." He took her left hand and laced their fingers together, then tugged her towards the soft seating on the terrace. The night air was still very warm and the only sound was the soft music from within the lounge and the waves of the inky ocean lapping the shore.

Miles guided her to the couches and she took a seat blindly, keeping her eyes trained on his tense expression. She'd never seen him so out of sorts, even when things were difficult or uncomfortable Miles had always made light of the situation. If something had angered him, he let it bubble under the surface but reined in his temper. His mood tonight was neither of these and Louisa felt a wave of uneasiness.

"Miles, you're scaring me. Did something happen?" She looked up at him, searching his handsome face for a clue as to what was passing through his mind. He gave her a lopsided tentative smile, then crouched down in front of her, pressing a kiss to her hand, which he was still holding.

"Yeah, it did," he said with a chuckle. "I fell in love with *just* Louisa."

Louisa's expression softened. "And I fell in love with *just* Miles."

"I think it was love at..." he squinted a little, then said, "*second* sight." Louisa chuckled at their private joke and Miles felt his nerves subside a little. "*Believe it to achieve it*," he said in a hushed voice, almost to himself. Louisa furrowed her brow at his words, unsure if she'd heard him, and missed him reach into the pocket of his shorts, then lift his fisted hand in front of her. Louisa's eyes shot to his hand, then back to his now sharply focused expression and her heart stopped. "I know I'm not your first love but you are mine. We are so very different, from different worlds with different pasts, but somehow our two different worlds collided and just fit so perfectly together. You are everything I'm not, but I promise I'll prove my worth to you."

Miles uncurled his fingers to reveal the engagement ring. Even in the dark evening, it captured the light of the lanterns and sparkled brightly. Louisa let out a gasp and clapped her free hand over her mouth. Miles pressed his lips to her hand and gave her a gentle smile. "Marry me, *just* Louisa. Marry me and I'll try every day to prove I'm worthy."

"Oh, Miles…" Louisa said shakily and he shuffled closer.

"I can't see a future without you in it. I don't want a future without you in it. I know your world is complicated but I'll adapt, follow your lead and always be with you, beside you all the way." Tears sprung into Louisa's eyes and she pulled her lips in and nodded, totally overcome with emotions.

"Is that a yes?" Miles said with his signature cheeky smirk.

"It's a yes."

Miles's smirk changed into a wide smile that lit up the moonless dark night sky and made his brilliant blue eyes sparkle brighter than the 2-carat diamond in his hand. He took her hand, slipped the ring on her finger, then kissed it, sealing the deal.

12

CHANGE OF PLAN

"**M**y Louisa." Miles kissed her palm rose up and gently, urging her back so she lay down on the couch.

"My Miles," she whispered as he blanketed over her.

"I've always been yours. I was a done deal from that first date. Signed and sealed. You in that red dress. I was blown away."

She smiled up at him as he tenderly pushed her hair off her brow. "Me too. I really wanted not to like you, but you were nothing like I expected. You threw me off with your charm and dazzling smile." She rubbed her thumb over his lips and he kissed it. "A total surprise."

"Yeah?" He gave her a lopsided grin.

"Yes. A good surprise. I can't believe you asked me." She gave her head a slight shake.

"You were never going to get rid of me." He dropped a kiss onto her lips and she slipped her arms around his neck.

"No, I mean, ask me today, with everything going on, on this trip. The meetings, the interview."

"I've been planning it for a while."

"You have?"

"I've had the ring with me, just in case. But I wanted to ask you here, just the two of us at my home. If there was a chance we couldn't make it out here, I would've asked you anywhere. I wanted us to be official by the concert." Louisa furrowed her brow at his revelation. She'd hoped he'd ask her and she thought that at some point he would, but she was surprised that he'd been ready to do it for a while. By his own admission, he wasn't classed as the marrying kind. That may have been true in the past, but Louisa had never seen any signs that it was true. To her he was perfect.

"No more hiding?" Louisa said, putting her left hand out and wriggling her fingers, causing the ring to sparkle.

"No more hiding." Miles chuckled and gave her a hard kiss.

"This was the perfect proposal," she said dreamily. It was intimate, private and as romantic as she could ever imagine.

"That's because you're perfect." Miles took her hand and kissed her ring finger, feeling a swell of masculine ownership seeing the ring he'd placed there. He couldn't believe how primal it felt, knowing that this was a symbol of her belonging to him. He hadn't realised how important it was to him that everyone knew she was his.

"It's beautiful," Louisa said softly.

"Do you like it? It's from a collection called Malibu."

"Really? I love it even more, then."

"It's why I wanted to propose here." Miles's gaze shifted from the sparkle of the diamonds to the glisten in her eyes.

"You're so thoughtful," she said earnestly, tears welling. From the very beginning, Miles had always put her needs first. Her life was restrictive and weighed down with duty and he not only understood her role, he accepted it. "That's a rare gift."

"Not as rare as the gift of you. I'm crazy about you, Louisa. I'm so in love with you."

And when he said those words, she knew they were the truest words he'd spoken. He'd always backed up his words with actions. She'd never doubt him and that was an even rarer gift. "Good, because I'm crazy in love with you too." She slipped her hand around his neck again and pulled their foreheads together.

"We need to seal the deal." Miles's brilliant blue eyes switched from lighting up with mischief, to darkening with desire.

"We definitely do. Time for that dessert I promised."

"You're sweeter than any dessert," Miles said, just before he branded his lips to hers and kissed her deeply. Louisa sighed and let her hands roam over his sculptured bare back. Miles pulled away, kneeling between where her legs had opened and Louisa frowned. "Robe off," he ordered hoarsely as his hands busied with the tie and within seconds, the robe was opened and pulled away from her body. With her lightly tanned body exposed and her hair dishevelled from the unceremonious disrobing, Miles let his eyes roam over her, taking in every curve of her flawless skin against the soft cream upholstery. Miles cupped her jaw and then trailed his palm over the column of her neck and down her décolletage, leaving a trail of goosebumps in its wake. He cupped her breast and dusted the pad of his thumb over the nipple, causing it to pucker. Louisa's eyes fluttered shut and she arched up into his touch, letting out a soft moan, snapping him out of his desire-induced haze. She'd hypnotized him, just looking at her laid out and naked, ready for him to take, to tease and to taste, had him mesmerized. She was a siren and he'd willingly fallen under her potent spell. He wasn't kidding when he said he couldn't see his future without her. Louisa had consumed his every thought and to know she would be his wife had his heart pounding. The warm pressure of his lips against her nipple elicited a gasp from her lips and Miles sucked a little harder.

"Ah, Miles."

"I need to taste you everywhere," Miles said gruffly, continuing his exploration with open-mouthed kisses down her body. Her fingers speared into his luxurious hair, gently tugging at the roots as each of his touches devastated her senses. Miles was an expert in the art of making love because with Louisa, that was what it always felt like. He lavished her with his undivided attention, worshipped and cherished her. She'd never felt so loved and at the centre of someone's world before. Sometimes it was a raw primal need when they were together, all grunts and frenzied coupling, their animal attraction being the untamed force between them. Other times it was playful, with teasing touches, laughter and sex-fuelled words swamped with sentiment that fused them together. But most times it was like tonight: intense, where few words were needed, connecting on a deeper level, where their bodies fell into a synchronized dance, to music only they could hear.

Miles's warm palms smoothed a path to her waist and down over her hips, cupping her behind. With a nudge of his hip he urged her legs to widen, further exposing herself to him. Seeing the evidence of her arousal glisten, triumph flared in his eyes and he lowered his mouth, just hovering over the apex of her thighs, then swiped his tongue through her folds. Louisa trembled beneath him. He loved how she reacted to him. For all her decorum and restraint in public, Louisa was the opposite in the privacy of their bedroom. Miles revelled in how she responded to him, how she let down her guard and surrendered herself totally to the moment. It was like quicksilver running through in his veins and now she was his, captured and totally at his mercy.

"Oh Miles…" Louisa let out a shaky gasp as he continued to his skilful ministrations that had her seeing stars and her body shaking within seconds. She'd never stood a chance and before her body even recovered and could come down from her high, Miles had stripped off his shorts and was entering her in one swift powerful stroke.

"Yes," Miles hissed, holding himself deep, giving himself a moment to adjust to her tight warmth. He rested his weight on his elbows and stared down into her eyes before leaning down to kiss her lips. "You feel incredible." Holding her gaze as he slowly began to move. Louisa moaned, relishing the heat of his skin over hers and his masculine scent that flooded her senses. He consumed her completely and she gladly drowned in his kisses as his body sank in deep and drew out of her, in a relentless rhythm. Their bodies were slick with sweat and the only sounds that could be heard over the waves of the ocean were their heavy breaths and the slap of skin on skin. Miles rose up sitting back on his heels, dragging Louisa towards him. He lifted her left leg and placed it over his shoulder and drove in deeper.

"Fuck," he called out, trying hard to control himself, but the sight of Louisa spread out in front of him, lips plump from his kisses, flushed skin and covered in a sheen of their combined sweat was too much. "Baby, I'm so close." He rolled his hips in a well-practised move and Louisa gasped.

She drank in his tanned, taut torso that rippled with every stroke. His hair fell messily, a combination of sweat and her frenzied tugging, while his eyes blazed white hot as they scorched a path from her face down to the point where their bodies joined. Louisa had never seen anything so beautiful and blatantly sexual in her life, a deadly combination that had her dissolving beneath him on a masterful stroke. Miles let his head fall back, feeling her tighten around him, calling out as his body shuddered through one of the most powerful and intense orgasms.

Miles slowly caught his breath and lowered himself, turning Louisa on her side so they could be face to face, holding her close.

"That was… wow." Louisa blew out a breath and Miles smiled lazily at her.

"Wow is the perfect word. Though every time with you is wow," he said, his chest still rising and falling as he levelled out his breathing.

"Well, now we'll have a lifetime of wow." Louisa grinned and Miles blasted her with his brightest smile.

"We will."

ALISTAIR SMOOTHED HIS HANDS over his pristine T-shirt and ran his fingers through his hair, then stole himself a second, before rapping his knuckles on the door. He could hear footsteps approaching and he took a deep breath just before the door opened.

"Morning," Amanda said with a smile. She was already dressed for the day in a white T-shirt, leggings and trainers. She'd pulled her dark hair into a high ponytail and had swung a small crossover bag over her shoulder. Alistair blinked at her, stunned for a second at how beautiful she looked, even casually dressed and makeup-free.

"Morning. I was worried you wouldn't be up after the late night." The whole team had been up until midnight, sorting out all the trailers for the various artists. Alistair had asked Amanda to be in charge but it had run on later than they'd anticipated.

"I'm used to ungodly hours. Grace and Louis don't quite understand the concept of sleeping in, so 6:30 is a normal morning for me," Amanda said stepping out into the corridor and shutting the door to her room behind her.

"I'm sure." Alistair held out his hand gesturing for her to follow him. "So, I thought we could have breakfast in my suite. It'll be a bit more casual but we can watch the interview in there. I already have it set up," Alistair said as breezily as possible. When he'd suggested that they have an early breakfast and watch Miles's interview streamed live together, he hadn't mentioned he'd set it up in his apartment in the east wing. The truth was he could've had it set up anywhere, but this was his attempt to steal some time alone with Amanda, without anyone noticing or staff interrupting. Alistair, like all the Blackthorns, coveted his privacy and in a house as big as Holmwood, with an army of staff and various relatives that came and left as they pleased, it often proved to be a challenge. He just hoped Amanda wouldn't feel uncomfortable.

"Casual is what I'm used to, Alistair. My breakfast usually consists of a toast and a mug of tea as I try to get the kids ready," she chuckled as she fell in step with him.

"Well, I might be able to lay on a bit more than that," Alistair said with a side glance and Amanda gave him an encouraging smile.

"Is anyone else awake?" The passageway to the east wing was quiet and only their footsteps could be heard against the thick carpet.

"Some of the staff. But the volunteers and my friends won't be up until eight."

"And Lady Blackthorn?"

"She's probably up but doesn't leave her suite until nine."

"Oh, so, it's just us walking around?"

"Yeah. I thought my apartment would be a bit more private. We always seem to have someone around," Alistair said quietly, coming to a halt outside a heavy double wooden door.

"We do. Sounds perfect," Amanda said feeling a little thrill at having him all to herself. For the last two days they'd been surrounded by Holmwood staff, his friends and CASPO staff. Everyone had made a huge fuss of her, making sure she was alright, which she found to be ridiculous and unnecessary. She was supposed to be there to help, not have everyone worrying over her. The few times she'd been with Alistair, there always seemed to be someone around. She was just glad that she'd mentioned she wanted to see Miles's interview to Alistair and he'd immediately suggested they watch it together while having an early breakfast.

"So, this is my home in Holmwood." Alistair opened up the heavy door and signalled her to go in ahead of him. The first thing that struck Amanda was how airy and light the apartment was. The light from the huge windows that led out to a terrace flooded the living space. Like the rest of the house, there were priceless paintings and antiques that decorated the soft blue walls and various period pieces of furniture but there was definitely a hint of Alistair's personality. There were modern couches that blended well with luxurious rare rugs. Framed family photos adorned the top of a baby grand piano and a dog basket sat by the huge ornate marble fireplace. The shelves on either side were filled with books and a number of models of helicopters and vintage airplanes. On a side table, an ornate chess set was set up that looked as though it was mid-game.

"It's huge," Amanda said as she walked towards the French

windows.

"I had it converted into a self-contained apartment. So I could have some privacy."

"Who are you playing with?" Amanda said pointing to the chess set.

Alistair smiled. "My friend and ex-colleague Martin. We served together. He's in Belize. We play via video call. This match has taken us four weeks, what with the time difference and how busy we both are."

"You're not afraid you'll cheat?"

Alistair let out a laugh. "Where's the honour in that? And anyway, I send him a photo of the board when we stop."

"So, he still has his doubts on your honour," she teased. "And you have a terrace too." She turned to the door and stepped up to it. Alistair reached for the handle and opened the doors and led her out to where there was garden furniture set up and huge planters filled with various flowers and plants.

"Yes. It means I can lock myself away, if I want to. I need to be able to have some outdoor space."

Amanda turned to look at him. He stood with his hands in the pockets of his shorts, looking a little nervous. Amanda hardly even notice his prosthetic blade anymore, even when the morning sunlight reflected off its shiny surface. It was just part of him and she was glad he hadn't felt the need to wear long trousers to hide it for her benefit. "It's really lovely up here. You have a view of the whole estate."

"I do. Holmwood is really the only home I've known."

"Well, it's beautiful," Amanda said sincerely and Alistair gave her a faint smile. She was the only woman he'd ever brought up to his apartment. He hadn't realised how nervous he was, until she started walking around his living room. Knowing she liked what she'd seen, went a long way to easing his nerves.

"Come, let's have some breakfast."

"Sure, as long as you let me help."

Alistair guided her to his kitchen. It was set to the side of the living room.

"Oh, wow, you have a fully equipped kitchen. You're actually going to cook?" Amanda said with amusement. She'd been used to the staff providing a buffet breakfast every morning in the conservatory and expected a kind of room service but by the look of the countertops, it seemed Alistair was going to actually cook for them.

"Don't sound so surprised," Alistair said with a chuckle. "Nothing too fancy. I had some help with the prep, but I will need to grill the ham and poach the eggs for the eggs benedict."

Alistair fired up the grill and placed the thick-cut smoked ham on the tray, then pulled out a poaching pan. Amanda busied herself setting up the dining room table where Alistair had wired up a TV screen. Once it was set she began bringing out the cut fruit, yoghurt, nuts and croissants plus all the accompaniments. Alistair warmed through the hollandaise sauce, dropped the eggs into the poacher, then put the kettle on to boil. Amanda reached for the milk and bumped into his back as he stepped back.

"Oh sorry," she said.

"No, it's me. I'm trying to make a good impression," Alistair said quickly, he'd stepped back from the stove in order to quickly get the kettle on. He wanted everything to be perfect.

"You don't need to try, Alistair." Amanda gave him a shy smile. She could feel his unease around her and she wasn't sure if he was just nervous she was there or of the unfamiliar situation.

"It's been a while for me to…" Alistair left the sentence hanging because he wasn't entirely sure how to end it, answering her unspoken question. It had been a while for him to entertain, cook with someone, have a woman in his apartment, feel something for a woman, be on a date – if this is was even a date – the list was long.

Amanda rested her hand on his forearm and gave it a slight squeeze. "It's been a while for me too."

Alistair's gaze dropped to where her hand was, then up to her face. In the past, before his accident, he'd have already had Amanda pinned to couch and breakfast be damned. He was a different man now, though. He spent most of his time alone and second-guessed the motives of the people he became acquainted with. But looking up into Amanda's large sincere eyes, he knew she didn't have any motive other than to spend time with him. He stepped closer and cupped her jaw, then lowered his lips to hers. He felt a sense of relief when she closed the last few inches to meet him and rested her hand on his hard chest. It was a soft tentative kiss, one that was born from pent up attraction and mixed with mutual respect.

"I've been wanting to kiss you for a long time. I was hoping that kissing you would calm me but my heart is racing," Alistair said hoarsely, betraying the effect she'd had on him.

"Mine too. I'm glad you decided to," Amanda said with a soft sigh and Alistair captured her lips with his again in a bolder deeper kiss that had Amanda gripping onto his biceps.

"You're so beautiful," he said as he pulled back. "I kind of messed up the order of the date. I'd planned to have our first kiss on the terrace," he said with a widening of his eyes and Amanda chuckled.

"You didn't mess anything up," She looked to the stove and added, "Well, except maybe the eggs."

Alistair whipped his head around to the stove where the poacher was almost boiled dry. "Oh shit!" He switched off the burner and lifted the pan into the sink and let the cold tap run over it. It sizzled loudly and filled the kitchen with steam. Amanda opened up the window and Alistair popped open the lid to reveal four very hardboiled eggs. Amanda put her hand over her mouth to stifle her giggle.

"Well, they're no good. Luna will be pleased; she loves hardboiled eggs." Alistair shook his head and laughed. "All your fault, you know."

"Mine?"

"Yes yours. Looking all beautiful and distracting me."

"Well overcooked eggs were definitely worth it."

"I'll say," he said with a lopsided smirk.

They both busied themselves preparing a new set of eggs, decidedly more comfortable around each other. The kiss had broken the ice. All the unease had been lifted and they moved effortlessly within the confines of the kitchen, allowing the odd touch or brush against each other without the awkwardness.

They ate their perfectly made eggs benedict, sitting next to each other while Jimmy Kimmel quizzed Miles on his life and career. Alistair took a sip of his tea and turned to Amanda. She'd been glued to the screen and it was obvious she was nervous for her brother-in-law. Today was a huge step for Miles and as the show finished, he saw her blow out a breath.

"He did good," Alistair said.

"He did. He was nervous. It's a big week for him." Her relief was evident.

Alistair nodded, then narrowed his eyes at her. "A big week for both of them: Louisa and Miles, I mean," he said with a hint of amusement and Amanda's eyes widened.

"You know, then?"

"I knew it was coming but Hugh confirmed it."

"I hope she said yes." Amanda twisted her mouth and Alistair let out a laugh.

"Of course she said yes. She's head over heels. I've never seen Louisa so happy."

"It'll mean that we'll be seeing more of each other," Amanda said with a lift of her brow.

Alistair shuffled forward so that his face was just a few inches from hers. "I'm hoping that we'll be seeing much more of each other anyway."

"Me too," Amanda said with a wide grin. "How about you show me your terrace again before we need to go."

"I'd love to." Then he pressed his lips to hers and kissed her thoroughly.

RING-RING, RING-RING, ring-ring.

"Who the hell is calling me at..." Miles squinted at his phone. "Seven twenty-three in the morning?" He silently cursed himself for not putting it on silent but they'd crawled into bed so late, he'd forgotten. The name Hugh came up and Miles's heart dropped. If Hugh was calling it must be important.

"Hugh, what's wrong?"

Louisa rubbed her eyes and yawned, having woken from the call.

"Sorry to wake you but I thought you'd need to know. A site has posted pictures of Lady Louisa sunbathing on your terrace."

"What? How the fuck?" Miles shot up in bed.

"What's happened? What is it?" Louisa said, trying to focus. She was exhausted and the rude wakeup call had her head spinning.

Miles put his phone on loudspeaker. "Say it again so Louisa can hear."

"Good morning madame, sorry to disturb but as I told Mr Keane, there have been pictures posted on a site of you sunbathing on his terrace."

Louisa's eyes widened in horror. "Oh no." Miles put his arm around her. He knew what this would mean. The press would be all over the pair of them and their chances of leaving the US undetected would be almost impossible.

"At present they haven't said who it is and from what I can see, your face isn't clearly visible but I just wanted to warn you before you went out there this morning," Hugh continued. Miles took a breath in relief, hopefully they hadn't gotten clear photos of her and they'd be able to keep her identity a secret. Then a horrifying thought passed through his mind.

"They're just daytime shots?" Miles asked and Louisa gasped. They'd been out on the terrace last night. Made love on the couch, skinny-dipped in the pool, celebrated their engagement on every surface of the terrace.

"Yes."

They collectively let out a relieved breath. "Okay, send me the link so we can have a look. Thanks." Miles put down his phone, then switched it to silent. He didn't want to be fielding calls from anyone about who was at his home. He wrapped Louisa in his arms and kissed the crown of her head. "Come on let's get up and check out what they got."

"Sure," Louisa said quietly. Her glowing good mood from the night before had been well and truly dampened.

"Shit. How the fuck did they get a shot of you?" Miles ground out. He knew he had cameras facing outward with motion sensors. His security system would make the secret service look like amateurs. He updated it every six months so he was assured things like this didn't happen. Amanda and the kids came here and they needed full protection.

"A drone?" Louisa suggested and Miles shook his head.

"No, they would've been spotted by the cameras and sensors outside. I need to see the angle so we can work it out." They quickly washed up and headed downstairs to Miles's laptop and opened up the site. The headline screamed, "Who's the new-flavour Keane?" and underneath were six grainy photos of Louisa on the sun lounger in a skimpy aqua bikini. The large umbrella obscured her head as well as a few trees that were around the edge of his property. The shot was taken from a height to the left of the house. The article reported that Miles was back in LA for an interview and that he'd obviously come with a female guest. They mentioned Amanda as being the possible guest and then speculated by adding a string of names of women that he'd been seen with in the past, including Lottie Price.

"Christ, well at least they haven't latched onto your name. Some of these women are married with children now!" Miles shook his head in disgust. They were forever going to dig up his past. Miles squinted at the photos and then furrowed his brow. "That's from the direction of Miguel's place next door. Why would he be taking photos?" Miles growled, picking up his phone.

"Who is Miguel?"

"He's the famous restauranteur, Miguel Ortiz. He has a few restaurants and this is his summer home. Fuck it, I'm going to call him," Miles said angrily.

"It's not eight o'clock yet," Louisa said in alarm.

"I don't care. The fucker needs to explain," Miles said, swiping his phone and scrolling to his name.

"Hey Miguel, how are you?" He said calmly, though his body was rigid. Louisa watched as Miles listened. "Oh, San Francisco?" His eyes darted to Louisa and she could tell that Miles's original thoughts on Miguel being the culprit were wrong. "I see, anyone staying in your home?" Miles shook his head at Louisa confirming that Miguel wasn't the photographer. "It's just that someone took some photos of my terrace yesterday and posted them and it looks like it was from the roof of your house." Miles listened to an agitated Miguel, who was obviously angry at what had happened. "I can have my security check if you like." Miles nodded and clenched his jaw. "Sure, I'll get them to call you." He finished the call and cursed.

"Well?"

"He's been in San Francisco for over a week, working on a new restaurant he's opening next month. There's no one at his home, so obviously some paparazzo got onto his roof and took the photos. He has cameras but by his own admission, his security isn't that top-notch. I'll ask Karl and Kurt to go and have a look."

Louisa nodded and slumped back into the couch. "Well, at least they only got shots of me from the shoulders down. No one knows who I am," she said quietly, then looked down at her ring and rubbed it with her thumb. *Way to put a dampener on their high. Was it always going to be like this?*

Miles called up Hugh and gave him the information Miguel had given him and asked for Karl and Kurt to go over and see what they could find. He sent him Miguel's phone number, just in case they found anything. Miles put down his phone and rubbed his face and then looked over at Louisa, who was looking deflated.

"Hey, let's get the guys in and see what we can sort out." Miles cupped her face and kissed her tenderly. He'd been so angry that he'd almost forgotten about how she must be feeling. "It's good that they didn't get your face," he said and she nodded. "The thing is, that means there's another problem. They know someone is here and if we try to leave they'll be around to find out who my 'new flavour' is," Miles said with more than a hint of sarcasm. This was his fault, wanting her to be with him. He'd exposed her to this violation of her privacy. He'd been so focused on her identity not being revealed he'd sidelined the other issue, photos of her body being plastered on some sleazy site. "I'm so sorry, baby. You shouldn't have to put up with this because of me." He held her to him and she sighed.

"This isn't your fault," Louisa said softly. She hated that he felt responsible. The sooner they were public, the sooner they'd be able to relax.

"This is because I did the interview. All the crazies know I'm here. Fuck!" He wanted to punch something, preferably the photographer and the owner of the site that published the photos.

"Let's make some tea. I need to wake up and then we'll get Hugh and Pierce in and see what we can do." Louisa pulled back, gave Miles a kiss and her best reassuring smile, then headed to the kitchen. This wasn't how she'd envisioned their morning going. They'd planned to laze around the pool until it was time for their flight. It wasn't even nine o'clock yet and she was exhausted. Miles came into the kitchen and started pulling out items for breakfast. They worked around each other quietly both of them lost in their own thoughts.

"Your phone's ringing," Louisa said, seeing it flash from the coffee table.

Miles cursed and stepped over to it and swiped the screen. "It's Hugh," Miles said and answered it putting it on loudspeaker. "Hugh?"

"We have some visitors." Hugh's steady voice came through the phone.

"See, I told you the place would be swarming." Miles gritted his teeth and shook his head.

"Er no, not that kind. It's your parents," Hugh said with a hint of amusement.

"What?" Miles closed his eyes and pinched the bridge of his nose, remembering he'd spoken to them before the interview. They'd said they would come and see them before they left. What with the proposal preying on his mind and then the photos this morning, Miles had totally forgotten. "Jesus, perfect timing. Well, let them in." Miles threw Louisa an apologetic look and she shook her head, letting him know it was fine. After all they were going to be her parents-in-law now.

Louisa looked down at herself and blanched, she couldn't be dressed in a robe and nothing else when they came in. "I'll go and put something on," she said, walking quickly past Miles.

He caught her by the waist and pulled her to him. "I'm so sorry, baby," he said stroking the hair from her face.

"It's fine, they're your parents. Of course they're going to come and see you."

"No, I meant about all the other shit."

"We'll work through it. Let me get changed." Miles gave her a quick kiss and a pat on her behind and she swiftly made her way upstairs.

Louisa pulled out her suitcase and looked at what she had packed. All her clothes were either formal, a bikini or beachwear she'd worn to lounge around in, apart from the jeans she'd travelled in. They would have to do. She washed up, put on her jeans and a camisole, then brushed her hair into a high ponytail. She looked down at her feet and scowled. Other than trainers she only had heels. Barefoot it would have to be, she thought to herself and headed out of the door.

"We just had to come and see you. We know you're busy but we couldn't not come. It might be months before you come out again," Louisa could hear Miles's mother Katy saying.

"We watched you last night." The deep voice of his father Richard chimed in. "You did good, son."

"You were brilliant! I always liked that Jimmy Kimmel; such a gentleman," Katy gushed and Louisa smiled to herself.

She liked Katy. She was vibrant, straightforward and obviously adored her son. Louisa slowly came down the steps, not wanting to intrude on their rare time together with their son, but Miles caught sight of her and made his way to the stairs. His brow rose, seeing her in jeans and barefoot.

"This was the best thing I had to wear," she whispered and Miles chuckled. Louisa hoped the next time she saw his parents she'd be more suitably dressed – they always seemed to catch her unprepared. They walked towards where Katy and Richard had taken a seat on the terrace but waited inside. They both rose up from their seats to greet Louisa with gentle hugs and kisses and Miles suggested they sit inside. He didn't need any more photos to be taken, even though Kurt and Karl were probably over at Miguel's house checking it out now.

"So, you fly out tonight?" Richard asked as Miles slid a coffee over to him. They'd moved to the dining table, where Miles and Louisa quickly laid out fruit, pastries, yoghurts and coffee as an impromptu breakfast.

"Yeah but we have a bit of a crisis on. We need to get out of here without anyone realising Louisa is here." Miles quickly explained about the photos as a concerned Katy and Richard listened. They knew what it was like and had experienced having their privacy violated first-hand. Katy patted Louisa's forearm in an attempt to comfort her. She didn't know her all that well but she could imagine how awful she was feeling, being exposed to the world in a private moment. Miles told them about Miguel and his theory and Louisa gave Katy a faint smile, appreciating the gesture. Richard furrowed his brow, clearly unhappy that they'd been subjected to another incident and Katy squeezed Louisa's hand, hoping that their presence would at least feel like support. Her eye caught sight of the beautiful ring on Louisa's finger and her eyes widened in surprise.

"Oh my god!" Katy said without any thought, cutting Miles off mid-sentence. "Is that what I think it is?" she asked, her eyes shooting up to meet Miles's stunned face.

Miles's eyes darted to Louisa, who was stifling a grin by pulling her lips in. "Mom, Dad, Louisa has graciously agreed to be my wife," Miles said proudly and grasped Louisa's other hand.

"Oh my God!" Katy repeated, clearly elated by the news. She jumped out of her seat and rushed to Miles to give him a hug. "I'm so happy for you," she said clasping his grinning face between her palms.

"Thanks, Mom," he said, overwhelmed at her reaction.

"I can't believe you didn't lead with that," she mock-chastised him, then turned back to Louisa. "Congratulations, this is just the best news." Katy hugged her tightly, then pulled back her eyes awash with tears.

"Thank you," Louisa said softly, her eyes welling up, seeing Miles and Richard hugging each other. With everything that had gone on that morning, Louisa was feeling overly emotional but was never happier to have Miles's parents there and share this moment.

"Congratulations," Richard said warmly and hugged Louisa. "As Katy said, this is really such good news. Welcome to the family."

"Thank you, Richard. It's an honour to be part of it," Louisa said sincerely and Richard beamed at her because the irony wasn't lost on him; it was Miles who was going to be part of her very distinguished and prestigious family.

"We should be celebrating but under the circumstances, I can understand that you've a few pressing matters to sort out." Richard turned his attention to Miles who blew out a breath.

"We will need to talk to our security soon. See how to navigate everything," Louisa said with a sigh because she was enjoying being excited about their news.

"Of course, don't let us stop you," Richard said, giving his wife a look that said they should leave.

"Please stay," Louisa said in a rush, seeing the disappointment on Katy's face. "We're family, after all."

"Yes, we are," Katy said enthusiastically and slipped her arm around Louisa's waist as if to confirm it.

"Okay, let's get the guys in and see what we're going to do."

Within a few minutes Hugh, Pierce, Karl and Kurt were sitting around the dining room table with Miles and Louisa. Katy and Richard played hosts by making refreshments and tidying up in the kitchen, all the while listening to them strategize.

Karl confirmed there had been some break-in on the grounds of Miguel's property. There was also evidence that the perpetrator had gone onto the roof. There were recently smoked cigarette butts left at the point that had the clearest view of Miles's terrace. They were scheduled to leave LAX at one and catch their flight from New York to London at eight in the evening, meaning they'd arrive in London in the morning. As Hugh pointed out, the flight from LA to New York wouldn't be a problem as they still had the private jet at their disposal. The problem arose when they arrived in New York. They'd both be checking in at the first-class lounge and there would be a high chance that there would be reporters waiting for a glimpse of Miles and anyone who was with him.

"The only way around it is to arrive at the check-in separately, Miles first, so the attention will be directed to him," Pierce said shooting a look at Miles who nodded.

"Not again. This isn't right." Louisa let out a sigh.

"It's fine, baby, really. Pierce is right. They're interested in me, so let them have me," he said as though it was the simplest solution. Louisa rested her head on her hand, feeling defeated.

"Then there's your arrival," Hugh continued, all business; he wanted the problem resolved quickly and didn't want to dwell on who's feelings were going to get hurt. He knew Miles well enough to know Louisa came first, every time, and that was a huge burden off the head of security's shoulders. "There's already all the hype about the concert and now with the photos, there's enough time for every journo to arrive at Heathrow and catch Miles arriving."

"We've done it before. I'll go out, be the distraction and then Hugh gets Louisa out before anyone sees her," Miles said firmly. From the kitchen, Katy and Richard listened, both horrified at what their son had to go through, and proud that he was taking it in his stride.

"What a mess." Louisa rubbed her forehead, then looked at her phone, which had started to vibrate against the table. "It's Celeste. Excuse me, I need to take this," she said and rose up from her seat and headed to the lounge, swiping the screen. "Hey sweetheart, are you ready to leave?"

"Hi Mum, not yet. I saw the photos."

"Oh goodness, already? I was hoping you wouldn't," Louisa said sadly. She didn't want her daughter subjected to media drama about her.

"Papa saw them and told me," Celeste explained and Louisa stiffened in her seat. Miles watched her reaction to the call and excused himself, stepping to where Louisa was sitting. She'd looked annoyed and he wanted to know what, on top of everything else, was upsetting her.

"Did he?" she said curtly, obviously unhappy that her ex thought it was wise to show their daughter gossip sites about her. "Well, as you can imagine, it's going to be quite a feat to get out of the US and into London without someone working it all out."

"I'm so sorry, Mum."

"It is what it is. Hugh is at this moment trying to sort it out." Miles lowered himself into the seat next to Louisa and studied her face, trying to get a grasp on what was being said.

"Papa wants to talk to you," Celeste said and Louisa answered quickly.

"Er, I don't think that's..." But before she could say any more, Gerard's voice came through the phone. "Oh, hello Gerard." Louisa gave Miles a tight smile as Gerard spoke. "Thank you, it is unfortunate. We're just sorting out our return..." Louisa furrowed her brow at whatever Gerard was saying and Miles narrowed his eyes, ready to rip the phone from her hand if need be and tell him to back off. "Oh, erm, well maybe you should speak to Hugh. He's the one who would know whether that would work. I'll pass you on to him." Louisa gave Miles a bewildered look and covered the phone with her hand.

"Gerard offered us his plane," she whispered, then took her phone to Hugh, asking him to talk to Gerard. Miles rose up from his seat and joined her at the table while Hugh talked quietly to Gerard.

"He said he would delay his flight that's scheduled to leave this morning, so that we can all fly in his plane together. Then it would look as though it was the family going back and you were... catching a lift," Louisa explained and Miles arched his brow.

"Catching a lift… you mean like plane pooling?" he said dryly.

"Yes, plane pooling." Louisa grinned at their private joke, pleased he could see the funny side. She'd been worried he wouldn't be on board with the idea but he seemed surprisingly at ease.

"Looks like Gerard has come to our rescue, as long as he isn't expecting me to fly in the cargo hold," Miles muttered and Louisa giggled.

"Is that alright? It's a long flight," she said wrapping her arms around his neck, not caring that there was a room filled with people. The last thing she wanted was for Miles to feel uncomfortable.

"You mean can I keep my mouth shut for the seven hours we're confined in a flying tin can?" he said with a heavy dose of sarcasm. "I think I can manage. I'll probably sleep."

"He's not likely to say anything with Celeste there anyway," Louisa said with a shrug, hoping she was right because otherwise, it was going to be very awkward.

"True. If Hugh thinks it's a good idea, then I'm sure I can graciously accept the lift. I wonder if he has a private room we can borrow too." Miles smirked and gave her a cheeky wink, causing Louisa to let out a light laugh, relieved he was on board with the plan.

"Miles, you're wicked."

"And you love it." He leaned down and gave her a swift kiss before they turned to their guests. Katy and Richard were smiling widely seeing their son and Louisa being publicly affectionate. It was the first time they'd ever experienced it and by the expressions on their faces, they really were getting a kick out of it.

Hugh was just finishing off his call to Gerard as Miles and Louisa took their seats again.

"So, change of plan," Hugh said with a sigh of relief. "A much better one."

"When do we need to be ready to leave?" Miles asked.

"I'll see if I can push up our flight to New York."

"Great, we'll get packing so we can leave as soon as possible." Miles looked at Louisa for approval and she nodded. The quicker they were out of here, the less chance anyone would find out she was there.

"I'll get on it." Hugh rose from his chair and Pierce, Karl and Kurt followed his lead. Hugh then stepped up to where Louisa and Miles had also stood up and put out his hand. "By the way, congratulations to you both." He shook Louisa's hand, then took Miles's.

"Thank you. You knew?" Louisa asked, a little surprised, looking between Miles and Hugh.

"It's a long story," Miles said dryly and Hugh chuckled.

"You all knew?" Louisa said, shifting her gaze to Pierce, Karl and Kurt, who were smirking just behind Hugh. They all offered their congratulations and shook the couple's hands. "You have some explaining to do," Louisa said narrowing her eyes at him and giving Miles a mock glare.

Miles pulled her to his side and kissed her temple. "I'll tell you all about it on the flight, baby."

13

ESCAPE FROM NEW YORK

"Wait a minute, so you're telling me *my* security knew weeks before that you were going to propose?" Louisa asked, eyeing Miles over her champagne glass. They'd managed to leave his home, say farewell to his parents, who had insisted on coming to the airport to see them off, and board their jet undetected. They were now cruising at 32,000 feet and enjoying a cool glass of pink champagne and canapes.

"Yep. Pierce helped me choose the ring. He knew *a guy*," Miles gave a knowing wink and Louisa giggled. She was already loving this story and as Miles had promised, it was a long one. She knew it would only get better. It was a perfect distraction from the troubles they might have to face in a few hours. "The jeweller was in Hatton Garden."

"Where all the best jewellers are," Louisa said with a fake sober nod and Miles grinned, enjoying their playful banter.

"Hugh had to find out your ring size, so he got to know too." Miles nodded to where Hugh was trying to nap. Louisa put out her hand for what must've been the 20th time, and admired the ring, sitting beautifully on her finger.

"It was a good choice. I love it."

"We're a good team, me and the boys," he said with a bit of swagger and Louisa laughed.

"Well, my mother will be pleased."

"Why do you say that?"

"She likes you," Louisa said pursing her lips, to keep her smile in check. She didn't need him getting big-headed.

"Hmm. I think she also knows," Miles said with a twist of his mouth.

"What! How?" Louisa furrowed her brow. *How could she know?*

"Well, I asked Alistair…"

"Hang on. You *asked* Alistair?" she said in a deliberate tone. Miles gave her a sheepish nod. "When?"

"After the press conference. Well, when I was at Holmwood after the press conference, to be exact," Miles clarified. He then explained that he thought he needed to ask for her hand, out of respect. He told Louisa he didn't know the protocol and seeing as she was the only person he could ask about it, he had to bite the bullet and ask Alistair.

"He was very kind and explained how your whole hierarchy worked." Miles rolled his eyes and Louisa chuckled. She could only imagine how surprised Alistair was and how uncomfortable he also must've felt. "He thought I was going to grill him about Amanda."

"Poor Alistair. I wonder how they're getting on," Louisa said, narrowing her eyes.

"Poor *me*. I just revealed my hand to someone I didn't need to," Miles huffed and Louisa laughed around her glass.

She took a sip and said, "Did he say anything about Amanda?"

"Other than he was being respectful and he had no intention of hurting her."

"Of course he wouldn't. He's a very honourable man. That was ages ago."

"I told you I wanted to ask you for a while. I wanted it to be the right time and the perfect proposal," Miles said taking her hand and kissing the palm.

"Well it was, thank you." Louisa leaned forward and dropped a chaste kiss on his lips. *This proposal story was the best.* "Anyway, why do you think Mama knows?" They'd gotten side-tracked and she wanted to know everything.

"Because, when I spoke to Celeste –"

"Celeste knows too?" Louisa's voice rose up an octave. "What the heck!"

Miles made a face and then made puppy dog eyes at her. "Ah yes, she kind of worked it out though, so I didn't technically tell her," he said in a rush, which earned him a mock glare. To be fair, Celeste was a clever cookie, so Louisa had no doubt she'd have worked it out. "In fact, she kind of kicked my ass about it."

"She did?" Louisa said, perking up at this piece of information.

"Yeah, she told me about the New York Gallery event and I kind of started making a plan because of that."

"How was that kicking your ass?"

"She said I had to make it happen and the fact she knew, Alistair and your mother knew meant I couldn't back down. Not that that was ever an option." Miles said the last sentence quickly, leaving her no doubt. Louisa smiled widely and tapped her glass against his.

"That's my girl," she said proudly and took a sip. "Maybe I should ask who doesn't know," she said dryly and rolled her eyes, though she was extremely entertained by the story of how Miles had managed to pull off surprising her with the proposal, with so many people knowing.

"I don't think Melissa knows. And the press of course." Miles sniggered and she lightly swatted his bicep.

"You are hilarious," she said shooting him a hard stare and he cupped her jaw.

"And charming and totally in love with you," he said, leaning down to give her a deep kiss that left her breathless.

"Stop distracting me and tell me how my mother knows."

Miles gave her a husky laugh and reached for the champagne bottle to top up their glasses. "Well, when I confessed to Celeste and I told her Alistair knew, she said that your mother would definitely know then and probably Margot too."

"She's probably right. Alistair is good at keeping things a secret but he would've told Mama, either to prepare her or because he knew she'd want to hear the good news. In this case it's the latter."

"Phew," Miles dramatically wiped his brow, causing Louisa to laugh. "I didn't want to have to deal with Lady Alice's temper."

"She'll insist you call her Mama now."

"Really?"

"Oh yes, Gerard used to call her *Maman*, the French version."

Miles nodded, then swallowed a large gulp of champagne at the mention of her ex-husband. "Speaking of Gerard…" He made a cringy face and Louisa's eyes widened.

"Do not tell me he knows too?" she said in disbelief.

"Yeah, he kind of does," Miles said carefully.

"My ex got to know before me?" she deadpanned.

"Look baby, it just slipped out."

"Slipped out? How the hell does that huge boulder of information slip out?" Louisa said incredulously.

"It was the day we did the fake photoshoot. I told him you were going to be my wife soon and he'd better get used to it and me," Miles said in a rush.

"Crap, well now a few things make more sense." Louisa drained her glass and pointed to her glass, wanting a refill. Miles wasted no time and filled up the flute. "No wonder he looked like thunder when you came back. Well, the flight back's going to be awkward." Louisa shook her head.

"Maybe we shouldn't say anything. After all, he's helping us out of a jam," Miles conceded. Though he would have loved to gloat, it didn't seem gentlemanly behaviour.

"Yes, I'll take my ring off," Louisa said with a sigh, looking down at it. "We can tell everyone… officially, not that there's anyone who doesn't seem to already know…" she said with a stifled smirk. "When we're at Holmwood. He's staying in the city and just coming to the concert."

"Absolutely," Miles said with a nod. If Celeste saw the ring, she was bound to blab and if Gerard saw it, he might not hold back. Miles took a sip from his flute, then put it down. "I'm kind of glad we'll have four security with us… at least they'll split us up if we end up fighting," he said dryly.

"Miles!" Louisa spluttered.

"I'm kidding!" he said playfully, then with a smirk, he added quickly, "I'd be too fast for him and knock him out with one punch. Hugh and the guys wouldn't have a chance to save him."

"You are so bad." Louisa poked his chest with her finger and Miles grabbed it.

"I know, I'm lucky you like bad, my lady," he said slowly kissing the back of her hand and giving her a sexy smouldering look.

"That and your super dick," Louisa said with a giggle and Miles let out a loud laugh.

"You'd better believe it."

THE SUN WAS LOW in the hazy sky as the jet landed at JFK's private terminal. Louisa waited in her seat with Miles while Hugh and Karl went to ensure there were no spectators and their limo was waiting to drive them to where Gerard's Boeing 737 was waiting. She slipped off her ring, leaving it on until the very last moment, and placed it carefully in an inside pocket of her bag.

"I'm putting it on the minute we get to London," she said quietly and Miles took her hand and kissed her ring finger.

"I was already getting used to seeing it there," Miles said with a wide smile.

"Me too." Louisa's eyes shot up to where Hugh had just stepped back into the cabin.

"All clear. But wear your sunglasses and keep the cap as low as you can," Hugh said to Louisa as she slipped her bag over her shoulder. She gave him a nod. "We'll go first and once Lady Blackthorn is in the car, then come out." Hugh directed his instructions to Miles. This was just a precaution. If anyone was waiting they'd see Louisa first and not know who she was, especially dressed in jeans, sneakers, a T-shirt and her face practically obscured. Once Miles came out, if they recognised him they would just get a shot of him and anyone who followed him out. In this case Kurt, Pierce would be in front.

"Sure. Here." Miles placed the C for C baseball cap on her head and pulled down the peak, she then fixed her sunglasses on her face. "There. No one will even guess," he said with his signature megawatt smile and Louisa grinned up at him, even though her stomach felt like it had a boulder lodged in it.

"See you in the limo," she sing-songed, trying to make light of the ridiculous situation they'd been put in. Miles watched her disappear through the small doorway and took a deep breath.

"You think we'll pull this off?" he asked Pierce.

"This bit's the easy bit. It's getting her in the other plane." The only sure way to secure total anonymity is if no one latched on to the fact Miles was at JFK. If he was spotted, then the paparazzi would be scouring for a glimpse of who was with him. They hoped that the change of plan and the speed in which they'd left LA would be enough to put anyone off the scent. Pierce nodded suddenly, meaning he had the go-ahead for Miles to leave the plane. "It's time. Keep your head down."

Miles quickly thanked the pilot and the stewards and headed out into the sunlight, shades firmly in place and a baseball cap covering his distinct dirty blond hair. The three men jogged quickly down the steps and jumped into the waiting car. Within seconds, it was driving to the other side of the terminal where Gerard's plane was waiting.

"Are you okay?" Miles asked a tense-looking Louisa. She nodded and gave a tight smile. "Okay, once the car stops, you need to get out as soon as possible and up the steps."

"I know."

"Don't look left or right. Hugh will be behind you and Karl up front." Miles looked out of the blackened windows, scouring the area as the limo began to slow down, searching for anyone or anything suspicious. Thankfully, where the plane was waiting was an area set away from buildings, minimising the risk of not only professional photographers but amateurs with a decent phone camera. They'd gone over the plan a few times and they all knew what to do, but Miles felt the need to repeat it. This was a new experience for Louisa. She'd never had to skulk or hide in her life, unlike him. Whenever she'd walked anywhere, it was with confidence and her head held high. Miles, on the other hand, had spent a lot of his time hiding and knew now how best to not draw attention to himself. He'd had his misconduct plastered over the Internet for years and made rookie mistakes in the beginning. Then later, he'd rebelled; his addiction fuelling his devil-may-care attitude. He'd been lucky that he had a team around him to minimize his exposure. Miles dreaded to think of how many situations he'd been in that had never been reported, all thanks to his security. His re-entry into the limelight now meant he had to be constantly alert, even more so because he had Louisa to think about.

The limo had just come to a stop, literally at the bottom of the stairs to the plane, and Miles was never more thankful for Hugh's attention to detail and thorough planning. Within an instant the door flung open.

"Okay, go," Miles said sharply and Louisa wasted no time, jumping out and speedily following Karl up the steps, her head down focused on the back of Karl's legs. It took all of ten seconds for them to complete the 20-odd steps, but to Miles it felt like an age. He kept his eyes fixed on Louisa until she cleared the doorway, then he looked back to Pierce. "We good?" He asked and Pierce gave a nod. Miles shot out of the car and raced up the steps, not waiting a second more. Once he was in the aircraft, he stopped and took in a deep breath. A steward was waiting to greet him. In his rush, to get into the plane, he almost didn't notice her.

"Good evening, Mr Keane," she said with a beaming smile.

"Good evening."

"Please, come this way." She signalled with her hand to follow her through what looked like a cloakroom area. Miles took off his cap and sunglasses and ran his fingers through his hair, affording him a moment to calm his pounding heart. A few seconds later, Pierce appeared beside him.

"You practising for the sprint in the Olympics?" he said with a smirk and Miles let out a laugh. If Pierce was making jokes, it meant they'd managed to escape any paparazzi attention.

"We good, then?"

"Yep, Kurt's just putting in the luggage and talking with customs. The officers will be in to check our passports in a minute."

"Thank you," Miles said in relief to Pierce and he gave him a nod. Miles turned his attention back to the steward, who led him to a plush lounge area.

Miles had flown in private planes throughout his career. He was used to luxury. Now he wasn't so drawn to it. He'd shied away from too much frivolous spending but he had to admit Gerard's airplane was next level. The lounge chairs and settees were upholstered in soft cream leather. There were rich wooden low tables and a bar area. Deeper in the cabin was a dining table. Beyond that was a closed-off section, where Miles presumed he had a bedroom and bathroom. His eyes focused on Louisa, who had removed her cap and glasses and looked so much younger dressed in jeans, sneakers and a T-shirt. She was standing next to Gerard and Celeste and for a split-second, Miles felt as though he was intruding on a family trip, until Louisa smiled widely and stepped up to Miles, slipping her arm around his waist.

"All okay?" she asked, searching his face for the answer.

"Yeah, it looks like we have managed to escape from New York undetected."

"Thank God." Relief washed over her beautiful face.

"Let me go and thank Gerard," Miles said quietly. Louisa nodded and followed him to where Gerard was sitting nursing a glass of red wine.

"Thank you, Gerard. This is very generous of you. We really appreciate your help." Miles held out his hand and Gerard stared at it, a little stunned. He stood up immediately, feeling a little uncomfortable with Miles towering over him.

"No thanks needed. I'm glad I could help. Please, make yourselves comfortable," he said, a little thrown by Miles's calm and genuine manner. "Dinner will be served once we're in the air."

Miles thanked him again, then turned to greet Celeste and Nicolas. Within 15 minutes, the plane was already taxiing down the runway heading for London. Both Louisa and Miles had never been so thankful that they had dodged yet another bullet.

Louisa leaned her head back against the headrest and looked out of the window, lost in her thoughts. It was almost dark and the plane had lowered its interior lights for take-off. Miles took her hand and played with her empty ring finger absentmindedly, and caught sight of Celeste watching him. She gave him a questioning look and he furrowed his brow for a second until she lifted her left hand and discreetly wiggled the ring finger. Miles chuckled, then nodded. Celeste's eyes widened in excitement. Miles immediately pressed his forefinger to his lips, signalling her to be quiet darting his eyes to where Gerard was sitting reading through what looked like a thick contract, his reading glasses perched on his nose.

Celeste gave a silent 'Ah', understanding why they hadn't said anything and nodded, then made an excited face and Miles chuckled softly. He just hoped she could keep the news to herself, or at least until touchdown.

"ON A SCALE OF one to ten, how awkward is this for you?" Celeste whispered to Miles and he considered her question for a moment. After a relatively amicable dinner, worthy of a five-star restaurant, Gerard had excused himself to the sectioned-off area, where he was working. Apparently, there was also an office too and he'd moved there with one of his assistants, who were also on the flight. Miles wondered if he'd used it as an excuse to be as far away from him as possible.

"You mean being in a confined space with your dad or that I accepted the lift to London from your dad?" He arched his brow at the tenacious Celeste and took a sip from his iced drink. Gerard had the bar stocked with what seemed to be every drink his guest favoured, including him.

"Ooh, I never thought of the last one. That's gotta sting a bit," she said, stifling a smirk, then added, "Both."

"Honestly, I thought it would be really bad but I'm good," Miles said honestly. It could've been awkward but with Celeste and Nicolas on board, along with the security and Gerard's two members of staff who were travelling with him, there were enough people around as buffers. Plus, it was late: Louisa, Nicolas and the security team were sleeping on the converted settees and chairs. Gerard had insisted that Louisa use the bedroom but she'd declined, so he had left his guests to rest in the main cabin and gone through the slim wooden door. That had been over an hour ago and Miles was still wired.

"That's because you know you've bagged the countess," Celeste giggled.

"Jesus, Celeste, how are you even a countess?"

"I can turn on the countess charm when I need to," she said in a mock-haughty tone and Miles clinked his glass to her teacup, chuckling. His gaze drifted to where Louisa was sleeping. She was exhausted after her busy schedule and the stress of leaving the US undetected.

"We should get some sleep too; we've a long few days in front of us," Miles said, draining his drink, hoping it would induce sleep, though he doubted he would, after the rush to get on the plane and the tension on board.

"How do you feel?" Celeste's question had him turning back to her. The softness of her tone was clarification that she was referring to the concert.

"I kind of put the concert out of my mind over the last few days, what with the interview, the proposal and then the media bullshit. Now that it's hours away..." He tilted his head to the left and then the right and said, "I'm a 50-50 mix of excitement and dread."

"It's a huge accomplishment. You and Konran have really made a massive difference," Celeste said sincerely, hoping it would ease any worries he might have.

"That helps with the dread," Miles said softly, appreciating her thoughtfulness. She was so much like her mother, it was uncanny sometimes.

"I'm off to have a sleep, I'm so tired. Nicolas can sleep standing up, I'm so jealous of him. I need my familiar surroundings," Celeste huffed and dragged herself up from the chair.

"Makes sense," Miles said with a smirk and Celeste's brows drew together in confusion. "Because you're a countess. We normal folk can sleep on concrete if we need to," Miles deadpanned and she mock-scowled at him.

"Anyone tell you you're hilarious?" she said and Miles chuckled.

"Funnily enough, yes. Your mother."

14

HOMEWARD TO HOLMWOOD

Louisa smiled as she looked down at her ring, which twinkled back at her. She'd slipped it on as soon as she'd taken her seat in their car. After thanking and bidding farewell to Gerard, they were all whisked away in waiting cars. LA was a distant dream and the only evidence that it had really happened was the 2-carat diamond ring that was now nestled on her ring finger.

"How are we going to break it to them?" Miles said, lacing her hand in his. Holmwood House had just come into view and they hadn't really discussed how they'd officially tell the rest of the family.

"We can tell everyone as we see them. They have an idea, so it won't be a huge surprise," Louisa said with a smirk. With the concert hours away, everyone would be distracted. They'd be able to celebrate afterwards. She didn't need a fuss; she was just happy they would finally become public.

There were reporters loitering just outside the gates and Louisa was thankful for the car's blacked-out windows. Holmwood had been closed to the public since Thursday afternoon, so no one was able to catch a glimpse of who was on the grounds or the preparations for the concert. Security was on high alert for the sake of both the artists who would be performing, and the Holmwood House residents.

The cars pulled up into the private entrance around the back of the house and everyone climbed out of the cars, glad to finally be home. Celeste and Nicolas quickly made it into the house, leaving Louisa and Miles behind. She'd called over her shoulder to them saying that she was excited to see Konran, who'd arrived late last night after his last tour date. Miles went to help with his bags but found Hugh already speaking to the security, who were already organising the various suitcases. Hugh turned his attention to Louisa.

"Excuse me, madame, but do you think I could have a quick word with you and Mr Keane in the conservatory, before you go to your suite?"

"Is everything alright, Hugh?" Miles asked, a little worried at his uneasy tone. The usually unflustered head of security was finding it hard to make eye contact.

"Yes, it's just a security matter I need to run by you both."

"In the conservatory?" Louisa said, frowning. She knew that for Hugh to be asking her, it must be important.

"Yes, that's where the issue is," he answered and before they could press him for more details, Hugh started to pace into the grand hallway and towards the conservatory with unusual speed, leaving Miles and Louisa trying to catch up behind him. Hugh disappeared through the large wooden door and the couple followed. Before they'd even cleared the threshold, they were met with a loud cheer.

"Congratulations!" The room full of people cried out to Miles and Louisa's surprise. They stood dumbfounded, taking in the room that had been decorated in flowers and balloons. Champagne glasses were waiting to be filled and a buffet had been set up for the surprise party. The Holmwood staff popped open the champagne and everyone cheered again. Louisa clapped her hand over her mouth, seeing Lady Alice, Margot, Alistair, Amanda, Melissa and Robert. Konran and his band were standing with Celeste and Nicolas, who had obviously known about the party. There were all the staff from CASPO and Holmwood, and at the rear, whistling loudly, Alistair's friends all stood.

"Security issue, eh?" Miles cast a sideways look to Hugh, who had a smug look on his angular face.

"It was the best I could come up with."

Grace and Louis ran to their uncle, their mother unable to contain them for much longer, and hugged him excitedly.

"Can I be a bridesmaid?" Grace asked, her wide eyes darting between the stunned couple.

"And me too. I want to be a bridesmaid!" chirped Louis and Louisa laughed lightly.

"You can't be a bridesmaid, silly. You'll be a page boy," Grace said deliberately. They'd obviously had this conversation before.

Miles laughed lifting up Louis. "Yes, of course," he said without hesitation. Both children beamed, then swivelled round to find Amanda and Alistair just behind them.

"He said yes," Louis said excitedly.

"Congratulations," Amanda said smiling widely. "It's been a real worry for them, since we told them." She smirked and Louisa chuckled.

"Well, of course they were worried, it's an important role." She bent down and gave Grace a smile. "I'm so happy you want to be my bridesmaid."

"Thank you. Me too," Grace said, suddenly feeling shy.

"Congratulations," Alistair said, thrusting out his hand for Miles to shake. "I see the proposal went without a hitch."

"Thanks, and yeah it did." Miles let his gaze drift over to his fiancée.

Alistair then pulled his sister into a tight hug, holding her close for a few seconds before letting her go. "Congratulations Lou-lou. I'm so happy for you," he said, his voice a little gruff with emotion. Lady Alice was next up to congratulate the couple. Amanda pulled Louis and Grace away from the bewildered couple, giving them some space.

"I always knew you'd come up trumps," Lady Alice said, taking Miles's hand in hers. "Congratulations and welcome to the family."

Miles gave her a small bow of acknowledgement and then accepted a kiss to his cheek. "Thank you. I have to say I'm a little overwhelmed."

"Well, we couldn't let such an important event go without being celebrated. We were lucky everyone was here already."

"How did you know?" Louisa asked after her mother had hugged her.

"Miles's parents called Amanda. Once she knew, she told Alistair and so we decided to do a small party."

"Small party?" Louisa said with a laugh, looking at the crowd of people eager to congratulate them.

"Well, it snowballed. It was just going to be family but then… well we couldn't not ask everyone that was already here," Lady Alice said, as though it was obvious. "So, we decided on a lunchtime engagement party. A little more casual than we're used to, but I rather think I'm getting to like casual events," she said, giving Miles a knowing look, and he blasted her with his bright smile, making the usually unflappable Lady Blackthorn blush slightly.

For the next 15 minutes, Louisa and Miles went around, receiving heartfelt and excited congratulations. The champagne flowed and the couple didn't have time to feel the effects of their jet lag.

After the initial excitement died down, everyone sat at their tables, giving the couple a breather. Louisa took a moment to look around the conservatory and shook her head in disbelief.

"Are you alright?" asked Melissa, who she was sitting next to.

"I should be asking you that. You're about to pop."

"Pop is exactly how I feel." She grimaced and rubbed her huge belly.

"I take it you also knew about the proposal." Louisa shot Miles a look but he shook his head, indicating he hadn't told her dearest friend.

"Margot told me."

"So, basically everyone knew about it before me." Louisa chuckled.

"Worst kept secret, ever," Miles muttered and they laughed.

"Shouldn't we be doing something more productive?" Louisa said with a frown. She was enjoying the party but they were hosting a concert tomorrow and everyone who was involved was in the room with them.

"Alistair, Amanda and everyone have been getting everything ready early so that we could have these few hours to celebrate. And to be fair, they all needed a break. It's been full-on."

"I hope you haven't been doing anything."

"Don't worry, Robert has turned into a rottweiler and won't let me do anything. Thank you for letting me stay here," Melissa said with a relieved sigh.

"Of course you should stay here. In fact, one more hour and we're taking you back to your room for a rest," Louisa said firmly and Melissa blew out a breath. "I need a debrief and then after you've rested, I'll come and we can have afternoon tea." The promise of time with her best friend perked Melissa up.

"You can tell me all about your few days away," she said with a widening of her eyes.

MILES'S HEAD WAS SWIMMING. He wasn't sure if it was the jet lag, the excited chatter he'd listened to at their surprise party or the hour-long meeting he was now having with Hugh and the security team. He had to hand it to Hugh, even while he'd been away with them in the US, he'd still ensured all security protocols were in place. Along with the extra security he'd commissioned, there were special security codes for access into Holmwood House that would be in place on the day of the concert. These would only be for family, Holmwood and CASPO staff and the few friends staying. They could also be changed at any time, if there was any security risk. The key Blackthorn family members would have a tracker and panic button on their person at all times, as well as a member of the security. Miles would also have Pierce throughout the whole day.

As the meeting progressed, the balance of feeling an excited rush of the concert ahead shifted to dread. When Miles had performed in the past, he'd never needed to know what security measures were necessary to ensure there was minimum risk. He and the band members were guided backstage then, after their performance, corralled back out again and straight to an afterparty or luxury hotel suite. All the arrangements were executed and he'd been blissfully unaware of the logistics. Things were different now; he was an independent celebrity, with close ties to the aristocracy. The risks were not only some crazed groupie or photographer trying to get that moneymaking shot any more – now there was a whole new set of threats that extended past him. They could get to him in order to get to Louisa, and there were kidnapping threats as well as political ones. What had set out to be a concert to help struggling single-parent families had ended up being the chief of security's nightmare and for that matter, his. This was what put a dampener on performing and was one of the reasons why Miles had avoided it for so long, the constant threats when being out there in the public eye. After the shooting, it became clear to him that it didn't matter how much security you had and what measures you took, once you were out there, on a stage, you were a target, a sitting duck. It only took one bullet.

Miles's heart rate started to rise and his eyes drifted around the room, shutting out Hugh's voice. He took in everyone who was listening to Hugh, standing at the front. Celeste had a blank look on her face, as though she'd heard it all before. Alistair and Louisa were both intensely focused, while Amanda looked worried. This had to be hard on her too, thought Miles. Hugh was talking about keeping everyone safe and the importance of vigilance, and Amanda must've been thinking about how, in Louis's case, it hadn't mattered. It was a mentally disturbed, failed graduate who'd pulled the trigger and killed Louis and eight other innocent people that fated day. The audience was small and made up of students, their families and university staff. A minimum risk venue having a maximum impact.

As Hugh wrapped up the meeting, Miles shifted his gaze to where Konran was sitting and saw that he was looking straight at him. 'You good?' he mouthed and Miles gave him a shrug because he wasn't good at all. Konran gave him a nod and made his way over to him.

"We need to do some sound checks and rehearsals." Konran said. "We can spend the next few hours going over our intros, or are you too tired, do you need some time and we can catch up later?"

"No, I'm not too tired. Sounds good," Miles said, trying to sound enthusiastic.

"We will," Konran said, then added, "sound good, I mean." He punctuated his play on words with a wide toothy smile and Miles grinned back at him. He was a thoughtful kid, thought Miles, thankful that they'd become friends over the last few weeks. Konran furrowed his brow and then added quietly. "Don't worry about all this." His hand waved vaguely in the air. "Let's focus on how much money we're going to raise."

Miles gave him a nod. "Let me just tell Louisa where I'll be. I think she's going to be spending some time with Melissa."

"Sure man, meet you in the orangery. We've set up our kit there."

"The orangery?" Miles let out a chuckle. He remembered when he'd researched Holmwood house and wondered what the hell an orangery was. He was pretty sure all the Blackthorn ancestors were turning in their graves knowing the majestic 300-year-old building that was meant to grow citrus fruits was now being used for a jam session by a rap star and rehearsal area.

"Yeah, you know where that is?" Konran, asked unsure as to why Miles was so amused.

"Oh, I know where it is. I'll see you there."

Fifteen minutes later, the golf cart Miles had used made a crunching sound on the surrounding gravel. The open windows let the melodic tune float out into the warm afternoon air and Miles smiled to himself, hearing Konran's distinct voice. He took a moment to listen to the now-familiar words, then hopped down from the cart before lifting out his trumpet case. He looked up at the vast building that was set to the southwest of the grand house, then stepped through the heavy glass doors of the majestic orangery. He was greeted by the sight of Konran playing on the keyboards. Margi, Ty and Roy were positioned around him, playing their instruments. Konran stopped immediately.

"Don't stop for me."

"I ain't playing anymore, man, not without you singing those beautiful words," Konran said from his seat.

"Well, let's see if we can make it work," Miles said to the four of them.

"We ain't sleeping until it's perfect." Ty's deep rumble of a voice came from the back where he was seated.

"Thanks guys."

"You're shittin' me, right? It's us that should be thanking you," Roy said with a huge grin and Miles felt a little more at ease.

"That's some trumpet you got there." Margi squinted at the slightly battered case, seeing the label, and Miles nodded, laying it onto one of the side tables and opening it up. Ty let out a low whistle when he saw the contents.

"Yeah, it's very special. It was a gift."

"Does it sound as good as it looks?" Ty asked.

"Absolutely," Miles said, pulling it out of the foam casing.

"Then let's hear whatcha got, man."

LOUISA STIFLED A YAWN and Melissa soon followed. "Stop it. You're making me yawn too."

"Don't let me sleep. I need to last until at least nine o'clock, otherwise my whole clock will be out of sync for tomorrow." They'd had their afternoon tea and were now sitting in the room next door to Louisa's, which she had arranged for Melissa and Robert to stay in. Darcy had just left and they were waiting for Lady Alice and Margot to come for a pre-dinner drink. Louisa had taken any meetings she had while keeping company with Melissa, which meant Melissa felt part of the organising but was still resting, all under Louisa's watchful eye.

"You didn't have to stay here all afternoon. I don't need babysitting." Melissa shot her a look.

"I'm not babysitting. I'm keeping you company and you're supposed to be making sure I don't fall asleep."

"You've always been terrible at adjusting," Melissa muttered. "Remember that Christmas you came over from New York and you slept through? You had to make a mad dash to put Celeste's presents from Santa under the tree as she woke up."

"Oh God, don't remind me. That Christmas was a blur but luckily Celeste didn't notice."

"A couple more hours and you can trot off next door to your fiancé. Where's he been all this time, anyway? I thought you two were inseparable," her friend said with a smirk.

"Rehearsing their intros with Konran and doing sound checks. He's going over the stage with the production people. Giving Alistair a break."

"Oh, I see. He has been working flat out while you've been away. Speaking of Alistair, he seems to be very cosy with Amanda."

"I know. I'm kind of excited about it but I don't know how far things have gone. Do you?" Louisa said suddenly perking up.

"All I know is that on Friday they had breakfast in his apartment."

"What! You mean she stayed overnight?" Louisa's jaw dropped open.

"No! They had a date?"

"A date?"

"Yes, an early date to watch Miles on Jimmy Kimmel. Alistair set up the live stream in his apartment and he made breakfast for her," Melissa explained.

"He made breakfast?" Louisa said in disbelief. She couldn't remember the last time Alistair had used his kitchen.

"Yep, that's what Robert said. Amanda wanted to see the interview so Alistair offered to set it up for her and make her breakfast... a deux. No staff, no family, just the two of them," Melissa said with a knowing look that left no room for any misunderstanding. Louisa made an excited face and was about to ask at least another 20 questions when there was a knock at the door.

"Come in," called Melissa, and Lady Alice, accompanied by Margot and a Holmwood staff member, walked through the threshold into the room.

"I hope you're not overdoing it," Margot said, seeing the two of them surrounded by laptops and scattered notes.

Louisa assured her godmother they were not and quickly collected everything, piling them on the antique console, next to the tray of drinks the Holmwood staff member had left for them. Louisa then passed around their various drinks as her mother and Margot took their seats around the now-cleared coffee table. They toasted Louisa's engagement again with their gin and tonics and Melissa took a sip of her plain tonic, sighing.

"I miss day drinking," Melissa said wistfully and Lady Alice chuckled.

"Get used to it. You'll be off the booze for a while. But it'll be worth it."

"It will, another couple of weeks and I'll get to meet the little so and so that keeps pressing on my bladder," Melissa said with a huge smile.

"Where's that lovely fiancé of yours?" asked Margot.

"Checking over the stage and rehearsing with Konran. I think he feels guilty for leaving Alistair to deal with it all," Louisa said.

"He has nothing to feel guilty about. Alistair loves the thrill and pressure of getting something organised. It's been a very long time to see him so focused and driven. This concert is the best thing that's happened to him in a long time," Lady Alice said.

"That and a rather lovely lady too, I think," Melissa said dryly.

"Yes, I think Amanda has certainly had quite an effect on him. It seems I have a lot to thank the Keane family for." Lady Alice gave Louisa a soft smile and she grinned back at her.

"I really hope they get together."

"Me too."

MILES QUIETLY CLOSED THE door behind him and flicked

the lock. He could hear the water running from the shower and he smiled to himself. *She was still awake.* It was well past ten o'clock and he had been sure Louisa would have fallen asleep by the time he'd made it back to their room. Though he knew how determined Louisa seemed to be when it came to beating jet lag. Konran and his band were true to their word. They hadn't stopped until Miles felt that everything was perfect, which inevitably meant they'd worked later than expected. It was good to have their positive energy around him. They had fuelled him, given him that boost he'd needed and had almost made the thoughts of any security threat and his anxiety fall away.

Miles stifled a yawn; the long flight and excitement of the day had caught up with him. His footsteps quickly ate up the distance to the bathroom, eager to spend as much time with Louisa as he could, before they both inevitably crashed. He leaned against the doorframe, taking in the beautiful sight of Louisa through the steam, rinsing out the last of the shampoo from her chestnut hair. His fiancée. Fiancée; he'd heard that word a lot today. It made his chest swell and his heart beat that much harder. She was finally his. They'd made their pledge, he'd sealed the deal and once tomorrow was over, everyone would know. He wasn't going to wait long before they were married, but that discussion was for another day. He pushed himself away from the door and paced towards her.

"You're back." Louisa smiled at the sight of him approaching from under the cascading water. Miles was already stripping out of his clothes and leaving them unceremoniously on the bathroom floor.

"I'm back and you're beautiful," he said, stepping into the huge shower and enveloping her in his arms.

"Ah, shush. The bags under my eyes are as big as suitcases." She yawned against his chest and closed her eyes, relaxing against him. It felt so good to hold him. He chuckled and kissed the crown of her wet head as the warm water poured down over them, washing away the long day they'd had. "I could sleep right here. I don't want to move."

"Baby, you're exhausted. Let me quickly shower and let's get some sleep."

"Hmm."

"Here, just sit for a moment." Miles slowly guided her to the large bench and she slumped down on it. Louisa scowled for a moment, unhappy he'd let her go, then leant her head back against the tiles and closed her eyes.

"I didn't want to let you go," she said mulishly and Miles chuckled.

"Me neither, baby, but I need to wash off the 12-hour flight and the rest of the day. I'll be quick, I promise." He gave her a quick kiss on the lips and she smiled dreamily.

"Don't fall asleep," he mumbled and she nodded.

Miles made quick work of his shower and then pulled the warm towels off the rack. He gently pulled Louisa up and wrapped her in one, then slung the other around his hips. "Come on, sleepy head, let's get you into bed."

Miles helped to dry her off and Louisa rubbed her hair. "I can't be bothered to dry it, I'm so tired." She yawned and settled for a comb through.

"I know, baby. Leave it, come on, get into bed."

Louisa slipped on her sleep vest and panties and crawled into the cool sheets, struggling to keep her eyes open. Miles dried off in double quick time and joined her. He turned off the lights and pulled her close, relishing the feel of her body tangled with his.

"Big day tomorrow," Louisa mumbled into his chest.

"Yeah," Miles said with a sigh. *It was going to be a huge day in every way.*

"Thank you."

"What for?"

"For being here. For doing this. For loving me for me."

"It should be me saying thank you, baby. You said yes." *He'd landed the jackpot; didn't she know that? Didn't she know what a catch she was?*

"I did." She smiled dreamily.

"You're mine."

"I'm yours and you are mine."

"I've been yours from the second time I set eyes on you, baby."

"That's because the first time you set eyes on me, you were a dick," Louisa teased and Miles let out a husky laugh.

"True, but now you *like* my dick." He flexed his hips and Louisa giggled.

"Correction, I loooove your *super* dick."

Miles let out a laugh at her crude comment. "Why, Lady Blackthorn, you have a very dirty mouth." He feigned shock and Louisa let out another giggle.

"Very true."

"I love your dirty mouth," Miles said, squeezing her tightly.

"I love you," Louisa said earnestly and in the semi-darkness of their room, Louisa could see Miles's brilliant blue eyes blaze.

"I love you too, so very much." Miles brushed back the damp hair from her face and kissed her tenderly. When he pulled back, she sighed and her eyes closed. "Go to sleep, baby."

15

THE BIG DAY

The day of the concert.

H olmwood House has been a hive of activity over the last few days in preparation for the summer Concert for CASPO. TuKon and his band arrived late Friday night from the final date of their sell-out world tour.

CASPO posted a video clip of the preparations on their Instagram account (see link below). The Earl of Holmwood and war hero has been at the heart of preparations alongside Miles Keane and CASPO employees. Lady Louisa Blackthorn and her daughter Celeste have also been hands-on with the preparations. It is over 12 years since Holmwood House hosted a concert. CASPO spokesperson Miss Darcy Aldridge said, "Everyone is pulling together to make sure the concert is a success." Forecast for the weather shows a 30 percent chance of rain but that hasn't deterred the spectators. Many have been camped out overnight to ensure they get a good spot. Staff of Holmwood House came out in the early hours and distributed hot tea and coffee, water and fruit juice to the guests, including Lady Louisa and Lady Celeste.

"It was a surprise to see the two of them handing out tea this morning," said Daryl Coombes who had arrived late last night from north London. "They both thanked us all for us coming and supporting the concert and took time to ask us how far we'd come."

Lady Louisa Blackthorn took over as patron to CASPO in July this year. This concert is the first major event since she took over from her mother Lady Alice. The concert is set to bring in over £10 million, which will fund many single-parent families. The late Earl of Blackthorn set up the charity with his wife and hosted festivals on the grounds. Lady Louisa Blackthorn seems to be intent on carrying on the tradition now she is patron.

"EVERYTHING ALRIGHT, HUGH?"

"Yes, my lady," Hugh said with a raised brow.

"Are you sure? You look tense," Miles asked. They were having a quick breakfast in their suite before they went down to the drawing-room for the final briefing. Hugh had just arrived and was ready to go over a few points privately.

"Impromptu visits to the waiting guests aren't a favourite of Hugh's," Louisa said with a stifled smirk.

"Impromptu *anything* isn't a favourite of mine, my lady," Hugh said dryly and Miles chuckled, then passed him a cup of tea. When Louisa had decided to go out that morning, Hugh had almost had a coronary. But she wouldn't take no for an answer. There were roughly a hundred people who had camped out overnight. She thought it was only right that she went out with her staff to give them some refreshment as a thank you. There were also three security with her, she pointed out, and no one would be expecting her there either. As soon as Celeste had found out, she also decided to help along with Nicolas. The 30 minutes the two Lady Blackthorns were out amongst the guests felt like a lifetime to Hugh.

"Well, it went well," Miles said, giving Louisa a wink. He really did feel for Hugh sometimes. "Everything else okay?"

"On the whole, but it's a big event. VIPs and their security detail; it can be a little taxing," Hugh said with a hint of annoyance.

"Ah, the security of musicians. They are a breed of their own," Miles said with a chuckle because he knew exactly what Hugh was talking about. Most musicians had a whole entourage who felt they were guarding some crown prince or politician. They could be difficult and often didn't reflect the wishes of the musicians.

"Almost as bad as the security of the aristocracy," Louisa added dryly, high-fiving Miles.

Hugh chuckled. "Quite. I'll be glad when today is over and done with, that's for sure," he said, taking a sip of his tea.

"We have four more hours before curtain up," Louisa said, checking her watch.

"And then 12 hours of a security nightmare, eh Hugh?"

"Something like that." Hugh reached into his jacket pocket and pulled out a velvet pouch. He then opened it up and tipped its contents into his palm. "Here you are," Hugh said handing Louisa a beautiful gold pendant with the Blackthorn coat of arms engraved on a purple inlay.

Miles furrowed his brow, seeing Louisa's face grow sober. "It's a family heirloom," she explained. Miles remembered this being explained to Eric when he came to stay at Holmwood. "Every countess of Holmwood has one."

"With a tracker fitted and a panic button," Hugh added sharply.

"Oh, Jesus," Miles muttered.

"We're not taking any risks. If you'll excuse me," Hugh said standing up from the table. "I need to deliver the Earl's, Lady Alice's and Lady Celeste's."

"Thank you," Louisa said, and her trusted head of security gave her a nod and strode out of the room, leaving the couple to their troubled thoughts. "Shit just got real," Louisa said with a huff, then shook her head. "Help me put it on?" She handed the pendant to Miles and he gave her a tight smile.

"Of course." They both rose from their seats and Louisa turned around and lifted her hair out of the way so that Miles could secure the fastening. "Alistair has a pendant too?"

"No, he has a signet ring. Hugh fitted a tracker and panic button to that too," Louisa said carefully, seeing Miles's face pale. "I'm not going to worry about anything. Today is a big day for CASPO and nothing is going to put a dampener on that," Louisa said firmly.

"You're right," Miles said softly, though his heart wasn't in his instinctual reply. Just the thought that Louisa had to wear a piece of jewellery that could save her from a potential threat was enough to not only dampen his excitement, it was like an ice-cold bucket of water dumped over him.

Louisa spun around with determination flaring in her dark brown eyes. "I mean it, Miles. Today is *so* important. Important for many families. I'm not talking about a critical success; this has to be a success for them. This is what my parents worked so hard to achieve and I want to carry on that work. No threats, nut jobs or paparazzi are going to spoil this. Alistair, our staff here and CASPO, Konran, Melissa, Amanda and all the bands have worked too hard, given up too much." She grabbed his face with her two hands. "You have worked so hard and given up so much. Nothing is going to stop this." She gave him a hard kiss and pulled back.

"I can't argue with that," Miles said, again awed by how strong Louisa was. Much stronger than anyone thought she was and he loved her that much more for it.

"This is just a precaution." She lightly touched the beautiful pendant. "You know Hugh; he's a belt and braces kind of guy."

"That's why I like him," Miles said with a grin, because it was true. He was so grateful Hugh was the man Louisa's safety depended on. He would give his life for her without a second thought.

"Exactly. So, we're not going to get angsty about this."

"It goes perfectly with your T-shirt," Miles said, smoothing his hand over her shoulders and down her arms. She'd dressed casually, by her standards, in a soft purple and cream striped top, fitted cream capri trousers and had paired it with some matching wedges. She didn't have the heart to tell him that she'd purposely chosen the top to match the pendant.

"Oh God, that reminds me, I have to get out my evening outfit, for a quick change."

"Evening outfit?"

"Yes. Darcy and Melissa said that I had to wear something casual for the first six hours, then change into something a bit dressier for the final six." Louisa blew out a breath. "All part of being a countess, blah, blah." Louisa rolled her eyes and Miles chuckled.

"Well, you'd better get your ass in gear," he said, patting her bottom affectionately. "A few hundred million people will be watching."

"Oh crap, way to make me feel even more nervous!"

"Welcome to my world baby," he drawled.

HUGH HUNCHED OVER TO check through the monitors in the security office of Holmwood House. There was a bank of them showing various camera angles throughout the house but he had now added another 10 for the entrance to the concert, and 15 which gave him a clear view of backstage, the VIP area, the area where the band trailers were set up and the purposely erected corridor that led from the VIP area to Holmwood House. This was only to be used by the family, CASPO and Holmwood staff and the few select friends. It ensured privacy for when they moved back and forth from the house. In addition, there was a monitor showing the live feed being streamed over the Internet that would be managed by the production company in a makeshift office behind the stage. They had a number of drones recording throughout the day, documenting the event. It was a huge set-up and Hugh had access to all the feeds from the drones too. The more eyes he had the better. His 10-man security team, employed for this task, would be monitoring every screen until the concert ended and every spectator had left the grounds. No one was getting to the Blackthorns, not on his watch.

The house had been closed off from six o'clock the night before and could only be accessed with the specific security code, which Hugh had already changed this morning. No one new would be entering the house until after the concert was finished, except for Gerard and his assistant. They were due to arrive in the afternoon via helicopter – another inconvenience for Hugh to manage. Why Gerard couldn't ensure he arrived the night before or early in the morning he didn't know but it would've made his life that much easier if he had. He now had to ensure Gerard could get to the VIP area from the helipad, which had been cordoned off. Hugh was pretty sure Gerard just wanted to make a grand media entrance. The whole world was focusing on Lady Louisa and Miles and it obviously didn't sit well with him. This was his way of having a moment in the spotlight too.

Hugh asked one of his men to switch the camera feeds to the points of entry of the concert. There were tens of thousands of people slowly making their way onto the grounds. All of them had to pass through a metal detector, which was a slow process, but Hugh wasn't taking any chances. Louisa had been adamant that no expense was spared on security and he had gone all out. He was glad he still had close ties with the military; a lot of the equipment he'd used wasn't legally readily available but with the Blackthorn name, and his connections, he'd been able to equip his team with the most sophisticated security systems.

Hugh shifted to the live feed and watched the swarm of people spread like locusts across the carpet of lush green grass. He fleetingly thought of the inevitable damage the hordes of feet treading over it would do, not to mention the litter that would be left behind. He watched the production team and stage management organise instruments on the huge stage, which was partially covered. The enormous monitors set around the grounds were showing the live feed from the drones too. Throughout the concert they'd zoom in on the performers or show videos in the 10-minute intervals. He pressed the intercom and spoke into the microphone.

"Mac?"

"Yes, Hugh." The production manager's voice came through the speakers.

"Give me an aerial on D1." Hugh watched the first drone screen. The screen showed the spectator area as the drone swooped around at a great height. "Great, now D2." The second screen was of VIP area which only had staff members at the moment but Hugh could clearly see the refreshment tables, seating and private restrooms. "D3," he said curtly. The third screen showed the front of the house where the thousands of spectators were coming in. As soon as they caught sight of the drone, they all cheered and waved up at it. Hugh chuckled. "Okay, give me D4." The fourth screen zoomed in on the crowds already in. They all cheered and waved up at it as it swept around the arena area. "Excellent. Thanks, Mac."

"No problem, boss," Mac answered and Hugh straightened. He'd checked and rechecked the cameras, entrances, the house and had his team complete a full sweep of the grounds every hour from midnight last night to just before nine when the entrances opened. He let his eyes move from one screen to the next, watching the people excitedly come in. He had the best team, the latest security systems and over 15 years of military and security experience under his belt and yet even he knew there was that slight chance of something going wrong. Hugh let out a sigh and checked the time. It was 10:43. In just over 12 hours, this nightmare would be over.

The whole concert was timed precisely; 20-minute sets, a 10-minute break to set the stage with a minute intro included. They had 16 bands, which covered eight hours, plus the starting speech, the final speech and laser show, which would be another hour and an hour for inevitable delays throughout the day, if all went to plan the concert would be over by 11:00.

Hugh pulled out his phone and tapped onto the tracker app. His screen immediately showed him the plan of the house and the grounds with four flashing icons in different colours. Lady Alice was red and was still in her suite, Alistair's blue icon was backstage and Celeste was green and heading down the corridor towards Lady Louisa's suite where Hugh could see her purple icon.

"COME IN," Louisa called at the knock on her door.

Celeste breezed in dressed in white jeans, a white T-shirt, her pendant hidden beneath and her standard pink converse. "Alistair said the first band members are already here. It's so exciting!" Celeste gushed and Nicolas chuckled at her enthusiasm.

"Aren't you going to go and meet them?" Louisa asked.

"In a bit. I don't want to look like a groupie and be too eager."

Miles laughed. "They'll probably get a kick out of meeting *you*," he said and Celeste furrowed her brow, indicating she found that hard to believe.

"Are you going to keep your ring on?" Celeste asked, seeing it sparkle as Louisa reached for her jacket.

"Yes," Louisa said, putting out her hand in front of her to admire it again.

"Wow, well that will definitely have the gossip sites in a frenzy."

Louisa and Miles shot each other a look. "We're going to become public after the concert, so if they suspect it won't matter. And to be honest, I'm fed up of all the secrecy," Louisa said and Miles stifled a smile.

The truth was Louisa felt a little uncomfortable with all the female attention Miles had been receiving. They'd walked around backstage and spoken to backing singers, stylists and various members of the bands' entourage earlier in the morning. They had shamelessly flirted with him and hung on his every word, this was all before the various VIPs, socialites and models arrived – then it would be even worse. Louisa had never seen Miles in his environment before and she was appalled at their brazenness, hugging and touching him at every opportunity. He, on the other hand, had been as respectful and distant as he could but they didn't seem to take the hint.

"Right then, I will go and sit with Melissa for a while, then come out when we're ready to start. Hugh wants me away until necessary and to be fair it's going to be a long day." Louisa let out a breath.

"I'll go down. I'm going to be with Konran backstage. Do the meet and greet." Miles gave Louisa a soft kiss. "Keep your phone close, so I can speak to you," he added before turning to Celeste and Nicolas. "Come on let's go. I think Dua Lipa just arrived."

"Oh my God, I love her!" Celeste cried and bounced with excitement. "This day is going to be epic!"

MELISSA WAS SPRAWLED OVER one of the couches in her room watching the live stream on a huge screen the production company had set up for her. She was dressed, made up and ready to leave, even though she knew it would be later on in the day, but one thing Melissa was excellent at was being prepared. She sipped her tea and eyed the various streams from the split-screen. The queues outside Holmwood seemed to go for miles and she was glad the local police force had brought in other officers from the surrounding area to help control the crowds. The show was going to start in an hour and a half; she just hoped that everyone got in on time.

"It's crazy, isn't it?" Louisa's voice pulled her attention away from the screen.

Melissa hadn't even heard her come in, she was so engrossed. "Absolutely. I just hope they all get in on time, otherwise they'll riot."

"They will. I have every confidence in Hugh and his team."

Louisa slumped into the armchair next to Melissa and looked at the various feeds. She had a view of everything and Louisa chuckled. "This isn't relaxing."

"I'm supposed to have my feet up." Melissa swept her hand towards where her feet were elevated on four cushions. "And watching TV." She pointed to the screen.

"That's not exactly what was meant by TV," Louisa said dryly.

"Are you joking! This is the event of the year. I wouldn't dream of missing it. Even if I wasn't involved, I'd still be watching it," Melissa said pursing her lips.

"Fine, but don't get all stressed if you see something you're not happy with. We have a great team. They know what they're doing."

"I know. Oh look, there's Celeste and Miles," Melissa said excitedly and picked up the remote, clicked it and enlarged the screen that was showing them. Louisa's eyes shot to the screen and she grinned. They were walking around backstage and towards where the trailers were. It took them a few minutes to get through because after every step, someone would come up to Miles and shake his hand or talk to him. He then, like a true gentleman, introduced Celeste and Nicolas and then moved on.

Melissa gave her a running commentary of who everyone was: "Oh, that's French Montana's backing singer," "That's Lewis Capaldi's manager," "See her in the green dress? She's Alicia Keys's agent." Louisa furrowed her brow, seeing Miles talk freely with anyone and everyone who came up to him. He was a superstar and Louisa had forgotten what that meant. He was an electromagnet with a powerful pull that drew everyone to him. He'd walked backstage, where the musicians were gathered, one more famous than the next, yet they were all drawn to him. Konran had joined him, standing beside him now, and though everyone spoke to him too, it was clear that they were all in awe of being in the presence of *the* Miles Keane. It was an eye-opener having this fly-on-the-wall insight to the world Miles lived in. She'd never been with him to any event that wasn't related to her. This is what it was like for him. This was what it meant to be a celebrity, a megastar and it was nothing like the attention Louisa received when she was out in public. Yes, she was recognised and occasionally photographed, but when people approached her it was with respect and reverence and they never touched her. Miles on the other hand had people rush up to him, hug him, have selfies taken and kiss his cheek, and these were people used to celebrities. *What must it be like to be in the presence of fans?*

Pierce stood a few paces away from Miles, keeping a watchful eye the whole time and Louisa swallowed hard. No wonder he had been so edgy about performing. Why this whole event had been a huge deal for him. Like he'd said many times, it was open season, and he was the sitting duck. Louisa felt her stomach tighten. He'd done this for her, for her cause and she'd never even thought of the sacrifice he was making. She knew he was anxious about being on stage, about the possibility of a threat and she'd put his nervousness down to that, but seeing him walk across the trailer area, she could see that this was also a huge sacrifice. He'd been away from this life for five years, he'd matured and learned to rely on himself, without the crutches of his brother, band members and drugs. Louisa had gotten to know Miles well and one look at his slightly stiff stature and the constant raking of his hair, she knew this was more than just difficult for him.

"I'm going down," she said suddenly standing up.

"What?" Melissa said surprised at her friend's reaction.

"I'm going down." She pointed to the screen. "It's unfair that Miles has to do all that on his own. What kind of a partner am I if I can't be by his side?"

"He has Pierce with him and Konran," Melissa said, understanding Louisa's concern.

"It's not the same."

"I know but he'd be horrified to know you were putting yourself in danger, just to be with him."

"I'm not in danger backstage! I'll be with all the musicians and their security and I'll have Karl with me too. He's outside that door now." Louisa threw her hands in the air. "Besides, I'll have to be there in an hour anyway, what can it hurt?"

"Hugh will be livid," Melissa said with a grimace.

"I'll let him know. He's got me tracked anyway." Louisa pointed to her pendant.

"Call him anyway. I'll feel better if he knows before you leave," Melissa pleaded and Louisa nodded.

"Fine."

THE VIP SECTION HAD filled up and Louisa could see the many family friends, business associates, socialites, donators, members of the aristocracy and tens of beautiful people she recognised but had no clue who they were. All she knew was they'd paid an enormous amount of money for the privilege of being so close to the performers. If Melissa had been here, she'd be whispering all their names and any juicy titbits she knew about them but unfortunately Melissa wouldn't come down until Konran came on stage. It had been arranged that she'd be brought down in a wheelchair and not allowed to stand at any time. They'd even sectioned off an area for her – to her total dismay, but Robert had put his foot down: if she wanted to see Konran on stage, this was the only way.

There were seats provided in the VIP area that everyone seemed to be ignoring, preferring to strut around and enjoy mingling. Louisa eyed the chairs and wondering if anyone would mind if she sat down. She'd been in the area for 20 minutes and, up until then, by Miles's side. He'd made a huge fuss of her when she'd arrived to his surprise, and caught sight of Hugh's steely expression and twitching jaw. This was not his idea and Miles once again felt for Hugh having to navigate Louisa's whims. Karl shadowed her the whole time and though Louisa enjoyed being introduced to all the bands backstage, they really weren't that interested in her, other than the fact it was because of her they were there. Louisa watched and listened to Miles do what he was good at: he schmoozed and networked, talking to managers, PR people and anyone of influence about CASPO. He really was a pro when it came to people; he had everyone eating out of his hand and had promises of donations and future collaborations.

Among the performers backstage were Mick and Josh from Keane Sense. They'd come to support Miles and were thrilled to meet Louisa again. They both enjoyed embarrassing Miles by bringing up that fated backstage incident over 10 years ago and were equally pleased to meet the grown-up Celeste, who was totally blown away that they remembered her.

Amanda had spent most of the time backstage, totally at ease with everyone. This had been her life for a long time and she was greeted like a celebrity. Louis had been respected in the industry and because of that, automatically so had Amanda. Her easy manner made her a perfect presence amongst the musicians; she was unfazed by their celebrity and was comfortable with the Holmwood residence and staff. Louisa watched her talk and laugh freely, then turn and speak carefully to one of the staff, then return back to her conversation. At one point, before the musicians went to prepare, she'd pulled Alistair over to introduce him to a band member and left her hand on his arm, as though she was anchoring him. He hesitated but with a little coaxing, he started to feel more at home talking to the many celebrities that were genuinely in awe of him. Louisa took a sip of her water and smiled to herself, seeing him looking so handsome in a pair of dark blue trousers and a white polo shirt that perfectly set off his tan from being outdoors. Amanda was exactly what her brother needed. She'd lived in the wings of her late husband's stage and thrived there, learned how important her role was and happily played it. She'd never needed to be the centre of attention, she'd only ever needed her partner's attention and from what Miles said, Louis had lavished her with it. Alistair laughed at something and Amanda smiled widely at him and he instinctively rested his hand on the small of her back and gazed down at her. The stunning singer they were talking to, her face fell and she blinked at them, realising that they were together. Alistair and Amanda were oblivious and after a beat turned back to the singer, whose expression was back to normal. Louisa thought to herself: *there are going to be a few people shocked today.*

Louisa had left Miles backstage so he could go over a few last-minute details with Konran and headed to the VIP section, along with Celeste and Nicolas, which had now almost filled up. The steady supply of refreshments was keeping everyone occupied and though they were very close to the stage, they thankfully couldn't get backstage. Three security guarded the entrance and only certain people could pass, namely Holmwood House and CASPO staff, the Blackthorns and a few of Alistair's friends. Louisa and Celeste made a point of talking to everyone and thanking them for their support. They were both well practised in small talk but Louisa found it hard to concentrate; her thoughts kept drifting backstage. They were minutes from starting and she knew Miles would be anxious. She was thankful when the screens, that had been showing the drone footage, changed to show a countdown clock for five minutes. The audience cheered loudly and Karl signalled to Louisa it was time for her to go backstage too for her small welcome speech. She hadn't wanted to do one but Melissa and Darcy insisted, saying that it was important for all the paying public to see her.

Louisa stepped past the security guards and was immediately met by Miles.

"Everything alright?" she asked as casually as she could, seeing Miles's set jaw.

"As ready as we'll ever be," he said with a well-practised air of confidence.

"In the words of Celeste, it's going to be epic."

Miles let out a husky laugh. Hearing those uncharacteristic words coming out of Louisa's mouth went a way to easing his tension and once again he marvelled at her composure. She was seconds away from addressing thousands of people in the arena and millions watching around the world, yet she seemed calm.

Louisa's eye caught sight of Darcy and the production manager. It was time for her to get on stage.

"Well, looks like I'm up."

Miles swivelled around to see, then turned back to Louisa. "Break a leg baby." He leaned down and gave her an unhurried kiss, then pulled back. "I love you," he said softly, his eyes focused solely on her.

"I love you too, so much."

He blasted her with his patented smile, then gave her his signature wink and said, "Showtime, baby."

16

LIVE FROM HOLLYWOOD

"*en, nine…*"

"Just this way, Lady Blackthorn." Karl guided Louisa up the flight of metal steps that led up to the back and centre of the stage. Louisa's heart began to race with every step. She was comfortable with public speaking. Her many years in New York speaking at various charity events had been an excellent training ground for her future role but she hadn't expected to be addressing millions of people at her first major event.

"*Eight, seven…*"

Hugh watched every monitor like a hawk as the screen countdown and the crowd shouted out each number. His eyes darted left, right, up and down, every which way, determined not to miss a thing, but even he knew he was only human.

"*Six, five…*"

Miles kept his eyes firmly fixed on Louisa as she stood and waited in the wings for her introduction and direction. One of the production assistants gave her an earbud to fit so she could hear the director tell her when to start, prompting her if necessary. There was an autocue too but they weren't taking any chances. The tens of thousands of fans counted down along with the screen and with every second that ticked by, Miles's anxiety crept up along with it.

"*Four, three…*"

Melissa's eyes were fixed on the monitors seeing the huge stage, the thousands of spectators and the various artists waiting backstage. She spotted Miles standing on the left side awaiting his cue and Konran on the right. Louisa was just hidden behind a concealed entrance and seeing her standing with Karl by her side, had Melissa feeling both proud of her dear friend and terrified. She couldn't even imagine how she must be feeling and yet her expression was the epitome of calm. She was definitely a countess through and through, born for this role.

"*Two, one!*"

The roar of the crowd was deafening and the image of a rocket blasting into space filled the screens around the arena. Louisa shook her head and shot a look at Karl, who smirked back at her, realising how monumental today's concert was. Alistair stepped up next to her and gave her shoulders a squeeze as the deep rumble of Ty's voice came over the speakers.

"Welcome to the first Concert for CASPO. The concert of the year, here at Holmwood House!" The crowd roared again and Louisa's chest swelled with pride at having put together the concert in such a short space of time. It was an immense achievement and she was ever grateful to her staff and family for making it possible.

"You did it, Lou-lou," Alistair said, squeezing her hand and Louisa shook her head.

"*We* did it, Action-man. We *all* did it." She gave his hand a final squeeze and took in a deep breath. Alistair took in her profile and marvelled at her ability to be so composed. She was about to address millions of people and she hadn't even broken a sweat.

"Can you please be upstanding for Lady Louisa Blackthorn, the Countess of Holmwood and patron of CASPO!" Louisa stepped out onto a small raised platform to thunderous applause, the volume increasing with every step she took towards the front of the stage. She waved to the audience and they cried out even more. A lone elegant figure. Her light clothing stood out against the dark stage and backdrop and all the lights shone directly on her, illuminating her for all the world to see. She stepped up to the waiting microphone and after a moment, the audience quieten a little and she smiled widely.

"Hello CASPO supporters, welcome to Holmwood and thank you

for being part of this monumental day!" The screens showed both a close up of Louisa and the crowds cheering her. "Today, with all your help, we will raise over £10 million." The split-screens changed to a glittery £10 million image and then various images faded in and out of the projects CASPO had funded. The crowd continued to cheer and clap. "Money that will help hundreds of single-parent families, and on behalf of them, and everyone at CASPO, thank you. These families will have a home they've only ever hoped for, an education they deserve and opportunities that were once unattainable. Today is both a celebration of the 20 years of CASPO's work and of an even more successful future." The crowd called out and whistled in appreciation and the image of Louisa's smiling face was transported around the globe. "So, without further ado, let me introduce your hosts for the day." Louisa tried to continue but there were screams from the crowds so she took a pause, chuckling at their excitement. "Two gentlemen that have worked relentlessly to make this special day happen. Hugely successful musicians in their own right and all-round amazing people. Please welcome our CASPO ambassador Miles Keane and the undisputed number one rapper, TuKon!" Louisa said enthusiastically, raising her voice over the roar of the audience and signalling first to the left and then to the right. Louisa didn't need to see Miles and Konran step out, she could tell the second they came onto the stage. The volume level doubled and there were screams, whistles and air horns blasting as the crowd went wild. The three of them stood on stage and while the crowd applauded them, Miles and Konran gave two hand waves to the fans around the arena.

In the control room, Hugh scoured the screens along with his team. The tense atmosphere in the room was miles away from the excitement out in the arena.

Karl's jaw set tight as he swept his focus to the VIP area and the wings of the stage, scanning for anything or anyone who looked suspicious. Nine times out of ten, an assailant was known to the victim. He knew Hugh and his team were checking the crowds but Karl focused on the area closer to Louisa. Close enough to get a clear shot.

Pierce also watched from the left wing of the stage, scanning the crowds for any inkling of danger. He swept his hawk-eye focus over the faceless crowds, looking for anyone or anything that sent up a red flag.

"That was some welcome!" Konran said, once the noise level dropped a little.

"I'll say!" Miles chuckled and the crowd roared again. The screens were filled with the faces of the three of them. An image that no doubt would be captured and sent to every media outlet, documenting this iconic moment when Miles Keane was back on stage, with a member of the aristocracy, and the top rapper in the world.

"Let's hear it for Lady Blackthorn," called out Konran, giving Louisa her chance to leave. He took her hand and lifted it into the air and the crowd cheered. Then she shifted her gaze to Miles, who gave her a subtle nod and a wide smile and she stepped back towards the wings, leaving the two megastars on stage.

Louisa let out a relieved breath and pulled out her earbud, handing it back to the assistant.

Alistair stepped up to her and gave her a hug. "You were brilliant," he said sincerely, in awe at how cool she'd been when in reality her heart was hammering in her chest. She thanked him and then shifted her look over to the stage where Miles and Konran were now standing. "Don't worry about him, he's in good hands with Konran. Come on, let's get backstage and out of the way." Karl gave Alistair a thankful nod. He wanted Louisa away from the stage and somewhere he could keep a close eye on her.

"So, we have quite a lineup for y'all today," Konran said in his familiar drawl. The screen above the stage, and high up, faded in all the various artists who were performing. He'd dressed for the role of host in an eclectic purple suit and white T-shirt, along with his customary white sneakers – his flair for striking design was as famous as the songs he wrote and performed. Miles, in contrast, wore a beautifully tailored, sand-coloured suit that showcased his tan. The blue shirt he'd paired it with made his brilliant eyes shine like priceless sapphires.

"We do. A huge thanks to all the bands who've made it out here especially for today. Like my man here," Miles said, gesturing to Konran. "He just completing his sell-out world tour.129 shows!" Miles played to the audience, who were happy to drink it all up.

"You've been busy too. Weren't you in LA 36 hours ago?" Konran asked, playing his role to perfection. The crowd lapped up their double act. "And haven't you got a few major projects coming up, er... like a series, a film and a Broadway and West End musical?" Konran made a show of ticking them off on his fingers and the crowd laughed and cheered. Konran was a born showman, his easy and familiar manner made Miles relax a little and their rehearsed introduction switched to being playful banter between friends.

"Okay, that's enough about us," Miles said to the crowd.

"Yeah, today is about who's here."

"And who better than an artist who is a Grammy, Billboard and Emmy award winner?"

"She's sold 40 million albums worldwide," Konran added.

"And flown in especially today to get... this... party... started!" Miles said, shouting out over the crowd's ever-increasing calls.

"Please welcome Pink!" both Miles and Konran called out, then jogged to their side of the stage and into the wings.

The audience whistled, shouted out and roared, the level increasing when the music to Pink's hit *Get this Party Started*, began and she ran on stage as the pyrotechnics burst upwards, sending bright pink sparkles skyward from the front of the stage.

Once Miles had cleared the wings, his eyes searched for Louisa. His gaze found her waiting at the bottom of the metal stairs, with a fully alert Karl by her side. The few production staff clapped him on his back and congratulated him on his first outing as a host and he graciously thanked them but headed straight to where Louisa was waiting patiently.

"You were so incredibly good," she said with a wide smile and he leaned down and pressed his forehead against hers and held her close, oblivious to the various artists and staff around. Louisa didn't seem to care either as her hands found their way underneath his jacket.

"You were amazing too," he whispered, then dropped a quick kiss on her lips.

"Come on let's get out of everyone's way," she urged and took his hand, leading him to the area set aside for the hosts. Konran burst around the back of the stage and jogged up to them.

"You killed it, man," he said excitedly and pulled his friend and co-host into a man hug. "They loved you!"

"They love *us*. Thank you," Miles said with sincerity, he would never have been able to do it without him.

"I told you. This is a dream come true for me." Konran gave him a toothy grin and then caught sight of Celeste who was bouncing with excitement.

The next few minutes consisted of everyone finding their way to the hosts to congratulate them on their opening. They didn't have much time to relax as they posed for backstage photos, to document the occasion and to prepare for the next intro. The crowds sang along with Pink and Miles had a chance to take a look at some of the set in the security production office.

He spotted Hugh looking at the monitors intently and furrowed his brow. They had a huge set-up and as Miles scanned the monitors, he wondered how the hell Hugh could keep tabs on every one of them.

"All good?" Miles asked quietly.

"Yes, sir," Hugh answered without taking his eyes off the screens.

"Good." Miles turned to leave, not wanting to take any of Hugh's attention away from the screens.

"You did good out there."

Hugh's words caused Miles to stop in his tracks. He looked back over his shoulder to where Hugh was still focused on the screens. "Thanks, Hugh," he said with a smile and the corner of Hugh's mouth lifted.

"Sir."

MELISSA SIPPED HER TEA and wished it was the champagne that all the VIPs seemed be knocking back with gusto. She rubbed her swollen belly and sighed as she looked over the monitors. All the high society and VIPs were rocking out to the Arctic Monkeys' *Do I Wanna Know?*, the final song of their set. They were the fourth band to play and the concert was already a huge success. Social media was exploding with video clips recorded on audience phones and uploaded. The media were scrabbling to get the latest scoops on backstage gossip, scouring social media accounts of all the artists and VIP guests. Melissa flicked through all the hashtags on her phone, checking for anything that would tar the event and up until now, there was nothing but praise. She chuckled at a photo on George Ezra's Instagram account: he had his arm around Kendrick Lamar and had captioned it with, *"Riding Shotgun with All the Stars!"*, a play on words of their hits' songs, and a show of how humble he was. He wasn't riding shotgun with anyone; his performance was that of a superstar.

Melissa checked the time and saw that they were now 13 minutes behind schedule. Her estimate of the concert running an hour over schedule looked to be spot on, though she'd much rather they'd prove her wrong. They were a quarter into the concert and though delays were to be expected, Melissa was twitching in her seat. She was a stickler for keeping to schedules and contemplated calling the production manager to insist he tighten up the changeovers. The last thing they needed was the concert going on past midnight. She'd have the local authority on her case for overrunning the time on their permit. Before she could call, her phone vibrated in her hand and the name 'Louisa' popped up and she smiled. She'd been calling her after every artist to check up on her.

"Hey, I hope you weren't rocking out," Louisa said dryly.

"Not quite; they're good but not my cup of tea. I'm looking forward to Alicia next, though."

"Me too. She's so lovely and is staying until the end, so you'll get to meet her. Apparently, she's a huge fan of Konran's. I think she wants to do a collaboration," Louisa said excitedly.

"Listen to you, getting the latest news on the music scene – who would've thought it?" Melissa chuckled.

"Yeah, I have to say the music scene is rubbing off on me."

"I wonder why?"

'Oh, shush."

"Talking of Miles, he's really doing great." Melissa clicked the remote and focused on the backstage area where Louisa was sitting and talking on her phone to her. She loved that she was able to check out everywhere without leaving her comfy seat or even break a sweat.

"He is. With every intro, he's getting less nervous and more relaxed. Okay, I'll let you enjoy Alicia. I'll call you after she's finished," she said in a rush. Obviously, there was something that had caught her attention and before Melissa could say goodbye, Louisa had hung up. Melissa focused on the screen and saw Miles step up to Louisa and take her hand. Melissa smiled to herself as she saw Louisa's face light up. If the world didn't know they were together by now, just one photo of how they looked at each other would be enough to tip them off.

LOUISA KEPT HER EYES fixed on Miles as he waited for the screen to fade out the latest video of CASPO's work. Alicia Keys and her band were waiting in the area behind him and she leaned forward and said something to Miles. He smiled widely and Louisa read his lips say, "Thank you," to Alicia, then he stepped onto the stage, back into the limelight, to a roar from the crowd. Louisa's eyes shifted to the screen that had been set up backstage and saw Konran enter the stage from the right. She couldn't be sure if it was the endless rehearsals the two men had had, the fact that they were both professional or that they were just so incredibly good at performing, that made their timing and introductions look effortless. *Probably all three*, she thought as she watched them interact with the audience with a well-thought-out play on words about Alicia Keys's opening song, *It's on Again*, with Kendrick Lamar. The roar as they introduced them was as loud as when they themselves had entered the stage. Louisa's gaze shifted to where Miles was about to appear from the left wings. He stepped through and said a few words to the waiting band as they rushed onto stage and he jogged down the steps, closely followed by Pierce.

DARCY CHECKED HER WATCH and cringed. They were now running 25 minutes behind schedule. She was bracing herself for another call from Melissa. The Foo Fighters had overshot their slot and even though Lewis Capaldi had somehow managed to get on stage in half the time, his performance was going to use every one of his minutes. Darcy shifted her attention to the screen and smiled. She loved this song and for a second, she forgot her role and took a moment to enjoy the distinctive refrain of *Before You Go*. The thousands of spectators sang along with him and Darcy felt the goosebumps scatter over her arms. How lucky was she to have been involved with such an impressive event, among the amazing talent she was surrounded by, for such a worthy cause? Her phone vibrated in her hand and she chuckled to herself and answered it, knowing full well who it was.

"MELISSA!"

Melissa's gaze shot up to where Robert was almost glowering at his wife. Almost, because he didn't want to be the killjoy she made him feel he was. He'd come to check up on her, knowing full well she'd been badgering Darcy and the production manager.

"I was just chatting with Darcy," Melissa muttered, immediately putting down her phone without even saying goodbye.

Robert narrowed his eyes at her – *guilty as charged,* he thought. "I call bullshit," he said waving his finger at her. "You're supposed to be relaxing with your feet up and watching the concert. Not shooting orders and getting stressed about going over schedule." He paced over to her and arched a brow, daring her to deny it.

Busted! "Okay, I'll promise to stop," Melissa said as convincingly as possible, but Robert knew unless he was physically watching over her, she'd be back on the phone again.

"Damn right you will. I'm staying with you to make sure," he said with a huff and flopped down on the couch next to her and lifted her feet onto his lap.

"You are?" Melissa was both delighted and unnerved.

"Yes. Alistair has everything under control. The gang are all here; they can manage without me for a while. Well, almost. Gordon forgot to bring his official T-shirt, so I had to get another for him. Thank goodness you ordered a few spares. I swear he becomes a teenager again whenever he's around Louisa," Robert huffed, clearly appalled at his friend's behaviour.

"He's no match for Miles."

"No, he's not. Anyway, forget about that oaf."

"Are you staying until Konran comes on and then taking me down?"

"I'll stay for an hour or so. I'll go back after Coldplay play our song." His gaze softened and Melissa smiled lovingly at him. He might have been coming to check up on her but he'd also wanted to keep her company.

"How do you know they'll play our song?" she asked.

"Because I went and asked them to." Robert answered nonchalantly, as though it was an everyday occurrence that he asked the huge band Coldplay to sing a song for his wife.

"You didn't!"

"I bloody did. It's the least they could do." He took hold of her hand and kissed it. "You, my darling, were a huge part of this. You, Melissa, love of my bloody life, were there, in a sky full of stars," he said sincerely, quoting the words from their song.

"I love you, Robert Hindley. You are one of a kind," Melissa said as her eyes filled with tears, moved by the romantic gesture and Robert kissed her hand again.

"Anything for you, darling. Come on, let me massage your feet. Who's up next?" he said with soft smile, prising off her shoes.

"Bryan Adams. Let's hope he's up and on fast," Melissa said, pulling in her lips and focusing back on the split-screen.

"Melissa." Robert mock-admonished her and she grinned.

"Just saying."

THE CLOUDS WERE GATHERING and even though the temperature was warm, what had been soft sparse clouds at midday were now turning heavier. It meant that the audience wasn't being subjected to the heat of the late summer sun but there was a distinct chance of rain. The slight darkening of the sky hadn't subdued their enthusiasm, though. When Dua Lipa started her performance of hit after hit, the drone flew over the crowds, honing in on them dancing around, waving madly at the camera and whooping loudly. The VIPs in the exclusive section were also now in full swing and party mode. The socialites, models, businessmen and donators, as well as members of CASPO's board, were enjoying the Blackthorns' hospitality. A few band members had also joined them, to the delight of the VIPs, and a constant taking of photos took precedent to actually watching the performers. Celeste and Nicolas watched on from their seats, a little disgusted at their blatant lack of decorum. She had a taste of their behaviour at the summer ball, but with the more relaxed atmosphere and a steady flow of alcohol, their inhibitions were thrown to the slight breeze that had cooled down the arena and stage. The thrill of seeing all the megastars had worn off for the young Lady Blackthorn, they were just nice accommodating people who were here to help raise money for a worthy cause. As Miles had said, it was her they seemed to be in awe of. They spoke to her with a sense of wonder that someone so young had a title and would one day be running Holmwood House and all that came with it.

Backstage, Alistair sipped his water and leaned back against one of the trailers, taking a moment away from all the musicians, managers, PR agents and production staff. He'd been on full alert since six that morning, almost 12 hours straight. He took a look up at the sky and prayed that it wouldn't rain until late into the night. His eyes scanned the specially erected covered lounge area, where a few musicians were seated watching the screens they'd set up. Among them was Amanda. He was still in awe at her unfazed behaviour around the various artists. She'd been mainly by his side but he'd slipped away, needing to take a moment on his own. He wasn't used to having so many people interested in him. He'd never been that good at small talk or even engaged in excessive social behaviour. The odd night out every few months with his friends was the extent of his social life, but it was obvious that Amanda had always been surrounded by an army of either an entourage or musicians, as well as various media representatives. She took it in her stride and he was grateful she was there to take on the brunt of it, when someone approached. He didn't even think that anyone had even noticed that he's slipped away until he felt someone come up behind him.

"You hiding?"

"Yeah, just for a minute. It's really full-on." Alistair smirked at Hugh. "How come you're out here and not hawk-eyeing the monitors?"

"Just needed a breather, plus your ex-brother-in-law will be making his big entrance and I want to make sure he gets into the VIP area without a hitch. I don't need *that* agro."

Alistair chuckled. He felt for Hugh. Dealing with Gerard was always delicate. Alistair had never had blows with him because Alistair refused to be riled by his arrogance, and to be fair, he'd been a huge help to him and his family when he was injured and his father died. That, though, was the extent of his loyalty. He knew how Gerard could be, particularly to anyone he felt wasn't up to his social standing. "What time does he arrive?"

"I timed it to be between sets. So, once Coldplay finish, he should land after five minutes. I didn't want to firstly, disrupt the set and secondly, rob him of his grand entrance," Hugh said dryly. Alistair let out a laugh, Hugh knew exactly what he was doing: pandering to

Gerard meant less hassle in the future. "Well, that's my cue to get back to the office," Hugh said and headed back to his production team. Coldplay were just starting to sing their closing song *Sky Full of Stars*. Thousands of tiny pieces of paper fluttered down around them as Chris Martin sang out the familiar song. Alistair grinned to himself and thought of Robert and Melissa, probably cuddled up on the couch, watching and listening together. He wondered whether one day he'd have an 'our song' and before he could ponder too deeply, he caught sight of Amanda watching him. She excused herself and headed straight to where he was standing.

"What were you grinning about?" She asked, once she'd reached him.

"This song. It's Melissa's and Robert's song. In fact, he asked them to play it for them."

"Really? Robert?"

"He'd do anything for Melissa," Alistair said with a soft smile and Amanda nodded.

"Are you alright?" she asked, searching his face.

"Yeah. I just needed five minutes away."

"It can be a bit a lot to take in and this, well this is just that bit... *extra*."

"*Extra*... yeah, that's exactly what it is." Alistair chuckled. It was *extra*ordinary and *extra*vagant he thought, taking in the scenes around him, from backstage, full of A-listed stars, to the VIP section with its extremely generous bar, which was being taken full advantage of. His thoughts shot back to Robert and Melissa; he'd give anything to be tucked up in Holmwood, away from all the attention.

Amanda tilted her head and narrowed her eyes, trying to judge his mood. "Just a few more hours and it'll be over."

Alistair nodded, a little surprised that she'd realised what he was thinking. "Do you miss all this?" he asked, waving his hand towards the bands, and she gave a soft laugh.

"Not at all. But it was nice to see some old faces and meet a few new ones." Alistair took in a breath, relieved at her answer. He wasn't sure he could endure this kind of life, even for Amanda.

The roar of the audience jolted them both. Coldplay were finished, which meant that backstage was going to be hectic for the next 15 minutes, getting the next stage up ready.

"Back to work," Alistair said with a roll of his eyes.

"I'll give you a hand," she said and he felt a sense of calm, knowing she'd be by his side again.

GERARD LET HIS GAZE skim the countryside as the helicopter approached Holmwood House. He'd been closely following the concert all day. He had to hand it to Louisa and Alistair, they'd really done a stellar job. Their father would've been proud that his legacy was being carried on. He'd also been surprised at Miles, not that he'd have ever admitted it. He'd certainly had glowing reviews so far on his role as host, even though the media was still persisting in their speculation of him performing.

The pilot swooped around the grounds, taking a much larger circle, so as to avoid flying directly over the central grounds, where the concert was set up. Gerard could see the thousands of people spread across the immaculate lawns, facing the huge stage. The helicopter's angle of flight gave Gerard a bird's eye view of the backstage area and trailers for the artists too. He shot his assistant a look and saw that he was smiling widely, clearly excited that he was also coming to the concert. One of the perks of working for Gerard Dupont. The crowd cheered, seeing the helicopter, obviously believing it was one of the performers arriving. Gerard furrowed his brow. They were certainly going to be disappointed when he stepped out of the door and Gerard second-guessed his actions for a split second. Maybe he should've arrived the night before, after all.

The pilot expertly landed on the helipad and powered down the helicopter, instructing Gerard to wait until security arrived. He was pleased to see that the helipad had been sectioned off by a high temporary wall, which afforded him privacy from the spectators. This meant they were safe from the audience, but the drones that circled the arena would catch them disembarking.

A Land Rover arrived, driven by one of the security team, and the pilot nodded to Gerard. He exited the door, closely followed by his assistant, then looked up and smiled at the passing drone before they both stepped into the waiting Land Rover. He'd gotten his grand entrance, his documented arrival and support of the Blackthorns, and that was all that mattered.

17

SHOT CALLER

R obert walked speedily down the corridor, making his way backstage. His eyes flitted up to the cameras and he felt a sense of calm, knowing that Hugh and his team were keeping an eye on every area. He'd never had to think about safety, he'd been lucky. The Hindley family were under the radar, extremely wealthy but understated, well connected but not well-known. Now with their baby due any day now, and Melissa's close connection with the Blackthorns, he might need to rethink and revise. His eyes caught sight of one of the huge screens that broadcasted the video feed from the drones, and he saw the smug face of Gerard appear for a few seconds. Robert tutted to himself. *He really is a pompous arse, wanting to make an entrance.* The security at the entrance to the backstage area opened the door for him to enter and after thanking them, he paced towards where Alistair was talking with the production manager and his assistant. Darcy looked decidedly nervous too. He'd happily place a bet that they were discussing the time slots, trying to shave minutes off wherever they could and stifled a smirk. His wife must've given them hell the moment he'd cleared the threshold of their room.

"Everyone looks a bit tense," Robert whispered to Louisa, gesturing to where Alistair was. He'd found her helping herself to a piece of cut fruit that had been laid out on the table of food for anyone backstage.

"That's Melissa's doing."

"Thought as much."

"Everything alright?"

"She's itching to come down."

"I know. Well, as soon as French Montana finishes, I'll go and change. Her orders," she added with a look and Robert chuckled. *Melissa was a force and law unto herself.* "I'll keep her company for a bit and then we can make our way down for when Maroon 5 come on."

"Excellent. You're an absolute sport." Robert squinted at something over Louisa's shoulder and Louisa turned to look. Her eyes widened as she watched Miles having his makeup touched up, ready for his next introduction. This in itself wasn't unusual – both Konran and Miles had their faces blotted and powdered to tone down the shine. What had caught Robert's attention was the open trumpet box next to Miles. "That's Papa's trumpet, the one he was gifted, years ago, by Miles Davis." He shot Louisa a look. "How does Miles have that?"

Louisa cringed. She hadn't realised that Robert didn't know she'd bought it from his father all those months ago.

"I bought it from your father and gifted it to him."

"You did?" Robert's brow furrowed.

"He's named after Miles Davis," Louisa said, hoping Robert would understand the connection.

"He is?" His eyes darted back to Louisa and she nodded, his expression softened and after a beat he said.

"Well, in that case, I suppose, it belongs with him."

"Thank you," Louisa said, placing her hand on his forearm. It was, after all, a family heirloom and Louisa had paid practically double what it was valued at. Bart Hindley, Robert's father, couldn't really refuse her.

"What's he doing with it here? I thought he wasn't performing."

Louisa's face dropped; she hadn't even thought about why Miles had brought the trumpet. She'd been so wrapped up in explaining how Miles had it, the fact he'd brought it to the concert hadn't crossed her mind. "I've no idea." Louisa quickly looked at the time. Miles and Konran were due onstage in the next couple of minutes. The last thing Miles needed was her quizzing him on his trumpet. The stage manager's assistant stepped over to Miles and said something to him and he nodded, then gave a questioning look to the makeup woman, who gave him a bright smile and indicated he was good to go. He stood up, ran his fingers through his hair and picked up his trumpet. Louisa stared at him. Her jaw almost hitting the floor when he caught sight of her, then gave her his signature wink and headed around the back of the stage.

"I think, I mean… I'm…" Louisa stuttered.

"Is he going to play?" Robert said in surprise. Throughout all the preparation for the concert, Melissa had rattled on about Miles not playing. Yet here they were, well past halfway and Miles was stepping up to the stage and holding his priceless Miles Davis trumpet.

"Shit. Did Melissa know about this?" Louisa asked Robert.

"If she did, she never mentioned it to me."

"Okay, I'm going out into the VIP area. If he really is going to perform, I want to be out front to see it."

"Me too."

"Y'ALL HAVING A GOOD time?" Konran called out to the audience and they cheered back. He beamed at them and the image of him filled the multiple screens.

"So, I have some good news and some bad news..."

The crowd gave a collective "ah", playing to his theatrics.

"And then I have some special news. Wanna hear it?"

A loud "yes!" resounded from the crowd.

"Okay the good news is our next artist is waiting to come on out." Cheers were heard across the arena. "The bad news is for his opening song, one of his musicians couldn't make it."

The crowd responded on cue with an "ah". Louisa watched in admiration as Konran played to the crowd and had them eating out of his hand.

"He's good at this," Robert said to Louisa, raising his voice over the noise of the crowd. She nodded but kept her eyes glued to the stage. Konran continued his sole introduction.

"I know, I know... but don't worry. The special news is that we found him an excellent substitute!" The crowd cheered and his eyes widened and his smile grew even more. "Our next artist is the multi-platinum record selling rapper, selling over seven million albums worldwide, all the way from California, especially for us tonight." Konran had to almost shout over the calling out of the audience but like the true professional he was, he didn't miss a beat. "Opening up with his debut single, *Shot Caller*, French Montana, featuring our very own Miles Keane!"

Konran ran off to the right of the stage to a roar. The screens went black and the stage was bare. It took the audience a few seconds to quieten down and Louisa could hear her heart thumping in her chest.

The seconds ticked by and Louisa began to feel the beginnings of panic. *What's happened? Is Miles alright? Has he changed his mind?* Her troubled gaze flitted to Robert, who looked equally worried. Then out of the still darkness came the clear vibrant sound of a trumpet, playing the distinct introduction to the hit. The screens spotlighted the exquisite trumpet being played by Miles, highlighting his fingers pushing on the valves. There was a collective gasp from around the arena as they were firstly in awe of Miles's skilful performance, then the realisation that this was his first time on stage playing music in five years. Their applause bubbled up and rose in volume with every note Miles played. Louisa gave an inward sigh of thanks to the heavens above, as goosebumps travelled the length of her body. Her eyes were fixed on the screen along with the millions of others around the globe. The piece perfectly showcased the talented musician he was, worthy of the awards and adulation he'd garnered over the years. The lighting only highlighted the trumpet – Miles wasn't fully visible, standing behind the central curtain at the back of the stage – yet the whole arena was now cheering, reaching a crescendo.

Miles played the third repeat of the piece and the distinct voice of French Montana came over the speakers as he strutted onto the stage, in time to the beat, the epitome of cool, singing the words to his debut hit. His band, backing singers and dancers filtered onto the stage waving to the audience from both sides, to another roar from the arena. Louisa's eyes were glued to the stage, oblivious to the crowd around her singing along to the famous song. She didn't want to miss it when Miles came on stage, because she knew that he would.

Louisa was so focused on the performance, she hadn't noticed Amanda, Alistair, Celeste and Nicolas had joined her and Robert in the VIP section. They obviously didn't want to miss Miles's comeback performance too. They chatted excitedly asking each other if they'd known he was going to play. Alistair asked Louisa, and she just shook her head but kept her eyes fixed on the screen. All of them had been clueless but at the same time were enthusiastic and nervous for him. This was a big deal. Huge. Robert lifted his vibrating phone to his ear and answered Melissa's call. Louisa vaguely heard him try and calm down her obvious excitement, telling her she shouldn't be getting worked up and Celeste came and stood by her mother, taking her hand

and giving it a squeeze.

Pierce stood a few feet away from Miles and watched in awe as his friend effortlessly played. Over their time together, his respect for Miles had grown exponentially, every time he heard him play music or listen to him sing as he composed in the privacy of his home. Today, though, Pierce was blown away at him playing under such stressful conditions. Konran stepped quietly up to where Miles was still playing. The trumpet piece was played throughout the rapper's hit, so it meant Miles didn't stop through the three-minute song. Konran beamed at his friend as he continued to play with constant vibrancy and gave him a double thumbs up. This was his cue. They'd rehearsed it over and over as soon as the lyrics "backstage" were said by French Montana, Miles had 15 seconds before he stepped out and made his way to where the singers and dancers would part, allowing him to make it down to the front and join French Montana. Konran counted the beat, holding up his fingers for Miles to see and take his cue. Fifteen seconds and he would be out on stage.

Ten... eleven.

Pierce shifted and took hold of the curtain.

Twelve... thirteen.

Miles turned towards the stage.

Fourteen... fifteen.

Pierce pulled back the curtain and Miles stepped out onto the stage, the spotlights pointing on him – but he didn't need them. He dazzled. He was born to be in the spotlight, to share his talent with millions, to show the world that nothing could stop him from doing this, what he loved. The screens split, showing a close-up of Miles's entrance and the dancers parting to let him walk to the beat, all the time playing the infamous trumpet, and the sonorous tune. The roar around the arena was almost deafening and Louisa's heart almost burst seeing him walk confidently towards the front, the spotlight bouncing off the brass instrument. .

Konran had managed to run back around and was now also with the rest of them, watching on. He bopped around, singing and jumping with such an incredible energy – it became infectious. It pulled them all out of their trance and soon they were all bouncing to the beat. Mike and Josh called out, punching the air and whooping in glee, seeing their last band member do what he did best. French Montana sidled up to Miles smoothly, singing the lyrics, and put his arm around him loosely, causing the audience to go wild. Cameras flashed, hands waved and punched the air. Miles Keane was where he belonged, on stage, in front of the whole world.

Hugh kept his focus on the monitors, shifting from one to the other and kept barking at his team to keep vigilant. The two stars at the front of the stage had both survived gunfire – the odds of them surviving a second attempt on their lives were heavily stacked against them. Hugh cursed under his breath and prayed that Miles got off the stage fast. There were roughly 15 people on stage, making it hard for security to keep a clear view of Miles. Konran had told him it would be a maximum of a minute playing time on stage. Hugh hoped that French Montana didn't keep them up there for much longer.

Pierce kept his gaze sweeping around backstage, up to the rigs and down into the front pit, checking constantly. The dancers had closed up behind Miles and he didn't have a good view of Miles, which also meant that anyone backstage didn't too. However, anyone at the front had a perfect view of him. Pierce shouted into his sleeve, alerting Karl. A second later Karl replied, assuring him he was at the front with two other security covering the front of the stage. Pierce blew out a breath, then looked at the huge monitor as Miles and French Montana finished the track. Miles pulled the trumpet away from his lips and a fresh batch of confetti fell from the top of the stage. The thunder of applause and cheering of the many thousand spectators was deafening. French Montana took hold of Miles's hand and lifted it in the air.

"Miles Keane calling the shots tonight!" he shouted out and the audience roared in approval. The rapper gave Miles a hard hug and said with his gruff Bronx accent, "We got shot but we the shot callers now."

Miles pulled back and gave him a nod in appreciation, glad he had someone with him on stage who understood. Miles turned to the audience and waved. "Thank you!" he called out and horns blasted, the shout-outs and applause rose again and though he appreciated all of it, his eyes searched the front of the VIP area for Louisa. The moment he found her, he smiled his megawatt smile, then gave a final wave and stepped backwards into the left wing.

Gerard watched the screen from his room window that overlooked the concert. He'd been led to Holmwood House to leave his few belongings, leaving his assistant at the VIP area to enjoy the concert. He wasn't particularly interested in the concert per se, other than wanting to make an appearance and be seen to be supportive, hence his late arrival. He'd planned to make his way down much later but after the huge impact Miles's performance had made, Gerard knew he was going to have to go down sooner. Firstly, he didn't want anyone thinking he was bothered by Miles's huge success, even though he felt it was a vulgar display of self-promotion. He'd always found anyone related to showbusiness a little crass: actors, musicians, they were always putting themselves out there, in the public eye. It was the very reason he'd never dated anyone from that type of circle. They couldn't be trusted. They'd find any way to promote themselves and he for one wasn't going to fall into the trap of being used. This was what he'd been trying to make Louisa see, Miles only wanted to be with her for his own gain. The second reason Gerard needed to go down to the concert, as well as wanting to be with Louisa and Celeste, was there were many business associates in the VIP section that needed to see he was still part of the Blackthorn family.

The security that had accompanied him gave him the passcode for entering Holmwood and strict instructions that only family, friends, Holmwood and CASPO staff were allowed in the house. Gerard resisted the urge to explain to the security that he was well aware of the thorough security measures. It irked him that the security had an inordinate amount of authority and say in how the people that paid them lived their lives but he wasn't about to rock the boat – not today, anyway. Gerard checked himself in the mirror, ensuring his immaculate white shirt and black trousers were free from wrinkles. He picked up the heavy crystal brandy glass, knocked back its contents in one, then headed downstairs.

THE FIRST TO HUG Miles as he appeared from behind the stage was Konran. He held onto him tightly for an extended moment, then slapped his back affectionately. "You were awesome! Man, you have mad talent."

Miles gave him a lopsided smile, a little taken back by the pure and sincere words. His new friend was unguarded, refreshingly honest and a positive bright beacon in the dark ocean of the often-fickle show business. "Thanks, I couldn't have done it without you."

"It's been a huge honour, and the best is yet to come, my friend. You're calling the shots!" Konran said, using French Montana's words.

Next up was Amanda, who had had to dab her eyes before getting to him. She'd been both moved by his outstanding performance and thrilled to see him playing, as well as being received so wholeheartedly. Seeing Miles back on stage brought back so many memories that she'd tried to forget, both good and bad. But now that she was seeing him off stage, it was obvious how much he'd missed this huge part of his life. He was a born performer and she was glad he'd finally come through the darkness to step back into the light.

Amanda wrapped her arms around him tightly, resting her head on his shoulder, and Miles squeezed his arms around her, holding her to him. She'd been in his life for nearing 20 years. There was no one who knew him better and he gave thanks to Louis every day for bringing her into their lives. "We're all so proud of you," she whispered and Miles knew she meant Louis too.

"Thanks, I'm so glad you're here."

"Me too. It's good to see you back." She pulled back from him and blinked away the tears that had welled up again. Miles gave her a soft smile and wiped them away with his thumbs and she laughed.

"Believe it to achieve it." Miles mouthed at her and she nodded, pressing her lips together as she heard her husband's mantra.

"Never forget it," she said with a teary smile, then gathered herself together, aware there were many others who wanted to speak to him. "Let me go. You have a lot of people who want to congratulate you."

One after another shook his hand gave him hugs and words of praise and genuine encouragement, understanding what a monumental achievement this had been for him. Pierce kept a constant watchful eye in and around the backstage area where everyone had gathered, and felt a sense of pride, seeing Miles tentatively embrace his re-entering into the music world. He noticed Louisa keeping a distance, allowing him to have his moment. They still weren't 'official' and he felt for her not being able to congratulate him on his performance. They'd had a few discreet moments behind the wings, where few people were allowed, but here in the backstage area, set up for the musicians and their entourages, there were too many people. Pierce caught Karl's eye and signalled to the rear of the stage. After a few minutes, Pierce stepped up to Miles and asked him for a moment. Miles excused himself and Pierce led him to an area around the back of the stage where only the artists went, when they were ready to go on stage.

"What's going on, Pierce?" Miles said, a little bemused.

"I thought you might want some privacy," Pierce said as they rounded the scaffolding, and Miles caught sight of Louisa waiting with Karl. "Five minutes, otherwise everyone will start looking for you," Pierce said with a smirk, then Karl stepped towards Pierce and they both moved far enough away so that the couple had some privacy.

"You looked pretty good up there. That was one hell of a surprise," Louisa said as she tried to look casual, leaning on one of the metal pipes. Miles's smile widened and he walked over at a leisurely pace to a few feet away from her and tilted his head to the side. He had an unworldly glow and Louisa realised it was the rush of performing. It elevated his good looks to godlike, and Louisa instantly understood how groupies felt. It was like the switch had been flicked on for an electromagnet, and she was powerless to pull away.

"A good surprise?"

"A fantastic surprise," she said immediately and in two strides he was up to her and lifting her in the air, spinning her around. She stifled a scream with her hand and Miles let out a laugh, then slowly let her slide down his body, until she was back on solid ground.

"Well, you always seem to surprise me so, now that we're engaged, I thought I needed to up my game."

"Up your game? You bloody smashed it!" Louisa said animatedly and Miles's face almost split in two hearing her praise. "Seriously, Miles, you were just amazing up there."

"Thanks to you."

"To me? No Miles; this, who you are, how you are, it's all you. To quote a wise man who I had the pleasure of meeting a long time ago, 'You believed it and achieved it'." She cupped his jaw and he leaned down and kissed her thoroughly.

"I love you, my Lady Louisa." He rested his forehead on hers and she closed her eyes.

"I love you too." A discreet cough from Pierce made them step back. Their time was up; someone was obviously looking for one of them. "Now come on, we've got a concert to be part of – though, to be fair, I don't think there's anything that can top *that* performance," Louisa said wryly, as they headed towards Pierce and Karl.

"You're biased," Miles said, taking her hand and kissing it.

"A bit. I think it was the trumpet, though. Pretty cool."

Miles let out a laugh and Pierce and Karl chuckled.

The next 15 minutes saw Miles being congratulated by everyone he came across, as well as multiple phone calls. The first was from his parents, who were watching the concert at their home. They were of course thrilled that he'd taken the plunge to get on stage and perform again. Eric called him too, both pleased and surprised he'd decided to do his first appearance in front of a worldwide audience.

"Well, you either go big or go home, right?" Miles joked. But Eric knew that Miles had picked the right venue and the right means to make his comeback performance. A charity concert that he'd been involved with from the start, and a three-minute musical piece, accompanying another singer. Eric had to give Miles credit for getting it one hundred percent right: maximum impact, minimum risk. The old Miles Keane had definitely been a risk-taker, he'd thrown caution to the wind and gone with his gut – maybe now he valued certainty more and calculated the risk. *It certainly paid off*, thought Eric.

GERARD CAME OUT FROM the back entrance and walked over to the large wooden door and pulled on the handle. It was locked and he cursed under his breath. In his haste to get down, he'd forgotten that the back entrance through the courtyard, that Holmwood House residents used, was closed off. For today, he was supposed to use the staff entrance, which connected to the corridor erected for the house residence and staff to use, as well as the CASPO staff and friends. This meant he'd now have to go all the way back, through the house and into the staff area. If he could just open this door, it would be a very short walk around the outside to where the corridor was.

He pulled out his phone to see if he could call up a member of staff to open it for him, when his eye caught sight of the small keypad by the door. He remembered that the member of the security had given him the passcodes used just for today, to access the house. He presumed that these were also for exiting the house too, though this hadn't been clarified. The worst-case scenario was that if they didn't work, he'd have to go the other way. Gerard checked the code he'd noted on his phone. It was an eight-digit code and he hadn't brought his glasses so he had to enlarge it on his screen before tapping it in. To his delight, it opened the lock on the door and he pulled it open and stepped onto the paving that ran around the outside of garages. He carefully closed the door, ensuring it was locked, then proceeded to the area that was sectioned off. There was a small hidden entrance, known only to Holmwood residents, which opened up to the grounds behind, and was where the corridor that led straight to the backstage area was.

Gerard looked up at the sky and frowned. The sky was turning grey and it looked as though there was a high chance of rain and he hadn't brought down his jacket. He paused for a moment wondering whether he should go back for it, then decided that the last thing he wanted was to get soaked, so he turned back to the locked wooden door and tapped in the code again. The door unlocked and Gerard pushed it back open and stepped into the courtyard again. His phone vibrated in his hand and saw the name Celeste flash and he smiled before answering it. "Hello, Celeste."

"Hey, Papa, where are you? I thought you were just dropping off your things; you've been ages," Celeste mildly chastised.

"I'm just going to get my jacket and I'll be there in a minute. I think it might rain."

"I hope not. We've another four hours left and Konran hasn't played yet."

"I'll be as quick as I can," he promised as he jogged up the stairs towards his room, then hung up. He grabbed his jacket, then decided that while he'd come all the way in, he might as well go through the staff area and out through the correct exit to the connecting corridor.

His phone rang again and he saw it was his assistant calling. He answered it and started going down the stairs.

"Scott."

"Sir, I just got a call confirming our meeting for tomorrow."

Gerard quickly went over the details, thanked him and hung up and headed back towards the courtyard, his mind on the meeting, when he realised he was going towards the wrong entrance again. He cursed to himself, annoyed that he'd instinctively come to the wrong exit again and almost bumped into a young woman coming in from the courtyard. "I'm sorry, I wasn't looking where I was going," he said, annoyed with himself for not paying attention.

"It's okay," said the young woman, dressed in the official purple CASPO T-shirt, which seemed a too large for her slight frame, and a baseball cap pulled down. Gerard stopped for a moment and narrowed his eyes at the young woman, who seemed a little nervy.

"Emily?" The woman's eyes darted up to Gerard and she gave an uneasy smile.

"Oh, it's you, Gerard," she said with a hint of relief.

"Yes, how are you?" The last time he'd seen Emily was with Gordon at a dinner Louisa had arranged in New York. He found the McKenzies a total bore but Gordon had ties to the British establishment and it never did any harm to keep channels of communication open. Gerard had also realised at that dinner that Gordon had strong feelings for Louisa, which made dinner awkward, especially as Gordon was useless at hiding it and it didn't take long for Emily to cotton on.

"I'm fine, good, you know," she stuttered, and shrugged noncommittally.

"What are you doing in here? Shouldn't you be out there having fun?" he asked. She seemed fidgety and a little gaunt, as though she hadn't slept well, and Gerard gave her a reassuring smile.

"I um… needed to, um, use the restroom," she answered quickly and Gerard mouthed 'ah'. Her fidgetiness now made sense.

"Well, I'll see you down there, then?" he said with a nod and Emily blinked at him and then headed for the stairs. Gerard shook his head and tutted, unsure of what to make of her, then headed back to the wooden door and tapped in the code for it to open.

18

UNFORGETTABLE

"**Y**es, I know, darling, he was great." Amanda smiled up at Alistair as she spoke to Grace and Louis on a videocall. They'd been allowed to stay up late to watch the concert while staying with Amanda's parents in one of the suites of Holmwood House. Amanda hadn't wanted them down in the crowds but at least they could watch and be close by. They of course had never seen their uncle play before, only in old videos and to be honest, they'd been too young to appreciate who their uncle and their father were, to millions of fans around the world.

"How many people are there?" asked Louis. "A hundred?" he said with wide eyes thinking that this number seemed fantastically large.

Grace rolled her eyes at her brother. "Nooo, there are thousands, isn't that right, Mummy?"

"Yes, sweetheart, thousands," Amanda confirmed.

"Is Alistair going to sing too?" Louis asked. He obviously thought that it was a free-for-all. Alistair stifled a laugh and Amanda signalled him to come into view.

"Hey, Louis, Grace. Are you enjoying the show?"

"Alistair!" they both shouted, clearly pleased to see him.

"Are you going to sing?" Louis repeated, ignoring the question and Alistair chuckled.

"No, I'm afraid I don't sing very well at all. I'm just helping the bands move their things around."

"Yes. That's because you're big and strong," Louis said sagely. "And you have that metal leg too, which makes you super-strong."

"That's right," Amanda said and Alistair bit the side of his cheek, trying hard not to laugh. "Okay, we need to go. Alistair has… things to move. We'll call you later." They all said bye and blew kisses, and Amanda quickly told her parents she'd pop up to see them before shutting down the call.

"So, no singing for you, then?" Amanda smirked.

"Maybe I will at the end – it'll be sure to clear the grounds," Alistair said dryly. "They seemed excited."

"Yes, it's a new experience for them seeing Miles play on a stage."

"Hopefully they'll get to see more of that."

"Yes, I hope so."

"Well, I need to get back to 'moving things,'" he joked, jerking his thumb in the direction of the stage. Amanda laughed at his air quotes. "Because you know I'm *that* strong." He put his hands on his hips and did his best impression of a Superman pose, which made Amanda giggle.

"You're an idiot," she laughed loving how much his sense of humour was coming out more and more.

"But a strong idiot though, right? And it must be true because Louis said so." Alistair carried on his act of being solemn, which made Amanda laugh even more.

"He loves you; they both do," Amanda said and Alistair's fake solemn face softened at her words.

"Good, because I love them too," he said sincerely and Amanda gave him a shy smile. He reached over and cupped her face gently. "I couldn't have done this today without you Amanda. Thank you, for everything."

"There's nowhere else I want to be, Alistair." Her words were so sincere it made his chest tighten. Without a second thought, he leaned down and kissed her softly, right in the middle of the backstage area with musicians, managers and various band entourage members moving around them.

THE FINAL MINUTE OF French Montana's set was ticking away and the audience sang along to his platinum hit 'Unforgettable'. The concert had a few more hours but true to the title of the song, it had already been an unforgettable day.

Gerard stepped into the backstage area and searched through the many people, milling around until he found who he was looking for. She saw him before he found her and her vigorous waving drew his attention to Celeste. He gave her a genuine warm smile before heading to where she was standing.

"You made it!" She hugged him and accepted his kisses to her cheeks. Gerard shook Nicolas's hand, then turned to Louisa.

"*Cherie*. It's a great event." He leaned in to kiss her cheek and she tilted her head to allow him.

"It is. But it was a team effort and Miles and Konran have been the force behind it."

Now that she'd mentioned Miles, Gerard had to acknowledge him. He was talking to Konran so he had to interrupt them to greet them both. He held out his hand and Miles was a little taken back. "Congratulations. I've been watching and today has already been a great success."

Miles took his hand and shook it. "Thank you. I'm glad you could make it." He'd omitted to say, "finally made it", seeing as Gerard had had the good grace to congratulate him, though he doubted he was happy doing it.

Gerard turned to Konran, who hugged Gerard without any hesitation. "Well done, son, you've made us all proud," Gerard said sincerely and Konran beamed back at him. Miles furrowed his brow, touched by the closeness that they had. He'd forgotten how close they must be, after all Gerard had been in Konran's life for over 10 years.

There was a huge cheer from the audience, marking the end of the set and suddenly backstage became a hive of activity. The band swept down the stairs and all the stagehands started to move things around as quickly as possible. The band members came over to where Miles was and shook his hand. They immediately steered him to where the official photographer for the event was waiting by the promotional backdrop with all the sponsors of the event and the Concert for CASPO logo. The photographer took a few promotional photos and a few candids – all would no doubt be all over social media. Gerard observed the tableau before him. He'd never witnessed this level of fame, adulation even, and though there was no love lost between Miles and him, he had to hand it to Miles, he handled it well.

"Crazy, isn't it?" Konran said, pulling Gerard out of his introspective thoughts.

"It is. How do you handle it?"

"Ha, I'm nowhere near his level. But it can be both flattering and scary. It's not too bad here because it's controlled and everyone here is used to it."

"I suppose," Gerard said, keeping his eyes focused on Miles and the band members.

"Miles, though, he's always a pro. Doesn't complain, takes time out."

"I can see... oh look, they're calling you up," Gerard said, seeing the photographer's assistant wave him over.

"Duty calls," Konran said with a grin and jogged to where they were waiting for him.

"I take it the reason why everyone is running around like blue arsed flies is your doing," Louisa said, answering her call from Melissa.

"I may have told them to get a wriggle on."

"Wriggle on? They look terrified."

"I may have used my pregnancy and high blood pressure as blackmail too."

"You're shameless."

"But effective. Anyway, I thought you'd like to know that social media is going bananas over your fiancé. They're hashtagging all over the place!"

"Excuse me?"

"You know; hashtag shot survivors, hashtag unforgettable Miles, that kind of thing."

"Oh, I see." Now that she understood the terminology.

"So, how much longer do I have to stay up here, alone? I really want to see Maroon 5!"

"Not long; I'm coming to get changed and we can come back together."

"Yay! Does Robert know?" Louisa could hear the cringe in her voice.

"I'm going to tell him now. Sit tight until I come," Louisa said, shutting down the call and pacing towards where Robert was talking with his and Alistair's school friends, Eddie and Tim.

"I better go and get her," she said to Robert as she pulled him to the side. "She's just getting worked up and she'll feel better down here. We can also keep an eye on her," Louisa said wryly and Robert huffed, not entirely sure Louisa was right – but he knew his wife, and she wouldn't last being cooped up until the last hour.

"You're right. I'll go and get her."

"No point, I have to change and I'll have Karl with me." Louisa motioned with her head in the direction of her trusted security and Robert nodded. "I'll just let Miles know that I'm off to change."

HUGH LOOKED AT THE time on the monitor: 7:32. There were five more sets of 30 minutes each, 20 minutes of stage setting for each, and the finale. If everything ran smoothly and Melissa's barking at the production team worked, they'd be just inside their permit time. That was a big *if,* though, and Hugh knew it. His eyes scanned the monitors as he sipped on his cold coffee, his eighth of the day.

The door of the security room opened and Miles stepped through holding a tray of hot coffees for the team. Hugh smirked to himself, thinking of the many times Miles had made him coffee and food in the past. He didn't think anyone would ever believe him if he ever told anyone, which of course he never would. This fact was confirmed by the wide eyes of his team, seeing the superstar with the tray.

"Here you go, guys. There's some protein bars, biscuits and fruit there too, to tide you over." After the initial shock, collective thanks were mumbled as the tray was passed around. "So, everything okay?" Miles said, letting his eyes scan the monitors.

"So far, so good. Let's hope we keep to our schedule."

"Hmm," Miles said, furrowing his brow.

"You were good up there." Hugh let his eyes dart for a second to Miles. "Really good."

"Thanks," Miles said, giving him a lopsided smile.

"Gave me a fucking heart attack until you were off the stage, but it was worth it," Hugh said gruffly and Miles chuckled.

"Another four hours and it'll be over."

"It can't come soon enough."

"Mind if I stay for a bit? It's a bit hectic out there."

"Yes, I can see." Hugh nodded towards one of the screens that showed Konran surrounded by various band members and their entourage. "Where's Pierce?"

"He had to pee." Hugh kept his eyes on the monitors and nodded, then raised a brow upon seeing Louisa heading towards the office on one of the cameras.

"Looks like your plan to hide has been kyboshed." A few seconds later Louisa stepped into the office and everyone immediately stood up.

"Oh goodness, please sit down," Louisa said mildly embarrassed at their excessive adherence to protocol. "I just came to let you know I'm going up to the house to change and bring down Melissa."

"You're taking Karl, right?" Miles said quickly.

"Yes, of course. I'll be 10 minutes, 15 tops. Just in time for Maroon 5," she said with a hint of excitement. Miles nodded. "All good?" She directed her comment to Hugh and he gave a curt nod.

"Yes, my lady."

"Good. See you in a bit." Miles gave her a breath-taking smile that had her blushing and she hurriedly exited the room, before anyone noticed, where she bumped into Robert.

"Whoa, there."

"Sorry."

"All good?"

"Yes, I'm just going now." Louisa jerked her head towards Karl. "Ready?" she asked him.

"Yes madame," he replied.

"Great, I'm just going in to see if the lads need anything." Louisa nodded, then set off towards Holmwood House.

LOUISA QUICKLY CLIMBED THE stairs with Karl a few steps behind. She'd hoped she'd have time to freshen up before changing but if they were to get Melissa down in time, she'd have to forego a quick shower. Louisa opened Melissa's door and found her talking brusquely on the phone. Melissa looked up guiltily at her dear friend, who had a disapproving brow raised. Melissa cringed and quickly ended the call.

"So, it doesn't matter what we say? You're like a sergeant major." Louisa tutted.

"We're running 40 minutes over. At this rate we'll be well past midnight," Melissa said in a rush, hoping to justify her actions.

"I know. They're cutting back the set changes to 15 minutes and Konran said he's going to forfeit a song if necessary. He doesn't want you worrying." Louisa explained, hoping this fact would appease and calm her.

"He's a good boy," Melissa said with affection and relief. It wasn't just the permit she was worried about. They had the worldwide live stream too and it wouldn't do to be cut short. The last thing they needed was worldwide disappointment.

"He is."

Then because she didn't want any more chastisement, Melissa waved her finger up and down towards Louisa. "Why haven't you changed?"

"That's why I came, to get changed and get you. Now relax, will you?" Louisa rolled her eyes. "I'll be five minutes. I'll ask Karl to get the wheelchair from the library."

"I will not need a wheelchair!" Melissa said adamantly.

"Robert's orders or you stay here." Louisa gave her a stern look and pursed her lips.

"He's becoming a tyrant," huffed Melissa.

"He learned from the best," Louisa countered, which earned her a second huff. "He adores you and wanted to come but it seemed silly, since I was already coming."

Melissa's expression softened. "Go on, then." She waved her away. "I don't want to miss Adam Levine!"

"Alright, alright. I'll be as quick as I can." Louisa left the room and found Karl waiting in the wide passageway. Even from within the house, Louisa could hear the crowds cheering to the various images of the crowds, VIPs and artists being displayed on the huge screens from the drones. She instructed Karl to retrieve the wheelchair from the library and bring it up from the service lift, while she quickly went to her suite to change. Louisa then pulled out her phone as Karl jogged down the stairs towards the library, to call Robert and let him know.

"Hey, Robert."

"Everything alright?" He sounded worried and Louisa smiled to herself. *He really is a model husband*, she thought, taking the 10 or so paces up to her door.

"Everything's fine, apart from her biting at the bit," Louisa said dryly as she opened the heavy door and Robert chuckled. "We'll be down in ten minutes. Just make sure... what the... Emily? What the hell are you doing?" Louisa's voice changed from light-hearted to horrified.

"Louisa?" Robert furrowed his brow and turned his head immediately in the direction of Miles and Hugh. Hearing the sudden surprise in his voice, they both instantly shifted their full focused attention on him.

"Emily, put the scissors dow–" A shriek was heard and then the phone went dead.

"Louisa!" Robert shouted down the phone and the colour drained from his face.

"What? What happened?" Hugh barked at him.

"Robert!" Miles shook him out of his milli-second stunned silence.

"I was talking to Louisa and then she started talking to Emily."

"Emily McKenzie?" Hugh said sharply, and pulled out his phone, checking where Louisa's tracker was. He could see it blinking in her suite on the floor plan. Miles pulled out his phone and called Louisa.

"I think so – she doesn't know any other one, does she?" Robert said, still a little stunned. By now, Hugh and Miles had exploded into motion, almost running to the door.

"She's not answering," Miles bit out.

Hugh barked out orders to his team and shouted into his sleeve at Karl. "Where are you?" He spat out.

Miles turned to Robert. "Call Melissa, tell her to keep her door locked."

"Of course, shit, yes. What the hell? Is she dangerous?" The question was left hanging as Miles and Hugh sprinted out of the office door, leaving a panicked Robert behind.

"Where's Karl?" called Miles as they rushed past various people backstage.

"He was getting the wheelchair. He's outside Louisa's now but the door's locked."

"Fuck!"

They were in the clear corridor now and as they ran, Hugh continued talking in his sleeve and listening to what his expert security team were conveying in his earpiece. He was glad Miles couldn't hear it all. Robert had told his team that he thought he'd heard Louisa mention scissors and that she screamed.

Miles heard footsteps behind him and looked over his shoulder. Pierce was running towards them. He'd obviously been brought up to speed by the team. An urgent bleeping start sounding from Hugh's phone and Hugh cursed under his breath as he increased his speed. "What's that?" Miles asked, knowing whatever it was, it couldn't good. His stomach tightened.

"Her panic button," Pierce said in an even tone but his face was like stone. *This is bad.*

"Is she dangerous?" Miles yelled as they entered the house, and Hugh put his finger to his lips, signalling them to be quiet.

"She could be. She's been at a facility," whispered Pierce.

"Fuck, fuck, fuck. How did she get in?" Miles hissed.

"I don't know but they're checking it now. Put your phones on vibrate," Hugh said in a very low voice. Miles realised that he was obviously getting information from his team through his earpiece. "The room's locked and Karl said he can hear them talking. I don't want him going in until we can evaluate the situation." They'd reached the grand hall where four security had gathered. Miles's eyes widened seeing them there with bulletproof vests on, headgear and carrying firearms. He paled. *Where were they and how did they get here before us?*

"Is Karl armed? What's he going to do?" Miles asked as his stomach contracted in panic at the thought of loaded weapons anywhere near Louisa.

"Yes, he is. Like I said, he's listening at the door. They're talking."

"Talking? She pressed the panic button," Miles said through gritted teeth. *Why aren't they storming the room?*

"Talking is good. It means the situation isn't as dangerous for Louisa," Pierce said quietly, trying to reassure Miles. "She's been trained on how to handle hostage and kidnap situations."

"Fuck." Miles raked his fingers through his hair in frustration. *Why the hell would anybody need training on how to handle being kidnapped? Has this happened before?* "Can't we just break the door down?"

Pierce put a hand on Mile's shoulder to try and calm him. "The door is heavy and dead-bolted. It's designed like that to keep her safe. If we blast it, we may injure Louisa or the assailant might panic and injure her or worse." His tone was calm and soothing as he explained and Miles furrowed his brow, taking in the information.

"Is she armed?" he asked, dreading the answer.

"We believe she has scissors."

Hugh shot Pierce a look but the man ignored him. Miles had a right to know what they were dealing with so he could understand their actions. He'd deal with Hugh afterwards, once everyone was safe.

Hugh signalled to his team to follow him up the stairs.

"I'm coming too," Miles said, in a tone that Hugh knew meant it wasn't for debate. He nodded and the three of them quietly climbed the stairs, closely followed by the rest.

"DARLING, WHERE ARE YOU?" Robert asked tentatively. The last thing he wanted was to make Melissa nervous.

"In my room waiting for Louisa. Don't worry, I'll come down in that blasted wheelchair," she said, clearly exasperated by his constant mollycoddling.

"Melissa, I don't want you to panic... but lock your door," Robert said in a measured tone.

"What! Why?"

"Emily McKenzie is in Louisa's room and she..."

"What? How? She's supposed to be in that facility," Melissa said confused.

"Well, she's not. Do it now. Hugh and his team are going to get Louisa out."

"Get her out? You're not making any sense."

Robert then carefully outlined what he believed had happened and that he was worried that Emily might also come to her. It was the first time Robert had heard Melissa a little unnerved.

"This is bad, Robert. She's suffered a kind of breakdown and had voluntarily checked herself in for therapy, after she lost the baby. I'll call and see how and when she got out – actually, find Gordon. If anyone can help, he can," Melissa said evenly as she waddled to the door of her room and locked the bolt. There was a good chance Emily would come for her, purely because she was pregnant.

"Oh God, I never thought."

"That's alright, that's why you married me, to do the thinking," she said and even though it was a tense situation, he smiled at her teasing, told her he loved her and went to find Gordon.

"SHE CHECKED OUT THIS morning," Gordon said after calling up the facility. He rubbed his forehead in frustration, clearly upset that they hadn't let him know. Though, to be fair, she had checked in voluntarily.

"The footage shows her coming in from the courtyard wearing the CASPO uniform." Kurt was speaking to Hugh from the security control room, where he was checking over the video footage with Robert, Gordon and Alistair. Robert had pulled Alistair aside to tell him what had happened and he'd immediately gone to the control room.

"Well, that explains where your T-shirt went." Robert said to Gordon and he nodded, his face ashen.

"She must've taken it when she came to visit last weekend. What on Earth is she thinking?"

"She's not. She's sick," Alistair said as calmly as he could. He'd seen many of his army buddies suffer from depression, paranoia, PTSD and many other conditions. It didn't need much to tip them over the edge. He looked over the different monitors and cursed that they couldn't see inside the suite. The tape had shown Emily coming in through the courtyard, where the large door hadn't been closed. She'd shut it behind her, then walked into the house. Everyone shifted uncomfortably, seeing Gerard talk to her in the hall and then make his way to the courtyard. No one mentioned the fact it was probably Gerard who had unknowingly let her in – they had more important things to focus on.

Robert called Melissa and told her what they'd found out.

"Robert, I'm scared."

"Don't be darling. I'm already on my way," he said exiting the office.

"Call for an ambulance."

"What? Why are you in labour?" He said beginning to jog towards the house, panicked at the thought of her giving birth under these circumstances.

"No, but Emily is going to need sedation and to be taken away."

"Right, yes, you're right. You really do think of everything. Let me call Alistair. He'll know what to do."

HUGH STOPPED AT THE top of the stairs and surveyed the corridor. He knew it like the back of his hand, from its lush deep-pile blue carpet to the ornate mouldings and antiques displayed on priceless console tables. Revered paintings hung on the walls, showcased by crystal chandeliers. It was the epitome of calm and the direct opposite of the feelings of the eight men on the outside and no doubt the mood of the women behind the two doors. Karl was standing like a statue by the door, listening intently. He made some hand signals that Hugh seemed to understand, then Miles whispered, "What does that mean?"

"They're calm, but Emily does have a weapon and the door is still bolted. We might have to go in from the window," Pierce said.

"What about the secret passage?" Miles said, turning to Hugh, and the head of security let out a breath.

"Shit yes," Hugh hissed in relief. *How had he forgotten?* "I hope it's not locked." He then signalled to his team to move up to the corridor, while he carefully moved quickly yet silently down the corridor towards the far room.

Miles watched for a moment, then turned to Pierce. "I'm going too." Before Pierce could object, Miles took off after Hugh. Pierce cursed under his breath and turned to the four men behind him. He quickly instructed them to come towards the door and he then took off after Miles.

Hugh gave a quick thanks to the heavens when he found the door to the room unlocked and he strode in and straight to the wooden panel. Before he popped the secret door open, he heard Miles come through the door. "What are you doing here?"

"I'm coming with you," Miles said, as though it was obvious.

Before Hugh could argue, Pierce appeared. Without another word, they all stepped into the secret corridor and quickly walked the length of it in silence. Once they got to the door, Hugh listened carefully, and when he was sure no one was there, he tried the handle. The three of them gave a collective sigh of relief when the door opened and they quietly stepped into Louisa's dressing room.

19

THE COVER-UP

T he first thing that struck Louisa was, *why is everything in such a mess?* It took her a millisecond to actually register that the mess was because Emily was plunging scissors into her bedspread, and ripping the ivory comforter to shreds. It took another millisecond for her to realise that the Emily who was ripping up her bed in a deranged frenzy was not the fun-loving, slightly spoilt Emily she knew.

"Emily? What the hell are you doing?"

When Emily had walked into Louisa's suite, she hadn't had a plan per se. She just wanted to damage something. Something valuable. Something that would break Louisa's heart, like hers had been. Of course, there was nothing of *that* value in the room. There wasn't a husband who she was madly in love with, or a baby. Those were valuable, precious, irreplaceable. She'd lost both because of Louisa and she hated her for it.

The room was exquisite, elegant and utterly beautiful, just like its owner, which only made Emily angrier. So angry in fact, that she was content to just destroy anything. She picked up the carefully laid out dress Louisa had left for her to change into, and pulled it apart, until the white silk material gave a satisfying ripping sound. Once the dress was thoroughly destroyed, she looked around frantically for something else to ruin. Her eye caught sight of an antique letter opener on her bureau and she rushed over and grabbed it. She then scanned the room at what else she could damage and contemplated ripping the heavy curtains but even in her deranged mind, she knew the antique letter opener wouldn't pierce the luxurious fabric. She rummaged through the drawers of the bureau and came across some large scissors and pulled them up in triumph. These would penetrate anything, she thought to herself. Emily ran to the bed and raised the scissors above her head, then, with all her might, she drove the points into the bedspread. The delicate material tore easily, letting the soft down spew out. Emily smiled wildly and began her frenzied slashing, imagining it was Louisa with every plunge of the scissors.

At the sound of Louisa's voice, Emily's attention was diverted from the bed to the doorway Louisa had just stepped through. Emily stopped and stood for a moment, breathing heavily. For a beat, she contemplated apologizing – an instinctual response so ingrained in her from her impeccable upbringing – until she took in the sight of the stunning woman.

"Emily." Something snapped in her, hearing Louisa's voice. "Put the scissors down," Louisa continued and Emily screamed, then ran towards her before the last word was out of Louisa's mouth. In that second, Louisa knew she wouldn't make it out of her room in time so rather than try and grapple with the heavy door, she ran to the side and took cover behind an ornate occasional chair. In her haste to grab the chair, she dropped her phone. It bounced away under a small display cabinet by the door.

"Emily," Louisa said as softly as possible, remembering the words of instruction from Hugh that the repeating of your assailant's name helped create a sense of familiarity. "It's alright; I'm not upset. Really." Louisa hoped her tone sounded sincere, rather than terrified. Her heart was hammering in her chest and her knuckles were white from the grip on the chair.

Emily's eyes moved from left to right, in jerky motions, as though she was trying to assess the situation. She then ran to the door and slammed the few inches it was open shut with a kick and dead-bolted it. Louisa swallowed hard, realising one of her escape routes was now blocked. She was trapped. *Why did I not run straight back out of my room once I saw Emily?* Was it shock? Confusion that had clouded her survival instincts to run? Or was it because she knew Emily and the whole disturbing scene had disorientated her thoughts? Whatever the reason, Louisa was on full alert now. Her only option for escape was through her dressing room and there was no way she'd be able make a dash to it with all the obstacles. Louisa caught sight of her beautiful dress, torn to shreds on the floor and she fleeting thought how mad Melissa would be that she hadn't changed yet and gone to fetch her. The blood drained from Louisa's face, thinking that Melissa was next door and was quite capable of coming to find her. If Emily heard her voice, or knew she was just next door, it might make matters worse. Louisa grabbed her locket and pressed it hard, praying the thing worked and that Hugh and his team came fast before Melissa unwittingly made things worse.

"Emily, please just put the scissors down and we can talk about why you're so upset."

Emily threw head back and cackled, which sent shivers up Louisa's spine. The woman in front of her looked like Emily but her demeanour, her movements and the look in her eyes were of someone entirely different. Someone sinister. The initial shock of what Louisa had stepped into had worn off and was now replaced with unmitigated fear.

"Upset!" Emily shrieked. "I'm not upset. I'm angry. Angry at you and your perfect life. Everyone loves you!"

"Emily…"

"No, don't interrupt! You listen to me. You don't have all your bodyguards all over you now. It's just you and me," she said inching towards her brandishing the scissors at her like a sword.

"Okay, but put the scissors down and you can tell me everything you're angry about." Louisa tried to keep her voice as steady and calm as she could and kept her eyes locked on Emily's wild ones. Hugh had told her to always look her assailant in the eye.

"You can't tell me what to do. I'm not your subject. You're nothing to me," Emily spat out.

"That's right. I'm nothing."

"I said don't interrupt! You think you're so fucking special, so perfect. In your house with hundreds of rooms and hundreds of staff. I hate you. You ruined my life. I'm going to ruin yours. Ruin you. Make you suffer." Emily was now only a few feet away. If she lunged, she'd easily pin Louisa to the wall behind her. Her wild eyes narrowed onto Louisa's left hand that gripped the chair.

"What's that?"

Louisa swallowed hard. Emily had noticed her engagement ring.

"I said what… is… that?" Emily used the scissors to point at the diamond.

"It's a ring."

"An *engagement* ring?" Emily said venomously.

"Yes." Louisa's voice was quiet.

"You're engaged? To…?"

"Miles."

"Miles." She let the fact settle for a moment and Louisa wasn't sure what she was thinking. "Give me your ring," she said sharply.

"Emily…"

"Give me your ring. It's precious; it means something to you. I want it. I want it now, so give me your fucking ring!"

"Okay, okay. I'll give it to you. Just please put the scissors down," Louisa said as she prised her beautiful ring off her finger and held it for a second. Emily opened her left palm and curled her fingers, indicating Louisa should put it in her hand. "I won't tell anyone what you did," Louisa whispered, dropping the ring in Emily's palm.

Emily snapped it shut and shoved the ring in the pocket of her jeans. "What I did? I haven't done anything." Emily furrowed her brow, trying to understand what Louisa was implying.

Louisa took this small window of opportunity and sidled away from the protection of the chair and backwards, just to widen the distance between them. If she could just move a little bit more, she'd be closer to her dressing room. "Of course, but you need to put the scissors down. I don't want you to injure yourself. Shall we call someone? Someone to come and collect you?" She needed to keep Emily talking, distract her from realising that she was moving away from her. Emily looked so maniacal, Louisa wasn't sure how long she could maintain her calm state. She was hoping that Hugh was either on his way or already there, and she was annoyed with herself for not pressing the panic button sooner. The truth was this was the first time she'd ever had to use it.

"I don't need anyone. They… they thought they could put me in rehab and forget about me," Emily said with a sad tilt to her tone, and for a second, Louisa saw the old Emily reappear and she felt a little bit of relief. Maybe her talking had helped.

Louisa stepped back a little more, closing the gap between her and the open door to her dressing room. "No one has forgotten about you. Your family loves you."

Emily's eyes narrowed into sinister slits. "They don't. I'm an embarrassment," she sneered, then something in her clicked and her features hardened. "Stop moving and stop talking! I know what you're doing, you're trying to escape to the bathroom. Move over there." She brandished the large scissors wildly, indicating the direction Louisa should go to. "Move! You're trying to distract me; I know what your plan is." She moved quickly towards Louisa, her whole demeanour suddenly becoming unhinged with a crazed look in her widened eyes.

Louisa shuffled away from her escape route and stepped back, circling away from her. Her mind going into overdrive as to where she could hide until help got to her. "You can't keep me here forever, Emily. Someone's going to come looking for me."

Emily stopped and considered what Louisa said for a beat and Louisa realised that she'd not thought an escape plan through. Then, as though a light bulb had been switched on in her disorientated brain, she said, "I'll take you with me. I've got a car. Yes, that's it. I'll take you away and they won't be able to find you. Then Gordon will stay with me, because you won't be here anymore. You'll have disappeared and no one, *no one* will know where you are." She gave Louisa a menacing smirk. "Yes, that's what I'll do," she said with determined finality.

"Emily, they'll come and find me and then you'll be in so much trouble," Louisa pleaded.

"Shut up! Just shut up!" Emily lunged at her, taking Louisa by surprise. She managed to dodge her but Emily grasped at her clothes and pulled her down to the ground. Louisa's knees buckled and Emily pinned her down with her knee. Before Louisa could try and get up, Emily slapped her hard across her face, stunning her, and pressed the scissors to her neck. Louisa froze, knowing that if she tried to struggle, her chances of escaping without an injury would be small. Her tears that sprang into her eyes stung as they spilt down her throbbing cheek.

"Get up!" Emily released her knee and grabbed her hair, yanking her up and backwards, so that her back slammed into Emily's front.

"Ah!"

Emily seemed to find a super-strength and gripped her tightly around her neck. "I'll drive this into your pretty neck if you scream or struggle. I've nothing else to lose so shut up," Emily sneered, pushing the sharp point into Louisa's exposed neck.

"Emily, please, you're hurting me," Louisa whispered. Her left cheek felt red raw from where Emily had hit her and her scalp pounded from hitting the floor and having her hair pulled violently.

"Shut your mouth and walk," Emily said, jostling her towards the door.

HUGH STEPPED CAREFULLY INTO the dressing room and crouched low, so as to hide his large frame behind the central island of drawers. Pierce followed suit and signalled to Miles to do the same. They could hear Louisa and Emily talking and Miles wondered why Hugh was taking his time. He should be storming the room. Miles made a frustrated gesture to Pierce, indicating they should just go in. Pierce shook his head and put his finger on his lips.

Hugh stretched his neck to see if he could see their exact position, then shuffled forward. He caught sight of Emily's back but his main focus was her right hand holding a pair of scissors to Louisa's neck. She was holding Louisa in a vice grip against her and was heading to the door. A quick sweep of the room showed him that there'd been some kind of tussle; the room was in disarray and there was white fluffy down scattered around the floor. Karl was on the other side of the door and if Emily opened it, he wouldn't be able to successfully tackle her without the risk of hurting Louisa. Hugh shuffled back and spoke quietly into his sleeve. "Karl, rattle the door handle and call Louisa's name."

Miles furrowed his brow, unsure as to why Hugh wanted to take away the element of surprise. Before he could ask why, he heard the door rattle and a hard knock on the door to Louisa's suite. After a beat, he heard Karl's voice. "Lady Blackthorn?"

Hugh shuffled forward, low to the ground, and watched Emily falter. She muttered something and then Louisa said, "Yes Karl, I won't be a minute. I'm just changing." Emily seemed satisfied with her response and backed away from the door.

Hugh shuffled back with his eyes still trained on the two women and whispered, "She's trapped. Her only escape is through here. Pierce…" Hugh pointed to a section of the room by the entrance. Pierce instantly understood what Hugh was thinking. He lay almost flat on the carpeted floor and crawled to the point where Hugh had pointed to, then slowly rose up and plastered himself against the wall by the right-hand side of the entrance, hidden from Emily's view. Miles looked to Hugh for instruction. Without looking at Miles, Hugh signalled him to hide behind the drawers. Miles crawled around the back and kept crouched down but kept the entrance in his eyeline. Hugh then crawled low along the floor to the left-hand side of the entrance and mirrored Pierce's position. They were relying on Louisa now to tell Emily of the escape route through the dressing room. If she didn't reveal it, Hugh would have to find a way to prompt her.

MELISSA PACED HER ROOM, gripping her phone and frantically thinking of ways she could help. The doorknob rattled and she froze.

"It's me," came Robert's hushed voice and she immediately ran to the door and unlocked it. Robert took her in his arms, and an overwhelming wave of relief washed over him as he hugged her tightly before ushering her back into the room.

"What's going on?" Melissa said as he moved her to a seat and coaxed her to sit.

"Hugh and Pierce are in the dressing room; Karl is at the door along with a few more security. How are you feeling? You're not overexcited, are you?" he asked, scanning her face and brushing back her hair.

"I'm fine. What did Gordon say?" she answered with an agitated frown. Right now, she was more concerned with her best friend's safety.

"Emily checked out today. He's livid that they didn't let him know."

"Maybe he should talk to her," Melissa suggested.

"I'm not so sure. Emily would probably like the idea of removing Louisa from his life for good," Robert said sagely. A quick revealing conversation with Gordon had cemented Robert's belief that Emily was more than just a little jealous of Louisa. "It seems she has a severe case of paranoia and has also been diagnosed as schizophrenic. Apparently, she's been on medication since her early twenties and has these episodes when she doesn't keep up her meds."

"Oh goodness, poor Emily," Melissa gasped. Her family had done a very good job of keeping that under wraps and out of the press.

"Poor Louisa right now, though," Robert said pursing his lips.

"Well, yes. Has Alistair arranged an ambulance?"

"There's a few on-site and a doctor, so it's just a matter of…" Robert blew out a breath, uncomfortable with completing his sentence.

"Restraining her?"

"Uh-huh."

Robert felt his phone vibrate in his pocket and he pulled it out. "It's Alistair." He swiped the screen and answered it. "Any news?"

HUGH STRAINED TO HEAR what Emily was saying but she was whispering to Louisa as they moved around the room. He could hear the pleading tone of Louisa, though he wasn't quite able to hear what she was saying. Miles kept the two women in his sight. He could see Emily's vice grip on Louisa around her middle, restraining her arms, and her right arm, which held the scissors, was tense as though one slight twitch and the points would penetrate Louisa's delicate throat. Miles couldn't wait any longer; he needed to do something. If they waited, there was a chance Emily might freak out and hurt Louisa or worse. She was clearly unstable. He had to find a way for her to urge Emily into the dressing room. Miles pulled out his phone and began typing a group message to Karl, Pierce and Hugh. Hugh narrowed his eyes and pulled out his phone to read it.

Get Karl to tell Louisa that I said to make sure she takes a waterproof jacket from her dressing room as it's going to rain.

Hugh's eyes shot up to Miles and gave him a thumbs-up sign. He then typed his response to Karl, instructing him to say it word for word and emphasising selective words, then Hugh signalled to Pierce to be ready.

"Stop struggling," hissed Emily.

"You're hurting me. I won't run. There's nowhere for me to go," Louisa said as softly as possible. She was trying to work out how quickly she could run to the dressing room, if Emily's grip loosened. It was her only way of escape. Her neck stung where the scissors kept grazing and her cheek was still throbbing.

"Looks like we've a long night ahead, *my lady*," Emily sneered, squeezing her harder, and Louisa gasped.

"It'll be worse for you. I won't say anything," Louisa said, hoping Emily would realise there was no way out. Hugh would definitely be here now, she just hoped he had thought of the secret passageway.

There was another knock at the door and Emily tensed. "Don't say anything stupid," she threatened, and Louisa gave a small nod.

"Yes," Louisa said tentatively, hoping it was someone to negotiate with Emily.

"Sorry to disturb, but Mr Keane messaged me and suggested you bring a waterproof jacket from your dressing room, as it's going to rain," Karl said with an ever-so-slight emphasis on the words 'dressing room'.

"Thank you, Karl, I will. I'll get it right now," Louisa called back.

"How very sweet. Is he worried you'll get wet?" Emily mocked sarcastically and pressed the points a little bit harder into Louisa's neck.

Louisa grimaced but the pain was worth the ray of hope Karl's words had given her. It was a message for her to reveal the secret passageway. She had no doubt Hugh was in there now. Karl's reference to Miles and rain were an added reassurance. Only Miles, Hugh and her knew about their moment in the rain. Louisa took a deep breath and prayed to the heavily clouded heavens she'd interpreted the message correctly. "Do you want us to get out of here, without anyone knowing?" She felt Emily tense as she asked.

"What do you mean?"

"There's a secret passageway that leads you out to another room."

"From here?"

Louisa nodded, then immediately regretted moving her head, as the sharp points dug in a little more. "The door to it is in my dressing room."

Emily shifted around so that she could see the entrance to the dressing room. She studied the dark open entrance and narrowed her eyes. "Is this a trap?" she hissed menacingly and Louisa shook her head ever so slightly.

"That's why I was edging to it," she explained and let her revelation sit for a second. "If you want to get out of here and to your car, that's the only way out."

"Who knows about it?"

"My mother, Alistair, Celeste and Gerard." Louisa omitted Hugh and Miles; she just hoped Emily hadn't worked out that her security detail and fiancé would also know every nook and cranny of Holmwood House too. She could feel Emily's hesitation. "I can go first, if you like, and show you. So you know it's not a trap."

Emily jerked her closer to her and sneered into her ear. "Oh no, we go through it together."

"It's right at the back, behind the mirror," Louisa said clearly, hoping whoever was in there could hear they were approaching.

"Okay, let's go. Slowly. Don't try anything, otherwise I'll hurt that pretty neck of yours."

"I promise I won't run. Just put the scissors down. They're hurting my right side," Louisa said a little louder, trying to give Hugh as much information as possible.

"Shut your whining and *move.*" Emily pushed her forward and they shuffled towards the dark room. Louisa prayed there was someone in there to help her, otherwise she'd just revealed her only way of escape.

"Where are the lights?" Emily hissed as they neared the threshold.

"They're just to the right. If you let my hand go, I can put them on," Louisa said clearly.

"Not a chance. I'll put them on with my elbow."

Louisa stepped into her dressing room and scanned the dark room, desperately trying to see if anyone was there. Emily hitched up her right elbow in the vague direction of the light switch as soon as she cleared the door frame.

Before Emily knew what was happening, Pierce grabbed her suspended right arm which held the scissors to Louisa's neck and yanked it forcefully back and away from Louisa.

"Ah!" Emily cried out in pain and shock, and instinctively loosened her left vice grip on Louisa.

"Louisa!" called out Miles at the same time as Hugh pulled her away from Emily's hold and shielded her from her assailant's frantic grabbing hand. Hugh all but lifted Louisa as he ran with her into the depths of the dressing room and to the secret door and away from danger.

"Get off me!" screamed Emily as Pierce repeatedly banged her hand with force against the wall so she would release the scissors – but she seemed to have some super-strength. She jerked and kicked in a frenzy, landing hard kicks to Pierce's legs. Miles, seeing Louisa was safe, ran to Pierce's aid. A few seconds before he reached Pierce, Emily scratched Pierce across his neck and kneed him in the groin.

"Fuck!" groaned Pierce and his two-hand grip on her arm relaxed and he buckled. Emily seized the opportunity and drove the scissors into his shoulder as he bent over and Pierce cried out.

Before Miles could even think, he raised his right hand and punched Emily straight in the jaw with a sharp jab. "Psycho bitch!" Miles ground out as she fell back against the wall, banging her head. She slumped to the floor unconscious. Miles turned to where Pierce was buckled up behind him. "Pierce, fuck. Are you okay?"

"Tie the bitch up before she comes around," Pierce ground out and Miles looked around for something to use. He flicked on the lights and headed to where Louisa had her robes. He yanked off one of the ties and ran back to where Emily lay. He pushed her onto her front and yanked her arms behind her back and began to tie them.

In the background, Miles could hear Pierce telling the team that they had the assailant controlled and that they needed a doctor. "Are you okay? Did Hugh take Louisa away?" Miles said. He shot a quick look at his friend.

"Hugh got her out. I'm fine; just winded. She got me good in the balls." Pierce coughed. "Tie up her legs too. She has a hard kick," he added with a grunt.

Miles looked back over his shoulder at his friend and narrowed his eyes. In the dark and the rush to get the robe tie, Miles hadn't noticed the blood that was seeping through Pierce's shirt. "You're bleeding!"

"Yeah, the bitch got me." Pierce straightened. "Tie her legs and open the door. The team can't get in and they don't need to break the door down." Miles nodded and attached another tie from a robe to Emily's hands and then tied up her legs, hogtie style.

"Good work," Pierce said wincing. "I'm going to the bathroom."

"Let me help you."

"Open the door, so the doctor can come in."

"Shit, yes, okay." Miles sprinted to the door and opened up the lock. He was faced with a stone-faced Karl and the four-security team and a young woman with a medical bag. "He's in the bathroom, through that door." Miles pointed to the bathroom and she immediately jogged towards it. The rest of the team came in, closely followed by Gordon and two other medics. Miles scanned the hall in search of Louisa, but the hallway was empty. He shut the door and headed to the dressing room where Karl had led the team. Miles was about to ask him if he knew where Louisa was, when she appeared from the secret door with Hugh.

Miles immediately ran to her. "Louisa, are you okay?" He scanned over her face and caught sight of a few cuts on the right side of her neck and he scowled, seeing her red cheek.

"I'm fine."

"Your neck. Your neck, it's bleeding. You need a doctor." His eyes shot to Hugh, who nodded his approval and his tense expression told Miles he'd already insisted Louisa see the doctor, but had obviously been ignored. Hugh walked over to where Emily lay and crouched down to talk to the medics.

Miles put his arms around her and held her close, relived she was alright. "I died a thousand deaths until I could see you. Are you sure you're okay? She didn't hurt you anywhere else? Why is your cheek so red?"

"She slapped me." Miles guided her towards the bathroom, past Emily slumped face down on the floor tied up, where the medics were checking her over while Gordon hovered.

"Is she...?" Louisa's eyes widened, seeing Emily's prone body and a small puddle of blood on the ivory carpet.

"No," Miles answered, understanding how it looked. "I just punched her."

"Oh." Louisa's eyes widened but before she could say anything Hugh appeared.

"Here you are, my lady." He held out her engagement ring and Miles furrowed his brow. "She took it from Lady Blackthorn."

Miles's expression hardened and he plucked the ring from Hugh's hand. "Fucking bitch," Miles muttered.

"Quite," Hugh agreed and gave a nod, before going back to where his team were.

Miles took Louisa's left hand and slowly slipped the ring back on her finger. "This doesn't come off." He lifted her hand to his lips and kissed her ring and finger and Louisa gave him a shy smile. "Come on, let the doctor look at you."

"It's just a scratch," Louisa said with a shake of her head and then she winced. Her head and scalp throbbed.

Gordon's attention was diverted to Louisa as she and Miles shuffled past. "Are you okay? I'm so sorry, she checked herself out. I had no idea," Gordon said in a rush, seeing Louisa uncharacteristically dishevelled.

"I'm okay, just shaken. A few cuts and bruises."

"What happened to her?" Gordon asked, looking back at Emily's motionless body.

"Miles punched her."

Gordon shifted his attention to Miles, enraged that he'd been so violent. "You punched her!"

"She had scissors at Louisa's neck, then stabbed Pierce in the shoulder. *And* she stole Louisa's engagement ring! So, damn straight I fucking punched her! Sue me."

LOUISA LOOKED AROUND HER suite and let out a breath. The place looked a mess but she hadn't wanted any of the staff to come in until Emily had been taken away and any evidence of a struggle had been removed. Though how she would explain the bloodstain on the dressing room carpet, she wasn't sure. Miles kept hold of her hand the whole time she explained to Hugh, step by step, what had happened. Louisa was mindful of Miles's reaction to each part she recollected. He'd cursed under his breath a number of times and shot Hugh looks. Her head of security kept his calm but his jaw was tense and Louisa knew he felt responsible for what had happened. The truth was: Emily had just gotten lucky. They'd been so focused on a stranger trying to get to either Louisa or Miles, when in the end it had been someone the family, friends and staff knew. And because her condition and previous altercation with Louisa had been kept quiet, no one outside of Louisa, Hugh and Miles knew she could be a threat.

Once Emily came around, she screamed and snarled, letting out a tirade of threats and bucked fiercely against her restraints. Any pity Louisa had for her quickly evaporated. The medics sedated her and took her away to a more secure facility. Gordon was left to inform her family of what had happened. Louisa didn't envy that task. He looked so forlorn when he left and she assured him that they would keep everything confidential, to Gordon's relief and Miles's and Hugh's irritation. She didn't want Emily's parents to suffer from any scandal. Even though she had escaped with minimum injuries, the same could not be said of Pierce, though. But he'd also refused to press charges against Emily and agreed to keep the incident to only those within the closed circle, with the proviso that if Emily came within 100 feet of him, he would report her.

Karl did the best job he could, tidying up the torn comforter and its insides that littered the room, putting everything in bin bags. Pierce received seven stitches from the doctor, who wanted him to go to a hospital, but he insisted on staying at Holmwood. Luckily, the scissors had had to go through his jacket, a shirt and a T-shirt, making the sharp points only penetrate the top layers of skin. The shot of painkiller the doctor gave would thankfully see him through to the morning.

Melissa had now moved Louisa to her dressing room for some privacy, while Robert had gone in search of a new shirt and jacket for Pierce to wear. Miles had been reluctantly ushered back to the stage, ready for his next co-introduction with Konran. They needed to carry on as though nothing had happened, so Hugh had also gone with him, leaving Louisa with Karl and a patched-up Pierce. The rest of the security team were situated outside Louisa's suite.

The doctor was checking over Louisa, at Miles's insistence. She shone a light in Louisa's eye. "Look up, look down, left, right," the doctor said and Louisa huffed.

"She just slapped me hard and pulled at my hair." The doctor nodded and then looked closer at the marks on her neck. There were three red nicks visible that were now dried blood, and the beginnings of a bruise forming. Louisa shifted in her seat and winced. The doctor narrowed her eyes at her. "My ribs feel tender. She held me down with her knees," Louisa said quietly and Melissa gasped.

"Good Lord, that's awful!"

"I'm fine, really. It's poor Pierce who got the worst of it."

"I'd like to see, my lady. Just to be sure."

Louisa took off her jacket and top and let the doctor check her back and sides. Melissa furrowed her brow and watched on, seeing the first bloom of bruises forming.

"They look bruised but no broken ribs. I'll give you some painkillers and I'd like to dress your neck."

"Oh God, how will that look, going out on stage with a huge bandage?" Louisa said wearily.

"You're going on stage?" Melissa said in surprise.

"Of course, I am. This is still CASPO's event. Emily's kidnap attempt isn't going to put a stop to that."

"Right, right, yes of course. That's the spirit. The show must go on and all that. Well, we need to find you something to change into," Melissa said, a little in awe of her friend. She was all business again and she rose from the Ottoman and started scanning the racks of clothes. "My lady, you've had a shock. I wouldn't advise you do anything other than take it easy."

"Thank you, but I'm a Blackthorn and we're notorious for being stubborn," Louisa said in a matter-of-fact tone and Melissa stifled a smirk. Louisa pulled on a robe, noting that the tie was missing, so she held it tight against her and said, "Melissa, see that purple dress?"

Melissa waddled to where Louisa was pointing and pulled out a rich purple, silky dress. It had one long sleeve that came over her right shoulder and was attached to a wide tie of the same material. The left arm was sleeveless and the tie was used to wrap around the wearer's neck to hold the sleeve and dress in place. The dress draped Grecian style around the bodice and had an asymmetric finish, with the longest point falling just above the ankle and the shortest point coming just above the knee. It was edgy and sexy but still looked suitable for a countess. The best thing about the dress, though, was that the wide tie covered up her neck beautifully.

"Perfect," Melissa said, then pulled out a pair of gold stilettoes and held them up. Louisa gave her a nod.

"Now, I need to see if my makeup can cover up my red raw cheek." Louisa thanked the kind doctor and asked her to stay on in the VIP section. She quickly instructed Karl to organise an escort for her, then she turned her attention to Pierce. He was slipping on a shirt

Robert had brought him. "You stay here with me until I'm ready to go down," Louisa said with affection.

"As you wish, my lady."

"Maybe have a cup of tea?"

"I think Robert went to sort out some for us all," Pierce said with a smirk. Louisa gave a nod and headed back into her dressing room, then shut the door behind her.

"Oh, crap." Melissa lay the dress and shoes across from her and slumped into her seat on the Ottoman.

"What's wrong?" Louisa asked.

"We missed Maroon 5. That's them singing their last song." Louisa strained to hear and sure enough, they were singing *Girls Like You*.

"If I hurry up, we'll get to see and hear The Spin Doctors, Ed Sheeran and The Police before Konran comes on," Louisa said, stepping up to the Ottoman and sitting next to her.

"Well, stop dawdling, then," Melissa mock-chastised and Louisa gave her a soft smile, then took a breath.

"Do you mind if I just take a breather?"

Melissa took hold of Louisa's hand, which she noticed had started shaking, and clasped it. Water flooded Louisa's eyes. "You take all the time in the world," Melissa said tenderly as Louisa let the tears run down her face. "Come here." Melissa wrapped her arms around her and let her friend sob into her shoulder.

"I was so scared. She was so deranged; nothing like the Emily we know. I was worried she'd come after you," Louisa said between sobs.

"I know. She was just sick. You heard what Robert said." Melissa held her and let Louisa release all the built-up tension. "Let it out. You're a tough cookie but that was next level." Louisa couldn't help but smile at her friend's comment. "I can't believe Miles punched her. He's badass."

Louisa chuckled. "Gordon was horrified," Louisa mumbled.

"I bet he was, but Miles did the right thing."

"He did. I think he likes the idea of being involved in the security. Hugh, Pierce and him are tight." Louisa sniffed, pulling back, and Melissa passed her a tissue.

"You feeling a bit better now?" She bobbed down to catch Louisa's gaze, and Louisa nodded. "That's my girl. Good. Well, you've a lot more to worry about now than covering up your red cheek," Melissa said dryly. Louisa turned to one of the mirrors and stared at her blotchy face and red-rimmed eyes.

"Oh crap."

20

IN THE SPOTLIGHT

"My lady, you look lovely," Pierce said, standing up as Louisa entered her suite from her dressing room. It took Louisa a little longer to prepare for her stage appearance. Melissa had suggested she take a warm shower to help relieve the tension and organised a cold compress for her cheek. An hour later, she felt less fragile. Her red-rimmed eyes were gone and her cheek had subdued enough that her makeup could tone it down.

"As do you. Where did you get that jacket?"

"I have no idea. Mr Hindley found it for me. It's a Tom Ford," Pierce said, looking down at himself, then opening up the jacket to reveal the label.

"Well, it suits you and it's a perfect fit. Melissa, remind me to order Pierce a few Tom Ford suits. It's the least I can do for being stabbed for me," Louisa said and Pierce chuckled.

"Of course. She's right, you look very dashing."

"Thank you, ladies." Pierce gave them a nod, then Karl pushed the wheelchair forward for Melissa to sit in. She rolled her eyes and lowered herself into it, clearly exasperated.

"Come on. We've missed The Spin Doctors too; at least we can catch the end of Ed Sheeran," Melissa grumbled. They'd both watched the concert on the TV while Louisa got ready. Miles and Robert had spoken to them both repeatedly throughout the performances but stayed in the VIP section so as not to raise any suspicion.

"Melissa, I promise you. When Maroon 5 have a tour, I'll take you," Louisa said, patting her shoulder.

"Pierce, you are my witness," Melissa said, looking up at him as Karl pushed the chair out of the suite.

"Yes ma'am."

"And you can come with us, of course," she added.

"It would be my pleasure."

"You sure you're alright?" Louisa asked him for the hundredth time.

Pierce nodded. "That doctor shot me up well. Those painkillers will be fine until the morning."

They paused at the door to the corridor and Louisa took hold of his right arm. "Thank you." Her words were heavy with sincere gratitude.

"You don't have to thank me, my lady," Pierce said gently, seeing the deep concern etched on Louisa's face.

"I do, Pierce, I really do."

HUGH KEPT HIS FOCUS on the monitors as Ed Sheeran sang the last few lines of his final song. He let his eyes dart to the monitor where Louisa and Miles were in view and a shiver ran up his spine at the thought of what could have happened. Pierce stood ramrod straight behind the couple as they sat with Melissa, Robert, Celeste and Nicolas. The young Lady Blackthorn knew nothing of her mother's ordeal and now wasn't the time. But she would have to be informed, if only for her own safety.

The VIP area had filled up with a few of the artists that had stayed on, as well as members of their entourages. The socialites and VIPs were having a ball mingling amongst them, thoroughly enjoying themselves, but Hugh was pleased to see that Louisa had stayed backstage, away from the crowds. The attack on her was still too raw and though she was putting on a brave face, he could see she was still shaken. It also didn't go unnoticed that Miles had stuck to her side like glue, only leaving her to do his introduction with Konran.

Hugh's attention shifted as the door to the control room opened. Alistair stepped up next to him and handed him a cool bottle of water. Hugh thanked him but kept his eyes on the monitors.

"Everything okay?"

"Yeah." Hugh checked the time. "An hour left. I'll be glad when it's all over."

Alistair smirked. "Looks like we might get away without getting rained on."

"If rain's the only problem over the next hour, I can live with it," Hugh said dryly. "I've had enough excitement for one day."

"You and me both. Pierce needs some time off," Alistair said, seeing Pierce roll his uninjured shoulder.

"I know; you tell him. He's hell-bent on sticking around."

"Well, after today, things should quieten down."

"I admire your optimism," Hugh said with a hint of sarcasm. "After today, Lady Blackthorn and Miles Keane will be the talk of the town – scratch that: the world."

"Oh, you mean after the concert? Yes, I suppose so but at least they won't need to be out in the public eye anymore."

Hugh let out a soft laugh. "You know that Miles's series comes out next month. He'll be asked on interviews and then he has the film and God knows what else. Things are going to get… livelier."

Alistair shifted the weight onto his right leg. "Crap, you're right. We're going to need more security."

"I'm already on it."

"Of course you are," Alistair chuckled.

"Go and enjoy the concert. Amanda's looking a little lonely." Hugh nodded to one of the monitors that showed Amanda prising herself away from one of the musicians in the VIP area and heading to the sanctuary of backstage.

"You're funny."

"One of my many talents," Hugh countered as Alistair headed to the door, stifling a grin.

"Hugh."

Hugh turned to look at him. "Yes sir."

"Thank you," Alistair said earnestly and Hugh understood exactly what Alistair was thanking him for. Hugh gave him a small smile and a nod and said, "No need, sir."

LOUISA STARED UP AT the stage from her sectioned-off position in the VIP area and smiled widely. She was finally getting to watch The Police perform live – and in her back garden, no less! She'd been a huge fan; in fact both she and Melissa had been diehard fans in their teens, with all that that encompassed: posters in their rooms, every album they featured on, doodling of their name and Sting's in a heart, the whole fan package. But they had never been allowed to go and see them perform. When they were both older, the group had stopped playing together and touring, so they'd never got to see their favourite band in concert. Once Louisa had married, it wasn't really something she could decide to do, so seeing her teenage crush sing *Every Little Thing She Does Is Magic* live was a dream come true.

"This is surreal," Melissa shouted to her over the music. "Twenty-five years we've waited for this."

"I know. It was worth the wait though, eh?" Melissa nodded and laughed.

"Having a good time?" Miles asked with an arch of his brow.

"The best. Did you ask them to play this song?" Louisa asked.

"I may have suggested to Sting that Lady Blackthorn liked this particular hit of theirs."

"You're a good fiancé," she whispered and Miles grinned.

"Anything for my lady."

THE CROWD WENT WILD as Konran ran up and down the stage, singing his latest number one hit single. His energy was contagious. He'd been on the go for over 15 hours and yet he was performing as though he'd just started. Miles was in awe of his newfound friend. The crowd sang along to every one of his rap songs and Margi, Roy and Ty were right there with their front man. This was a huge night for them too, rubbing shoulders with musical legends and musicians they'd only ever listened to. Today had elevated them all to equal status and it was both overwhelming yet thrilling.

Ty beat out the last few bars of music on the drums and the song ended with pyrotechnics shooting up from the front of the stage. The crowd roared as Konran raised his hands high in the air and looked up to the heavens, the ultimate showman. Silver confetti fell from the sky like stardust and the crowd chanted for more.

Konran looked out to the audience and beamed his patented toothy smile. "You guys are awesome!" The crowd roared back in reply. "Today has been about raising money and having a good time!" Everyone cheered. "Today has been about getting amazing musicians together and making a difference!" Airhorns blasted along with the cheers. "Today happened thanks to the Blackthorn family and to you guys." He pointed to the audience around the arena. "Coming here and supporting Concert for CASPO! Thank you!" Everyone cheered again and Konran beamed at them. "Now, as you all know, I had a little help from my friend and legend, Miles Keane tonight." There was a deafening roar and screams from the audience and Konran chuckled. "Man, he's still got it, right?" The crowd laughed and cheered. "Well tonight, as a thank you from us to you, we have a special something for y'all." The audience roared and Konran ran back to his piano and took a seat.

Louisa furrowed her brow as she looked up at the stage as Konran spoke. She turned to where Miles had been standing next to Alistair behind her, and saw that he wasn't there. She swivelled round to see where Karl was and she spotted him at the front of the stage area with two more security. Louisa then turned and caught Pierce's eye and she gave him a questioning look. Pierce just gave her a one-shoulder shrug and a knowing smirk.

Before she could say anything to Melissa or Celeste, who were sitting next to her, the stage darkened and the crowd gasped, then let out cheers and whistles in excited anticipation of what was about to happen. There was shuffling on the stage but it was too dark to make out what was going on and then over the speakers the deep rumble of Ty's voice hushed the crowd.

"Ladies and gentlemen, live at Holmwood at Concert for CASPO, Miles Keane."

A spotlight lit the centre of the stage, where Miles sat on a stool with his guitar around his neck and a microphone in front of him.

The crowd went ballistic. Louisa jumped up from her seat, quickly followed by Melissa and Celeste.

"Did you know about this?" Louisa asked Melissa.

"No! Oh my God, he's going to sing," Melissa said, at the same time as Celeste said, "Mum, he's going to sing!"

Amanda jumped up from her seat and turned to Alistair, clearly in shock. "He's going to sing. This is huge!"

"Uh-huh," Alistair said, equally surprised, taking in the stunned faces in the VIP area. Miles Keane was going to sing after five years of being a recluse. This wasn't huge – it was monumental.

Miles waited, allowing the audience to express their surprise and joy that he was back on stage and to take a moment to absorb the enormity of what he was doing. He took a deep breath and gave a small smile and repeated his brother's mantra to himself. *Believe it to achieve it.* And then he said, "It's been a while."

The crowd cheered and Miles grinned back at them, that megawatt smile that had his fans swooning and had earned him the title of Sexiest Man on the Planet. His image blasted around the arena on the huge screens and across the whole world via satellite. There was no doubt that Miles Keane belonged on the stage. Just sitting on a stool on a huge blacked-out stage, he somehow managed to command the audience's full attention. His magnetism was thermonuclear; there wasn't a person who wasn't spellbound by his presence.

Lady Alice gave Margot a pat on her arm, where they were both sat in her private sitting room, enjoying the show. "I knew he'd come through," she said with a self-satisfied smile.

"He certainly has," agreed Margot.

Across the ocean, Katy and Richard Keane stared at their widescreen TV at their son on stage again. His appearance was both heart-stopping and heart-rending in equal parts and his parents were filled with an enormous sense of pride and apprehension.

"I'D LIKE TO PLAY you a song, specially written for tonight for a special someone," continued Miles, and the audience whooped and cheered loudly, but soon quietened when Konran played the intro and Miles shuffled forward to strum the first chord on his guitar.

Before it felt empty
Nothing but dark
Shrouded in the
Blackness of my heart
Moments of sadness
In between the pain
My life and soul
Never the same

You came to me
I kissed you in the rain
No one's watching
And I kissed you again
I loved you then

You crossed my battlefield
My black heart taken
Signed and sealed
My life changed then
Signed and sealed

Show me how to wash
Away the stain
Hold me until
I'm without the pain
My love is strong
Worth the price
Pure addiction
More than any vice

You came to me
I kissed you in the rain
Everyone's watching
So I kissed you again
I'll love you always
My heart healed
Just by you
Signed and sealed
Always you
Signed and sealed

You taught me how
To live again
Breathed life and blood
Into my damaged veins
So beautiful
So kind and true
My lady love
I live for you

You came to me
I kissed you in the rain

They keep on watching
I'll kiss you again
My heart wide open
All revealed
My love for you
Signed and sealed
Forever and ever
Signed and sealed

Throughout the performance, Louisa stood mesmerised, like every person in the concert and no doubt around the globe. It was a love song, dedicated to her, and he was declaring his feelings to the whole world. His husky voice and heartfelt performance had everyone transfixed. Louisa blinked her tears back, totally overcome with the overwhelming and raw sentiment he was expressing, the fears he was overcoming, for her, always for her. Before she realised what she was doing, she had made her way to the side of the stage where Kurt was waiting. The crowd was going wild and as if it was a sign, a few specks of rain started to fall.

Hugh turned to his crew in the control room and told them to keep watch, then he strode out of the control room and jogged up to the side of the stage, grabbing an umbrella en route. He raced up the stairs and stood beside to Louisa.

"Whenever you're ready, my lady," he said and she shifted her attention from the front of the stage to the man she'd owed her life to, and held his gaze for a beat and smiled.

Miles stood up from the stool and waved to the audience as they cheered loudly. Konran rose from his piano and punched the air, whooped loudly. *He'd done it!* He'd finally made it back on stage and wowed the crowd, just like he always had and how Konran had known he would again. Konran cheered along with the crowd, revelling in his friend's success. Miles Keane was back and what a way to come back, live on stage at a worldwide concert.

It was starting to drizzle and Miles looked up at the heavens and laughed. He looked to the right and saw Louisa standing undercover in the wings with Hugh and he beckoned her to come out. Hugh opened up the umbrella and led Louisa out on stage. Miles grinned, seeing

Hugh shielding Louisa from the light rain. It was only fitting that Hugh shared the limelight with him and Louisa. He always seemed to be around at their most pivotal moments. The audience cheered, seeing Lady Blackthorn on stage again and Miles reached out, took her hand and kissed it.

"My lady love, my fiancée, Lady Louisa Blackthorn!" Miles said into the microphone and the audience collectively gasped and immediately cheered loudly.

The image of Louisa and Miles on stage together, being shielded by an umbrella held by Hugh, would no doubt be flashed around the world on every media platform. They were finally out of the darkness and into the light for all to see. There'd be no more hiding, no clandestine meetings or secrecy. Lady Blackthorn had brought Miles back into the spotlight; he wasn't behind her in the wings, he wasn't out in front of her either, but he was right beside her, exactly where she wanted him to be and where he belonged.

21

SIGNED AND SEALED

Miles Keane has definitely Signed and Sealed *his top-ranking position in both his professional and private life, after last night's outstanding Concert for CASPO and surprise engagement announcement. Originally, the popstar and idol was only set to co-host the concert with the number one rapper TuKon, but Miles Keane surprised the worldwide audience with his exceptional and renowned trumpet playing, accompanying fellow musician French Montana and survivor of a shooting (see video below).*

After a five-year absence and major speculation, Miles Keane took to the stage in an unforgettable finale performing a heartfelt ballad, Signed and Sealed, *written especially for the concert and for his fiancée, Lady Louisa Blackthorn. The double whammy had audiences stunned and surprised, as well as all media outlets. It has to be one of the best-kept secrets this year.*

Lady Louisa Blackthorn sported a huge cushion cut diamond engagement ring (see picture left), as Mr Keane announced their engagement to the world. Not even the light drizzle could dampen their obvious happiness. The couple met while Miles Keane volunteered at CASPO earlier this summer, and later became ambassador to the charity, a source close to the family revealed. Lady Blackthorn and Miles Keane have been working closely together on a number of fundraising projects and Mr Keane has been instrumental to the success of last night's concert.

The concert held at the stately home of the revered Blackthorn family, Holmwood House, is set to raise over £15 million from ticket and merchandise sales. The charity's spokesperson Darcy Aldridge said the figure is expected to rise with future donations, The charity was started by the late Earl of Holmwood and his wife Lady Alice. CASPO has helped fund struggling single-parent families and give their children equal opportunities. Amongst the bands that played at last night's concert were The Police, Ed Sheeran, Dua Lipa and co-host, organiser and number one rapper, TuKon.

Miles Keane revealed recently that he has a number of projects. His first TV series, Keane's Interest, *airs in two weeks and filming of his new film starts early next year. Speculation now is on when the couple will finally tie the knot, with such a busy schedule. Let's hope the happy couple don't keep us waiting for too long.*

GERARD CLENCHED HIS JAW as he scrolled through the many posts and sites documenting and reporting on last night's concert. He was still holed up at Holmwood. He'd arranged to stay for the morning so he could spend time with Celeste, but even spending time with his beloved daughter seemed like an ordeal in the light of last night's revelation. His grand entrance had been forgotten and every media outlet was talking about Miles. Miles's comeback, Miles's bound-to-be-a-worldwide-number-one hit song and performance, Miles's excellent co-hosting and, the last nail in the coffin, Miles's and Louisa's engagement.

Gerard had seen the number of floral deliveries arriving all morning for the happy couple. The grand hall was covered in arrangements when he'd gone out for his morning ride and after he'd arrived back, an hour later, the number had easily doubled. The heady scent of the blooms filled the vast entrance. Gerard looked out of his window and wondered whether this was the last time he'd be welcome here.

The grounds were teeming with staff, clearing the debris left behind by the hordes of spectators. Alistair had wasted no time in getting the stage dismantled and the various temporary walls they had erected taken down. Holmwood House had to get back to business and even the light late summer rain of last night hadn't stopped the workmen working throughout the night.

Lady Alice looked out over the grounds as she sipped her tea. By the looks of it, Holmwood would be ready for business tomorrow. It was good to have a house full of guests. Over the last 10 years, only close family had stayed, and the occasional friend of Alistair's. The Blackthorn family was growing, though. Miles was now part of the Blackthorns and if Melissa's meddling had done the trick, Amanda and her adorable children would also be regular, if not permanent residents too. Breakfast this morning had been reminiscent of the many times the late Earl had had members of his staff over for parties. The look on Amanda's parents' faces was priceless as their grandchildren showed them around the breakfast buffet in the conservatory like seasoned pros. It didn't go unnoticed that Alistair went to extraordinary lengths to make them feel comfortable too. He was definitely his father's son.

A light knock at the door drew Lady Alice's attention away from the window and her thoughts. "Come in."

One of the house staff stepped into the room and Lady Alice gave her a smile. "Mr Dupont will be leaving shortly, my lady. You asked me to let you know."

"Yes, thank you. Ask him to come up to see me."

"Of course, my lady."

It didn't take long for Gerard to find his way to the west wing and the private suite of Lady Alice to bid her goodbye. He sharply knocked on her door and waited for her to beckon him in.

"Gerard, thank you for coming. I didn't have chance to speak to you yesterday and breakfast was quite a busy affair," she said as he kissed her on both cheeks.

"It was my pleasure, *Maman*. You have a good many guests to attend to; there was no need for you to worry about me. We're family, after all," he said with a slick smile.

"Precisely. That's why I wanted to see you before you left," Lady Alice replied and directed him to a chair. They both took their seats and Lady Alice continued. "In the light of Miles and Louisa's announcement yesterday..." Gerard sat up a little straighter but kept his expression neutral. He wasn't sure where this conversation was going to go. "I wanted to clarify that you would always be welcome at Holmwood." Gerard gave her a nod and a small smile. He hadn't expected her to cut him out but he wasn't entirely sure what pull Miles had on the Blackthorns. "You have been part of the Blackthorns for 20 years and are the father of the future heiress."

"That might change," Gerard said carefully. There was a good chance Louisa might have another child. She'd always wanted more children, just not with him. She'd told him that quite succinctly, he remembered bitterly.

"It might, but Celeste will still be a countess," Lady Alice answered, her meaning clear that Celeste would always be the heiress, unless she didn't want the responsibility.

Gerard gave a nod, then furrowed his brow before saying. "Forgive me, but may I ask you something?"

"Of course."

Gerard took a second before carefully asking, "Do you approve of the match?"

"I do," Lady Alice answered without missing a beat. "That surprises you?" His expression had given him away. "Gerard, you know I have the greatest affection for you. You have stood by the Blackthorns in their hour of need and we will never forget that." Gerard gave Lady Alice a slow nod in acknowledgement. "Louisa was never supposed to be the heiress and her marriage to you was, we all believed, the perfect match. But as you well know, Louisa's role suddenly changed, which meant her partner would also need to… adjust accordingly."

Gerard tried hard not to clench his jaw at the implication Lady Alice was not so subtly making. "I don't understand."

"You were never going to let her take the lead or stay in the background when she took on her role as heiress. That's not who you are. And your… interests would eventually cause her – and therefore the family – embarrassment."

Gerard blanched at the reference to his extramarital affairs, ones he was sure no one knew about, especially his mother-in-law. "And you think the American won't embarrass you or Louisa?" he countered defensively.

"I can't guarantee it but if I was a betting woman, the odds would be firmly in his favour. You see he loves Louisa, in spite of her title. She always comes first to him and he's happy to be in second place," Lady Alice said evenly.

"He's a popstar, permanently in the limelight! You saw the stunt he pulled yesterday, announcing their engagement to the world." Gerard's voice rose a little, betraying his emotions.

"Yes, he did, but they've been together for over four months and nobody even guessed. He stood back and let her take the lead. He didn't want any scandal attached to her, didn't want speculation, or anything to taint her reputation and when she agreed to be his wife, that was the green light for him to announce it. In his own way, maybe, but he'd earned that privilege. He'd proved his worth."

Gerard found it hard to hear his ex-mother-in-law defend Miles. She'd always been supportive of him and the idea of losing her affection was bad enough, but losing it to Miles was unthinkable. "He has a sordid past," he shot back.

"Better than a sordid present," Lady Alice said with a knowing look and Gerard had the good grace not to refute it. It would do him no good to open up an argument with Lady Alice. Seeing him back down, Lady Alice gave him a soft smile. She knew this was hard for Gerard to accept. He wasn't accustomed to losing, especially to someone he deemed as a lesser man. "Miles has earned his respect; it wasn't given to him. He is a fighter and he fought for Louisa, and won. He hasn't had it easy like us, Gerard. Everything he has, he worked for, earned it and he's lost a lot too. That's a quality our circles don't appreciate, but I do. Remember, my family didn't run in high society or the aristocracy," she said pointedly. She let that fact settle for a moment before adding. "Now I know you're a gentleman; you've always had the family's interests at heart. So, I'm expecting your loyalty to *all* our family to continue."

"Of course, *Maman*," Gerard said with not an ounce of sincerity.

"*Bien*." Lady Alice rose from her seat and Gerard immediately followed. He'd had his audience with Lady Alice and she'd outlined what she expected from him. In return, he'd be welcome at Holmwood. The ties to the aristocracy he fiercely coveted were not being cut, as long as he played by their rules. Gerard hardly ever lost but he wasn't a total fool. He might be the superior man, in his eyes, but maybe now he wasn't the right man. "Celeste tells me you're leaving for New York today."

"Yes, I have some pressing matters to attend to, otherwise I would've stayed on a little more. Gils and I have some family business to discuss. He'll be leaving with me."

Lady Alice saw Gerard to the door of her suite, continuing to make small talk, before he kissed her cheeks again and said his goodbyes. She shut the door and breathed a sigh of relief. One by one, she was tying up all the loose ends. Now her next task was to secure a wedding date.

LOUISA'S SUITE WAS BACK to its pristine self. The comforter had been replaced and the bloodstain had somehow miraculously disappeared and every piece of furniture was in its place, as though the awful ordeal the night before had never happened. Louisa had gone to speak to Celeste and Lady Alice about what had happened. Hugh and Alistair had joined her, giving them all the details of how Emily had managed to get into Holmwood, as well as where she was now and the measures put in place to ensure she didn't escape.

Miles had been bombarded with calls but had only spoken to his parents, who were full of praise and pride at seeing him on stage, and Eric.

His manager and friend had been thrilled at seeing Miles back on stage and singing new material. "What does this mean? Are you going to write more? Perform again?" Eric had asked during their video call.

"I have a lot of material. I never stopped writing. I'm not sure yet. I cannot perform under the name of Keane Sense. Keane Sense had Louis and it doesn't feel right without him."

"Okay. Maybe a solo career, then?" Eric pressed.

"Maybe. And a few collaborations." Miles was already thinking of working with Konran.

"Well, I've had a huge interest already. My phone and mailbox have been red hot."

"Yeah, well don't promise anything... yet," Miles said warily. He needed time for everything to sink in still.

"Treat them mean to keep them... Keane?" Eric chuckled and Miles huffed.

"Not quite."

"You did good, kid. It was good seeing you do what you do best," Eric said earnestly.

Miles nodded at the screen, moved by his manager's obvious emotion. "Thanks."

Miles put down his phone and slumped back into the couch. It was all a bit too much. He'd enjoyed being on stage and performing; that buzz was addictive but it was still clouded by anxiety and he wasn't sure he'd ever be rid of it. He'd focused on a point on the stage and took the deep breaths his therapist had instructed him to do. It had helped, but having Louisa there was what had made him take that leap of faith. For her, the risk was worth taking. He'd never had any reason to perform before, until now. Financially, he was set up for a few lifetimes, and he was over the thirst for attention and adulation that had somewhat driven him while he was with Keane Sense. He found satisfaction in his composing and playing but his need to perform, be centre stage, had decidedly lessened. He'd made the decision to perform solely for Louisa, to sing the song he'd written for her and to let the world know who she was to him. Miles knew his performance would make Concert for CASPO the most talked-about concert since Live Aid. His motives were not for him but for Louisa and the charity she patroned and worked so hard to make a success of.

His attention was drawn to the door opening and Louisa stepped into the suite with Celeste. From the look on Celeste's face and the way she scanned the room, Louisa had obviously told her what had happened.

"Are you alright?" Celeste asked, stepping up to him, and Miles stood up immediately. Before he knew it, Celeste threw her arms around his middle and hugged him tight.

Miles stared at Louisa over Celeste's head, clearly surprised but hugged her back. "I'm fine."

"Thank you," she said quietly and pulled back.

"Hey it's okay; it's over. And it was Hugh and Pierce who did all the work – I just helped." Miles bobbed down to catch her gaze and Celeste nodded, though worry was still etched over her face. "She's going to be looked after in a more secure facility until she's well enough."

"Yeah, Mum said."

"Come on. Don't let Emily ruin our *epic* concert buzz," Miles said with a wide smile and Celeste giggled at his choice of words.

"It was pretty epic," she said, smiling back at him.

"Mama's arranged for us all to have a family lunch. Amanda's parents will be leaving afterwards, so I think she wants to give them a good send-off," Louisa said as she walked towards him.

"I think Amanda's parents are going to be a little overwhelmed," he muttered. They'd been wowed by Holmwood when they'd arrived on the day before the concert. It was a lot to take in, as Miles knew first-hand.

"Well, they're going to have to get used to it if things get more serious between Amanda and Alistair," Louisa said with a shrug.

"A birdy told me that Amanda didn't sleep in her room last night," Celeste said, stifling a smirk.

"Celeste!" Louisa said, shocked at her candid remark, though she was secretly pleased at the news.

"It's true," Celeste said.

"Who told you?" Miles asked, narrowing his eyes at her.

Celeste shook her head. Gerard had seen Amanda and Alistair in his apartment early in the morning out on the terrace, while he rode around the grounds, and had mentioned it to Celeste at breakfast. But she wasn't about to out her father as her source. "It doesn't matter who told me; what matters is that it looks like they're finally together!" she said and pulled an excited face.

"It's been quite a weekend," Louisa said, widening her eyes.

"I'll say," agreed Miles.

LUNCH WAS A LIGHT-HEARTED affair. Most of the guests and friends had left Holmwood after breakfast, which meant it was just the family, Amanda, her parents and the children, Konran and his band as well as Melissa and Robert. By the time Amanda's parents drove away in the early afternoon, they were decidedly more comfortable being around the Blackthorns. Konran and his band also left for a much-earned holiday, with promises of being in touch soon.

The sun had broken through the thin veil of cloud and Lady Alice suggested they have coffee out on the terrace, while the children played on the lawn. Amanda had decided to take up the offer of staying on for a few more days with the children, at the request of Alistair, seeing as there were still a few more days of school holidays left.

Melissa sat with her feet up, scrolling through all the sites on her iPad. She read out titbits whenever she came across any that she either found amusing or interesting. There were endless posts about all the performers and specifically how well Konran and Miles co-hosted. There were facts and figures banded about on how many people watched the concert around the world, and Melissa was hellbent on ensuring she had the accurate figures. She'd already liaised with Darcy to put up the total money collected so far and the various video feeds up on CASPO's website.

Robert frowned at her as she tapped away. "This isn't relaxing, Melissa," he chided.

"I'm reading, with my legs up and enjoying the good weather on the terrace. This is as relaxed as I get Robert," Melissa said in a matter-of-fact tone and Robert sighed. He was fighting a losing battle and he knew it. He slumped back on the settee next to her, lifted Melissa's feet and started to give her a foot rub. She gave him a shy smile and mouthed that she loved him, then went back to reading her iPad and let out a gasp. "Well I never. The cheek of it. One below-par site has dubbed you two as the Lady and the Tramp!" Melissa said incredulously.

"Oh wow! That's a bit much," Robert said, shooting his gaze over to where Louisa and Miles were sitting. Lady Alice frowned. She didn't like anyone belittling a member of her family or friends.

"I don't know. It sounds about right," replied Miles with a shrug. "I always liked that film and we can't deny that I'm a little rough around the edges." Miles gave Louisa a grin, seeing her concerned expression. "I'm used to being criticised. They can take a shot at me anytime. Besides, didn't Tramp get Lady in the end?"

"He did," Louisa said with a grin.

"Well, there you go." Miles took her left hand and kissed it.

"While we're on the subject, have you thought about the wedding at all?" asked Lady Alice, accepting a cup of coffee from Margot. A shriek of laughter from Grace, who'd managed to tap her ball under the croquet hoop, caught Miles's attention for a moment and he clapped. Grace waved frantically at him and he beamed back. The children were playing with Alistair, Amanda, Celeste and Nicolas in a game of girls against boys and, by the scowl on Louis's face, the girls were winning.

"Mama, we've only just got engaged," Louisa said with a sigh. She knew her mother would be biting at the bit.

"These things need planning and with both your schedules, it makes sense to start early," Lady Alice said with a pointed look.

"I'll fall in with whatever you want. Though I'm a 'sooner rather than later' kinda guy," Miles said, picking up his coffee cup and taking a sip.

Celeste came running up with Nicolas for some refreshments at the end of their game, leaving the children to wander up with Alistair and Amanda.

"I'm with you, Miles. No point in waiting, plus it'll shut up all those nay-sayers," Margot said with a purse of her lips. Melissa nodded and threw a sympathetic look to Louisa.

"No point waiting for what?" asked Celeste, pouring herself some iced lemonade.

"The wedding," Margot answered.

"Oh, any idea when?"

"We were just discussing timing," Lady Alice said, before Louisa could answer.

"You should do it when I have time off university. Then I can be part of it, rather than just coming in a day or so beforehand," suggested Celeste.

"You mean at Christmas?" Melissa asked.

"Well, I actually meant at any holiday time, but a Christmas wedding sounds like a good idea, actually."

"Holmwood will be shut to the public too," added Lady Alice, thinking it would be an ideal time for a grand wedding.

"And most people are on a break anyway. It's the perfect time, between Christmas and New Year," Melissa said encouragingly.

While everyone discussed the merits of a Christmas wedding, Miles turned to Louisa and said softly, "It'll mean we're married before I start filming in New York." Louisa scrunched her nose and nodded.

"How does a Christmas wedding sound?" Lady Alice said to Alistair and Amanda as they stepped up to the terrace.

"Erm…" Alistair widened his eyes and shot a look at Amanda. "Well…"

Louisa burst out laughing, seeing her brother thrown off-kilter and misunderstanding their mother's comment. "Mama meant *our* wedding, Alistair. No need to look so panicked."

"Oh right, you caught me on the hop there," Alistair replied in relief and everyone laughed, including Amanda.

"Unless you guys want a double wedding," Miles added and Amanda mock-glared at him.

"Steady on. Anyway, Louisa would hate for us to steal your thunder," Alistair countered, which earned him a chuckle from everyone.

"Nice dodge," Miles mumbled to Alistair and he nodded.

"What about a New Year's Eve wedding? We can all see the new year in together as well," Melissa mused, while Alistair and Amanda took their seats and helped themselves to drinks.

"That's actually a great idea," Celeste said.

"It'll be easier for my parents to come out then too," Miles added.

"Right, then. We need to start getting a guest list." Melissa swiped her iPad and began to type.

"Melissa, will you just calm down and take a breath!" Robert chided.

"This will be the wedding of the year! And I'm going to be the matron of honour. I am, aren't I?" she asked, whipping her head around towards Louisa.

"Yes, of course you are."

Lady Alice put her hand up to halt Melissa. "*I'll* put together a list and each one of us will add to it. Margot will take charge until you can." Margot immediately started naming guests and Melissa added to it, while Lady Alice and Celeste came up with a few wedding ideas.

Louisa knew she was going to have to put her foot down at some point, but seeing them all so excited, she let them have their say – she'd revise and adjust later.

"Are you alright with all of this?" Louisa said, catching Miles's slightly surprised expression.

"I'd fly to Vegas tonight, baby, but somehow I don't think your mother, Melissa or any of them will be on board for that," he said dryly. "What about you? It's not too soon for you?" he said taking her hand and giving it a squeeze.

"I'm kinda liking the idea of Vegas too," she said, gesturing to the four women, making all the arrangements. "But I don't want Mama to have a coronary. New Year's Eve sounds perfect."

"Whatever my lady wants." Miles lifted Louisa's hand to his lips and kissed it and gave her a sultry look. "New Year's Eve it is, then: signed and sealed."

Celeste came over to the settee they were sitting on and plonked herself down and said, "This wedding is going to be epic!"

"EVERYONE GOT A DRINK?" Louisa said, looking around the media room at Blackthorn Mansion. They'd all gathered to watch the first airing of Miles's series *Keane's Interest*. The last two weeks had been hectic after the concert at Holmwood. The media had gone into a Miles-Louisa frenzy, from speculation on the wedding date and all-star guest list, to dragging up ex-hook-ups of Miles, and Louisa's marriage to Gerard. It was, as Miles had said time and time again, open season. Surprisingly though, his ex-hook ups had kept quiet, apart from giving the couple their congratulations, and the Gerard camp had been tight-lipped, apart from releasing a statement that he wished the couple a happy future together. With a complete lack of feedback, the press had changed tactics and focused on the future of the couple, rather than their past. Miles wondered how much interference or power over the media the Blackthorns had, for the stories to be so quickly quashed. Either way, Miles was happy that his name wasn't being dragged through the mud or causing embarrassment to Louisa or her family.

"Hurry up, Mum!" Celeste said, almost bouncing in her chair. She was self-crowned manager of the remote control and was growing more impatient with every minute that past. Louisa was trying to make sure the handful of guests were all comfortable. Melissa and Robert were there, alongside Amanda, Alistair and Nicolas.

"Come on, Freddy's asleep and goodness knows how long he'll give me before I have to feed him," Melissa groaned. A few days after the concert, Melissa had given birth to Frederick Matthew Hindley, an eight-pound two-ounce baby boy, named after Robert's and Melissa's grandfathers. Today was his first outing and was presently sleeping in the adjoining room.

"Okay, okay I'm here," Louisa said, taking her seat next to a nervous Miles. She passed him his drink, then took hold of his hand and squeezed it. This was the first social event they were hosting as an engaged couple.

"Finally," Celeste said and pressed a button to dim the lights.

"Eric just texted me," Miles whispered. "It's the number one series in the US," he said with disbelief.

"Already? That's amazing!" Louisa said and repeated the news to the rest of their guests. Melissa was straight onto her phone, researching the facts.

"Well, according to USA Today, The New York Times and the Los Angeles Times, you're definitely up for an Emmy. Listen to this: 'The insightful and candid *Keane's Interest* does not just shine a spotlight on its hard-done-by by-gone stars, it brings a new talent onto our small screens. The sensitive and empathetic performance in the role of presenter has surely cemented Miles Keane as a multi-faceted artist and entertainer, and no doubt secured him an Emmy nomination to add to his Grammy collection.' High praise indeed, Miles."

"Let's not get ahead of ourselves, shall we? The series was only released yesterday in the US and today worldwide," Miles said with a chuckle. He'd learned to take both scathing and praising from the media with a pinch of salt. All he cared about was what his family thought and what Louisa thought, and if he'd proved his worth.

"Okay, everyone hush up, I'm pressing play," Celeste said and the screen lit up with the opening credits.

Louisa made an excited face and clinked her glass against Miles's, and he revelled in her childlike enthusiasm. "Can you imagine: an Emmy!" she whispered.

Miles chuckled and kissed her hand and said, "Showtime!"

Epilogue

1

NEW YEAR'S EVE

Lady Alice ran her fingers over the picture of James Clementine Blackthorn, the late earl and her beloved husband. His eyes, full of mischief, stared back at her, like they always did. His handsome chiselled face, which was so like Alistair's, kept her company on her bedside table. She missed him terribly and on days like today, where she knew he'd be in his element, even more so.

"Oh darling, Holmwood is full of life again. You'd love it. Celeste is so excited and has been bouncing around, saying it was wedding eve. She's a card, that one! Alistair, well he's the happiest I've ever seen him. We'll all miss you tomorrow, more than ever, but I know you'll be looking down on us." She spoke to him every night and every morning, as though he was lying beside her. When he'd died, she'd been told that, in time, she'd get used to him not being there but the truth of the matter was, she hadn't. She didn't want to get used it – whyever would she want to? Every night she reached for him and whenever she wanted to share some excited news, she turned to where he would normally sit, to tell him.

He would've loved all the wedding preparations, loved hosting his whole family and close friends over Christmas and New Year – he had always been so social. Tomorrow was such a happy day, yet Lady Alice would feel his absence more than ever, and though she wouldn't let it show, for her there would be a little bit of sadness.

"Good night, my love. See you in the morning. Celeste says that tomorrow is going to be *epic*. Whatever that means. I can't keep up with her sometimes." Lady Alice chuckled and turned off her bedside lamp and reached out to the cold empty left-hand side of her bed.

"THEY HAVE EIGHT CHRISTMAS trees. Eight! And not just little ones, huge ones. Each one is decorated in keeping with the décor of the room and they're all real – no imitations for the Blackthorns, oh no. Can you imagine, all those pine needles dropping!" Miles stifled a smirk listening to his mother talking to Eric over the breakfast table. It was New Year's Eve morning and Miles and his parents were set up in one of the suites on the east wing that Alistair occupied. In keeping with wedding tradition, Miles had slept away from Louisa and was as far away from her suite as possible. He'd vowed to stay out of sight until the time of the wedding. Eric had arrived the evening before and was also staying in the east wing, along with Amanda, Amanda's parents and the children. "Plus, the smaller ones they've put up in everyone's suite. The children ran to each tree to collect presents on Christmas morning – it was chaos!" Katy continued.

Miles's parents had arrived just before Christmas and had had the full Blackthorn experience. Lady Alice had lavished them with attention and treated them to every type of quintessential British tradition, from carol singing in the drawing-room on Christmas Eve, with Miles playing piano, while decorating the final tree in the lounge together, to a huge Christmas lunch with board games and charades. Then on Boxing Day, the Blackthorns held an open house party for friends and family to drop by. The weather was unusually mild for December and though they'd missed out on a white Christmas, they at least could enjoy the grounds.

"I think the Blackthorns are just happy to have the house full again," Miles said.

"House full, that's an understatement," Richard muttered buttering his toast. Over the last week, there had been a steady flow of new guests coming to stay. The latest count at dinner last night was 42. Miles's father wondered how many more guests would be taking advantage of the Blackthorn's hospitality.

"Did you see the grand dining room? It's like something out of a fairy-tale, so elegant, and they have their own chapel too. My friends back home are going to burst a blood vessel when I show them the pictures," Katy gushed, pouring herself some coffee from the antique coffee pot. She'd been snapping photos continuously on her phone the whole stay.

"Mom, don't show them anything about today. You can show them when you get back home, not a minute before. We've done everything we can to keep the press out of it," Miles said with a frown. There had been a complete blackout of media opportunities in the run-up to the wedding. Anyone leaving or entering the grounds rode in blacked-out cars, and all guests to the wedding had been instructed not to release any information regarding the day. The Blackthorns would publish an official press release and photos after the wedding. There were going to be members of the world's aristocracy and entertainment industry at the wedding, so apart from the Blackthorns wanting privacy, there was also security to think of too.

"Hush now, I'm not stupid. I meant when we get back," Katy said, patting Miles's arm. She'd been well versed in the protocols of privacy throughout the hype of Keane Sense and when any scandals were revealed.

A knock at the door drew their attention and Richard called out for whoever it was to come in. Amanda, the children and her parents came through the door and settled around the large table to enjoy the pre-wedding breakfast with the Keanes and Eric.

"It's been too long for us all to be together," Richard said as he poured champagne into the beautiful crystal flutes.

"It has," agreed Miles. He looked around the table at his family and felt a wave of sadness pass over him. Miles took a breath and stood up. "I'd like to make a toast," he said, taking his champagne flute in his hand.

"Aren't you supposed to do that at the reception?" Eric asked.

"I have another one for that, this is just for us," Miles said, and swept his gaze across the expectant faces of his family. "Thank you for being here for me. The last five years have been tough and if it wasn't for you all, I don't think I would be here today. You all never gave up on me and because of you, I'm a better person." Miles took a breath to unclog his throat of emotion. "I wish Louis was here to see what we've all achieved and though he's not here to be my best man on the happiest day of my life, I know he'd approve of his substitute." He gave Eric a smile, and Eric reciprocated it with a nod. "This toast is for all of you and Louis. Thank you, I promise never to let any of you down again."

Everyone stood up and said, "To Louis," and clinked their glasses together in the centre of the table. Katy and Richard had tears in their eyes and Amanda blinked back hers, not wanting the children to see how moved she was.

"Now, no more tears of sadness. Only happy tears," Miles said and everyone immediately sat back down to the lovely spread of food the Blackthorn staff had brought up for them.

Amanda leaned against Miles and he gave her a tight hug. "That was a lovely thing to say. He'd be so proud of you."

"I know."

LOUISA STEPPED OUT OF her luxurious bath and wrapped herself in a towel. Her suite was so quiet and felt empty. There was no Miles humming as he moved around the rooms. He hardly ever sat still. If she was in the bathroom, he'd usually join her. While she dressed, he lounged on the chaise and keep her company. Over the last few months, she'd become used to him being with her. They were rarely apart and for Louisa, who'd had a lonely marriage of convenience and been void of a partner's company, it had been blissful. After the dinner last night, they'd parted ways; Miles walked off to the east wing and Louisa stepped into her suite and she hadn't heard or seen him since. It surprised her how much she missed him and it had only been 12 hours. Miles Keane was her addiction. It was unexpected how, in such a short space of time, he'd become part of her everyday life. After today, their lives would be intertwined forever and Louisa couldn't wait.

It was going to be a long day, though it was their wedding day, they'd combined it with New Year's Eve celebrations. After the midday wedding, the 322 guests would be served lunch. Holmwood was pulling out all the stops, laying on its finery and using the majestic banquet room and ballroom, bringing them back to their former glory. Once the lunch was over, the speeches were said and the cake cut, some of the distinguished guests would leave. The rest of the guests would stay on at Holmwood and be joined by a few selected families from CASPO, to join in the combined wedding and New Year's Eve party. It was a full day that combined the elegance and style synonymous with the Blackthorns' aristocratic heritage, as well as the warmth and generosity of the newer generations.

Louisa collected her velvet robe and slipped it on, then stepped into the sitting room of her suite, where breakfast had been arranged. She checked the time and sat down, knowing that at any moment Celeste, her mother, Melissa, Alistair and Margot would be here. She took a moment to appreciate the last moments of calm before the whirlwind of wedding preparations started.

"IS EVERYTHING ALRIGHT?" Miles asked as Alistair stepped into his suite with Lady Alice. He'd just changed into his wedding suit and was in the process of tying his cravat in readiness for the photographer to arrive. When he'd heard the knock, he'd assumed it was him, but was faced with an extremely well-groomed Alistair and an elegantly dressed Lady Alice. Miles blinked at them, suddenly realising the level of grandeur he was marrying into. Alistair looked every part the earl in an immaculate black three-piece suit and silver cravat that matched Miles's. The magnificent sapphire necklace Lady Alice was wearing perfectly matched her eyes and dress, and sparkled so brightly, it almost eclipsed her wide smile.

"Everything's perfect. We just wanted to give you this." Lady Alice said, holding out a purple velvet box. Miles looked at it, then shot his gaze up to Alistair and Lady Alice. He took it from her hand and opened the box. Nestled in the cushioning was a gold and purple signet ring with the Blackthorn coat of arms engraved on it.

"You're part of the Blackthorns now," Alistair said and Miles blew out a breath.

"Thank you. It's... well it's an honour."

"Put it on. It should fit," Lady Alice said and Miles plucked out the ring and slipped it on his right-hand ring finger, the same finger that Alistair had his identical signet ring on. It fit perfectly. He held out his hand to look at it and then looked up at Lady Alice and Alistair.

"Perfect. We had it specially made," Alistair said and Miles nodded, overcome with the significance of what this meant.

"If you and Louisa ever have a son, he'll inherit my James's ring," Lady Alice explained. "Only Blackthorn heirs can have the ring or pendant. That honour also extends to their spouses."

"No pressure," Alistair chuckled, seeing Miles's eyes widen at his mother's words.

Miles grinned back at his soon-to-be brother-in-law. "Thank you for entrusting me with the honour," he said to Lady Alice and she leaned up and gave him a kiss on the cheek.

"We'll leave you to finish getting ready. I think the photographer is waiting outside."

"ARE YOU READY?" Louisa called from her dressing room. Celeste, Lady Alice and Melissa were seated in the lounge area waiting for her to come out, from where the stylist had finished her hair and makeup.

"Come on, Mum, I'm dying to see you in your dress!" Celeste said impatiently and Louisa let out a giggle, then stepped through the door of her dressing room and walked carefully out to her audience of three. "Oh my God, you look amazing. Miles is going to freak!" Celeste said, jumping up out of her seat. The dress Louisa had chosen was a column gown in duchess silk satin. A modern ivory dress with no nostalgia or sense of revival – in part to avoid comparisons with her first wedding dress but also more to her matured taste. The gown itself folded out to a short, slim train in keeping with the silhouette. But the striking feature was the fully-embroidered, five-metre-long train that cascaded from the crossover neckline. The slim silhouette was simple and elegant, but the train and the embroidery gave the "simple" dress the grandness it needed for the wedding of the aristocracy. Swarovski crystals, mother-of-pearl teardrops, and gold stones completed the floral intertwined embroidery on the gown, which flowed like a chandelier from the top to the bottom of the gown to circle the shorter train, as well as the trim of the longer train and its central section. As Louisa walked, the light caused the gown to shimmer with every step. Her veil was simple and was attached to the most magnificent diamond and ruby tiara, a Blackthorn heirloom, the priceless gemstones dating back 300 years.

"It's been a very long time for me to wear a tiara," Louisa said, and her mother rose up from her seat.

"I know. We need to have more occasions to wear them." Her voice was heavy with emotion.

"Granny's right," Celeste said taking hold of her mother's hand.

"You look positively regal." Melissa carefully hugged her dearest friend. "Well, it covers the something old and borrowed. Your dress is the new," Melissa added.

"Something blue?" Celeste asked.

"Melissa stitched a blue flower on the inside seam of my train," Louisa said.

"Didn't want a tacky garter, did we?" Melissa gave a shudder and they all laughed.

"Everyone's already in the chapel. Come on let's do a wedding selfie. Come on, Granny," Celeste said, getting out her phone. They all huddled together and Celeste took at least half a dozen photos as the official photographer stood back and chuckled, seeing the countesses behaving in such a carefree manner. He then proceeded to take a few official photos of the bride and then a number of photos of the rest of them. Both Melissa and Celeste wore red velvet gowns, styled individually, that matched the rubies in Louisa's tiara.

At five minutes to twelve, Alistair knocked on the door to Louisa's suite and walked in.

"You look absolutely beautiful, Lou-lou," he said clearly overcome with emotion.

"Thank you," she said as he carefully kissed her cheek.

"Everyone's waiting for you, are you ready?" he asked, taking her hand.

"Absolutely."

Lady Alice gave her daughter a kiss on the cheek, then lifted her veil over her face. She then patted Alistair's bristly cheek and said, "Your father would be so proud of you two."

"JEEZ, THERE ARE ACTUAL royals here. I mean like crowned princes," Eric muttered under his breath as he scanned the congregation in the private chapel.

"Shut up. I'm nervous enough as it is," Miles whispered back at him. He knew who was on the guest list, he'd been over it a hundred times with the Blackthorns. There was a not-so-subtle divide of the guests. On the groom's side were musicians, a few actors and music industry executives. On the side of the bride were members of the aristocracy, military and politicians. Hugh and his security team were scattered around and Miles could only imagine what a tactical nightmare today must've been for him.

"I may have to modify my speech," Eric said with a cringe and Miles chuckled. "This is… surreal."

"Yeah, shit just got real," Miles said, widening his eyes.

"You're not going to bail, are you?" Eric said, worried that his friend looked overwhelmed.

"Are you kidding me? She's the real deal."

"She is." The soft organ music stopped and after a beat, *The Wedding March* started to play and the whole congregation stood up. "This is it, kid," Eric said and they both stepped up to the front and turned. Grace walked in front with Louis, holding hands, looking adorable in a red velvet dress and a suit that matched Miles's, but Miles only had eyes for Louisa. Images of her flashed through his mind, their date at Blacks, that had him flustered, Louisa arranging flowers in the wine bucket the first time she'd visited his house and her standing in the rain under the umbrella held by Hugh – so many snapshots of *just* Louisa, before he'd known who she was. But as she glided down the aisle on the arm of Alistair, he marvelled at how blind he'd been. She was magnificent, a sight to behold and her radiance eclipsed the brilliance of the precious stones of the tiara that crowned her regal head. *How had he not realised she was a cut above the rest?* She was a priceless diamond, someone who should be treasured and revered. Both *just* Louisa and The Countess of Holmwood were going to finally be his and it was up to him to prove he was worthy of both sides of her. When she reached the front, Miles smiled his patented megawatt smile and Alistair released her, then stepped back.

"You look breathtaking, like…"

"A countess?" Louisa said with a shy smile, and for a second it was *just* Louisa and Miles.

"Yeah, exactly like a countess."

"Then that means you're…"

"The best £50,000 you ever spent?" Miles said with a cheeky smile.

Louisa laughed softly. "And worth every penny."

2

OPENING NIGHT

A year later.

T onight sees Grammy and Emmy award-winning Miles Keane return to the centre stage as Don Lockwood in Singing in the Rain. *After a sell-out six weeks on Broadway, the cast of the revered musical perform their opening night in front of a London audience. The six weeks at the Dominion Theatre have been sold out since the dates were released. Miles Keane's performance has wowed the audience stateside and there is speculation he will add a Tony and a Laurence Olivier Award to his many accolades. Is there no end to his talent?*

Since their marriage last year, Miles Keane and Lady Blackthorn have been splitting their time between their stately home, Holmwood in England, and the US over the last year. Miles Keane has been promoting his film, playing the legendary Chet Baker in the biopic and his film acting debut, Time After Time, *due for release in the next two weeks. The ex-popstar and front man of Keane Sense made a huge splash in Cannes, proving he is more than just a singer-songwriter. Word on the glittery streets of Hollywood believes he will be nominated for an Academy Award.*

"LADY BLACKTHORN, OVER HERE!"
"This way, look to your right!"
"Who are you wearing?"
"How's Miles feeling tonight?"

Louisa smiled her practised and well-rehearsed countess smile and ignored the persistent calls of the world press. She had to admit it wasn't as bad as it had been in New York and she was thankful that the ever-present Hugh and his team were with her. Over the last year, they'd been hounded by the press. Living in New York while

Miles was filming *Time After Time* and rehearsing for *Singing in the Rain* had meant they'd fed both sides of the Atlantic with endless newsworthy stories. The press hounded Miles every time he went to the theatre. Fans crowded around outdoor sets while he was filming, and when he went for a run at five in the morning, he was followed by photographers on bikes. The upside was that CASPO had more exposure and donations than ever before, but it had been a hefty price to pay. Louisa was glad to be back home again, back at Holmwood and at Blackthorn Mansion. There, at least they had their privacy, especially now it was late Autumn and Holmwood was closed to the public.

Louisa blinked as the flashlights went off one after another, happy in the knowledge she didn't have to endure the red carpet for much longer. Hugh ushered her into the foyer of the theatre, where she greeted the management and staff in a line-up, before being led up the stairs to her private box and where her mother, Alistair, Amanda, Melissa and Robert waited.

"Here you go." Alistair passed her a champagne flute. "How was it?" he said with a smirk as she smoothed her hand over her purple velvet gown.

"Thank you. Hectic. I'm just glad there wasn't so much pavement and the walk-in was quick," Louisa said, taking a welcome sip after kissing her family and friends. They'd arrived earlier and with less fuss. The world's press wanted to see Lady Louisa, the woman who'd tamed Miles Keane, and the last thing Louisa wanted was the people she loved were also hounded by the press.

"Well, you gave them the pictures they wanted," Lady Alice said.

"Yes. Now I hope they'll just leave us alone for a bit," Louisa said, taking her seat, then handing her champagne glass back to Alistair. "Better not have any more." She made a face of disappointment.

"How are you feeling?" Amanda asked.

"Absolutely fine." Louisa rested her hand protectively over her practically flat tummy. She'd just passed her first trimester and had yet to officially announce her pregnancy. "It's nothing like I was with Celeste. No sickness at all."

"Fingers crossed, then," Melissa said and Louisa crossed her fingers and held them up and nodded.

Louisa picked up the program and began to flick through it, until she got to the pictures of Miles. She'd been with him when he'd done the photoshoot in readiness for the show. There were some stunning candid shots of him while rehearsing, but the one Louisa loved the most was of him broodily looking at the camera, wearing a thick cream woollen jumper that contrasted with his tanned face and dishevelled hair. He looked every bit the bad boy, a little rough around the edges but sexy as hell.

The lights dimmed and the audience clapped in anticipation. Louisa knew they were going to be in for a treat. The production was spectacular, full of glitz and glamour and the famous dance scene in the rain, which had stretched the technical team of the production to its limit, managed to even top Gene Kelly's original performance. The New York reviews had had nothing but praise for Miles's interpretation of a more modern Don Lockwood. He'd added his well-known stamp of style and flair of showmanship that had had audiences spellbound from the second he came on stage to when the curtain came down. Miles was more than a star, he was a whole solar system, and his stage presence had everyone mesmerised and drawn into his magnetic orbit.

The show's opening scene was of an opening night. The stage was set as though it was the front of the Dominion Theatre, mirroring what had only just transpired earlier, a clever twist on the original show. The announcer called out to the audience, "It's opening night and here are the stars of the night, Don Lockwood and Lana Lamont!" The announcer looked out to the audience and to everyone's surprise, Miles and the leading lady appeared walking down the aisle with an entourage of bodyguards and photographers flashing cameras at them. Miles was in a cream tuxedo and the actress playing the leading lady shimmered in a silver sparkly dress. The audience gasped, then clapped and cheered loudly and to the delight of the few, Miles even managed to shake a few hands of the audience before stepping up onto the stage to where the actors playing the reporters were. It was clever and unique, and set the tone for the rest of the performance.

"You've come a long way, Don," said the actor who played the reporter.

"Why, thank you," Miles drawled.

"Tell us your story, Don."

"Oh no, not in front of all these people." Miles made a show of sweeping his hand out towards the audience and the audience cheered.

"But your story of success is an inspiration to young people…" the reporter continued.

Louisa smiled at the words she'd heard hundreds of times, when Miles practised at home, in rehearsals and finally on stage. She got a kick out of how apt those opening lines were. How much they echoed Miles's real life. He was more than an ex-popstar, a singer-songwriter, an entertainer, he was Miles Keane, an inspiration, the love of her life, husband and soon-to-be father of the next earl of Holmwood.

3

TIME AFTER TIME

Eighteen months later.

*A*ll eyes are on the first official sighting of the Countess of Holmwood after the birth of her son James Richard Blackthorn-Keane. Miles Keane and Lady Louisa Blackthorn flew out to their Malibu home with their one-month-old son, the ninth Earl of Holmwood, on Friday, in preparation for the Academy Awards tonight at the Dolby Theatre in Hollywood.

Miles Keane's film, Time After Time, *is nominated for six awards, including best actor and best motion picture. Can Miles Keane add Oscar to his many accolades? The odds are definitely in his favour. He will share the coveted title of having won every entertainment award, EGOT (Emmy, Grammy, Oscar, Tony) and take his place in history next to Audrey Hepburn, Mel Brooks, Andrew Lloyd Webber and John Legend. If Miles Keane wins tonight, he will be the youngest artist to have won all four awards, at the age of 37.*

Is there nothing Miles Keane cannot do?

GERARD CLENCHED HIS JAW and turned away from his computer in disgust. For the last year and a half, Miles Keane and his success had hounded him. Gerard scoured the media sites for any trace of scandal, hoping he'd finally be proved right about Miles being a liability to the Blackthorns but the fact was, he was squeaky clean. He'd fallen in with the aristocratic lifestyle with ease. Miles had been featured in magazines as the new look of the aristocracy; he'd even learned how to ride a horse and was learning to play polo. As if that wasn't enough, his career seemed to be going from strength to strength. He had the Midas touch when it came to all things entertainment. Apart from his awards for his series, *Keane's Interest*, and Broadway, he'd released an album which featured various collaborations with artists as well as his own solo hits. The album had been a worldwide success, staying in the top 10 for 12 weeks. Miles Keane was everywhere. There wasn't a magazine, newspaper or site that didn't have a feature about what he was doing and where he was heading next.

The charity work he championed was the cherry on top of the cake. Holmwood had hosted another summer concert, bigger and better than the last. Miles Keane could do no wrong in the eyes of the public and the media, and what infuriated Gerard even more was that Miles could do no wrong in the eyes of the Blackthorns too. His past had been forgotten and easily forgiven; he'd proved his worth in both his professional and his personal life and had secured the Blackthorns' future with an earl.

Gerard swirled his cognac in its glass and looked back at the picture of Louisa and Miles on the red carpet outside the Dolby Theatre in Hollywood. Louisa looked radiant in a dramatic red velvet gown with a slit to the knee and gold satin lining that flashed when she walked. The neckline was off one shoulder, with a sculptured wave that rose over her left shoulder, revealing more rich gold satin. The necklace and earrings she'd paired with her dress were of her own antique collection and were made of priceless diamonds and rubies and the envy of all the women on the red carpet. She looked elegant and regal with an extra dose of serious glamour but what caught Gerard's eye was the ring Miles was wearing. On his right-hand ring finger, Miles wore the coveted signet ring of the Blackthorns. It was a ring Gerard had never been given because at the time he'd married Louisa, she hadn't been the heiress of Holmwood. Gerard knocked back his cognac in one gulp and put the crystal glass down with a bang.

Miles Keane had taken his place next to Louisa and been welcomed into her world. He was undoubtedly part of the revered Blackthorn family now, accepted in all the aristocratic circles and the presence of the family signet ring, placed on his right hand for the world to see, was validation enough that Miles Keane had proved his worth, signed and sealed.

"EVERYTHING ALRIGHT?" Miles asked nervously as Louisa took her seat next to Miles. She'd just left to see how James was doing. This was the first time she'd ever left him. He was in excellent hands.

They'd hired two nannies and both Karl and Kurt were on hand too. Hugh and Pierce were instructed to get her if there was a problem and were seated a few rows behind them.

James and his entourage were in a suite at the Four Seasons, a five-minute drive away. Along with them were Katy and Richard Keane, who had volunteered to watch over their grandson while they attended the award ceremony. So baby James had six adults watching over him. Louisa had first suggested she stay behind at their home, but Miles wouldn't hear of it. On such an important night he wanted her next to him. So, they compromised. James would be closer than the hours' drive to their home and they could all leave after the ceremony. No afterparty for them; they'd be happy with their own little afterparty, just the three of them in their home by the ocean.

Miles looked around the packed-out theatre and nodded his hellos to the few people he knew or recognised. They weren't the musicians he usually saw at award ceremonies. These were talented, seasoned actors, celebrated and respected directors and he felt like an imposter sitting here amongst them.

It was going to be a long night. The award Miles was up for would be announced towards the end of the show, which meant he had to sit through a few hours, and Louisa was going to be calling every half an hour to check on James. He was already nervous and though the chances of a debut actor winning an Oscar were slim, he felt proud of his performance of the tortured trumpet player.

"How're you feeling?" Louisa whispered, taking his hand and squeezing it.

"Shit scared," he said without missing a beat, and Louisa giggled.

"You know it doesn't matter either way, don't you? You were brilliant in it."

"I know. But call me self-indulgent, I really want to win it."

"Yeah, you're such a prima donna! I want you to really win it too."

"Oh, here we go. It looks like it's about to start."

"AND THE AWARD GOES to… Johnny Moritz for *Time After Time*!" Miles jumped out of his seat and hugged the director who was seated across the aisle from him. They'd worked hard together on the film and Miles hoped his extraordinary work would be awarded.

"Congratulations, man, this is just so great. We've won four Oscars. I can't believe it!" Miles said, truly thrilled. Their film had won another three awards and was already causing a stir. Miles watched his friend and director take to the stage and collect the gold statue to huge applause.

His speech was short but heartfelt and he was clearly emotional when he dedicated it to his parents. Miles shifted in his seat, knowing that the next award announcement was for best actor. He was up against some of the world's most famous and talented actors and when the presenters started to introduce each one of them, Miles realised he was already a winner, just being in the same category as them. The audience cheered loudly after each clip that was shown of each of the films. The scene they'd chosen of Miles was, of course, of him depicting Chet Baker playing his trumpet in a nightclub. It was smoky and atmospheric and the round of applause when it finished seemed to be that much louder and longer than the other clips.

Louisa took hold of Miles's hand and waited with bated breath as the presenter of the award, last year's best actress, opened up the envelope and smiled widely.

"And the award for best actor goes to… Miles Keane in *Time After Time*!" Miles sat for a split second, stunned that he'd won.

Louisa gasped out and turned to him. "You won, baby." Her voice jolted him and he immediately turned to her. She threw her arms around his neck in an unguarded moment and he kissed her, holding her close. "Go get your award. We're all so proud of you," she said in his ear, so he could hear her over the deafening cheers that resounded around the theatre.

"Thanks baby," he muttered, still stunned. As soon as he was out of his chair, his fellow actors and members of the team that had worked alongside him were over to congratulate him.

In a flat in Edinburgh, Celeste jumped up and down and whooped loudly with Nicolas, as they watched the live feed in the early hours of the morning, while on a video call with Konran. Konran cried out in joy as he heard the presenter say Miles's name and ran around his hotel room in Chicago, whooping loudly with Margi.

"My man did it! He won the fucking Oscar!" They all cracked

open champagne and toasted Miles's success via video, then quickly sent her mother and Miles messages of congratulations.

In the early hours on Monday morning, while most of the residence of Holmwood House were still asleep, Lady Alice clapped and smiled at the TV screen and nudged Margot to wake her up. They'd stayed up specially to watch the award ceremony.

"He won, our Miles won the Oscar!" she said excitedly, and Margot blinked and rubbed her eyes.

"Well done, Miles. What a result!" she said, patting Lady Alice's lap, and lifted up her sherry glass, clinking it against Lady Alice's.

In the east wing of Holmwood, Alistair and Amanda sat up in bed and watched as Louisa and Miles hugged and kissed. "He won! He bloody won; I can't believe it!" Amanda gasped and Alistair air punched the air.

"Bloody marvellous!" He called out and Amanda clapped her hand over her mouth and shook her head in awe. Louis would've been so proud of him. Tears welled in her eyes as she thought of how far Miles had come. Alistair pulled her close to him and gave her a squeeze. "He did good, eh?"

"Yeah, he really did."

In the sitting area of the suite in the Four Seasons, Katy and Richard Keane jumped out of their seats, hearing Miles's name. They somehow managed not to make a sound, knowing that baby James was sleeping just a few feet away from them in the adjoining room. They did however jump about, to the amusement of Karl and Kurt. Richard hugged Katy and whispered, "He did it, our boy did it."

"He sure did," she said, then they high fived Karl and Kurt.

MILES MANAGED TO FINALLY make his way to the staircase that led up to the famous stage and stepped up to where the beautiful actress stood with the glittering golden statue.

"Congratulations, Miles," she said and gave him a kiss on the cheek before handing the award to him. It was heavier than he'd expected and he clutched it hard, scared he'd drop it.

Miles stepped up to the podium and looked out over the vast audience, who were still cheering and clapping for him. This was a huge moment and their reaction only underlined the significance of it.

"Thank you, thank you," Miles said, hoping the audience would cease their cheers. He knew he was on a time limit and he wanted to use every second of it.

"As you all know, my life has had some very dark moments and there were times I thought I'd never see the light. I have many people to thank for showing me the way back to that light, time after time… excuse the pun." The audience chuckled at his reference to the film title. "My parents, for being strong for me when I couldn't be. Eric my agent and good friend, who never gave up on me. To Amanda, my beautiful sister, who showed me what real courage is." The audience cheered at the mention of his much-loved sister-in-law and he smiled widely, pleased she was being acknowledged. "To Louis, man I miss you every day. Everything I am is because of you."

The audience cheered and clapped and before Miles could carry on, the whole of the theatre was up on their feet, giving Louis a standing ovation, honouring his beloved brother. Tears welled up in Miles's eyes and he scanned the front rows to find Louisa. He found her within a second, standing and clapping with everyone else.

"Believe it to achieve it: his mantra. I hear him say it every time I step on stage, sit in front of a camera, pick up and play an instrument and when I wake up in the morning," Miles called out over the noise of the crowd. He waited a few seconds, blinking back his tears, until there was a lull. Then he added, "And finally, to the love of my life." He gestured to where Louisa was standing. "I lost my Louis but he sent me Louisa to show me what true happiness is. From the first time… okay, second… I met you" – Louisa laughed at their private joke and the audience joined in – "I knew my fate was signed and sealed. This is for us." Miles held the golden statue in the air and the theatre went wild, the noise level nearly blowing the roof off.

Miles Keane had achieved everything he'd believed in and so much more. He ran down the stairs to deafening applause and straight into the arms of the woman who had been with him every step of the way, by his side, his lady love and the love of his life, his *just* Louisa.

THE END

NOTES FROM THE AUTHOR

One of the best things about writing novels is the interesting things you find out about while doing research. I came up with the subplot of Alistair being a war hero and losing his leg, who had now thrown himself into running his family's estate. I wanted him to find another purpose, so I decided he would fall in love with Amanda.

I like to visualise places and people when I write, so my next task was to find stately homes that would be suitable for Holmwood House. I came up with a few and took elements from each one but the main estate I used was Wrest Park. It's a gorgeous stately home with fabulous grounds. Reading up on it, I found out that it had been used as a military hospital in World War I and that a soldier, who had lost his leg, found love with a member of staff from the house. I was totally blown away by the uncanny coincidence.

ACKNOWLEDGEMENTS

Signed & Sealed was supposed to have been published before the summer but if there's one thing I've learned, it's that however good your intentions and plans are, there's always a good chance things won't work out as you'd hoped. To be honest, I was kind of happy that Miles and Louisa's story stayed with me longer than I anticipated.

Writing, as any author will tell you, is a lonely business, so I personally get a thrill from any feedback I get during the writing process.

I'd firstly like to thank my mum, Helen. She is my first sounding board for all my books and without her support, I probably would never finish anything!

I lost my father, George, during the writing of *Signed & Sealed*, which was hard. It was also one of the reasons I was unable to motivate myself to write. But my father wasn't a quitter, and I'm thankful for his work ethic he instilled in me, to never give up. Thank you, Dad.

To my crew, Mary for your overwhelming praise and faith in me, to Xenia who always knows exactly what to say to fire me up, and to Voula for our years of friendship and your relentless support. I am forever grateful for your love and endless encouragement, and seeing me through thick and thin. I love you girls.

This book wouldn't be here without the talented James Millington, Roi Ioakeimidou and Lou Stock; a huge shout out to them for being so patient with me.

A special thanks to Adrian Otten at **Dexter Signet Rings** who created, photographed and sent me the images of the magnificent signet ring and seal for the cover of this book. It's everything I ever imagined it to be and am in your debt.

I am forever grateful for my husband Marios and my sons George and Michael, who have put up with my mood swings and general craziness whenever I'm writing but really, they should've gotten used to it by now!

Finally, I'd like to thank you, the readers. I love writing, putting my imaginary friends down on paper and watching them come alive. Without you, your constant support and feedback, I would just keep them in my head. I am forever grateful.

PLAYLIST

- Pink – *Let's Get This Party Started*
- George Ezra – *Riding Shotgun*
- Kendrick Lamar – *All the Stars*
- Alicia Keys/Kendrick Lamar – *It's on Again*
- Lewis Capaldi – *Before You Go*
- Coldplay – *A Sky Full of Stars*
- French Montana – *Shot Caller*
- French Montana – *Unforgettable*
- Maroon 5 – *Girls Like You*
- The Police – *Every Little Thing She Does Is Magic*

ABOUT THE AUTHOR

Anna-Maria Athanasiou is originally from Leeds in the UK but for the last twenty-six years she had lived in the heart of the Mediterranean on the island of Cyprus. Limassol is her adopted town where she lives with her husband, two sons, Golden Retriever and seven cats. She had her debut novels, Waiting for Summer Book One and Two published in 2013 and 2014 having written the series in secret, never expecting to finish them or to be published.
Since then Anna-Maria has completed her La Casa d'Italia series and been asked to guest write articles for The Glass House Girls, an online magazine for women. She has also contributed to a number of charity anthologies, They Say I'm Doing Well, Break the Cycle, Poems to my Younger Self and Elements.
Anna-Maria has recently started to also write restaurant reviews for the Cyprus in Style Magazine and is a member of both the Association of Authors and Global Woman. In 2021 she was nominated as Global Woman Inspirational Woman at their annual awards.

Loved Signed and Sealed?

Book reviews are always appreciated.
Find Anna-Maria on Goodreads and Amazon

Connect with Anna-Maria:
Facebook: www.facebook.com/annamariaathanasiouauthor
Twitter: @AMAthanasiou
Instagram: annamariaathanasiou

OTHER BOOKS BY ANNA-MARIA ATHANASIOU

Waiting for Summer Duet
Waiting for Summer Book One
Waiting for Summer Book Two

La Casa d'Italia Series
For Starters
Heavenly Fare
Just Desserts

Blackthorn Series
Bought and Paid For
Signed and Sealed

Printed in Great Britain
by Amazon